A Treatise On the Rules of the Law of Personal Succession, in the Different Parts of the Realm: And On the Cases, Regarding Foreign and International Succession, Which Have Been Decided in the British Courts

David Robertson

A

TREATISE

ON

THE RULES OF THE LAW

OF

PERSONAL SUCCESSION,

IN

THE DIFFERENT PARTS OF THE REALM;

AND ON

THE ·CASES,

REGARDING · FOREIGN AND INTERNATIONAL SUCCESSION,

WHICH HAVE BEEN DECIDED IN THE
BRITISH COURTS.

BY

DAVID ROBERTSON,

OF THE HONOURABLE SOCIETY OF THE MIDDLE TEMPLE.

EDINBURGH:

THOMAS CLARK, LAW-BOOKSELLER.

MDCCCXXXVI.

LONDON:
Printed by A. SPOTTISWOODE,
New-Street-Square.

TO THE

RIGHT HONOURABLE

THE LORD BROUGHAM AND VAUX,

THIS TREATISE

IS,

WITH HIS LORDSHIP'S PERMISSION,

MOST RESPECTFULLY INSCRIBED.

A 2

More than a quarter of a century has passed, since the author of the following Treatise called the attention of the Profession to the decisions of the House of Lords, in cases of appeal from Scotland. Up to that period, the early decisions had remained in a great degree neglected and unknown. The collection of them, which he then published, has since been continued by Mr. Craigie, and Mr. Stewart, of the Scottish Bar.

In the course of his professional life his attention has been directed to the subjects, which are treated of in the following pages. Unavoidable circumstances have delayed the publication to a later period than he had at one time anticipated; but he now gives the result of his labours in a new field of inquiry, under a strong impression that a revision and consolidation of the Law of Succession, in regard to Personal Property, would be attended with effects highly beneficial to every part of the Empire.

November, 1835.

CONTENTS.

INDEX OF CASES.

ERRATA.

Page 232. line 25., *for* " remembrances," *read* " incumbrances."
364. line 1., *for* " Sir James Stewart," *read* " Sir John Nisbet."
384. note (o), *for* " Ovory," *read* " Ivory."

*** The case of *Doe on the demise of Birtwhistle* v. *Vardill* (noticed p. 86.) has again attracted the attention, which is due to its importance, as a question of international law. — On the 2d of September, 1835, the House of Lords, on the motion of Lord Brougham, ordered the cause " to be further argued before the Judges *in the next Session.*"

A TREATISE

ON THE

LAW OF PERSONAL SUCCESSION.

INTRODUCTION.

THERE is no branch of the law of more general interest, than that which relates to the right of *Succession* in moveable, or personal estate. In modern times, this species of property has attained to a degree of importance which was formerly unknown, by reason of the vast increase of the public securities of the nation, and of its agriculture, commerce, and manufactures.

It is now the general rule, in every part of the realm (*a*), that the law of that part of the kingdom in which the person dying possessed of personal estate had his residence, or legal *domicil*, at the time of his death, shall regulate the right of succession to such personal estate. This rule, in regard to the domicil, was not assented to or fixed in Scotland without much inquiry, and many conflicting decisions, in the courts of law of that country.

The other rules of the law of succession in personal

(*a*) It will be seen in the sequel, that an exception must be made in regard to the succession of a freeman of London, under the custom of that city.

estate differ widely in the several parts of the kingdom, in England and in Scotland; and there is this peculiarity in regard to this branch of the law, that, by a permanent change of residence, a person may effect the greatest alterations upon the rights of himself, and of those who are most nearly connected with him. In this respect, the conflicting rules in the law of succession in personal estate are more inconvenient, than those relating to the succession in real estate. While, in regard to the former, the rules of law are subject to the most important alterations as the owner changes his domicil; it has never been matter of dispute that, in regard to the latter, they remain fixed and permanent, and attached to the property.

A very considerable period has elapsed since two distinguished writers on the law of Scotland, Sir John Nisbet of Dirleton and Sir James Stewart, had pointed out what appeared to them to be defects in this branch of the law, and the expediency that then existed of effecting changes upon it in some important particulars. But in after times this expediency of a change ceased to attract the attention which the subject merited. (b)

In England many important alterations have been made upon the law of succession in personal estate in modern times; but in Scotland the law remains now nearly as it has stood from an early period, while the circumstances of the country have changed very materially, augmenting in

---

(b) Under the title, " *If a mother and her friends may succeed,*" Sir John Nisbet asks (*Direleton's Doubts,* p. 129.), " If in no case *cognati* " on the mother's side can succeed ? " and he answers, " It is thought " that they ought to succeed." — " But in this our custom is lame, " and *opus est vel constitutione vel decisione.*" Sir James Stewart, in his *Answers* to Dirleton's Doubts (p. 210.), assents to the view taken by Dirleton of the lameness of the custom, and adds, " *eget constitutione,*" probably being of opinion that no judicial *decision* could remedy what he considered to be defective.

a high degree the inconveniences which existed in the times of Dirleton and Stewart.

There is still much of anomaly, and much requiring consideration, in the law of succession in England, particularly in regard to the local *customs* still obtaining in that country. But some of the alterations which have been made in the law of succession in England have now stood the test of long experience; and it is worthy of consideration whether similar alterations, to some extent at least, may not be introduced into the law of Scotland with great benefit to the public.

In recent times, the intercourse between the different parts of the kingdom has become much more frequent than it was even at no distant period. This is increasing rapidly, as new facilities of every kind arise for promoting it. The changes of domicil must thus become more frequent every year.

Already it has become ambiguous in what part of the realm some of the principal families of the kingdom, possessing estates and places of residence in England, in Scotland, and in Ireland, have their fixed or legal domicils; and it is in the necessary course of events that this ambiguity should, in process of time, be more generally extended.

It is the object of the present Treatise, to bring into one view the various and conflicting rules which affect the succession of this species of property in the different parts of the United Kingdom. The right understanding of these may tend to bring about such changes, connected with this subject, as may remove many inconveniences arising, and likely to increase, from the state of the law as it now exists. (c)

(c) In giving judgment in the case of *Somerville* (to be afterwards noticed), Sir R. P. Arden, Master of the Rolls, remarking the incon-

In prosecuting the present inquiry, it is proposed to examine into the state of the ancient law of succession in personal estate in England and in Scotland; to show the changes which have been introduced in these countries into this branch of the law by statute, by lapse of time, or by other causes; to trace downwards the cases which have arisen from the conflicting rules in regard to the succession in personal estate, and which have been the subject of discussion and decision in the courts of law in both countries (d); and to conclude with a statement and review of the parallel rules, in the law of personal succession, which now exist in the different parts of the United Kingdom.

It gives an additional interest and importance to this subject, that many of the questions which have occurred, and which are afterwards noticed, belong rather to the law of nations than to the municipal law of either country.

---

veniences which resulted from the then state of the law, in questions of international succession, expressed his hope, that the legislature would interpose to assimilate the laws of the two countries. This was upwards of thirty years ago, and nothing has yet been done upon this subject.

(d) *Succession* is the word used by the writers on the civil law, and on the law of Scotland, when treating of this subject; it is used in a narrower sense by Blackstone (2 Com. 430.), and is applied to the *succession* of *corporations* only. In the present treatise, it is applied not only to succession under a will, or disposition to take effect *post mortem*, but to succession *ab intestato*.

CHAPTER I.

OF THE EARLIER RULES IN THE LAW OF SUCCESSION IN PERSONAL ESTATE IN ENGLAND AND IN SCOTLAND.

BEFORE proceeding to consider the state of the law as it now is upon the subject of succession in personal estate, it is not unimportant to see how it stood in more remote times. The chief object of entering into this inquiry is to endeavour to discover, whether or not there was, at that period, a coincidence between the laws of the two countries in regard to personal succession.

SECT. I.

Early Rules of Succession in the Law of England.

THE power of bequeathing personal property by a will or testament, appears to be coeval in England with the first rudiments of the common law. (e)

We find it stated in *Glanvil*, in the reign of Henry II., that every free man, not being involved in great debts, might make a will of his personal estate; but under certain regulations: — " Quod dominum suum primo de me-
" liore, et principaliore re quam habet, recognoscat; *deinde*
" *Ecclesiam;* postea vero alias personas pro voluntate
" sua." (f) In a subsequent part of the same chapter it is laid down, that a wife and children were entitled to certain parts of the personal estate, of which they could not be de-

---

(e) Co. Litt. 111., and note (1) by Hargrave.　2 Bla. Com. 491.
(f) Glanvil, lib. 7. c. 5.

prived by will. Upon this subject Glanvil says, " Cum quis
" in infirmitate positus testamentum facere voluerit, si de-
" bitis non sit involutus, tunc omnes res ejus mobiles in
" tres partes dividentur æquales, quarum una debet hæredi;
" secunda uxori; tertia vero ipsi reservatur. De qua tertia
" liberam habebit disponendi facultatem. Verum si sine
" uxore decesserit, medietas ipsi reservatur." (g)

In the Great Charter of King John, it is laid down in
regard to the tenant of a lay fee holden of the Crown, that
in case of his death none of his chattels were to be removed
till his debts to the crown were paid; it is added, " et re-
" siduum relinquatur executoribus ad faciendum testa-
" mentum defuncti; et si nihil nobis debeatur ab ipso,
" omnia catalla cedant defuncto, salvis uxori ipsius et
" pueris *rationabilibus partibus* suis." (h)

In the immediately subsequent chapter of the same
Charter, there is this regulation in regard to the intestacy
of a *free man :* — " Si aliquis liber homo intestatus deces-
" serit, catalla sua per manus propinquorum parentum et
" amicorum suorum, *per visum ecclesiæ*, distribuantur, salvis
" unicuique debitis quæ defunctus ei debebat." (i)

Again, in the Great Charters of the 1st and 9th of
Henry III., the provision in regard to the deceasing tenant
of a lay fee holden of the Crown, is adopted in the same
words as in the Charter of John. (k) But the equitable pro-

(g) Glanvil, lib. 7. c. 5.
(h) Magna Carta Joannis, c. 26.   (i) Ibid. c. 27.
(k) Great Charter, 1 Henry III. c. 20. Magna Carta, 9 Henry III.
c. 18. In another great charter of Henry III. granted in 1217, as
printed by the commissioners of the public records, there is a difference of expression from that in the other two charters of the same
king, in the head referred to. The words in that charter are, " Salvis
" uxori ipsius rationabilibus partibus suis :" — The words " et pueris"
are omitted, apparently from mistake, as they are necessary to the sense
of the passage.

vision in regard to the succession of a free man in case of intestacy, contained in that Charter, is not stated in either of the Charters of Henry.

Bracton, who wrote in the reign of the last-mentioned king, gives it as the general law of the realm of England, that after debts and other necessary charges were deducted, the whole residue of the personal estate of a person deceased should be divided into three parts, of which the children, if there were any, should have one part; the wife, if she survived, another part; and that the third part should be at the disposal of the deceased. If there were no children, one moiety went to the deceased, the other was reserved to the wife; if no wife, but only children survived, then the deceased was to have one moiety, and the children were to have the other; if a person died without wife or children, the whole was at the disposal of the deceased. (*l*)

In the time of Bracton also, in making a will, it was necessary for the testator to acknowledge his lord " de " meliori re quam habuerit, *et postea ecclesiam* de alia me- " liori." He might then bequeath his effects (as far as they were at his disposal by will) to his relations, and to such other persons as he should see best.

The same rules are given by the author of *Fleta*, almost in the same words; and he says, as Bracton had said before, that this was the law, unless there were any local custom to the contrary. (*m*)

Thus, the common law of England, regulated by the Great Charters of John and of Henry III., appears to have been, that a widow and children (where such existed) were entitled in their own right to certain parts of the personal estate, and that the father had only the power of disposing

---

(*l*) Bracton, lib. 2. 60, 61.　　　(*m*) Fleta, lib. 2. c. 57.

by will of that portion of it which was not affected by the rights of his wife and children. (n)

But these lay authorities alone do not give a clear view of what were then the rules of the law of England, in regard to personal succession. At this period, all questions relating to wills and testaments, and to the disposition of the personal estates of intestates, had become matter of ecclesiastical jurisdiction in England. Formerly the jurisdiction, in matters of this kind, appears to have been part of the royal prerogative; and it was granted as a franchise to many lords of manors and others, some of whom, to this day, have a prescriptive right to the granting of probates of wills, and administrations of the estates of intestates, in their own courts baron, or other courts. (o)

But it was chiefly conferred upon, or assumed by, the bishops, in their respective dioceses, who were thence termed the *ordinaries*, as if the other judges were in this behalf incompetent or extraordinary. (p)

In that system of laws, which had been compiled, and promulgated to the western Christian world, under the influence of successive Popes, and which was known under the title of the *Canon Law*, all matters regarding personal succession were specially regulated. In England the authority of this body of laws, however, was at all times much restricted. Coke lays it down as a conclusion, and for this he cites the authority of Glanvil, that no foreign

---

(n) Sir Edward Coke, I am aware, states that this *reasonable partition* never was a rule of the common law (2 Inst. on Magna Carta, p. 32.); but all the early authorities as quoted above are against him; and Blackstone has no doubt upon this subject: he shows that Sir Edward Coke had misapprehended the meaning of a passage in Bracton. (2 Bla. Com. 493.)

(o) 2 Bla. Com. 494. Report to His Majesty of the Commissioners on Ecclesiastical Courts, 1832, p. 24.

(p) Swinburne, 684.

canon or constitution made by authority of the Popes, was binding in England, if it was *contra jus et consuetudinem Angliæ.* (*q*)

We have, therefore, to look for the actual state of the law, less to the general rules of the canon law, upon this subject, than to those particular rules which were made by ecclesiastical persons of competent authority in England at this period. (*r*)

In the legatine Constitutions of *Otho* and *Othobon*, made in the English national councils, in the thirteenth century (*s*); and in the Constitutions of the archbishops of Canterbury, made in their provincial synods, as collected by Lyndwood (*t*), we see in contemporary authorities many of those canons of the ecclesiastical law in regard to personal succession, which prevailed in England in those days. The clergy not only laid down rules which were to be binding in all matters in regard to the probates of wills,

---

(*q*) 2 Inst. (on the Statute of Merton) 97.

(*r*) Blackstone, in his Commentaries, notices a gloss of Pope Innocent IV. (*in Decretal.* lib. 5. t. 3. c. 42.), as laying it down [for established canon law, about the middle of the 13th century, that in Britain *a third part of the goods of intestates* was to be dispensed for the use of the church and of the poor. Though the name of Blackstone is never to be mentioned but with respect, it is proper to state, that the words of this gloss are not very correctly given by him. Innocent, alluding to customs in various places, which, if existing, were to be enforced, says, " ut sicut in *Venetiis* solvitur in morte decima mobilium, " in *Britannia* tertia, in opus ecclesiæ et pauperum dispensanda." But he does not apply this to cases of intestacy only, but to a case of *death.* Such a rule is not alluded to in any of the English constitutions that I have seen.

(*s*) Constitutiones legatinæ D. Othonis et D. Othoboni Cardinalium, &c. Cum annotat. Joannis de Athon. Oxon. 1679. Othobon was afterwards Pope, by the name of Adrian V.

(*t*) Lyndwood's Provinciale, Oxon. 1679. These were constitutions of the province of Canterbury, but were received by the province of York, in convocation, in the year 1463. (1 Burn's Eccles. Law, pref. p. 27.)

but took upon themselves the entire disposition of the personal estates of those who died intestate.   A person dying
intestate was considered as one whom death had arrested,
before he had had time to provide by his last will for the
health of his soul.   The church, therefore, interposed
mercifully towards the deceased in thus disposing of his
personal estate, " cum res temporales quæ illius fuerint,
" per distributionem *in pios usus* ipsum in juvando se-
" quuntur, et coram cœlesti Judice pro ipso propitiabiliter
" intercedunt." (*u*)

Many of the Constitutions thus made were of a very
equitable nature (*x*); and Othobon appears to have given
his sanction to that chapter of the Charter of John, which
related to the distribution of the estates of intestates after
payment of their debts. (*y*)   But this was lost sight of;

(*u*) Constit. Othoboni, 121.   It is an inquiry of some curiosity
what the church, in such cases, considered to be *pious uses.*

In the gloss of John of Athon on this constitution, he describes
them as being to perform the seven corporal and seven spiritual alms, of
which he gives the examples.

Archbishop Stratford, in a provincial constitution made about the
year 1342, given by Lyndwood (p. 180.), considers a disposition of the
goods of intestates, after payment of debts, " decedentium consan-
" guineis, servitoribus, propinquis seu aliis," to be pious uses, and for
the good of their souls.

Lyndwood, in a gloss upon this constitution, describes pious uses as
including generally every thing which related to the good of the soul of
the deceased; but he mentions a number of other matters (some of
them of a public secular nature), which had also been included under
this description of pious uses.

(*x*) John de Athon, " De bonis intestatorum."   Lyndwood, " De
" testamentis," *passim*.   These legatine and provincial constitutions,
guarded as they were with the pains of ecclesiastical censures
(Gladium Ecclesiæ), were then probably not of less weight than the
charters of our kings.

(*y*) The conclusion of the constitution of Othobon, " De bonis intestatorum " (122.) is in these words : " Proinde super bonis decedentium
" ab intestato provisionem quæ *olim a prælatis regni Angliæ cum approba-*

great abuses were introduced, and the clergy took to themselves the personal estates of intestates, without payment of their debts or other charges, and applied them as they saw fit, without any responsibility but to God and themselves.

There is no reason to doubt that great abuses prevailed in England in this branch of the law during a long period. A learned judge in the reign of Elizabeth, according to Plowden, gives this statement in regard to these abuses: — He says, " Before the statute of Westminster 2. c. 19., " if a man died intestate, the ordinary should have had his " goods, to dispose of in *pios usus.* For it was to be pre- " sumed that the ordinary, who had the care of his soul " in his lifetime, would be the fittest to have the care and " disposal of his goods *in pios usus* after his death; and, " therefore, the ordinary might seize them, and keep them " without waste; and he might have given, or aliened " them, or have otherwise disposed of them at his pleasure,

---

" *tione regis et baronum* dicitur emanasse, firmiter approbantes dis- " tricte inhibemus, ne prælati vel alii quicunque bona intestatorum " hujusmodi quocunque modo recipiant, vel occupent, contra pro- " visionem prædictam."

John de Athon, in his gloss upon this constitution, applies it to the statute of Gloucester, in the 6th of Edward I., and the statute of Westminster the second, in the 13th of the same king; but the consti- tution was made in 1268, in the 52d of Henry III.   Bishop Gibson in his Codex, and Burn, notice this mistake; and Burn applies the re- ference in this *Constitution* to the great charter of Henry, (4 Burn's Eccles. Law, 323.)   It has been already noticed, (supra, p. 7.) that it is only in the great charter of John that any thing is said in regard to the goods of intestates.   It is amusing to remark how Othobon, a foreign churchman, describes the making of this great charter of our liberties, " as made *by the prelates* of the realm of England, with the " approbation of *the King and the barons.*"   On this John of Athon gravely observes: " *Nota* — Discretam et ordinatam provisionem in " parliamento regni *debere primarie incipere a prælatis,* maxime super " contingentibus opera pietatis."

" and the money arising from them he was to dispose of
" in *pios usus ;* and, if he did not, he broke the confidence
" and trust reposed in him, for which he stood *charged in*
" *conscience to God ;* but nevertheless, the gift or alienation of
" the goods by the ordinary was good by the law of the realm.
" And although the law committed the goods to the ordinary,
" yet it did not make the ordinary chargeable to actions
" of creditors for debts due to them by the intestate ; but
" the charge of the ordinary was only to employ them in
" *pios usus,* and in acts of charity ; and the common law
" did not make him, being a spiritual governor, subject to
" temporal suits for such things. And this was a great
" defect in the common law, there being no remedy to
" come at the debts of the intestate." (z)

It is not necessary to prosecute this inquiry further, or
to adduce the sentiments of others, at a later period, to the
same effect. Not only were the rules of law, connected
with this subject, most unjust in themselves, but great
abuses were exercised in carrying these rules into effect.
It will be seen in the sequel, how and by what means these
abuses were corrected.

Sect. II.

Early Rules of Succession in the Law of Scotland.

The antiquities of the law of Scotland are in much
obscurity. This has arisen from a great variety of causes,
particularly from the unsettled state of the country, and
its constant wars maintained during so many centuries
with the powerful kingdom of England; but nothing has

(z) Mr. Justice Weston, in Graysbrook v. Fox, East, 7. Eliz.
Plowden, 277.

tended more to render the ancient law of Scotland obscure and uncertain, than the opposite statements made upon this subject by the two eminent writers, *Skene* and *Craig*.

Skene, the clerk register in the reign of James VI., had opportunities of informing himself upon the state of the ancient law of Scotland at least equal to those which can be enjoyed by any modern. He was selected to publish the ancient books and statutes of the Scottish law. Among those he has given the well-known book, termed (from its initial words) "*Regiam Majestatem*," and other books and treatises, as forming the ancient and authentic law of Scotland.

Unfortunately Skene had an hypothesis to support, connected in some degree with the much agitated question of the independence of the Scottish monarchy. It was his object to show that the books of *Regiam Majestatem* were of an antiquity more remote than the work of Glanvil on the law of England. On comparing those two books, it is obvious that both cannot be original works, and that one must either be (in great part) a transcript of the other, or that the plan of both must have been taken from some common source. Skene wished it to appear, that the *Books of the Majesty* were of the age of David the First of Scotland. Glanvil wrote in the time of Henry the Second of England, at a period somewhat later. (*a*)

It is obvious that Glanvil's book is in great part a compilation, and it is by no means improbable that some treatise of the same kind may have existed in the time of

---

(*a*) The superior antiquity which Skene thus wished to maintain for the *Books of the Majesty* may not extend over a very considerable period. David died in 1153. Henry II., in whose time the treatise of Glanvil is understood to have been written, began his reign i-·· ·· lowing year, 1154.

David I. That there was a writer on the law of England prior to Glanvil is well known. *Ricardus de Lucy*, justiciary of England from 1162 to 1179, appears to have composed some treatise of a nature similar to Glanvil's. In the epistles of *Bishop Grosseteste* to *Walter de Ralegh*, Chief Justice of the King's Bench, in the time of Henry III., a reference is made to a treatise of this Richard de Lucy (*b*), showing his strong opposition to the introduction into England of the law of legitimation *per subsequens matrimonium:* and in a manuscript of the Regiam Majestatem, presented by the Earl of Cromarty to the Library of the Faculty of Advocates in Edinburgh, Ricardus de Lucy is specially referred to, together with Glanvil (*c*), as an authority in the law. (*d*)

At that period the minds of the learned were much directed to the books of the civil law. (*e*) In the reign of Stephen, with whom David was contemporary, the books of Justinian had been introduced into England; a struggle for the mastery arose between the civil and the common law; and Stephen, by a royal proclamation, prohibited the study in England of the laws then newly imported from Italy. (*f*)

Though the writers on the common law of England

(*b*) Selden ad Fletam, p. 538.

(*c*) Cromarty MS. lib. 2. c. 33. I take this on the authority of Lord Hailes, in his *Examination*, noted *infra*.

(*d*) I do not find that any treatise of Ricardus de Lucy exists. In the Harleian Library (No. 2.) certain conventions of Henry II. regarding Thomas a'Becket and the then pope are addressed from Normandy, "Ricardo de Lucy, Justitiario," and others.

(*e*) In one of the treatises published with the Code Napoleon,— "Projet du code civil, discours preliminaire," it is thus remarked, in regard to the Corpus Juris:— "La decouverte que nos ayeux firent de la compilation de Justinien fut pour eux *une espèce de revelation*."

(*f*) Selden ad Fletam, p. 508.

were opposed to the introduction of the civil law, yet in their treatises (as noticed by Selden) they adopted much from the books of Justinian, as well in substance as in form. (g) It was their fashion, in the commencement of their books, to keep in view the *proeme* of the Institutes of Justinian. This is to be noticed in Glanvil, in Bracton, and in Fleta, compiled in England in three different reigns.

The same thing was done by the author of Regiam Majestatem, to whatever age that work must be attributed.

Sir Thomas Craig, the distinguished writer on the feudal law, had a very different opinion in regard to these books of the Regiam Majestatem from that of Skene. (h) Instead of considering them as exhibiting the ancient and authentic law of Scotland, he appears to have held them almost in horror; he treats them merely as a transcript from Glanvil, and considers that the theft was manifest. He adds, " Sufficit hoc jam monuisse nullam auctoritatem eos libros " habere, nihil unde causæ decisio quæri potest continere, " et nunquam in foro pro authenticis consuetudinibus ha- " bendos : *imo ne nominandos quidem.*" (i)

In another place he breaks out almost into an execration against him who first held out these to be genuine books of the law of Scotland ; he says, " Male sit illi, quicunque " is fuit, qui nobis leges Normannicas pro nostris obtru- " sit." (k)

(g) Selden ad Fletam, p. 463. *Wood*, in his Institute of the Imperial, or Civil Law (Preface, p. 6.), speaking of the early English writers, says, " Fleta and Bracton, and the most ancient of their writers, would " look very naked if every Roman lawyer should pluck away his " feathers."

(h) Craig was born in 1548, and died in 1608, consequently he never saw Skene's edition of the Regiam Majestatem, which was printed in 1609.

(i) Craig, lib. 1. d. 8. s. 11.

(k) Ibid. lib. 1. d. 11. s. 1.

It would be very much out of place here, to enter at large into this celebrated controversy. Lord Hailes (*l*) has clearly detected some of the proceedings of Skene in editing these ancient books. It is not distinctly known what manuscripts were used by Skene in preparing his printed edition; but in the existing manuscripts of the Regiam Majestatem a reference is made in various places to Glanvil *in the text*, showing clearly that those manuscripts at least were of a date later than Glanvil. These references Skene has retained. Instead of keeping them in the text, however, he has placed them in the shape of notes in the margin of his book, amidst numerous other marginal references of the same kind. So in these existing manuscripts there are also references *in the text* to certain authorities in the canon law, to a gloss on the decretals of Gregory IX., and to the decretals of Boniface VIII.; but the decretals of Gregory were not published till 1230, nor the decretals of Boniface till 1298, the former 77 years, and the latter 145 years, after the death of David; and to have given the text correctly would have militated against Skene's hypothesis as to the book being compiled by David I. These quotations, therefore, are also expunged from the text, and thrown as notes into the margin. No doubt can thus exist that Skene merited the character given him by Lord Hailes of " a careless, if not an unfaithful publisher."

But even that admirable person Lord Hailes appears to treat the question in too confined a shape, as one merely in regard to the relative antiquity of the two *treatises* of Glanvil and of Regiam Majestatem. The real question in this matter is of more importance. Does the Regiam Majestatem, from whatever source taken, exhibit a view of

---

(*l*) *Examination of some of the arguments for the high antiquity of Regiam Majestatem.* Edinburgh, 1769.

the ancient laws of Scotland; or is it to be treated, as Craig treats it, merely as a *theft* and a *forgery?*

Notwithstanding the high celebrity of Craig, and his opinion so strongly given, there is reason to conclude that he was mistaken upon this subject, and that this body of *Scoto-Norman* laws had been of authority in Scotland during a very considerable period. Craig had been educated in France at a time when the French and Scottish nations were intimately blended together, and long after some of the most important legal institutions of Scotland had been borrowed from France. In various parts of his book, he appears to have had no partiality for the law of England; and he notices that he had little acquaintance with the English courts. (*m*) It is not to be wondered at, therefore, that in some places he is under misapprehension when stating the law of England. (*n*)

It is not unimportant to notice, that some of his objections to the Regiam Majestatem are clearly founded in error in regard to the state of the ancient law of Scotland. Craig, when treating on the subject of *reversions*, says, " Mirum tamen est quod in toto nostro jure antiquo, viz.

(*m*) " Nam ut ingenue fatear fori Anglici formam vix ipso in limine salutavi."— Craig, Epistola nuncupatoria, p. 6. edit. 1732.

(*n*) Some instances of this may be noticed. When treating of the law of descent in real estate, he appears to have considered, that as in Kent, where *gavelkind* prevailed generally, so in Essex, Norfolk, Suffolk, and other places, there were *general* rules in the law of descent different from those of the common law of England (lib. 1. d. 7. s. 18.). Again, when treating of bastardy, and noticing that the law of England does not admit of legitimation *per subsequens matrimonium*, he says, the English law calls a son born before the marriage of his parents a *mulier:* " Mulierem per contemptum appellant." (lib. 2. d. 13. s. 27.) But this is also an error; the English law terms such a son " *bastard* " *eigné.*" The son born *after* marriage is termed " *mulier puisné.*" Co. Lit. 399. 2 Black. Com. 248. The law is stated upon this subject in the *Regiam Majestatem* as it still exists in England; lib. 2. c. 51.

c

" libris Regiæ Majestatis, de Judicibus, Quoniam Atta-
" chiamenta, Legibus cum Burgorum, tum Forestarum,
" de reversione aut regressu nulla fit mentio ; de re inva-
" diata aut mortuo vadio, plurima, quod longe a reversione
" differt ut mox dicemus ; nisi forte quis putet reversio-
" num usum, cum hi libri scriberentur, ad nos nondum
" pervenisse. Ego, sane, illum librum Reg. Majest. a
" nostris hominibus scriptum fuisse vix possum induci ut
" credam. Anglorum enim leges et mores potius sapit ex
" omni parte quam nostros." (o)

But Lord Kaimes apparently more than solves this
difficulty of Craig; he says, " Saving the respect due to
" an author of established reputation, the wonder may be
" justly retorted upon him that he should be so ignorant
" of the laws and constitutions of his own country. It
" need not be surprising that no mention is made of a
" reversion in our first law books, when it was a late
" invention in the days of James III." (p)

In another place, when noticing the tenure of *villenage*,
Craig says, " Tenendriam de villenagio omnino præterii
" propter ejus apud nos *insolentiam ;* nullus enim apud
" nos ejus usus, et inauditum nomen, nisi quod nonnulla
" in libro Regiæ Majestatis de *nativis*, et ad libertatem
" proclamantibus, proponantur ; quæ et ab Anglorum
" moribus sunt recepta, et nunquam in usum nostrum
" deducta." (q) Nothing, however, is now clearer than
this, that villenage was at one period common in Scotland,
as it was in England. This appears from numerous royal

(o) Craig, lib. 2. d. 6. s. 25.

(p) Statute Law abridged, Historical Notes, p. 429. He refers to
the statute 1469. c. 27., which introduced *reversions* into the law of
Scotland.

(q) Craig, lib. 1. d. 11. s. 32.

charters and transcripts of deeds in the chartularies of the Scottish monasteries. It is quite unnecessary to quote at length the numerous authorities upon this subject. (*r*)

Grounds, however, exist, upon which there appears to be reason to conclude that the Regiam Majestatem, notwithstanding any blots and uncertainties with which it may be charged, contains an outline of what was at one time the law of Scotland.

1. For several centuries after the Norman Conquest the connexion between England and Scotland was most intimate. During this period the Scottish kings had great fiefs in England, numerous Anglo-Norman families settled in Scotland, and the crown of that country was successively held by two of those families, the Baliols and Bruces. In the absence of all evidence it would be reasonable to conclude, that, while this state of things remained, there should be an approximation of the laws of the two countries.

2. The offices of sheriffs and coroners, and the practice as to justice-ayres, and the brieves or writs issuing from the Chancery, which were common to the laws of both countries, all tend to show that such approximation once existed. Some of these have disappeared from the law and practice of Scotland, but enough of them remains to show the landmarks of the ancient legal institutions of that country. (*s*)

(*r*) 1 Lord Hailes's Annals, p. 304. Robertson's Index of Royal Charters, pp. 16. 47. 66. 81. 91. 96. 134. &c. The chartularies referred to are specified in Chalmers's Caledonia, vol. i. p. 719. *et sequen.*

(*s*) Daines Barrington, in his " Observations on the more ancient " Statutes" (p. 126), when treating of the *writs* contained in the *Register* in England, says, " I have likewise compared them with the " forms in that ancient book in the Scotch law entitled *Quoniam* " *Attachiamenta*. The comparison of these writs seems most fully to " prove the great authority which is due to our *Registrum Brevium*, and

3. The copies of deeds preserved in the chartularies of the Scottish monasteries strongly confirm the position that their ancient laws, in regard to real and personal estate, and the forms of their legal instruments of all kinds, nearly coincided with those of England at the same period. (*t*)

4. Upwards of four centuries ago, the legislature of Scotland recognised the books of Regiam Majestatem and Quoniam Attachiamenta as ancient books of the law of Scotland. In a statute of James the First of that kingdom, of March 1425, it is thus enacted : — " It is sene " spedful and ordanit be the king and the parliament, that " sex wise and discrete men of ilkane of the thre estatis, " the quhilkis knawis the lawis best, sal be chosyn, quha " (sen fraude and gyll awe to help no man) sal se and " examyn the bukis of law; that is to say, Regiam Majes- " tatem and Quoniam Attachiamenta, and mend the lawis " that nedis mendment." (*u*) At that period the books thus noticed by the Scottish parliament, according to all fair construction, must have been reputed as of some considerable antiquity.

" likewise that the law of Scotland, as hath before been contended, " agreed anciently, not only with the principles of the law of England, " but in its practice, though there might be some variances of no great " importance."

(*t*) I have examined many of those deeds transcribed from the Macfarlane MS., and meant to have been used in a *Monasticon Scoti-canum*, for which large collections had been made by a distinguished lover of antiquities, Mr. Spottiswoode of Spottiswoode. In the 12th, 13th, and 14th centuries these appear to differ little, if at all, from the deeds of the same period, printed in Madox's *Formulare Anglicanum*. The tenures, the structure of the instruments, and the forms of their testing clauses, appear to be all precisely the same. Nothing could throw so much light upon the state of the ancient law of Scotland as a publication of these chartularies, or of a selection from them; and I rejoice to learn that some publications of this nature are in progress.

(*u*) From the edition of the Record Commission ; 1425, cap. 54. of the common edition of the Scottish Acts.

The same thing was done in the parliamentary commission for revising the laws in the reign of James the Third in 1469 (*x*), and in the commissions for the same purpose in the reign of Mary in 1566, and in the regency of Morton in 1574 (*y*), all tending to the same conclusion, and apparently much overweighing the objections of Craig to the authority of this body of our ancient laws.

Though it may be impossible to fix with precision the period when the Regiam Majestatem was compiled, or adopted as of authority in the law of Scotland, it appears to be not unlikely that this took place some time towards the end of the reign of Edward the First. As it refers in the text to the decretals of Boniface, which were not published till 1298, it follows that this compilation must have been of a date posterior to the publication of these decretals; and this hypothesis also concurs with all that is known of the policy of that most sagacious prince. The author of *Caledonia* states the same opinion upon this subject, and considers that the true origin of the Regiam Majestatem is to be sought in the famous ordinance of Edward in 1305, " *Super stabilitate terræ Scotiæ.*" (*z*)

(*x*) Erroneously printed in the common edition of the Scottish Acts of Parliament as of the year 1487, cap. 115. (4th Report of Mr. Thomson, deputy clerk register, in 1810.)

(*y*) *Ibid.*

(*z*) Caledonia, vol. i. p. 732.

The discovery made some years ago of an ancient manuscript in the library of the canton of Berne, containing collections of the laws of England and of Scotland, excited some new interest upon this question. This book is now in the General Register House at Edinburgh. For the possession of it we are mainly indebted to the author of *Caledonia.* According to the description of it given by Mr. Chalmers, it contains copies of Glanvil de Legibus, of the Leges Marchiarum, the English *Brevia*, and the Statute of Marleberge. These occupy the greater part of the volume. Then commence some collections of

It may thus probably ever remain uncertain at what distinct period Scotland adopted this body of laws, with some intermixture, no doubt, of Celtic customs (*a*), and local regulations; but there appears to be no difficulty, on the whole, in coming to the conclusion of Lord Kaimes, that " one must' be ignorant of the history of " our law who does not know that the laws of England " and Scotland were originally the same, almost in every " particular." (*b*)

After this deduction it appears that we may safely quote the Regiam Majestatem as an authority in the ancient law of Scotland in regard to the succession to personal estate. The law is thus laid down in that work : —

" 1. Cum quis in infirmitate positus testamentum facere " voluerit, si debitis non sit involutus, omnes res ejus mo- " biles in tres partes dividentur æquales.

" 2. Quarum una debetur *hæredi*, secunda uxori, tertia " reservetur testatori.

Scottish law, corresponding, though not strictly, with those on the same subjects contained in the Regiam Majestatem. It also contains the *Leges Quatuor Burgorum*, nearly in the same form as given by Skene.

As this collection makes no mention of the Regiam Majestatem, Mr. Chalmers considers that it affords " additional proofs that the *Regiam* " *Majestatem* was unknown in the age of this manuscript, at least to " that curious collector." But there is great uncertainty in founding much upon the silence of these early compilers. As far as I have observed, Bracton says nothing of Glanvil; and the author of *Fleta* is silent as to Bracton, while he borrows so largely from that earlier compilation. Nothing can show more strongly the state of our Scottish legal antiquities than the importance attached to this anonymous book obtained from *Berne*.

(*a*) Witness the chapter relative to *Cro*, which *Skene* considers not to be genuine, though it be contained in the Berne MS.—(Caledonia, vol. i. p. 729.)

(*b*) Statute Law abridged, historical notes, p. 429.

" 3. De qua tertia parte, testator liberam disponendi
" facultatem habebit.

" 4. Verum si sine uxore decesserit, medietas ipsi re-
" servetur." (c)

That this is almost in the very words of Glanvil appears to add to, instead of detracting from, its authenticity,
or indeed its authority in the ancient law of Scotland.
Where the two books differ, there is more reason to
enquire into the grounds of difference, and into the authenticity of such parts of the Regiam Majestatem as do
not coincide with the work of Glanvil. (d)

Whatever differences have since arisen in the laws of
England and of Scotland, it may be remarked, that as far
as the law of succession in personal estate is laid down in

(c) Reg. Majest. lib. 2. c. 37.   We find also in a preceding chapter
of the Regiam Majestatem, the same regulations as to making a will
which were laid down in Glanvil : — " Potest liber homo, debitis non
" involutus majoribus, de rebus suis in infirmitate sua facere ration-
" abile testamentum.
" 2. Sub hac forma secundum patriæ consuetudinem, videlicet, quod
" primo Dominum suum de meliore et principaliore re quam habet
" recognoscat.
" 3. Deinde ecclesiam, postea alias personas pro sua voluntate."
Lib. 2. c. 36.

(d) It affords some evidence to the same effect, that the legatine constitutions of Cardinal Othobon (ante, p. 9.) were addressed to England,
Scotland, Ireland, and Wales, as if the same rules in matters ecclesiastical
applied at that period to all of those countries. (Præfat. Constitut. Othoboni.) But we know that the labours of Othobon were considered too
expensive by the Scottish clergy : he claimed six marks from each cathe-
dral, and four marks from each parish church, for the expenses of his
visitation.   The King, with the advice of his clergy, forbade the contribution to be made, and appealed to Rome.   The Scottish clergy gave
the King 2000 marks for defraying the charges of the appeal. (Fordun,
lib. 10. c. 21.   1 Hailes's Annals, 178).   In the subsequent year, however, the clergy appear to have made their peace with Othobon :
" Ipso anno pacavit clerus Scotiæ Ottobono, legato in Anglia commo-
" ranti," by paying part of the demand. (Fordun, lib. 10. c. 22.)

Glanvil and in the Regiam Majestatem, it has always had effect in Scotland, and remains in full force to this day. It is true that we see nothing in the Regiam Majestatem of the communion of goods between husband and wife, and some other peculiar doctrines of the more modern law of Scotland on this subject. (e) The introduction of these into the law of Scotland will form the subject of consideration in the sequel.

(e) At the present time, this enquiry into the state of our ancient law is not without interest : if the laws of the two countries were the same (as there is reason to believe) six centuries ago, this gives additional reason for considering whether they may not be again consolidated into one body, with infinite advantage to the community of both countries.

CHAP. II.

OF THE CHANGES IN THE LAW OF SUCCESSION INTRODUCED INTO THE LAW OF ENGLAND, BY LAPSE OF TIME, AND BY STATUTE.

IT is matter for observation, that though the rules of the common law in England were of a general nature in regard to the division of personal estate into the dead's part and the *partes rationabiles* of the wife and children, as laid down in Glanvil and other writers from a very early period, yet there appear to have then existed customs of a different kind in some parts of England. After laying down the general rule of law as already stated, Bracton says, " Et ea " quæ dicta sunt locum habent et tenent nisi sit consuetudo " quæ se habet in contrarium, sicut in civitatibus, burgis, " et villis ;" and then he goes on to cite the custom of the city of London in regard to dower, as controlling the general rules of law in this matter (*a*) : and the same thing appears in Fleta in the same words. (*b*)

There is a good deal of obscurity in regard to the introduction of that important change into the law of England, which converted the law of *reasonable partition* into a custom of particular parts of the kingdom, instead of being one of general observance. This change appears to have been made silently, and by lapse of time, without any statute or general regulation to this effect.

Some brief notices appear upon this subject in the *Natura Brevium* of *Fitzherbert*. (*c*) He mentions that the writ *de rationabile parte bonorum*, by the statute of Magna

---

(*a*) Bracton, 61.   (*b*) Fleta, lib. 2. c. 57.
(*c*) Fitzherbert, N. B. 122. ed. 1794.

Carta, seemed to be the common law of the realm, and that the same so appeared in Glanvil.   In 31 Edward III. a woman demanded the moiety of her husband's goods because he had no children, and *counted* upon the general custom of the realm.   This was adjudged to be good. But in after times, and by degrees, it became the practice to *count* for the same upon the special customs of particular places.

Accordingly in the *Register* the writs of partition rehearse only the customs of particular counties, and not the general law. (*d*)   Any more minute enquiry into this subject would be more curious than profitable.   In the lapse of time it came to be well understood that the law *de rationabile parte bonorum* had ceased to obtain in the greater part of the province of Canterbury, where a person might grant or dispose of his whole personal estate by will.   But it still continued in some parts of the principality of Wales, in the province of York, and in the city of London, mixed up, in these districts and places, with various local differences and regulations.

Thus England, in regard to personal succession, became divided between the *general* and the *customary* law.   This division appears to have existed during several centuries, while personal estate was of less importance, without attracting observation in regard to its manifest inconvenience.   The distinctions between the general and the customary law still remain in full force, though both have been modified by the statutes to be afterwards mentioned.

While this very important change was silently taking place in the common law of England, several other

---

(*d*) Even as late as the reign of Charles I., Sir Henry Finch lays down the law of the *rationabiles partes* as the common law of the land.   Finch's Law, 175.

important changes were also introduced by statutes passed
from time to time. The first of them was made by the
statute of *Westminster the second* in 1285. (*e*) It had by
this time, probably, become intolerable, that the goods of
a person dying intestate, should be seized by the ordinary,
and disposed of as he saw fit, without being subject to the
payment of the debts of the deceased.

It was therefore thus laid down in this statute : " *Cum
post mortem alicujus decedentis intestati, et obligati aliquibus
in debito, bona deveniant ad ordinarius disponenda, obligeter
de cætero ordinarius ad respondendum de debitis quatenus
bona defuncti sufficiunt, eodem modo quo executores hujusmodi respondere tenerentur si testamentum fecisset.*"

Sir Edward Coke observes upon this statute, that it was
made in affirmance of the common law (*f*); and it has been
seen that an equitable provision to the same effect had been
contained in the Great Charter of John. In the turbulent
period which had intervened, this had probably been lost
sight of.

In the 31st of Edward III. two acts were passed of
great importance in regard to the law of succession in
England. The first of them was for " *redressing of extor-
tion in bishop's officers in proving of wills.*" (*g*)

In this statute, on the recital, that, " *the ministers of
bishops, and other ordinaries of holy church, take of the
people grievous and outrageous fine for the probate of testaments, and for the making of acquittances thereof, the King
hath charged the Archbishop of Canterbury, and the other
bishops, that they cause the same to be amended; and if they
do not, it is accorded that the King shall cause to be enquired
by his justices of such oppressions and extortions, to hear them*

(*e*) 13 Edward 1. c. 19.   (*f*) 2 Instit. 397.
(*g*) 31 Edward 3. c. 4.

*and determine them, as well at the King's suit, as at the suit
of the party, as in old time hath been used."*

The next statute which was then passed was very remarkable, being that which first introduced administrations
and administrators into the law of England; it is in these
terms : — (h)

"*Item, It is acorded and assented, that in case where a man
dieth intestate, the ordinaries shall depute the next and most
lawful friends of the dead person intestate to administer his
goods; which deputies shall have an action to demand and
recover as executors the debts due to the said person intestate
in the King's Court, for to administer and dispend for the
soul of the dead; and shall answer also in the King's Court
to other to whom the said dead person was holden and bound,
in the same manner as executors shall answer. And they shall
be accountable to the ordinaries, as executors be in the case of
testament, as well of the time past, as the time to come."*

Thus the powers which the ordinaries had before exercised by themselves or their own officers, were now to
be deputed to the next and most lawful friends of the
deceased. This must, at that period, have been an improvement of great importance. The ordinaries, from
their high rank and sacred character, must have been
exempt from suits (i): it appears, also, from several of the
legatine and provincial constitutions, that the extortions
were committed more by the officers of ordinaries, than by
the ordinaries themselves.

After this period, and for a considerable while down-
ward, the persons deputed by the ordinary were termed
executors and *executors dative* (k); but the word *administer*
having appeared first in this statute, the persons so ap-

(h) 31 Edw. 3. c. 11.   (i) Plowden, *supra*, p. 12.
(k) *Snelling's* case, 5 Rep. Swinburne, p. 684.

pointed were afterwards termed *administrators*, to distinguish them from the executors of a testament; and this description has now, and for several centuries, been in universal use.

In the reign of Henry V. an act was made (*l*), again taking notice of the oppressive fees exacted for proving of wills, and it was ordained, that ordinaries should take no more for proving of testaments with their inventories, than was taken in the time of Edward III.; but this act was only to last for a year, and was not renewed.

Matters remained upon this footing till the act was made in the reign of Henry VIII. (*m*), as well in regard to the expenses of probates and of letters of administration, as for regulating, in all future cases, to whom letters of administration, in cases of intestacy, should be granted.

This act recites the before-mentioned statutes of the 31st of Edward III. and 3d of Henry V., in regard to the expenses of probates, and the oppressions and exactions practised in regard to the same, and " *that the said unlawful exactions of the said ordinaries and their ministers be nothing reformed nor amended, but greatly augmented and increased, against right and justice, and to the great impoverishing of the king's subjects.*" — The act therefore proceeds to lay down rules in regard to the fees of probates and administrations, which were to be observed from the 1st of April, 1536, in time coming.

But the most important part of this statute is that which relates to the parties, to whom administration was to be granted, in case of intestacy. Before this period, at common law, no person had a right to obtain administration of the goods and effects of a party deceased; but it

---

(*l*) 3 Hen. 5. c. 8.   (*m*) 21 Hen. 8. c. 5.

was in the breast of the ordinary to grant it to whom he pleased.

By this statute, however, the ordinary was required to grant the administration to certain connexions of the deceased to the exclusion of all others. Upon this subject the statute enacts : —

And in case any person die intestate, or that the executors named in any such testament refuse to prove the said testament, then the said ordinary, or other person or persons having authority to take probate of testaments, as is above said, shall grant the administration of the goods of the testator, or person deceased, to the widow of the same person deceased, or to the next of his kin, or to both, as by the discretion of the same ordinary shall be thought good, taking surety of him or them, to whom shall be made such commission, for the true administration of the goods, chattels, and debts which he or they shall be so authorised to minister; and in case where divers persons claim the administration as next of kin, which be equal in degree of kindred to the testator or person deceased, and where any person only desireth the administration as next of kin, where indeed divers persons be in equality of kindred, as is aforesaid, that in every such case the ordinary to be at his election and liberty to accept any being one or mo making request, where divers do require the administration : or where but one or more of them, and not all being in equality of degree, do make request, then the ordinary to admit the widow, and him or them only making request, or any one of them at his pleasure.

This statute introduced a vast improvement into the law of succession; and it regulates in regard to the grant of administrations to this day. There were some uncertainties and cases not provided for in this act; and it has been the business of the proper courts to provide remedies for these, as they became evolved in future times.

But the greatest alteration in the law of personal succession in England, has been that which was made by that well known act termed the *Statute of Distributions*. (n)— The causes which led to the passing of this statute are mentioned briefly by the writers who have treated upon this subject.

The ordinary was now obliged to grant the administration to some of the connexions of the deceased; yet whoever took administration was entitled to the surplus of the estate of the deceased, after payment of debts, although the ecclesiastical courts claimed the power of making distribution to the next of kin. The objects, therefore, to be obtained by the statute of distributions were, to oblige the administrator to distribute the surplus of the estate of an intestate, instead of retaining it to his own use, and to fix the rules by which he was to be guided in making such distribution. (o)

A case had arisen upon the point, whether the Ecclesiastical Court had the power, or not, of making distribution of the effects of an intestate. Dr. Charles Hughes of London had died worth 12,000l. of personal estate, leaving a son and daughter. (p) Administration was granted by the ordinary to the son. He refused to give his sister any part of the personal estate; and he was thereupon called into the Court Christian by his sister claiming her share of the personal estate of her father. The Ecclesiastical Court appears to have been favourable to this claim; but the case was removed by prohibition into the Court of Common Pleas, and was argued in Trinity Term, 18 Charles II., and in the subsequent term, before Sir Orlando Bridgman Chief Justice, and the other judges of that court. In this prohibition Sir Walter

---

(n) 22 & 23 C. 2. c. 10.
(o) Humphrey v. Bullen, 1 Atk. 458.
(p) Hughes v. Hughes, Carter, 125.

Walker, a distinguished civilian of those days, was heard, by permission, in support of the power of the Ecclesiastical Court to make distribution. The arguments of the counsel and of Sir Walter Walker are given at large in the report in Carter; but the decision of the Court is not there mentioned.

A farther account of this is given in a speech of Chief Justice Holt, in the cause *Rex* v. *Raines,* or *Pett* v. *Pett,* T. 1700., reported by Lord Raymond. (*q*)   Chief Justice Holt (in that case) says, " Bridgman, Chief Justice, in- " clined in opinion to Sir Walter Walker, but the other " Judges opposed it, and it never obtained in Westminster " Hall; but prohibitions were granted upon the first " motion, and when he could not obtain his point in the " courts of law, *he procured an act of parliament.*" (*r*)

This act, all expedient as it was, does not appear to have excited much attention in parliament at the time. The discussions upon it are not mentioned in the parliamentary history of that period. It was introduced into the House of Lords on the 18th of March 1670-71, while Sir Orlando Bridgman was Lord Keeper. In the House of Commons there must have been some discussion upon the bill, for at the second reading it was carried upon a division of 28 to 13, but the nature of this discussion does not appear.

By this statute it is thus enacted : —

All ordinaries, as well the judges of the prerogative courts of Canterbury and York for the time being, as all other ordi-

---

(*q*) 1 Lord Raymond, 574.

(*r*) Carter, at the end of the case of *Hughes* v. *Hughes,* says, " Et puis " per act del Parliament pur melieux settlement des Intestates Estates " fuit contrived." The arguments of counsel in this case are curious. It is to the honour of those practising in the Ecclesiastical Courts, that this great improvement appears to have originated with them. The then state of things must have been almost intolerable.

naries and ecclesiastical judges, and every of them, having power to commit administration of the goods of persons dying intestate, shall and may, upon their respective granting and committing of administrations of the goods of persons dying intestate after the 1st *day of June* 1671, *of the respective person or persons to whom any administration is to be committed, take sufficient bonds, with two or more able sureties, respect being had to the value of the estate, in the name of the ordinary, with the condition in form and manner* (as therein specified).

Which bonds are hereby declared and enacted to be good to all intents and purposes, and pleadable in any courts of justice; and also, that the said ordinaries and judges respectively shall and may, and are enabled to proceed and call such administrators to account, for and touching the goods of any person dying intestate; and, upon hearing and due consideration thereof, to order and make just and equal distribution of what remaineth clear (after all debts, funerals, and just expences of every sort first allowed and deducted,) amongst the wife and children, or children's children, if any such be, or otherwise to the next of kindred to the dead person in equal degree, or legally representing their stocks pro suo cuique jure, *according to the laws in such cases, and the rules and limitation hereafter set down; and the same distributions to decree and settle, and to compel such administrators to observe and pay the same, by the due course of his Majesty's ecclesiastical laws; saving to every one, supposing him or themselves aggrieved, their right of appeal, as was always in such cases used.* (Sect. 3.)

Provided that this act, or any thing herein contained, shall not anyways prejudice or hinder the customs observed within the city of London, or within the province of York, or other places, having known and received customs peculiar to them; but that the same customs may be observed as formerly; any

D

thing herein contained to the contrary notwithstanding. (Sect. 4.)

Provided always, and be it enacted, that all ordinaries, and every other person who by this act is enabled to make distribution of the surplusage of the estate of any person dying intestate, shall distribute the whole surplusage of such estate or estates in manner and form following; that is to say, one third part of the said surplusage to the wife of the intestate, and all the residue by equal portions to and amongst the children of such persons dying intestate, and such persons as legally represent such children in case any of the said children be then dead, other than such child or children (not being heir at law) who shall have any estate by the settlement of the intestate, or shall be advanced by the intestate in his lifetime, by portion or portions equal to the share which shall by such distribution be allotted to the other children to whom such distribution is to be made; and in case any child, other than the heir at law, who shall have any estate by settlement from the said intestate, or shall be advanced by the said intestate in his lifetime, by portion not equal to the share which will be due to the other children by such distribution as aforesaid, then so much of the surplusage of the estate of such intestate to be distributed to such child or children as shall have any land by settlement from the intestate, or were advanced in the lifetime of the intestate, as shall make the estate of all the said children to be equal as near as can be estimated; but the heir at law, notwithstanding any land that he shall have by descent or otherwise from the intestate, is to have an equal part in the distribution with the rest of the children, without any consideration of the value of the land which he hath by descent or otherwise from the intestate. (Sect. 5.)

And in case there be no children, nor any legal representatives of them, then one moiety of the said estate to be allotted to the wife of the intestate, the residue of the said estate to be distributed equally to every of the next of kindred of the intestate who are in equal degree, and those who legally represent them.   (Sect. 6.)

Provided that there be no representations admitted among collaterals after brothers' and sisters' children ; and in case there be no wife, then all the said estate to be distributed equally to and amongst the children ; and in case there be no child, then to the next of kindred in equal degree of or unto the intestate, and their legal representatives as aforesaid, and in no other manner whatsoever.   (Sect. 7.)

Provided also, and be it likewise enacted, to the end that a due regard be had to creditors, that no such distribution of the goods of any person dying intestate be made till after one year be fully expired after the intestate's death ; and that such and every one to whom any distribution and share shall be allotted shall give bond, with sufficient sureties, in the said courts, that if any debt or debts truly owing by the intestate shall be afterwards sued for and recovered, or otherwise duly made to appear, that then and in every such case he or she shall respectively refund and pay back to the administrator his or her rateable part of that debt or debts, and of the costs of suit and charges of the administator by reason of such debt, out of the part and share so as aforesaid allotted to him or her, thereby to enable the said administrator to pay and satisfy the said debt or debts so discovered after the distribution made as aforesaid.   (Sect. 8.)

Provided always, and be it enacted, that in all cases where the ordinary hath used heretofore to grant administration cum testamento annexo; *he shall continue so to do, and the will of the deceased in such testament expressed shall be performed and observed, in such manner as it should have been if this act had never been made.*   (Sect. 9.) (s)

(s) I do not give the statute in a more abridged form; it is important that it should be most attentively considered before coming to any

The following remarks may be made upon this statute:—
1. Its primary object appears to have been to give those powers to the ecclesiastical courts, for which Sir Walter Walker had unsuccessfully contended in the Court of Common Pleas; and to fix the rules which were to guide these courts in the distribution of intestates' estates.
2. The customs of the province of York, of the city of London, and of other places, having known and received customs peculiar to themselves, were specially reserved; and thus it followed, that, according to these customs, the wife and children were still entitled to their *partes ratio-nabiles;* and the same restraints as to making a will remained within the districts or places over which those customs extended as before the making of the statute.
3. The children of an intestate, advanced by him in his lifetime, were obliged to bring their advancements, whether of land or goods, to account, before sharing in the surplusage; but the heir at law was not to abate in respect of the land which he had by descent, or otherwise, from the intestate.

This statute appears to have been very inaccurately penned; it soon received amendments by other statutes; and it will be seen in the sequel that it has in numerous cases required the construction of courts of equity under various heads of the statute. (*t*) When the Statute of Frauds and Perjuries was passed in the 29th of Car. 2. (*u*), a clause was introduced into it, to explain the former statute, in regard to the goods of a feme covert, which had rendered the law upon this subject doubtful. By this last-

conclusion in regard to the alterations which ought to be made upon the law of Scotland.

(*t*) See the judgment of Lord Hardwicke in Stanley v. Stanley (May 1739), 1 Atk. 458.

(*u*) 29 Car. 2. c. 3. s. 25. made perpetual by 1 Jac. 2. c. 17. s. 5.

mentioned statute it is declared that nothing contained in the former act *shall be construed to extend to the estates of feme coverts that shall die intestate ; but that their husbands may demand and have administration of their rights, credits, and other personal estates, and recover and enjoy the same as they might have done before the making of the said act.*

Before the making of the statute of the 22d & 23d Car. 2. it had been clearly understood that the *administration* of the goods of a married woman of right appertained to her husband, *as her next and most lawful friend* within the statute of administrations of the 21 Hen. 8. c. 5. (*x*) Having thus the right to the administration, the surviving husband had also under the law, before the statute, a right to retain the whole property to himself; but as a doubt arose under the words of the first statute of distributions whether the personal estate of the wife did not go to her next in kin, exclusive of her husband, this doubt was removed by the declaratory act of the 29 Car. 2. last mentioned.

In an act passed in the reign of James II. (*y*) a clause was introduced for removing a doubt which had occurred in regard to the rights of a mother under the statute of distributions.   According to the interpretation of that last-mentioned statute, in the event of failure of descendants the father and mother were in the first degree of kindred. If the father survived, he took the whole estate of a child predeceasing, in his own right ; and if the father had died, leaving the mother surviving, she would also have become entitled to the whole personal estate of her child.   This was regulated by the before-mentioned act of James II., by which it is enacted, *that if after the death of a father any of his children shall die intestate without wife or children in*

(*x*) 1 Roll's Abridgment, 910.   (*y*) 1 Jac. 2. c. 17. s. 7.

the lifetime of the mother, every brother and sister, and the re-
presentatives of them, shall have an equal share with her, any
thing in the last-mentioned acts to the contrary notwithstanding.

When these important statutes do not reach every case
that occurs, great respect is paid in England to the three'
first chapters of the 118th novel of the Emperor Justinian,
not only because these contain the latest improvements of
the civil law, in regard to the disposition of intestates'
estates, but because the statute law of England, on the
subject of distributions, is understood to have been mo-
delled in great part on these chapters of the *jus novissimum*
of the civil law. (*z*)

It would be out of place here, where the object is chiefly
to show the general policy and bearing of the law, to enter
into a statement of the numerous cases which have occurred in regard to the distribution of the estates of intestates in England since these acts were passed. These
have gone to settle points which were not distinctly regulated by the statutes, or which were left in doubt from the
expressions used in them. It must probably always occur,
even if a code of the law were made with the greatest
diligence and care, that the courts would be called upon
to apply the principles of such code to other cases which
had not, at the time, been fixed or contemplated.

A very important alteration in the law of England connected with this subject has been introduced at a recent
period. It was long a settled rule of law in that country,
that if there was no residuary legatee appointed by the
will of a testator, the surplus or *residuum* devolved to
the executor for his own use, by virtue of the executor-
ship. This restriction to the rule was afterwards introduced
in courts of equity—that although, where the executor

(*z*) 4 Burn's Eccles. Law, 410

had no legacy, the *residuum* in general should be his own; yet where there was enough on the face of the will, *by reason of a competent legacy, or otherwise,* to imply that the testator intended that his executor should not have the residue, the undivided surplus of the estate should go to the next of kin; and if there were no kindred, then to the crown. Thus frequent cases occurred in the courts of equity in England, upon the interpretation of wills, as to the meaning and intention of the testator in this respect. Lord Thurlow stated the rule to be " *that the executor shall " take the residue, unless there is an irresistible inference to " the contrary* (a);" and it was often extremely difficult to see clearly what the meaning and intention of a testator, in such cases, truly were.

The difficulty and uncertainty upon this state of the law, however, have happily been removed by a recent act of parliament of the 11 Geo. 4. & 1 Will. 4. (*b*), which enacts, *that when any person shall die after the first day of September next after the passing of this act, having by his or her will, or any codicil or codicils thereto, appointed any person or persons to be his or her executor or executors, such executor or executors shall be deemed, by courts of equity, to be a trustee or trustees for the person or persons (if any) who would be entitled to the estate under the statute of distributions, in respect of any residue not expressly disposed of; unless it shall appear by the will, or any codicil thereto, the person or persons so appointed executor or executors was or were intended to take such residue beneficially.* (Sect. 1.)

Provided, that nothing herein contained shall affect or prejudice any right to which any executor, if this act had not

---

(*a*) Bowker v. Hunter, 1 Brown's Chanc. Cas. 328.
(*b*) 11 Geo. 4. and 1 Will. 4. c. 40.

been passed, would have been entitled, in cases where there is not any person who would be entitled to the testator's estate under the statute of distributions, in respect of any residue not expressly disposed of. (Sect. 2.)

It may be remarked of this statute, that it had no retrospect, but went to regulate the wills and codicils of persons dying within a limited time after the passing of the act; and that in regard to the crown, in a case of escheat, by reason of bastardy or otherwise, the old common law was still allowed to prevail.

It was specially enacted that the act should not extend to Scotland; and it will be seen in the sequel, that, to a certain extent, the matter had already been regulated in that country.

CHAP. III.

OF THE CHANGES ON THE CUSTOMARY LAW OF SUCCESSION
IN ENGLAND, MADE BY VARIOUS STATUTES OF LOCAL
OPERATION.

IT had followed, from the reservation contained in the first
statute of distributions, as already remarked, that the customs known and received in Wales, in the province of York,
and in the city of London, were specially preserved to them.
Thus, within those districts and places, the same rule of distribution among the wife and children, by the *partes rationabiles*, obtained after the statute as before it; and the power
of bequeathing by will was confined to the dead's part, as it
had been according to the ancient common law of England.
But it has been found necessary further to modify these
local customs by the statute law.

SECT. I.

Changes on the Custom of the Principality of Wales.

LITTLE is stated distinctly in the books of authority in
the law, as to the extent and nature of the local customs
observed in regard to the succession of personal estate
within that part of the kingdom. By the *Statutum Wal-
liæ* (a), Wales was annexed and united to England, so as to
form part of the same kingdom: but in Wales they still
retained much of their ancient policy, particularly their rule
of inheritance, that the lands were to be divided among all
the issue male, and not to descend to the eldest son alone;

(a) 12 Edw. 1.

and the law of the *partes rationabiles* in regard to succession in personal estate.

By subsequent statutes, particularly by that of the 27th of Henry VIII. (*b*), these local customs were done away, in so far as regarded the law of inheritance in real estate, which was made conformable to the common English rules of descent; but the law of succession in personal estate remained unaltered by statute till a later period. At last, however, the statute of the 7th & 8th of William III. (*c*) gave the power to the inhabitants of the principality to dispose of their whole personal estate by will. The act is in these terms : —

Whereas in several counties and places, within the principality of Wales and marches thereof, the widows and younger children of persons dying inhabitants therein have often claimed and pretended to be entitled to a part of the goods and chattels of their late husbands or fathers, called her and their reasonable part, by virtue or colour of a custom or other usage within the said principality and marches thereof, notwithstanding any disposition of the same by their husbands' and fathers' last wills and testaments, or by deed in their lives-time, and notwithstanding a competent jointure, according to the agreement made for the livelihood of the said widows by their husbands, which have often occasioned great troubles, disputes, and expences about and concerning such custom and usage, whereby many persons have been and are disabled from making sufficient provision for their families, younger children, and relations ; and great disputes, troubles, and expences have often happened concerning the same, to the great damage or ruin of many ; for remedy thereof be it enacted, that from and after the 24th day of June 1696, it shall and may be lawful for any person or persons inhabiting or residing, or who shall have

---

(*b*) 27 Hen. 8. c. 26.   (*c*) 7 & 8 Will. 3. c. 38.

*any goods or chattels within the principality of Wales or
marches thereof, by their last wills and testaments, to give,
bequeath, and dispose of all and singular their goods, chattels,
debts, and other personal estate, to their executor or executors,
or to such other person or persons as the said testator or testators shall think fit, in as large and ample manner as by the
laws and statutes of this realm any person or persons may
give and dispose of the same within any part of the province
of Canterbury or elsewhere; and that from and after the said
24th day of June 1696, the widows, children, and other the
kindred of such testator or testators, shall be barred to claim
or demand any part of the goods, chattels, or other personal
estate of such testator or testators, in any other manner than
as by the said last wills and testaments is limited and appointed; any law, statute, custom, or usage to the contrary in
anywise notwithstanding.* (Sect. 1.)

*Provided always, that nothing in this act contained shall
extend to take away any right or title which any woman now
married, or younger children now born, may have to the
reasonable part of their husband's or father's estate, by virtue
or colour of the said custom or usage.* (Sect. 2.)

It is not distinctly known what particular grievance gave
rise to this statute.   The custom does not appear to have
been fixed and clear, as in the cases of the province of York
and city of London; this appears from the language of
the preamble of the statute.   It appears to have passed
without much discussion, while Sir John Somers was Lord
Keeper of the Great Seal of England.   The proviso at the
end of the act, saving the rights of wives or children then
existing, is worthy of observation; it was added to the bill
in the Committee of the House of Lords. (*d*)   In this respect it differs from several of the other acts which have

---

(*d*) Lords' Journals, 8th April 1696.

been passed in England, regulating the law of succession in personal estate.

SECT. II.

Changes on the Custom of the Province of York.

THE ancient limits of the province of York, over which the custom extends, comprehend the counties of York, Nottingham, Cumberland, Northumberland, Westmoreland, and Durham, and part of the county of Lancaster, a great extent of country, with a vast population, and an immense mass of property. (e)

Soon after the first statute of distributions was passed, some doubts arose as to its meaning and intention, in regard to the reservation contained in it of the custom of the province of York. The administrator in that district appears to have contended, that, according to the ancient law or custom, he was entitled to retain that portion of the estate to which he had administered, and which was not subject to partition (viz. the *dead's part*), without distribution; and the same doubt arose as to the custom of the city of London. This was remedied by a clause in the before-mentioned act of the 1st of James II. (*f*), by which the law is thus declared :—*For the determining some doubts arising upon* the said statute, *it is hereby enacted and declared, that the clause therein, by which it is provided that that act, or any thing therein contained, should not any ways prejudice or hinder the customs observed within the city of London and province of York, was never intended, nor shall be taken or construed to extend to such part of any*

(e) I take this from an anonymous writer in the Scots Law Chronicle, vol. i. p. 328. I have not observed the limits of the custom laid down in any book of authority.

(f) 1 Jac. 2. c. 17. s. 8.

intestate's estate as any administrator, by virtue only of being administrator, by pretence or reason of any custom, may claim to have to exempt the same from distribution, but that such part in the hands of such administrator shall be subject to distribution, as in other cases within the said act.

But the great and important alteration upon the custom of the province of York, was that by which the inhabitants of that province were enabled to give and dispose of their whole personal estate, by their last wills and testaments, in as ample a manner as any persons could do within the province of Canterbury or elsewhere. This was effected, as to all parts of the province except the city of York, by an act of the 4th of William III. (g), in these terms : —

Whereas by custom within the province of York, or other usage, the widows and younger children of persons dying inhabitants of that province, are entitled to a part of the goods and chattels of their late husbands and fathers (called her and their reasonable part), notwithstanding any disposition of the same by their husbands' and fathers' last wills and testaments, and notwithstanding any jointures made for the livelihood of the said widows by their husbands in their lifetime, which are competent, and according to agreement, whereby many persons are disabled from making sufficient provision for their younger children ; for remedy whereof be it enacted, that from and after the 26th day of March 1693, it shall and may be lawful for any person or persons, inhabiting or residing, or who shall have any goods or chattels within the province of York, by their last wills and testaments to

---

(g) 4 Will. 3. c. 2. This act was prior in date to that already noticed, in regard to the principality of Wales. It does not appear that it excited much attention at the time; it is not noticed in the parliamentary history. It was brought into the House of Commons by Sir Christopher Musgrave, on the 5th of December 1692; and, after going through the usual stages, was read a third time, in the House of Lords, on the 7th of January 1692-3.

give, bequeath, and dispose of all and singular their goods, chattels, debts, and other personal estate, to their executor or executors, or to such other person or persons as the said testator or testators shall think fit, in as large and ample manner as by the laws and statutes of this realm any person or persons may give and dispose of the same within the province of Canterbury or elsewhere; and that from and after the said 26th day of March 1693 the widows, children, and other the kindred of such testator or testators shall be barred to claim or demand any part of the goods, chattels, or other personal estate of such testator or testators, in any other manner than as by the said last wills and testaments is limited and appointed; any law, statute, or usage to the contrary in anywise notwithstanding. (Sect. 1. & 2.)

Provided always, that nothing in this act contained shall extend or be construed to extend to the citizens of the cities of York and Chester, who are or shall be freemen of the said respective cities, inhabiting therein, or within the suburbs thereof, at the time of their death, but that every such citizen's widow and children shall and may have and enjoy such reasonable part and proportion of the testator's personal estate, as she or they might or ought to have had, by the custom of the province of York, before the making of this act. (Sect. 3.)

From some of the expressions used in the first section of this statute, by which it is enacted, that " it shall be lawful " for any person or persons inhabiting or residing, *or who* " *shall have any goods or chattels within* the province of " York, by their last wills and testaments to give, bequeath, " and dispose of all and singular their goods, chattels, " debts, and other personal estate," there is reason to suppose that the framers of the statute considered that the *lex loci rei sitæ* was of some importance in questions in regard to the custom. (*h*)

(*h*) See the speech of the Master of the Rolls in the case of Somerville v. Somerville, *infra.*

In the exception in this statute with regard to the free-men of the cities of York and Chester, there was a mistake in mentioning Chester; the custom had never extended to that city. Till the erection of the see of Chester, in the time of Henry VIII. (*i*), the archdeaconry of Chester was not within the province of York, but formed part of the diocese of Litchfield and Coventry within the province of Canterbury. (*k*) The statute subjecting the see of Chester to the Archbishop of York is silent as to the custom; thus it never obtained in the bishoprick of Chester. When this proviso came to be done away with respect to the city of York, by the statute to be immediately mentioned, it thus was not necessary to repeal the same proviso in regard to the city of Chester.

It is not known why, when this power of making a will of the whole personal estate was given to the inhabitants of the province of York, the city of York should have been excepted. This had probably some reference to the local custom which still subsisted in the city of London; and the inhabitants of York might wish to preserve their own peculiar customs also, in the second city of the nation. But they appear soon afterwards to have altered their views upon this subject; and a similar power of disposition by will was given to the inhabitants of the city of York, by an act of the second and third of Anne, in these terms: (*l*)

Whereas by an act made and passed in the fourth year of the reign of their late Majesties there is a proviso that nothing in the said act contained should extend or be construed to extend to the citizens of the cities of York and

---

(*i*) 33 Hen. 8. c. 31.

(*k*) 4 Burn's Eccles. Law, p. 456. Lord Alvanley's observation in Pickering v. Stamford, 3 Ves. 338.

(*l*) 2 & 3 Ann. c. 5.

Chester, who were or should be freemen of the said respective cities, inhabiting therein, or within the suburbs thereof, at the time of their death, but that every such citizen's widow and children should and might have and enjoy such reasonable part and proportion of the testator's personal estate as she or they might or ought to have had by the custom of the province of York, before the making of the said act: And whereas notwithstanding the mayor and commonalty, on behalf of the inhabitants of the said city of York, have humbly desired that the said proviso may be repealed, so that the freemen of the said city may have the benefit of the said act of parliament, as well as all other persons inhabiting within the said province; be it therefore enacted, that from and after the 26th day of March, in the year of our Lord 1704, the said proviso, so far as the same concerns the citizens of the city of York, shall be repealed, and is hereby repealed, and made null and void; so that from thenceforth it shall and may be lawful for all and every the citizens of the said city of York, who are or shall be freemen of the said city, inhabiting therein, or within the suburbs thereof, at the time of their death, by their last wills and testaments to give, bequeath, and dispose of their goods, chattels, debts, and other personal estates, to their executor or executors, or to such other person or persons as the said testator or testators shall think fit, as any other person or persons inhabiting or residing within the said province of York may lawfully do by virtue of the said act; and that from and after the said 26th day of March the widows, children, and other kindred of such testator or testators, shall be barred to claim or demand any part of the goods, chattels, or other personal estate of the testator or testators, in any other manner than as by the said last wills and testaments is limited and appointed; any thing in the said act, or any other law, statute, or usage to the contrary in anywise notwithstanding.

This had been first introduced as a private bill, upon

the petition of the mayor and commonalty of the city of York (m), stating that the proviso in the act of the 4th of William III. had been found to be very prejudicial to the citizens of that city. In the committee on the bill, a clause was added that the same should be deemed to be a public act, as it now stands in the statute book.

As modified by these statutes, the custom of the province of York subsists in full force to this day. The power of disposing of the whole personal estate by will, within the province, is now universal; and thus the peculiar rules of law applicable to the distribution of intestates' estates are less felt in their operation; but these differ in several very important and intricate particulars from the general law. This shall be further explained in the sequel.

SECT. III.

Changes on the Custom of the City of London.

THE doubt raised as to the operation of the first statute of distributions, in regard to the claims of the administrator to appropriate to himself the residue of the dead's part under the ancient law, applied equally to the custom of the city of London, as it did to the custom of the province of York. As already noticed, this doubt was removed by the clause in the act of 1 James II. c. 17.

It appears that the restriction on the powers of making a will, which had already been abrogated by the legislature in the principality of Wales, and in the province of York, had been felt as a grievance in the city of London. In the 11th of George I. a bill had been introduced into parliament, upon the petition of the mayor and commonalty of the city of London, for the regulation of their

---

(m) Commons' Journals, 26th January 1703–4.

E

elections, and a variety of other local matters. An opportunity was taken of introducing into this bill, clauses placing the power of making a will upon the same footing in London, as it then was in all other parts of England. This bill was the subject of much anxious discussion, upon many of its clauses, in both houses of parliament; and particularly upon that part of it which related to the alteration of the custom, in regard to the power of making a will.

At the third reading of the bill in the House of Lords, several protests were taken against different parts of it. (n) In one of these protests the objections to this part of the bill are thus expressed: " 4. Because this bill abolishes " the custom relating to the distribution of the personal " estates of free citizens, which is a custom not only of " great antiquity, but seems to us to be wisely calculated " for the benefit of a trading city, and has been acquiesced " under for so many years, without the least complaint of " any one free citizen that we have ever heard of, that the " taking it away in this manner cannot but appear to us to " be too rash and precipitate, and may too probably, in our " opinion, be very detrimental to the true interest of this " ancient, populous, loyal, and hitherto flourishing city, " the preservation of whose good order and government, " the bill itself very justly and judiciously allows to be of " the greatest consequence to the whole kingdom."

And in the other of those protests we find the following objections to this alteration of the custom : — " 5thly, We " are of opinion that the abolition of the ancient custom " of the city touching the personal estates of freemen is a " dangerous innovation, tending to let into the government " of the city, persons inexperienced and unpractised in

---

(n) Lords' Journals, 13th April 1725.

" the laudable and beneficial trade of the city and king-
" dom, and unfit for the magistracy of the city, and may
" thereby introduce improper and pernicious influences
" over the citizens; and we think that the strength, riches,
" power, and safety of the city of London have been
" hitherto in a great measure supported by this and other
" customs of the city, as the walls thereof; and we fear
" that the decay of trade, and with that of the grandeur of
" the city of London, and the diminution and loss of the
" great excises and duties arising from the trade of the
" city, on which the support of his Majesty's government
" so much depends, may be the consequence of the abolition
" of this ancient custom and privilege of the freemen of the
" city of London."

The opposition to the bill, and to this part of it, did not
however prevail; and clauses regulating this matter now
appear in the act (o), which was then passed, in these
terms : —

*Whereas great numbers of wealthy persons, not free of the
city of London, do inhabit and carry on the trade of merchandize and other employments within the said city, and
refuse or decline to become freemen of the same, by reason of
an ancient custom within the said city, restraining the freemen of the same from disposing of their personal estates by
their last wills and testaments.* (Preamble.)

*And to the intent that persons of wealth and ability, who
exercise the business of merchandize and other laudable
employments within the said city, may not be discouraged from
becoming free of the same, by reason of the custom restraining
the citizens and freemen thereof from disposing of their
personal estates by their last wills and testaments, be it
enacted, that it shall and may be lawful to and for all and*

(o) 11 Geo. I. c. 18. s. 17, 18.

E 2

every person and persons who shall, at any time from and after the 1st day of June 1725, be made or become free of the said city, and also to and for all and every person and persons who are already free of the said city, and on the said 1st day of June 1725, shall be unmarried, and not have issue by any former marriage, to give, devise, will, and dispose of his and their personal estate and estates to such person and persons, and to such use and uses, as he or they shall think fit; any custom or usage of or in the said city, or any by-law or ordinance made or observed within the same, to the contrary thereof, in anywise notwithstanding. (Sect. 17).

Provided nevertheless, that in case any person who shall, at any time or times, from and after the said 1st day of June 1725, become free of the said city, and any person or persons who are already free of the said city, and on the said 1st day of June 1725 shall be unmarried, and not have issue by any former marriage, hath agreed or shall agree by any writing under his hand, upon or in consideration of his marriage or otherwise, that his personal estate shall be subject to, or be distributed or distributable, according to the custom of the city of London; and in case any person so free, or becoming free as aforesaid, shall die intestate, in every such case the personal estate of such person so making such agreement or so dying intestate shall be subject to, and be distributed and distributable, according to the custom of the said city; any thing herein contained to the contrary, in any wise notwithstanding. (Sect. 18.)

As in the statute relative to the alteration of the law in the principality of Wales, so this act of the 11th of George I. had no operation upon the rights of wives and children, in the city of London, then existing. In this respect, it differed also from several of the other acts which have been already mentioned.

Thus, throughout England, the power is now universal

in every person to give and bequeath the whole of his personal estate by his last will and testament, as fully as he formerly could any part of such personal estate; and it does not appear that such power has been, at any subsequent period, objected to as inconvenient or inexpedient. This obviously must have tended to prevent all collision between the conflicting rules of distribution of intestates' estates, which still subsist in the different districts of England; such collisions, it will be seen afterwards, have been little known as matters of discussion in the courts of law.

According to the customs of the province of York and city of London, as modified by these acts of parliament, it will be seen in the sequel, that a great degree of intricacy has been introduced into the law of succession where these customs prevail. In a case of intestacy, the widow and children take their rateable proportions according to the ancient customs; but the dead man's part is distributed by the statutes of distribution.

There is this further intricacy in regard to these customs, that it has been decided in various cases (p), that the customs do not extend to grandchildren. Thus, though grandchildren would represent their deceased parents, and take the distributive shares of such parents under the statute, they would be cut out from all distributive share under the customs, in regard to which their uncles and aunts would be preferred to them.

It could not have been contemplated, that such intricacies should have resulted from the statutes of distribution. It is matter of surprise that they have been allowed to exist in England till the present day; but the universal power of making a will of the whole personal estate, ap-

---

(p) 1 Vern. 367; 1 P. Williams, 341; 2 Salk. 426.

pears to have operated so as to have made these intricacies little felt. Except for this power of bequeathing by will, it is not too much to say, that the variety of customs, and the intricacy of the rules thence resulting, still subsisting in England, must long ago have become intolerable.

The differences between the rules of distribution, prevailing respectively in the province of Canterbury, in the province of York, and in the city of London, shall be further stated and contrasted in a future part of this treatise.

CHAP. IV.

OF THE LAW OF SUCCESSION IN PERSONAL ESTATE IN IRELAND.

IT does not appear that this part of our inquiry is attended with much difficulty or intricacy. At an early period the law of succession in personal estate, with other branches of the common law of England, was introduced from England into Ireland. Henry III. appears to have sent to his subjects in Ireland a charter, in the first year of his reign, containing clauses and privileges similar to those contained in the charter then also granted to the people of England. This, as already noticed (*a*), directed that the division of the personal estate to the wife and children should be *per rationabiles partes.*

The charter sent to Ireland comprehended that country and Henry's Irish subjects, in the same way that the original charter comprehended England and the English people. In the conclusion of the writ, transmitting the charter to the chief justiciary of Ireland, there is this clause: "Vo- "lentes ut eisdem vos et cæteri fideles nostri Hiberniæ "gaudeatis libertatibus quas fidelibus nostris de regno "Angliæ concessimus, et illas vobis concedemus et cofir- "mabimus." (*b*)

The law was laid down in similar terms in *Magna Carta*, in the ninth of the same King (*c*); and this, amongst other

---

(*a*) Supra, p. 6.
(*b*) Blackstone on the Great Charter, &c., Introduction, p. 44.
(*c*) 9 H. III. c. 18.

E 4

ancient English statutes, was extended to Ireland by an act of the Irish Parliament of Henry VII. (d)

This extension of the English statutes to Ireland included those of the 13th of Edward I. and 31st of Edward III. in regard to the granting of administrations, already mentioned in a former chapter.

But even at this period, and for a considerable while afterwards, the laws thus introduced from England had a very partial operation in Ireland. They were confined to the English settlers, and those within the English pale. (e)   In the other parts of Ireland the ancient local customs, termed the *Brehon* law, which had been handed down in Ireland from the earliest period, prevailed among the native tribes, and was administered under their own chieftains. (f)

In the twenty-eighth year of the reign of Henry VIII. an act was passed in Ireland, regulating the mode of granting administrations in that country, nearly in the same way as this had been regulated in England by the statute of the 21st of Henry VIII. c. 5. (g)   The administration was to be granted to the widow, or to the next of kin of the intestate, or to both, as the ordinary should think fit, taking security of them for the true administration; and where divers in equal degree of kindred made claim, or where only one claimed while there were several in equal degree, the ordinary might accept one or more of them making request; and where divers required administration, and but one or more of them in equal degree, the ordinary might admit the widow, and him or them making request,

---

(d) 10 H. VII. c. 22. Ir. Stat.; one of the acts of the Parliament held at Drogheda before *Sir Edward Poynings*, the King's deputy.

(e) Edmund Spenser's View of Ireland, *passim.*

(f) Gabbett's Abridgment of English and Irish Statute Law, *Preface*, p. 6. It appears that the English laws did not overspread the country generally till the reign of Elizabeth and of James I.

(g) 28 Hen. VIII. c. 18. Ir. Stat.

or any of them, at his pleasure, taking nothing for the same.

At a subsequent period, by an act of the Irish parliament of the 7th of William III. (*h*), the law of succession in Ireland appears to have been fully regulated, and put upon the footing on which it stands at the present day. This Irish statute embodied in it, and nearly transcribed, the English act of the 22d & 23d of Charles II. c. 10., already quoted, in regard to the sureties to be granted by administrators, the rules of distribution, and the time of making distribution to be observed by them; it also adopted the regulation contained in the act of the 29th of Charles II. c. 3. in regard to the estates of feme coverts, and the rule contained in the act of the 1st of James II. c. 17. in regard to the mode of distribution as between a mother and children; and it entirely abolished the custom, which apparently had obtained in Ireland till that time, in regard to the partition among a wife and children *per rationabiles partes*, and by which a person, having a wife and children, could only dispose of one third of his personal estate by his last will and testament.

This important alteration of the law in Ireland, does not appear to have excited discussion in the parliament of that country. It was almost simultaneous with the statute passed in England in regard to the disposal of personal estate by will in the principality of Wales; but it went further than was done by this last-mentioned statute (*i*), inasmuch as by the English statute, though the power of bequeathing by will is given throughout the principality of Wales, yet the custom (though of a doubtful nature) is left in other respects as it then stood; whereas in Ireland not only a

---

(*h*) 7 Will. III. sess. 1. c. 6. Ir. Stat.
(*i*) 7 & 8 W. III. c. 38. already stated.

power was given of bequeathing by will, but the custom as to the division *per rationabiles partes* was altogether abolished.

Thus, by this Irish statute, the law of succession in personal estate was put upon the same footing in that country, as it already was in the province of Canterbury in England, and upon that footing it now remains at this day. (*k*)

(*k*) There is thus but one rule for the whole of Ireland, and it is, in respect to the law of succession and distribution, in a more desirable state than any other part of the realm.

CHAP. V.

OF THE LAW OF SUCCESSION IN SCOTLAND FROM ITS EARLY PERIOD TILL THE PRESENT TIME.

IN a former chapter we left this subject with what appeared to be the reasonable conclusion, that at the period to which the inquiry had then extended, the law of succession in personal estate had been nearly the same in England and in Scotland.   In our last chapter, it appeared that the law of succession in Ireland had been placed upon the same footing, as it was in England by the charters of Henry III.   We have traced downwards, the alterations which have been introduced in England and in Ireland upon this branch of the law.   The same thing is now proposed to be done, as far as any lights appear, in regard to the law of Scotland.

From the period above mentioned, and a considerable time afterwards, the same obscurity continues to exist in regard to the history of the law of Scotland.   We have no series of authentic writers, as in England, through whom our legal history may be deduced; we can only proceed, therefore, to trace this in the scanty notices which we find in the other books published by Skene, and in our early undoubted statute law.

1. In the statutes of William the Lyon, who reigned in the end of the 12th and beginning of the 13th century, as published by Skene, we see it thus laid down: " Gif ane " free man decease intestat, his gudes sal be distribute be " the sicht of his friends, parents, and be the provision of " halie kirk, reservand to all creditors the debts auchtand " to them be the defunct. 2. After the decease of anie " man intestat, and awand debts to creditors, his gudes

" sould be disponed be his ordinar; and the ordinar sal be
" oblissed to answer for the debts, sa far as the gudes and
" geir will extend. 3. In the samine maner that the
" executors sould doe in case the defunct had made ane
" testament." (a)

But it will be seen that the first section of this act is a
translation, almost word for word, of that chapter in the
great charter of John, in regard to the goods of intestates,
which we have already noticed (b); and the second section
of this act appears to be verbatim the same with the act of
the thirteenth of Edward I. in England upon the same subject, and was in all probability copied from it, though given
as the production of an earlier age. (c)

2. In the Leges Burgorum, also published by Skene,
and stated to have been made by David the First, the law is
thus laid down as to " the division of ane burges gudes." (d)
" The custome is, within the burghes of this realme, *passed
" memorie of man, quhereof there is na memorie in the contrair*
" that quhen ane burges hes children begottin with his awin
" wife, and thereafter deceisses, the thrid parte of all the
" gudes and geir perteines to the sonnes and dochters
" lawfully begottin.   2. And the eldest sonne and heire
" of that man and wife sall have the like parte and portion
" as the other bairnes, that is, equal with any of them,
" except he be forisfamiliat be his father."

According to this statute, it would appear that there had
been a custom in the burghs of Scotland relative to the law
of succession different from the general law, as there was
in various parts of England.   For a long period no trace
of such custom has been known in Scotland, and there has
been but one rule of law in that country, in regard to the
succession in personal estate.

(a) Statutes of William, c. 22.   (b) Supra, p. 6.
(c) 13 Edward I. c. 19.   (d) Leges Burgorum, c. 124.

From the expression, " passed memorie of man, quhereof " there is no memorie in the contrair," there is strong reason to conclude that this had had an English origin. This is precisely the mode in which their writers describe the *legal memory* of the English law. (*e*)

3. The other notices of the law of succession in personal estate in our statute book are very scanty. In 1540 an act of parliament was passed in these terms (*f*): *For sa-meikle as oft-times zoung persones dies that may not make testamentes, the ordinares usis to give their executoures datives to their gudes, quhilkis intromettis therewith, and withdrawis the gudes fra the kin and friendes that suld have the samin be the law, it is statute and ordained be the three estates of this present parliament, that quhair ony sik persons dies within age that may not make their testamentes, the nearest of their kin to succeed to them sall have their gudes, without prejudice to the ordinares anent the quote of their testamentes.*

In this act it appears, that, by the law as it then stood, the next of kin were entitled to the personal estate of persons who died before they were capable to make testaments, and that the ordinaries were in use to make grants thereof, to the prejudice of such next of kin. To remedy this was the object of the statute; and by this act the law appears to have been placed upon a better footing in Scotland than it was in England till the statutes of distribution were passed in that country in the 17th century.

This act is also to be noticed in regard to the expression which it contains of " *executoures datives.*" The law language of Scotland had been then settled in the distinction of *executors testamentary* and *executors dative*, which has continued to our time. These in England had been long described respectively as *executors* and *administrators*. (*g*)

(*e*) 1 Instit. s. 176. (*f*) 1540, c. 120.

(*g*) In every country (except Scotland) which uses the English

Something as to the state of our law of succession may be discovered in the *instructions* given to the commissaries with regard to the confirmation of testaments in 1610. In laying down the rules for ascertaining the quantity of the *dead's part,* which was liable in payment of the *quot,* or composition payable to the commissaries and their officers for granting confirmations, and after specifying what debts were to be deducted from the inventory, the instructions proceed thus: " Quhilkis deductiounis beand maid be the " persoun deceist, he leivand behind him wife and bairnis, " gif ony of the bairnis, be unforisfamiliat, the testament (*h*) " dividis in thre partis, and the thrid of the fre geir payis " quot; gif all the bairnis be forisfamiliat the testament " then dividis in twa partis, and the half of the fre gear " payis quot; gif there be na bairnis, the testament dividis " likewayis in twa, and the half of the fre geir pays quot; " gif the persoun deceist be singil, and hes na bairnis un- " forisfamiliat, in that cais the hail fre geir payis quot, but " ony divisioun." (*i*)   At this time the law appears to have

---

language, — in England, in Ireland, and in the American States, — the words *executors* and *administrators* have now a precise and technical meaning ; the first, denoting the *executors testamentary,* and the other the *executors dative* of the law of Scotland.   The word *administrator* in the above sense is unknown either in the civil or canon law.   It was introduced, as already noticed (supra, p. 28.), into the law of England by the statute of 31 Ed. III. c. 11.   It would be a matter of some convenience were the words executors and administrators adopted in Scotland in the same sense.   I have observed the expression *executors,* used in the sense of the Scottish law, leading to misapprehension at a very recent period.

(*h*) At this period the word *testament* appears to have been commonly used instead of moveable succession, or personal estate.   This was very different from the *Testatio mentis* of the civil law (Inst. lib. 2. tit. 10.) ; the expression is still so commonly used in Scotland in the same sense, that its anomalous nature scarcely attracts attention.

(*i*) Instructions to the commissaries in 1610, printed in Balfour's Practicks, p. 666.

been clearly understood. If the deceased left a wife and children, or a child not forisfamiliated, the division was into three parts; but if the children were forisfamiliated, or had accepted provisions from the father, the division was to be bipartite, and in the same way as if he had left only a wife, and no children.

In the reign of James the Sixth an important statute was passed in Scotland, for further settling the law of succession in that country. (*k*) This statute was in these terms: *Our Soveraigne Lord understanding that a great number of ignorant people, the time of their sicknesse and disease, or otherwise at the making of their testaments and latter wills, do nominate certain strangers to be their executors, meaning only to commit the care of their goods, and diligent ingetting thereof, to the saids strangers, and that to the behoof of their children, or other persons who are nearest of kin: whereas, by the contrary, the said office of executry, by the interpretation now observed, doth cary with it the whole profit and commoditie of the defunct's part of the goods contained in testament; which his Majesty findes to be altogether against law, conscience, and equity: therefore his Majesty, with advice and consent of the estates of parliament, finds and declares, that all executors, already nominate in any testament not as yet confirmed, or to be nominate in any testament to be made hereafter, are and shall be obliged to make count, reckoning and payment of the whole goods and geare appertaining to the defunct, and intrometted with by them, to the wife, children, and nearest of kin, according to the division observed by the laws of this realm; reserving onely to the saids executors the thrid of the defunct's part, all debts being first payed and deduced, without prejudice always to the saids executors of whatsoever legacies left to them by the saids defuncts, which shall no wayes be pre-*

(*k*) 1617. c. 14.

judged by this present act; but the saids executors shall have full right to their saids legacies, albeit the same exceed the said thrid of the defunct's part; and in case the saids legacies exceed the whole thrid part, the saids executors shall have right to the whole legacie, and no part of the thrid; with this expresse declaration, that where legacies are left to the executors, they shall not fall both the saids legacies and a thrid by this present act, but the saids legacies shall be imputed and allowed to them in part of payment of their thrid.

This is a very important statute, in various points of view; we see from it the state of the law at the time when the act was passed. The executors testamentary claimed the whole *residuum* to themselves, after payment of debts and legacies; but by this *just act* (as it is termed by Sir George Mackenzie in his observations upon it) the residue is directed to be paid to the wife, children, and nearest of kin, reserving to the executor the third of the deceased's part; and if any legacy was given to the executor, such legacy was to be imputed to account of his third part.

Under the provisions of this statute, which is still in full force, the law was regulated more equitably than it had been in England, down to the period when the recent act of the 11th of George IV. and 1st of William IV. (already noticed) (*l*) was passed. This last mentioned act appears to have put this matter upon its proper footing.

In one of the acts of the parliament of Scotland in 1644, an ease is granted to clergymen surviving their wives, in regard to their *books* falling under the *executry* of the predeceasing wives. (*m*) The act is in these terms: " The " estates of parliament presently conveened by vertue of the " last act of the last parliament holden by his Majestie and " three estates, in anno 1641, Finding ministers to be much

---

(*l*) Supra, p. 39.   (*m*) 1644. c. 19., rescinded acts.

" prejudged *that their books* in their own life times should
" fall in their wives executorie; therefore the saids estates
" liberates and exeemes all ministers surviving their wives
" from confirming their books in their wives testaments,
" and from giving up inventar thereof; and declares their
" books no wayes to fall in the executorie of their wives
" whom they survive."

This was repealed by the acts rescissory of Charles II.,
and the matter again returned to the regulations of the
common law; but it is worthy of notice, as touching upon
a point of great importance in the law of Scotland at this
day, namely, the rights accruing to the personal representatives of a wife on her predeceasing her husband; and
this appears to be the only mention of this point in the
statute law of Scotland.

The only other act which it is necessary to notice upon
this subject is of very recent date, — that of the 4th of
George IV. c. 98, relative to " the better granting of confirmations in Scotland."   It had been a maxim of the law,
that *confirmation* was necessary to vest the moveable estate
of a person deceased in his or her representatives; and
that if such representatives died before confirmation, all
their rights died with them, and accrued to the other next
of kin of the deceased.   By this act it was intended to
remedy this inconvenience: it is accordingly enacted (sect.
1.) that *in all cases of intestate succession, where any person
or persons, who, at the period of the death of the intestate,
being next of kin, shall die before confirmation be expede, the
right of such next of kin shall transmit to his or her representatives, so that confirmation may, and shall be granted to
such representatives, in the same manner as confirmations
might have been granted to such next of kin, immediately
upon the decease of such intestate.* (n)

(n) Some doubts have been suggested as to the efficiency of this

F

As we do not discover from these statutes how the law of
Scotland came to differ so widely from the law of England,
as it now does, in regard to the rules of succession in personal
estate, neither can we find this matter explained in any writer
on the Scotch law. The earliest *name* of a writer on the law
of Scotland, is that of Sir James Balfour, of Pittendriech. (o)
In the compilation termed " Balfour's Practicks," the ancient law, as laid down in the Regiam Majestatem, is often
referred to, but no deduction is given of the various changes
of the law which had taken place in the intervening period.
This appears to be a book of very doubtful authority, composed of many miscellaneous matters, more resembling a
common-place book, than a digested treatise on the law.
Indeed the author, whoever he was, in a good many instances, cites " *ex meo albo libro.*" There is no internal
evidence, nor evidence of cotemporary authority, to show
that this book was compiled by the person whose name it
bears; and several of the matters contained in the book,
(particularly the *Injunctiones to the Commissaries in* 1610,)
are of dates a good many years after the death of Balfour. (p)

---

statute, to carry into effect the very proper and beneficial objects which
were intended, when it was framed (*Stair by Brodie, p.* 597. *in notis*);
but it is hoped that the statute will be found to operate as it was meant
to operate, namely, to preserve to the representatives of a party dying,
all those rights to which such party was entitled, and which, by the
want of confirmation, would have gone over to others. The right of
obtaining confirmation, which belonged to the party dying, is transmitted to his or her representatives. Upon their obtaining confirmation, could any remoter next of kin enter into competition with them?
We think not; but if there be any ambiguity in regard to this very important matter, such ambiguity should not be allowed to remain.

(o) In the fourth report of Mr. Thomson, the deputy clerk register,
to the commissioners on the public records in 1810, he says (speaking
of this book), " I am not, at present, aware of any authority for ascrib-
ing it to Sir James Balfour, more ancient than the reign of Charles II."

(p) Sir James Balfour appears to have been a most extraordinary
person. In Goodall's preface to the printed edition of Balfour's Prac-

In Craig's time the law of succession in personal estate
in Scotland, does not appear to have differed materially
from what it is at this day.   His book chiefly related to real
estate, but from time to time it notices also the rules of law
in regard to personal estate.   It may be noticed that at that
period the rule of law, in regard to the division of the succession of a person deceasing, under certain circumstances,
between his relations by the father's and mother's side,
(*materna maternis et paterna paternis*,) does not appear to
have been fixed as it is at present: it is now well understood that no such rule obtains in the law of Scotland in
the succession of personal estate, though Craig appears to
have been of a contrary opinion. (*q*)

Sir John Nisbet in his *Doubts* appears also to have
been inclined to this rule of succession in personal estate,
of *materna maternis et paterna paternis*. (*r*)   But Sir James
Stewart is clearly of opinion that it had no place in the
law of Scotland. (*s*)

Neither do we find in the reported decisions, nor in the
institutional writers on the law of Scotland, any deduction
of the alterations of the law upon this subject.   In both

---

ticks (Edinburgh, 1754), the date of Balfour's birth is not mentioned,
but he is said to have died in 1583.   In 1546, he appears to have been
implicated in the murder of Beaton; he was carried to France as a pri-
soner, and, according to Knox (b. 1. p. 77.), was sent to the French
galleys, where he continued for some time.   He appears afterwards to
have been a favourite with Mary; he was successively parson of Flisk,
Commendator of Pittenweem, Clerk Register, some time President of
the Court of Session, Deputy Governor of Edinburgh Castle, and a
Privy Councillor.   Certain of the *Black Acts*, printed in the reign of
Mary, bear his signature.   At his death he appears to have been under
forfeiture for accession to the murder of Darnley.   His talents must
have been of an extraordinary kind to have fitted him for these various
offices, in a period so stirring and turbulent.

(*q*) Craig, l. 2. Dieg. 15. sect. 6.
(*r*) Nisbet's Doubts, p. 123.
(*s*) Stewart's Answers, p. 205.

we find the rules of law laid down as they subsist at the present day.

In Burn's Treatise on the Ecclesiastical Law of England, he states an hypothesis, in regard to the law of Scotland, on the subject of the succession in personal estate, that it had been borrowed from the custom of the province of York, which it resembled in several particulars, because, as he says, "the whole kingdom of Scotland, when this custom of the province of York took place, was within and a part of that province." And in aid of this hypothesis, he notices several points in which the law of Scotland agrees with the custom of the province of York. (*t*) It does not appear, however, that this hypothesis is well founded. In the reign of William the Lyon, in 1188, the independence of the Scottish church appears to have been declared by a bull of Pope Celestine the Third. (*u*) At a period, as we have endeavoured to show (*x*), considerably later, the law of the division of personal estate, *per rationabiles partes*, prevailed, as the general law, in England, in Scotland, and in Ireland.

As far as appears, some of the most important rules in the law of succession in personal estate in Scotland, have been at all times unknown in every part of England; particularly the doctrine of the communion of goods between husband and wife, and the important consequences thence resulting to the parties and their children. These

---

(*t*) 4 Burn's Eccles. Law (*Custom of the province of York*), p. 475. I have occasion often to cite this work, which is done from Tyrwhitt's edition of 1824.

(*u*) 1 Hailes's Annals, 130. Though there were great disputes afterwards as to the independence of the Scottish church, there is no reason to believe that an archbishop of York could, at a period subsequent to this, have impressed the custom of York on the kingdom of Scotland.

(*x*) Supra, pp. 7. 24.

have been adopted in Scotland, and remain in full force in that country at the present day.

If an hypothesis is to be sought for, it appears to be not unreasonable to conclude, that we have to look to a continental source for the origin of our present system of the law of succession *in mobilibus,* and for the introduction of that modification of the Roman law of succession which now obtains in Scotland. It belongs to our civil history to deduce, from their origin, the intimate political relations which subsisted for so many centuries between Scotland and France. England and Scotland, in the lapse of centuries, had become almost *natural enemies;* and the connexion between France and Scotland, arising from their mutual interests, was cemented by the closest alliances. During this period the legislature had, in 1532, instituted the College of Justice, on the model of the Parliament of Paris (*y*); and, soon after the marriage of Mary to the Dauphin, in 1558, Frenchmen and Scotchmen were mutually naturalised in the two countries. The royal *ordonnance* of Henry II. of France, granting these privileges to Scotsmen within the realm of France, is printed in our statute book, along with the act of the Scottish parliament, granting similar privileges to Frenchmen within Scotland. From this ordonnance, Henry appears to have considered, that by this marriage the realms of France and Scotland were to be for ever inseparably united: He says, " Au moyen de quoy estans les subjects des deux royaumes, (qui ont jusques icy & des long temps ordinairement communiqué ensemble, vescu en mutuelle amitié & intelligence, favorisé & secouru les uns les autres,) par l'approche des maisons de France & d'Escosse, tellement unis ensemble, *que nous les estimons comme une mesme chose."* (*z*).

(*y*) Mackenzie's Institute, b. 1. t. 3. s. 7.

(*z*) 1558, c. 66. (A striking instance of the uncertainty of all human affairs!) It appears from a memorial printed by Sir George Mackenzie,

It is reasonable to conclude, that with all this intimacy of connexion, the laws of succession in personal estate had become gradually approximated to each other in the two countries. When we find at that period in France several of those modifications of the civil law which are in full force in Scotland to this day, it is not unreasonable to conclude that we have derived them from that country.

But although some of the chief doctrines of the law of Scotland, such as the communion of goods between husband and wife, and various consequences resulting from this communion of goods, appear to have been universal in France, we have not been able to discover in any part of that country the same rules of law, in the succession of personal estate, obtaining, *as a whole*, which now prevail in Scotland.

Down to a very recent period all France was divided " en pays coutumiers, et en pays de droit ecrit." There were, besides, the royal *ordonnances*, which were common to both divisions of the kingdom. (*a*) But in the *pays de droit ecrit*, where the Roman law prevailed, that modification of the law of succession which is contained in the three first chapters of the 118th novel of the Emperor Justinian was constantly followed as the rule. (*b*) These chapters introduced new regulations in regard to the succession of *descendants*, of *ascendants*, and of *collaterals*, which never appear to have obtained in Scotland. The first chapter

---

in his *observations* upon this act, that down to the reign of Charles II. the privileges thus granted to Scotchmen were claimed as being them still in force in France.

(*a*) Projèt du Code Civil, Discours Preliminaire, p. 16.

(*b*) Code Civil " Rapport fait au Tribunal, par Chabot, sur la loi re-" lative aux successions." He says, " Et cette novelle, qui forme le " dernier etat de la legislation Romaine, etait constamment suivie dans " le pays de droit ecrit."

of this celebrated novel, in regard to descendants, lays down the rule of succession *per stirpes*, and the right of *representation* of the descendants of deceased children. The second regulates the rights of ascendants, particularly of the mother, whom the ancient law of the twelve tables had rejected from the succession; and lays down the rule of law of dividing the succession by *paterna paternis et materna maternis*. The third chapter regulates the rights of collaterals, provides for the representation of brothers' and sisters' children, and settles the preferences of the *whole* and the *half blood*.

The customary laws of France were of prodigious extent and intricacy. (c)   These were full of rules, differing in the several parts of the kingdom upon almost every point regarding the disposal of and succession in real and personal estate.   Some of them contain rules by which the succession was confined to agnates, or relations by the father's side, to the exclusion of the mother and the maternal relations, as in the law of Scotland.   Whether there were any of these customs which agreed precisely with the rules of personal succession now observed in the law of Scotland, has not been observed; and it would be unprofitable to pursue the inquiry more minutely.   Neither are there any means by which we can discover why, when we adopted the rules of the civil law in regard to succession in Scotland, we appear to have rejected so much of the *jus novissimum* as was contained in this novel of Justinian. Several of these rules are of a very equitable nature.   There

---

(c) The " Nouveau Coutumier de France, et des Provinces connues sous les noms des Gaules," contains a statement of these customs, to the number of *five hundred and forty-seven*. These must have occasioned intricacy almost intolerable in regard to succession in France. In recent times the whole have been swept away by the " *Code Napoleon* " and the " *Code Civil.*"

can be no doubt, that, when we come to revise the state of
the law of succession in Scotland, much benefit will result
from minutely considering the matured wisdom of the ·
Roman law upon this subject. Accordingly, in England (d),
and in France (e), we see the great attention that has been
paid to it, in settling the respective laws of succession in
personal estate in those two countries.

(d) By the Statute of Distributions.
(e) Code Civil, " Des Successions."

CHAP. VI.

OF THE CASES WHICH HAVE ARISEN IN SCOTLAND UPON
QUESTIONS OF INTERNATIONAL SUCCESSION, BEFORE IT WAS
SETTLED THAT THIS SHOULD BE REGULATED BY THE LAW
OF THE *DOMICIL.*

For a long period, the difference between the rules of law
in the succession of personal estate in the several parts of
the British empire, between themselves, or as respected the
personal property of foreigners situated in Britain, appears
to have attracted little attention.   These rules had not
then come distinctly into collision in any case which has
been noticed.   Foreign jurists, however, have long been
familiar with the doctrines resulting from the conflict of
laws in the different countries of Europe, in regard to the
succession of persons dying, having *bona mobilia,* or *nomina
debitorum,* in different countries, where the rules of the law
of succession are different.   This had arisen out of the
great variety of the rules of law which had sprung up in
the different countries of Europe, and often in the same
country, since the fall of the Roman empire.

In the *corpus juris,* or body of the civil law, there is nothing very distinctly laid down, on the subject of international law.   One chief reason for this is stated to have
been, that at the time when that body of laws was promulgated, the Roman empire, which contained the whole
civilised portion of the globe as then known, was governed
by the same laws. (*a*)   Though this may not be admitted

(*a*) Huber says, " In jure Romano non est mirum nihil hac de re
" extare, cum populi Romani per omnes orbis partes diffusum, et æqua-

in its fullest extent, it is certain that the doctrines of the foreign jurists on questions of this nature have grown up in comparatively modern times; and that they have drawn little of these from the works compiled by Justinian. (b)

It is a principle flowing from the independence of nations, that the law of one country can have no intrinsic force, *proprio vigore*, except within the territorial limits and jurisdiction of that country. The maxim "extra territo- " rium jus dicenti impune non paretur" (c), is applied to the

---

" bili jure gubernatum, imperium conflictui diversarum legum non æque " potuerit esse subjectum." (Huber, prælect. jur., pars 2. lib. 1. tit. 3. s. 1.) But there seems to be no reason to doubt, that as well before the time of Justinian as afterwards, there existed different rules of law in the different parts of the Roman world. (1. Hertii opera, sec. 4. de collis. leg.) In the Digest, there are traces of the existence and operation of the *lex loci*. (Digest, lib. 50. tit. 1. l. 21. s. 7. tit. 3. l. l. tit. 4. l. 18. s. 27. tit. 6. l. 5. s. 1.) In the argument on the case of *Somerville*, to be afterwards mentioned, it is stated as matter of doubt, whether in the time of Justinian the succession to the personal property of a citizen of Jerusalem would have been regulated by the Roman law, or by that of the Jewish people. (Somerville v. Somerville, 5 Vesey, 780.)

(b) An exception should be made in regard to the definition of Domicil, which, it will be seen in the sequel, forms an important matter of inquiry in all cases of international law. Whether domicil was to be held as regulating only in regard to offices, or otherwise, we find many texts in the civil law bearing upon this subject; among others, the following, which are often quoted, may be noticed here : — " Et in eodem " loco singulos habere domicilium, non ambigitur, ubi quis larem rerum- " que ac fortunarum suarum summam constituit; unde (rursus) non " sit discessurus, si nihil avocet; unde cum profectus est peregrinari " videtur; quod si rediit, peregrinari jam destitit." (Cod. lib. 10. tit. 39. l. 7.) " Eum domum unicuique nostrum debere existimari, ubi " quisque sedes et tabulas haberet, suarumque rerum constitutionem " fecisset." (Dig. lib. 50. tit. 16. l. 203.) " Si quis negotia sua non " in coloniâ, sed in municipio semper agit; in illo vendit, emit, con- " trahit, eo in foro, balneo, spectaculis utitur, ibi festos dies celebrat; " omnibus denique municipii commodis, nullis coloniarum fruitur; ibi " magis habere domicilium quam ubi colendi causa diversatur." (Dig. lib. 50. tit. 1. l. 27.) " Domicilium re et facto transfertur, non nuda " contestatione." (Ibid. lib. 50. tit. 1. l. 20.)

(c) Dig. lib. 2. tit. 1. l. 20.

municipal laws of the different countries in the world, as the Romans held it to be applicable in relation to the authority of their magistrates. But the comity of nations, with a view to the comfort and convenience of their respective subjects, has rightly conceded that there should be some exceptions to this strict rule of the territorial law; and these exceptions form the subject of international law. They present many questions of great difficulty which have long exercised, and still continue to exercise, the ingenuity of the most acute minds, conversant with all that exists of the mass of accumulated learning upon matters of this sort.

International law has never been treated at large as a system, by the writers on the laws of these realms. It is only in modern times, that questions of this kind have attracted the attention of our courts of law; several centuries after the wants of continental Europe had made the subject of international law familiar to their writers.

In their disquisitions upon matters of international law, and the rules by which these were to be governed, the continental writers have endeavoured to get rid of many of the difficulties of their subject, by classing it under the heads of *personal*, *real*, and *mixed statutes*. They use this word *statute* in a different sense from that in which it is used by British writers: with us it is commonly applied to acts of the legislature, in contradistinction to the rules of the common law: with them it is applied to the whole municipal law of any particular state, from whatever source derived. (*d*) *Personal* statutes are held by the continental writers to be of general obligation, in so far as the *person* or *status* of

---

(*d*) In some writers the word *statute* is used to signify the particular municipal law of any state, by way of distinction from the Roman imperial law, styled the common law. Voet. de Statutis, c. 1. s. 4., defines a statute to be *jus particulare, ab alio legislatore quam Imperatore constitutum.*

any individual is concerned. *Real* statutes are applied to property, whether moveable or immoveable, and are not otherwise connected with individuals: they are held to have no force *extra territorium* within which the property is situated. *Mixed* statutes are those which at once concern persons and property of any description.

In the application of this classification to particular cases, there has been a great diversity of opinion among the most distinguished of the foreign jurists, from Bartholus and Baldus in the fourteenth century, to Heineccius and Boullenois in the eighteenth. They were never able to lay down any certain and satisfactory rules for distinguishing personal from real statutes; nor to show, in regard to mixed statutes, whether the personal or real portions of these should have preponderance.

It would be out of place here, to enter into any inquiry in regard to the conflicting opinions of civilians upon this intricate subject (*e*); their doctrines upon personal, real,

---

(*e*) In the treatise prefixed to Mr. Henry's Demerara case of *Odwin and others* v. *Forbes*, we have, for the first time in the English language, an explanation of the *personal, real, and mixed statutes* of the continental jurists. (Chap. 1, 2, 3, 4.)

But in the United States of America we find these subjects treated more at large, and in a more scientific way. The same causes which have made the doctrines of international law familiar upon the continent of Europe, have rendered it necessary to study them in America. There appears to be a great diversity in the municipal laws of the several states forming the American Union, some of these having been transplanted from the different countries of Europe, which originally gave law to those territories.

This has already produced among them writers who have treated of these important subjects, of distinguished name. We have learned the respect that is due to Professor Kent, the late chancellor of the state of New York, author of the " Commentaries on American Law," a name probably not inferior, as a legal writer, to any of the present day. The treatise of the late Samuel Livermore, of New Orleans, " On the " Contrariety of Laws," and the commentaries of Dr. Story, " On the

and mixed statutes, have very rarely been matter of inquiry in the British courts of law.

It may be noticed, however, that Huber, a distinguished writer of the seventeenth century, and much referred to in the British courts, has laid down certain axioms, which appear to have received very general concurrence; and which apply, amongst others, directly to the doctrines of international succession in moveable estate. The *first* of these axioms is, that the laws of every state are of force within its own bounds, and towards its own subjects, but no farther. 2. That those are to be held subjects of any state, who are found within its limits, whether their residence be permanent or temporary. 3. That the rulers of nations act with comity, when they admit that the laws of every people exercised within their own limits should have every where the like force, in so far as they do not prejudice the power or rights of other states, or their citizens. (*f*)

" Conflict of Laws, Foreign and Domestic," are still in few hands in this country. They introduce us to the study of the foreign jurists, in a way hitherto unknown in our common language. These writers have the additional advantage of bringing to the consideration of these subjects, an intimate acquaintance with all that has been written and decided in regard to the different systems of laws obtaining in Great Britain. Their works form an important accession to the legal knowledge of the present age. Inquiries of this kind present a new field for the generous rivalry of kindred nations.

(*f*) " 1. Leges cujusque imperii vim habent intra terminos ejusdem " republicæ, omnesque ei subjectos obligant, nec ultra. 2. Pro sub-" jectis imperio habendi sunt omnes, qui intra terminos ejusdem repe-" riuntur, sive in perpetuum, sive ad tempus ibi commorentur. 3. " Rectores imperiorum id comiter agunt, ut jura cujusque populi intra " terminos ejus exercita teneant ubique suam vim, quatenus nihil potes-" tati aut juri alius imperantis, ejusque civium præjudicetur." (Huber, lib. 1. tit. 3. de conflictu legum, s. 2.) These axioms are disputed by other writers. Hertius appears to have been opposed to them. After quoting them he asks, " Si sola populorum conniventiâ id niti dicamus,

These axioms may be applied to all the variety of topics which have arisen, or may arise, upon the subject of international law. In a particular manner they are applicable to the subject of our present treatise.

It relieves this part of our subject from difficulty, that the Continental writers appear to concur in their views upon questions of international succession. It is clearly laid down by them all, 1. That immoveable or heritable property is in all things to be governed by the law of the country in which it is situated; 2. That in regard to moveable or personal property, it is held, by a fiction, that it has no *situs*, but that it is attached to the person of the owner, and is subject to the law of that country in which the owner had his domicil at the time of his death, if the law of the country of the domicil be not contrary to some special rule of law of the state within which the property may happen to be. (g)

" quæ juris erit efficacia." But they appear to have obtained in our own courts, in other questions of international law.

Livermore, the American jurist, objects strongly to the idea of a court of justice acting upon *comity;* he thinks that it is their business solely to administer justice according to law. (Livermore " On the " Contrariety of Laws," p. 26.) But what law can have effect *extra territorium* unless *ex comitate?*

(g) I am not aware that there is any difference of opinion among the Continental jurists upon this subject. A few of their dicta may be stated here.

Paul Voet says, " Ut immobilia statutis loci regantur ubi sita." (De Statut. et eor. concursu, § 9. c. 1. n. 3.) Again, " Verum mobilia ibi cense- " antur esse secundum juris intellectum, ubi is cujus ea sunt sedem atque " larem suarum fortunarum collocavit." (Ibid. § 4. c. 2. n. 2.) Again, " Verum an quod de immobilibus dictum, idem de mobilibus statuendum " erit? Respondeo quod non: quia illorum bonorum nomine, nemo " censetur semet loci legibus subjecisse. Ut quæ res certum locum non " habent, quia facile de loco in locum transferuntur, adeoque secundum " loci statuta regulantur ubi domicilium habuit defunctus." (Ibid. § 9. c. 1. n. 8.)

John Voet writes on the same subjects: " In successionibus, testandi " facultate, contractibus, aliisque, mobilia ubicunque sita regi debere do-

By this fiction as to the *situs* of the moveable property, the Continental jurists have avoided the operation of their own

---

" micilii jure; non vero legibus loci illius in quo naturaliter sunt con-
" stituta." (Voet. ad Pandectas, lib. 1. tit. 4. pars 2. de statut. s. 11.)
Again, " Sed considerandum quadam fictione juris, seu malis, præsum-
" tione, hanc de mobilibus determinationem conceptam niti; cum enim
" certo, stabilique hæc situ careant, nec certo sunt alligata loco, sed ad
" arbitrium domini undequaque in domicilii locum revocari facile ac
" reduci possint, et maximum domino plerumque commodum adferre
" soleant cum ei sunt præsentia, visum fuit hanc inde conjecturam sur-
" gere, quod dominus velle censeatur, ut illic omnia sua sint mobilia,
" aut saltem esse intelligantur, ubi fortunarum suarum larem, sum-
" mamque constituit, id est, in loco domicilii." (Ibid.)
When treating of what was considered moveable by the law of the
domicil, but immoveable by the *lex loci rei sitæ*, he says, "Quo posito,
" necesse fuerit, ut quæ in domicilii loco mobilia habentur, immobilia
" vero illic ubi sunt, regantur lege loci in quo vere sunt, magistratu ne
" ex comitate quidem permissuro ut quasi mobilia domicilii dominici
" sequerentur jura." (Ibid.)
Again, " Etenim regulariter mobilia ubicunque naturaliter exsiterint,
" illic censentur esse, ubi dominus domicilium fovet: immobilia illic,
" ubi vere sunt; indeque immobilia regenda lege loci in quo sita
" sunt; mobilia vero ex lege domicilii domini." (Ibid. lib. 1. tit. 8.
s. 30.)
Huber, when treating of the same matters, says, " Communis et
" recta sententia est, in rebus immobilibus servandum esse jus loci in
" quo bona sunt sita; quia cum partem ejusdem territorii faciant di-
" versæ jurisdictiones legibus adfici non possunt." (Præl. Jur. Civ.
pars 1. lib. 3. tit. 13. s. 21. de success.)
Again, " Verum in mobilibus nihil esse causæ cur aliud quam jus
" domicilii sequamur, quia res mobiles non habent affectionem versus
" territorium, sed ad personam patrisfamilias duntaxat; qui aliud quam
" quod in loco domicilii obtinebat voluisse videri non potest." (Ibid.)
Vattel says, on the same subject, " Puisque l'étranger demeure ci-
" toyen de son pays, et membre de sa nation, les biens qu'il delaisse
" en mourant dans un pays étranger, doivent naturellement passer à
" ceux qui sont ses heritiers suivant les loix de l'état dont il est mem-
" bre: mais cette règle générale n'empêche point que les biens immeubles
" ne doivent suivre les dispositions des loix du pays où ils sont situés."
(Vattel, Droit des gens, liv. 2. c. 8. s. 110.)
Pothier writes on the same subject: " Pour sçavoir à l'empire de
" quelle coutume une chose est sujette, il faut distinguer celles qui ont

doctrines as to *real statutes*, which otherwise would have subjected even this species of property to the law of the country within which it was situated. (*h*)   It is now to be seen how these important questions have been treated by our own writers, and in our own courts.

It appears that several centuries ago questions of this kind had presented themselves to the Scottish legislature. Thus, in a statute of James I. (*i*), regulations were made

---

" une situation véritable ou feinte, et celles qui n'en ont aucune. Les " choses qui ont une situation véritable sont les heritages, c'est à dire, " les fonds de terre, et maisons, et tout ce qui en fait partie." Then he goes on to describe the rights connected with land and houses which had " une situation feinte;" and he adds, " Toutes ces choses " qui ont une situation réelle ou feinte, sont sujettes à la loi ou coutume " du lieu où elles sont situés ou censées l'être." (Coutumes d'Orleans, c. 1. s. 2. n. 23.)

Again, " Les choses qui n'ont aucune situation sont les meubles " corporels, les creances mobiliaires," &c.   " Toutes ces choses qui " n'ont aucune situation suivent la personne à qui elles appartiennent, " et sont par consequent régies par la loi ou coutume qui régit cette " personne, c'est à dire, par celle du lieu de son domicile." (Ibid. n. 24.)

And Denisart also states to the same effect : " C'est le domicile qui " règle le partage des successions mobiliaires."   (Denisart, tom. i. tit. Domicile, n. 3. p. 513.)

Again, " A l'égard des immeubles, ce n'est pas le domicile de celui " qui le possedoit, qui règle à qui ils doivent appartenir dans la suc- " cession et comment ils se doivent partager : c'est la *coutume* dans le " ressort de laquelle les biens sont situés." (Ibid. No. 5.)

Bynkershoek, after stating that personal property is subject to that law which governs the person of the owner, but that immoveable property is regulated by the lex loci rei sitæ, says, " Adeo recepta hodie " sententia est, ut nemo ausit contra hiscere." (Quæst. Jur. Priv., lib. 1. c. 16.)

·   (*h*) That distinguished writer, Mr. ex-Chancellor Kent, observes, that Mr. Henry and Mr. Livermore had become so completely initiated in the Roman law, as to use the terms *real and personal statutes* as familiarly as an English lawyer would the words real and personal property. He protests against the introduction of such a perversion of the word statute, so long as we can find other and more appropriate terms to distinguish foreign from domestic law.   (Vol. ii. lect. 39. p. 456.)

(*i*) 1426, c. 88.

strongly resembling those which in recent times have been found to result from the rule of the law of the domicil. In that statute it is thus decreed: "Quod causæ omnium mercatorum et incolarum regni Scotiæ in Zelandia Flandria vel alibi extra regnum decendentium, qui se causâ mercandisarum suarum peregrinationes, vel aliqua quacunque causa (dummodo causa non morandi extra regnum), se transtulerunt, debent tractari coram suis ordinariis infra regnum, a quibus sua testamenta confirmantur, non obstante quod quædam ex bonis hujusmodi decedentium tempore sui obitus fuerunt in Anglia vel in partibus transmarinis." Though this statute relates rather to the mode of confirming the testaments of Scotsmen dying abroad than to the distribution of their personal estate, the expression, "dummodo causa *non morandi extra regnum*," shows clearly that the difference between a temporary and permanent residence abroad, and its effects in questions of this nature, must have been then well understood. It has been inferred from this statute, that, in terms of it, the effects of Scotsmen were to be governed by the law of Scotland, wherever such effects should be situated. (k)

When Sir John Nisbet wrote, he appears to have entertained doubts as to the doctrines of the law on this subject in Scotland. Under the word *mobilia* he asks, " If *mobilia* has *situm*, when they are here *animo et destinatione domini;* so that when they belong v. g. to Englishmen, they are to be thought *res Scoticæ*, and to be affected by the laws of Scotland, and he cannot dispose of them by a nuncupative will; and *e contra* if he should change their *situm*, and transport them to stay in England?" In a subsequent paragraph, under the head

---

(k) In the case of Hog v. Lashley, *infra.*

mobilium · vilior possessio, in which he makes a quotation
from a foreign jurist, (Hering. de molend. quæst. 8. n. 58.
& sequen.) it is thus stated : " Mobilia sequuntur condi-
tionem personæ sive domini, adeo et *ejus ossibus adhæreant*
active et passive : Immobilia autem cohærent terri-
torio." (*l*)

Sir James Stewart, in his Answers to the Doubts, under
the head *mobilia,* has these observations : " If *mobilia* has
situm seems to be an improper question; for it is more
proper that *mobilia sequuntur personam.* And as to the
question, whether an Englishman in England could make
a nuncupative testament as to moveables in Scotland, to
me it is without doubt, and that even a Scotsman residing and dying in England may also make a nuncupative
testament reaching his moveables in Scotland. But in
our law we have a rule as to the probation by witness,
limiting the same to one hundred pounds Scots, which
being a rule of judgment, might incline our judges to
reject a nuncupative testament, though made in England." (*m*)

In this passsage he appears to have alluded to the case
of *Shaw and Lewins,* to be hereafter noticed, with regard
to a nuncupative will made by a Scotsman in London,
which by the Scotch judges was found to be null *in substantialibus.* Though it is not difficult to see that the
principles which ought to regulate in a matter of this kind
had not been very clearly defined in Scotland in the time

(*l*) Sir John Nisbet's Doubts, p. 126. The quotation from *Heringius*
accurately expresses the state of the law, which is now universally
assented to, almost in the fewest possible words.

(*m*) Sir James Stewart's Answers, p. 208. Upon the questions
arising in regard to *nomina debitorum* and *strangers' debts,* it appears
that there were various points upon which these eminent persons were
both in considerable doubt. (Stewart's Answers, pp. 68. 227. 279

of those writers.　Yet both appear to have been well acquainted with the doctrines, now well established, that real estate was subject to the *lex loci* only; while personal estate was subject to the law of the domicil.　Sir James Stewart also puts the case of the nuncupative will upon what appears to be its true principles.

When our institutional authors wrote, the law still remained in some degree of uncertainty upon these important questions.　Stair, indeed, appears to have understood the rules of law to be totally different upon these subjects from what they are now fixed to be at the present day.　In his section on the effect of *testaments made abroad* (*n*), he notices several cases which had occurred prior to his time, particularly the case of the nuncupative will made by a Scotsman resident in England, which had been found to be null in Scotland. (*o*)　And when treating of the law and customs of England, and of foreign countries, he says, " Yet the custom of these places cannot constitute any right of succession not allowed by the law of Scotland."　Thus he appears to have rejected the distribution by the law of the domicil, and the doctrine that *mobilia non habent situm.*

Bankton also appears to have had erroneous views upon this subject.　When noticing the before-mentioned case of the nuncupative will, he says, " And though such testament was made abroad, according to the custom of the place, we would not otherwise sustain it, because the laws of foreign countries can never constitute a right of succession, which must have its force from the laws of the place where the subject lies; and the maxim *mobilia sequuntur personam* is

---

(*n*) Stair, b. 3. tit. 8. s. 35.

(*o*) Case of Shaw *v.* Lewins, *infra*, p. 89.

not to be understood of one's effects without the jurisdiction where the person resides." (p) Thus he also appears to have rejected the distribution by the law of the domicil; and he gives a very limited interpretation to the rule, that *mobilia sequuntur personam.*

Erskine appears to have had correct views upon this subject in general; but upon the details the law in his time was not yet fixed in its present state. He says (q), "Where a Scotsman dies abroad *sine animo remanendi,* the legal succession of his moveable estate in Scotland must descend to his next of kin, according to the law of Scotland; and where a foreigner dies in this country *sine animo remanendi,* the moveables which he brought with him hither ought to be regulated, not by the law of the territory in which they locally were, but by that of the proprietor's *patria* or domicil whence he came, and whither he intends again to return. This rule is founded in the law of nations; and the reason of it is the same in both cases, that since all succession *ab intestato* is grounded on the presumed will of the deceased, his estate ought to descend to him whom the law of his own country calls to the succession, as the person whom it presumes to be most favoured by the deceased." But he adds, " Yet we must except from this general rule, as civilians have done, certain moveables which by the destination of the deceased are considered as immoveable. Among these may be reckoned the shares of the trading companies, or of the public stocks of any country, *ex. gr.,* the banks of Scotland, England, Holland, South Sea Company, &c., *which are without doubt descendible according to the law of the state where such stocks are fixed.*"

(p) Bankton, b. 3. tit. 8. s. 5.
(q) Erskine, b. 3. tit. 9. s. 4.

At the present day, these would clearly be held to be subject to the law of the domicil. (r)

While the institutional writers in Scotland held these various and conflicting opinions, as was to be expected, the decisions of the courts of law could not proceed upon any fixed and certain principles. (s)

The earliest case appearing upon this subject is that of *Purvis* v. *Chisholm*, 1st February 1611. (t) This was a case of succession to the estate of a bastard. " A Scotsman born bastard, dying in England, his goods will fall under escheat to the King, and his donatar will have right thereto, notwithstanding any testament alleged made by the bastard, and confirmed in England, and that though bastards be alleged to have *testamenti factionem* there; especially if it be offered to be proved that the bastard has rents, resort, and traffic in this country as a Scotsman, and not as an Englishman naturalised or made denizen."

In various respects, in the present state of the law, this is an important case. It does not distinctly appear what the domicil of the bastard was, but his will had been admitted to probate in England. As far as is known, this is the only case which has occurred in regard to the effect of bastardy, in opposition to a will made by the bastard in another country, where he had the power of making a will. The testator in this case, as far as appears, was born before

---

(r) *Pothier* appears to have had the same view in regard to the public stocks of any country, that Erskine had. He considered that these were to be subject to the *real statutes* of the country, in which the *bureau public*, by which they were managed, was situated. Pothier, Cout. d'Orleans, c. 1. s. 2. n. 23.

(s) I have deemed it better not to pass over those cases which were decided before the law was better understood. We see in them the state of the law at the time, and several of them contain matter for important observation and consideration at the present day.

(t) Kaimes's Dict., i. p. 320. Haddington MS. Morrison, p. 4494.

the union of the crowns, and thus an alien in England, though this would not have prevented his holding personal estate in that country. (*u*) But the question might be raised, whether, even at this day, the will of an English bastard could extend to his personal estate in Scotland, and if the rights of the Crown would be thereby cut off. They adopt *ex comitate* the law of the domicil in the general case; but they have a special rule of their own, regulating in regard to the testaments of bastards, upon which this case was decided. (*x*)

In *Henderson's Bairns* v. *Murray*, 9th December 1623 (*y*), a will made in a foreign country was held to be effectual only for the heritage and goods in that country; not for those in Scotland. Colonel Henderson, by birth a Scotsman, but settled in Holland *animo remanendi*, where he had married, and where his children were born, had lent out

---

(*u*) *Calvin's* case, where the question as to the rights of *postnati* in regard to *real estate* excited so much attention, was decided in England in the following year, 1612. *Coke's* Seventh Report.

(*x*) In the recent English case of *Doe on the demise of Birtwhistle* v. *Vardill*, 5 Barn. & Cres. 438., it was found by the Court of King's Bench, that a person born out of wedlock in Scotland, but legitimated *per subsequens matrimonium* in that country, did not succeed as heir to real estate in England. That case suggests considerations connected with this case of bastardy. In both, a person might be held legitimate *quoad effectum* in one country, and illegitimate in the other. This appears to be one of the most important cases on the conflict of laws, which has been agitated in modern times. It was brought by writ of error to the House of Lords; it was argued in 1830, and several questions were put to and answered by the judges thereon; but a new series of questions was put to them on the 16th of July, 1830, which have not yet been answered, and the case still remains undecided: the chief difficulty appears to be, whether Birtwhistle could be said to have been born out of wedlock, as the law of Scotland, by a fiction, in such cases presumes that the marriage had taken place between his parents before he was born; and whether the question of legitimacy or illegitimacy ought not, therefore, to have been left to be decided according to the law of Scotland.

(*y*) Durie, p. 88. Lord Kaimes's Dict., i. p. 320. Morrison, p. 4481.

money upon heritable bonds in Scotland; these bonds were left in the hands of Murray, " who had employed the moneys, and to whom the trust and handling and employing thereof was committed by the said Colonel." The Colonel made his will or testament in Holland, according to the forms of the Dutch law, instituting his bairns as his universal heirs, and dividing his moveables, lands, and heritages among them, in certain proportions, as therein specified. He afterwards died at the siege of Bergen-op-Zoom.

After his death, his two sons and three daughters sued Murray, the factor, and the debtors in the bonds, to hear and see them decerned to make payment to the pursuers. In this action the Court of Session " found, that albeit by the laws and custom of the country where the testator died the defunct might institute all his bairns heirs, and divide his heritage among them, yet that testament could not be valuable but for the goods and heritage which were within that province where the testator made his testament, *and could not extend to any goods and gear* which were within another kingdom or territory, where the goods would not fall under that division and testament of the defunct, by the law of the kingdom within which the goods and lands lay; but the said goods ought to be asked by that person, who would be found to have right thereto, by the law of the kingdom within which they were, and not the laws of any other kingdom; neither could any other country law have place in Scotland for any thing being within Scotland, but the proper law of the country itself; and therefore found that none of the defunct's bairns could pursue for their obligations, the same being heritable, but only the heir, and who must be retoured and served heir after the laws and custom of Scotland."

Of this case it may be remarked, that though the judgment related to real or heritable estate, which clearly, and upon the principles recognised at all times by foreign jurists, as well as by our own, could only be given away from the heir according to the rules of the law of Scotland; still it lays down the law as to goods, or personal estate, upon principles now admitted to be erroneous, namely, that the *lex loci rei sitæ* was also to regulate as to these. Lord Haddington remarks of this case, that the Judges were equally divided in opinion upon it. (*z*)

It does not appear that any question occurred in this case, on the doctrine of *election*, or of *approbate and reprobate*, as to the right of the heir to take the heritable estate, and also his share of the moveables under the testament (*a*), though, from the circumstances stated, it appears likely that such a question, if noticed, might have been raised.

In *Melvil v. Drummond*, 3d July 1634 (*b*), the succession as to *bona tam mobilia quam immobilia* was held to be regulated by the *lex loci rei sitæ*. Mr. Drummond, residing in England, had money lent on a heritable bond in Scotland, and, by his will or testament made in England, gave this particular heritable bond to his wife. In an action brought thereon by her and her second husband, the Court found, " that albeit by the law of England, where the *infeftment* (*c*) was made, which bore that legacy, the testator might leave legacies of heritable sums, and that the heir could not quarrel the same, but that such legacies are effectual; and albeit the heir was born in England, and so was alleged behoved to be subject to the English laws; yet, seeing the money left was addebted in Scotland, and was a sum which could not be disponed upon by way of testament, and so came not under legacy, according to the Scottish laws, therefore that the relict had no action to pursue for the

---

(*z*) Lord Haddington's MS., 2945.
(*a*) See the case of Brodie *v.* Barrie, *infra*.
(*b*) Durie, p. 723.
(*c*) Apparently meaning the *will*.

same, by the practique and laws of this realm, for *bona tam mobilia quam immobilia regulantur juxta leges regni et loci in quo bona ea jacent et sita sunt;* for this legacy was *in corpore individuo,* of another nature than what was testable in Scotland, being of a particular heritable bond."

Thus the decision, so far as it regarded the subject matter or heritable bond, appears to have proceeded upon those principles which are now universally recognised; but, by the *dicta* in the judgment, the *lex loci rei sitæ* is recognised in moveable as well as in heritable succession.

In *Shaw* v. *Lewins,* 19th January 1665, a *conflictus legum* occurred, in regard to a nuncupative testament. (*d*)

William Shaw, a native of Scotland, but described in one report as " a factor at London," and in another as " a residenter at London," by a nuncupative will, made at London, nominated Anna Lewins his sole executrix and universal legatee, and declared that he meant to leave her all, and to his relations in Scotland nothing, because they had dealt unnaturally with him. Shaw died possessed of personal estate in England and in Scotland.

Of this nuncupative will Anna Lewins obtained probate " in the Court of Probates of Wills in England." (*e*) Adam and William Shaw, the cousins of the deceased, his nearest in kin, obtained themselves confirmed executors dative to him in Scotland, before the Commissaries of Edinburgh. A competition thereupon arose between the parties, in regard to the personal estate in Scotland. Anna Lewins, the executrix under the nuncupative will proved in England, claimed the whole property as universal legatee. She appears to have admitted, that if it had been a case of in-

---

(*d*) Stair's Dec., vol. i. p. 252. Morrison, p. 4494.

(*e*) I have not found this probate in the registry of the Prerogative Court of Canterbury. There are no calendars of wills or administrations in the Consistory Court of London between the years 1642 and 1670.

testate *succession* merely, the law of Scotland must have regulated; but she contended that the *nuncupative will* being valid, according to the law of the country where it was executed, must carry the whole succession to her; and she referred to the validity given in Scotland to instruments executed in foreign countries, without the solemnities of the law of Scotland.

The next of kin contended that a nuncupative will could have no effect in this case upon the funds and effects in Scotland, and that though a legacy might be left by word of mouth, yet it could not by the law of Scotland be allowed to exceed 100*l*. Scots (8*l*. 6*s*. 8*d*. sterling.)

" The Lords " (according to the report in Stair) " having considered the reasons and former decisions, preferred the executors confirmed in Scotland; for they found that the question was not here of the manner of probation of a nomination, in which case they would have followed the law of the place, but it was *upon the constitution of the essentials of a right*, viz. a nomination, although it were certainly known to have been by word; yea, if it were offered to be proven by the nearest of kin that they were witnesses thereto, yet the solemnity of writ not being interposed, the nomination is in itself defective and null *in substantialibus.*"

It is not stated distinctly in this case whether Shaw the testator was domiciled in England or not at the time of his death; the decision appears to have been founded solely on the nullity of a nuncupative will, according to the Scotch law, for a larger sum than 100*l*. Scots, a rule of law which had been already repeatedly recognised in the courts of that country, in the cases of *Russel* (Had.), 24th November, 1609, and *Wallace v. Mure*, 7th July, 1629.

This is a curious case, and has been noticed by almost

every writer on the law of Scotland. (*f*) Assuming that
the maker of the *nuncupative* will was domiciled in England, as the words " residenter at London" appear to
import, a direct *conflictus legum* occurred, upon which
different opinions might be formed, even at this day. If
he had not been domiciled in England, according to what
is well understood, his nuncupative will might have been
challenged even in regard to the property in England,
as made by a Scotsman, and contrary to the law of Scotland. (*g*)

In *The nearest of kin of Adam Duncan competing*, 16th
February 1738 (*h*), it was held that the personal succession in Scotland of a Scotsman born, who died domiciled
in Holland, was to be regulated by the Scotch law. Adam
Duncan, a Scotsman, had resided for forty years in Holland, and died there. He left moveables and debts in
Scotland, and after his death a competition arose before
the Commissaries of Edinburgh, for the office of *executors
dative* to the deceased, between James and Ann Duncan,
his surviving brother and sister, and his nephews and
nieces by other brothers and sisters deceased. The Commissaries preferred the surviving brother and sister. On
a bill of advocation to the Court of Session, by the
nephews and nieces, complaining that the Commissaries
had preferred the brother and sister to the office of executor, and refused to conjoin them, though the defunct
had his residence more than forty years in Rotterdam, and
died there, and that " by the law of Holland (which by the

(*f*) I see that it has also attracted notice in America : in Story's
" Commentaries on the Conflict of Laws," (p. 395.) both this case and
that on the bastardy in *Purvis* v. *Chisholm* (supra, p. 85.) are noticed
and commented on.

(*g*) Nasmyth *v.* Hare, *infra*.

(*h*) Elchies' Decisions and Notes v. *Succession*.

law of nations must regulate the succession) nephews and nieces succeed *jure representationis et per stirpes*, in place of their parents deceased, jointly with their surviving uncles and aunts," the Court refused the bill, reserving to the advocators " to be afterwards heard upon their right to the succession as accords."

Though this related to a question of confirmation, which does not form the subject of our present inquiry, yet the Court appear to have given an opinion on the question of succession, founded upon the *lex loci rei sitæ*, in opposition to the law of the domicil. Lord Elchies says, " The Lords thought that the *succession to moveables and debts in Scotland*, and the office of executor, must be regulated by the law of Scotland, and not by the law of the place where the defunct proprietor had his residence and died. They did not determine that point." (*i*)

In *Brown* v. *Brown*, 28th November 1744 (*k*), the succession to Irish personal securities, belonging to a Scotsman at the time of his death, was held to be regulated by the law of the domicil, not the *lex loci rei sitæ*.

The general question between the law of the domicil, and the *lex loci rei sitæ*, appears to have been very fully discussed in that case. Captain William Brown of the Scots Royals, son to Adam Brown, late provost of Edinburgh, having died at Edinburgh without issue and intestate, John Brown, his only surviving brother, was

---

(*i*) In a case of Fullerton *v.* Kinloch (Ct. of S., July, 1739. H. of L., 13. Feb. 1740. 1 Craigie and Stewart, 265.) a question of some importance in international law was decided: Dr. Fullerton died domiciled in England; he had a heritable bond due to him on a Scotch estate. His simple contract debts incurred in England, though they did not affect his heir, or his real estate in that country, could be recovered in Scotland against the heir in the heritable bond.

(*k*) Kilkerran, *voce* Foreign, No. 1. p. 199. Falconer, p. 11. Elchies, *voce* Succession, Decisions and Notes. Morrison, p. 4604.

confirmed his executor dative.   He gave up in the inventory certain personal securities which the deceased had acquired while the regiment to which he belonged had been quartered in Ireland, and which he had with him in Edinburgh when he died, consisting of two Irish government debentures, and bonds and promissory notes, all granted in Ireland.

Thomas Brown of Braid, nephew of the deceased by a deceased brother, brought an action against the uncle before the Commissaries of Edinburgh; he insisted to have it declared, that the half of the debts for which securities were granted in Ireland belonged to him, on this ground, that by the law of Ireland the *jus representationis* is admitted in the succession of moveables, and that the succession was to be governed by the law of the country where the effects happened to be situated.

The law of Ireland was admitted, and the question turned upon this general point: " By the law of what country the succession to a defunct's moveables was to be governed; whether by the law of the country where the moveables happened to be at the time of his death, or by the law of the country where the defunct had his domicil ? "

The Commissaries of Edinburgh decided " that the deceased Captain Brown was *origine* a Scotsman, and never had any proper or fixed domicil elsewhere, having only attended his regiment in the different places to which it was called from time to time, until he at last returned to Scotland, his native country, where he resided some months before his death at Edinburgh ; and that the said debentures and other *nomina* in question were found in his possession at his death : that the succession to the said Captain Brown's moveable estate is to be regulated by the laws of Scotland, and that the right to his *nomina*

belongs to the defender, as his sole nearest of kin, whether these *nomina* are granted by single persons or bodies
politic, and whether the granters of them live in Scotland
or Ireland: and having considered the debentures in
question, which pass by indorsation, and are payable to
executors, &c., together with the act of parliament 5 G. 2.
referred to in the said debentures, and that the funds
appropriated in the said act for payment of the 300,000*l.*
(thereby authorised to be borrowed) are of a personal
and moveable nature; and that the time for demanding
the capital sum, as well as the annual rent thereof, was
elapsed several years before the indorsation to the defunct,—find that the sole right to the said debentures,
and sums thereby due, belongs to the defender, and therefore assoilzie him from this process."

This judgment was brought under the review of the
Court of Session by bill of advocation, and the case
was fully debated on the import of the former decisions,
and on the law as laid down by foreign jurists.   The
uncle contended, that, as the question was new in respect
to the custom of Scotland, and as nothing was to be found
in the decisions, or law books, directly determining it,
recourse must be had to the laws and practice of other
countries, and to the testimonies of foreign lawyers;
especially as the question might not improperly be said
to concern the law of nations.   And he stated, that the
general and received doctrine of foreign lawyers on this
subject may be reduced to these propositions: " 1st, That
in all countries the succession to heritage is to be governed
by the *lex loci ubi res sita est.*   2dly, That proper *mobilia*
are not considered *habere situm,* but to follow the law of
the country where the owner has his domicil, and to
which it is presumed that, sooner or later, he intended to
transfer them. 3dly, That the same thing is true con-

cerning *nomina debitorum ;* that these are governed by the law of the domicil of the creditor, and not of the debtor. 4thly, That there are certain moveable subjects *quæ habentur loco immobilium."* And, in support of his argument on these points, the uncle referred to Voet, and the many authorities cited by him, Appendix to the Title, *De constitutionibus principum,* § 11., and *de rerum divisione,* § 30. ; stating, from these authorities, that it would be absurd to suppose that, where a man had money or effects in all the different parts of the world, his presumed will, upon which the succession *ab intestato* was founded, should be held to be as different as the peculiar laws or constitutions of the several parts of the world where his effects were, or his debtors lived.

The Court confirmed the decision of the Commissaries, and " remitted to the Lord Ordinary, to refuse the bill of advocation." And this, apparently, is precisely the decision which would be pronounced, in such a case, at the present day. It appears, however, to have been at that time admitted on both sides, that capital stock of the Bank of England, the South Sea Company, or any trading company, fixed by their charters in a certain country, would be accounted among *mobilia quæ immobilium loco habenda sunt.* (*l*)

In *Machargs* v. *Blain,* 22d July, 1760 (*m*), the will, made in Scotland, of a Scotsman born, who died domiciled in Antigua, was interpreted by the law of Scotland. John Blain resided for some years as a merchant in Antigua;

(*l*) The principles in this case appear to be so clear, that it is matter of surprise that they were not adopted in future cases; but we see (*infra,* p. 101.) that they were then generally rejected by the Scottish judges. Lord Kaimes, in his " Principles of Equity" (p. 359.), assents to this case of Brown, and to the principles contained in the decision.

(*m*) Fac. Coll.

he afterwards came to Glasgow, and, after a few years'
residence there, returned again to Antigua, where he lived
about twelve years, and died.

When residing at Glasgow, before his return to Antigua,
he executed his last will, written with his own hand, by
which he appointed his brother Gilbert Blain, his executor;
he gave legacies of 100*l.* to his executor, 200*l.* to his sister,
Margery Blain, and 100*l.* to Anthony and James Machargs,
his nephews by his deceased sister Jean. The will contains
this clause: " And all the rest, residue, and remainder of
my estate and effects I leave and bequeath equally amongst
my brethren and sisters, or other nearest of kin, that shall be
alive at the time of my decease." When he left Scotland,
he committed this will to the care of a friend.

The testator at his decease left a considerable personal
estate, chiefly situated in Antigua. After his death Anthony
and James Machargs, his nephews, brought an action in
the Court of Session against Gilbert Blain, the executor
nominate, claiming a share of the residuary bequest, under
the description of the testatator's " *other nearest of kin.*"

It was admitted, that if the deceased had died intestate,
the law of England, which takes place in Antigua, would
have regulated his succession *ab intestato,* and would have
given a share *jure representationis* to his nephews. But it
was contended, that the will, having been made in Scotland,
was to be interpreted *according to the sense of the country
where it was executed,* and that if the question had been tried
in Antigua it must have received the same interpretation
there. The Court " found, that, after payment of the
special legacies contained in the testament, the residue of
the estate and effects of the defunct belonged to the defender and his sister Margery; and therefore assoilzied the
defender."

This appears to be a very doubtful decision. The domicil of the testator had been in Antigua for twelve years

after the date of his will; the law presumes that he must have known the rules of succession in that country. The will was written by the testator himself. The expressions in the will, upon which the case was founded, are precisely such as might have been used in an English will. It must be presumed that the testator recollected the words of his will. What meaning could he, domiciled in Antigua, and familiar with the law of succession there established, have given to these expressions? (*n*)

The next case, in point of date, is that of *Mortimer v. Lorimer*, February 1770. (*o*) " In a question about the succession of William Lorimer, a Scotsman, who had passed the greatest part of his life in Scotland, but for some years before his death had resided chiefly in England, though sometimes in Scotland, and died at sea in a voyage to Italy, whither he was going for his health, the Lords found that his succession must be regulated by the law of Scotland."

Nothing appears here as to the *situs* of his property, nor any thing very distinctly as to his domicil; and the case is mentioned, less for any importance belonging to itself, than as having been referred to in other cases, as one of the series of this class of decisions.

In *Davidson v. Elcherson*, 13th January 1778, the *lex loci rei sitæ* was applied to the effects of a Scotsman dying at Hamburgh. (*p*)   William Murray, a Scotsman, having, " in the course of business, left Scotland in 1768, and

---

(*n*) See the case of *Anstruther* v. *Chalmer, infra*, where a different decision was given by the Master of the Rolls in a case strongly resembling the present.

(*o*) Not reported, but briefly noticed in a note to Erskine (ed. 1773), p. 601.

(*p*) Fac. Coll. Morrison, 4613.

gone to Hamburgh, died there soon after, without making any *settlement.*" (*q*)   Mr. Parish, a Hamburgh merchant, took the custody of his chest, in which effects were found to the value of 300*l.*, consisting in part of bank-notes.

The uncles and aunts of Murray took out a confirmation to him before the commissaries of Edinburgh, and transferred to Davidson, an assignee, their right to the effects of the deceased. Marian Elcherson, the mother of the deceased, claimed the property in the court at Hamburgh, as belonging to her by the law of that country.

To settle this question, Parish brought a multiplepoinding in the Court of Session, in which the parties appeared for their interests. It appears to have been admitted, that the deceased was not at Hamburgh *animo remanendi*, and that his domicil still continued in Scotland; but the discussion turned upon the question, whether or not the property should go according to the *lex loci rei sitæ*. The Court decided, " that the distribution of the moveables in this case must be regulated by the laws of Hamburgh, where those moveables are and were situated at the death of William Murray; that no action for such distribution lies, or is competent before this Court; therefore dismisses the foresaid process of multiplepoinding and competition relative thereto." On a reclaiming petition, which was answered on the point of the *situs* of the bank-notes, the

---

(*q*) *Settlement* in Scotland is an expression in universal use, meaning an instrument in the nature of a will, or *mortis causa* deed, *settling* the affairs of a person deceased. It has thus obtained a species of technical meaning, but very different from what is known by the name of a *settlement* in England. This last is a deed *inter vivos* (*e. g.* a *settlement* in contemplation of marriage), by which any property, real or personal, is *settled* for certain specified purposes. As real estate cannot be disposed of by a last will in Scotland, the *settlement*, in which both real and personal estate may be joined, appears to have nearly superseded the last will altogether in modern times.

Court adhered.　Thus the mother took the property by the *lex loci rei sitæ*.

So far as this decision went upon the *situs* of the moveables, it appears to have been contrary to those principles which are now clearly established. (*r*)

In *Henderson v. Maclean* and others (13th January 1778), a will made by a person born in Scotland, who died in India, in the military service of the East India Company, was effectual against a claim of *jus relictæ* of his widow. (*s*) The facts were these:—John Maclean, a captain of artillery, in the service of the East India Company, having been mortally wounded in an engagement in the Mogul country, immediately before his death executed a will, by which he bequeathed his whole estate and effects to his father and a brother and sister in certain proportions, and named executors in India.　The will was proved by the executors in common form in the Mayor's Court of Madras. The executors recovered the funds, which were all in India, and remitted them to the legatees in Scotland.　Afterwards Helen Henderson, the widow (*t*) of the deceased, brought an action against the legatees in the Court of Session, claiming her share of the moveables of the deceased as her *jus relictæ*.

The same point was argued here as in the last case, namely, whether the law of the domicil, or of the place where the effects were situated, regulated the succession. The point of domicil is not much discussed in the report. The widow contended, that having died in the Mogul's

---

(*r*) Apparently there is scarcely any country in Europe where the *successio tristis* of the mother is not received, except Scotland.

(*s*) Fac. Coll. Morrison, 4615.

(*t*) In England, from the name, a conclusion would be drawn that the widow had married again; but in Scotland the maiden name is not changed at marriage for legal purposes.

country, where the law was unknown, and the effects being now in Scotland, in the hands of the legatees, the Court had jurisdiction over them, and the widow's claim to her *jus relictæ* ought to be sustained.

On the other hand, the defenders contended, 1st, That they were in possession, by the law of the place where the effects were situated at the time of the death of the deceased; that therefore no claim of succession to them could be sustained by the law of Scotland; and that if they had been brought to Scotland without authority, the law of the country where they were situated at the death of the deceased, would regulate the succession to them. 2d, That the British residing in the East Indies, whether in a civil or military capacity, are under the law of England, and every question as to their persons or effects must be governed by that law, as received in the English courts there. As Captain Maclean died upon an expedition into an enemy's country, the law of that country could not regulate his succession while in the British camp.

The Court found, " that the pursuer has no claim to a *jus relictæ* out of the estate and effects of the said Captain Maclean, conveyed by the said will."

Though the same decision *in rem* was given here that would be pronounced at this day, the principles upon which the decision proceeded were not then settled; thus it does not appear whether the judgment proceeded upon the law of the domicil, or the *lex loci rei sitæ.*

In the case of *Morris v. Wright* (10th January 1785) (*u*) a decision was given in favour of the *lex loci rei sitæ,* against the law of the domicil. A person, domiciled at the time of his death in England, had effects situated in Scotland. These were intromitted with by Robert Wright,

---

(*u*) Fac. Col. Morrison, 4616.

a relation of the deceased, who was *executor* by the law of Scotland. (*x*)   Mary Morris, as next of kin according to the law of England, brought an action against Wright to account for the property to her.

The general question again occurred, whether succession in moveables should be regulated by the law of the place in which the deceased proprietor resided, or by the law of the country in which the effects were situated at his death. The case was taken to report upon informations; and the Court, without entering into a particular discussion of it, *considered the point as now firmly fixed that the* LEX LOCI *ought to be the rule.*   Accordingly, the defences were unanimously sustained.

It was noticed on the Bench at the decision of this case, that the case of *Brown v. Brown* (*y*) was the only one that could be adduced in support of a contrary doctrine; that it was given by a thin Bench upon a verbal report; and though not altered, because never brought under review, " *was exploded by the most eminent lawyers of the time.*"

It is not a little singular to see that, at this comparatively late period, a doctrine had been established in Scotland, contrary to those principles which had long been clearly laid down by the foreign jurists, and by their own early writers.   This was the last of the decisions reported before the law was settled upon its proper basis, in the case of *Bruce v. Bruce,* to be afterwards mentioned.

At a subsequent period it was made matter of inquiry (*z*), how it had happened that the doctrine of succession, in moveable property, by the *lex loci rei sitæ* had been thus

---

(*x*) It does not appear that there was any will in this case; the *executor* here mentioned must have meant the *executor dative qua* nearest in kin, of the law of Scotland.

(*y*) *Supra,* p. 92.

(*z*) In the case of Hog *v.* Lashley, to be afterwards stated.

recognized, in the decisions of the courts of law in Scotland. It is stated as matter of legal anecdote, that this train of decisions had been introduced in consequence of an opinion given by Sir *Dudley Ryder*, when Attorney-General of England, in regard to the succession of Alexander Lord Banff, who died at Lisbon in November 1746, without making a will. Lord Banff appears to have had personal estate in England, as well as in Scotland. There were, of competitors for his succession, an *aunt* by the *father's side*, who was next of kin according to the law of Scotland, and three *brothers uterine*, who were preferable by the law of England. It was stated, that Lord Banff's *principal domicil* was in Scotland, and that he never had any settled domicil in England; but it is said, that Sir Dudley Ryder having given an opinion " that the *succession* to effects *situated in England* was to be governed by the law of England," it came to be taken for granted in Scotland, that, in England, the courts of law regarded only the *lex loci rei sitæ*. Accordingly it is said, that in the case of *Lorimer v. Mortimer*, mentioned above (a), it was laid down by one party, and not controverted by the other, " that by the law of England, effects, as well heritable as moveable, situated in England, do descend *ab intestato*, agreeably to the rules of descent established by the laws of England, without any regard to the *lex domicilii*."

And in like manner in the case of *Davidson v. Elcherson*, decided in 1778 (b), the same erroneous statement was made in the following words: " if a Scotsman leave effects in England, the person entitled by the law of England will obtain *letters of administration* in Doctors Commons; and it will be in vain for an uncle or an aunt to compete with a mother, no such thing being known in the law of England;

(a) *Supra*, p. 97.   (b) *Supra*, p. 97.

and in conferring the office in Doctors Commons, *the civilians there will not give themselves the trouble to inquire what the law of Scotland is with regard to succession."*

It is obvious that the matters alluded to in these two cases are very different; the first related to *succession,* the other to the right of obtaining *administration,* points in themselves totally distinct, but confused in the statement here given. There appears never to have been any doubt in either country, in recent times, that a right of administration, or confirmation, was to be treated of, and discussed, in the courts of the *lex loci rei sitæ.* It seems likely, from the confusion of these two different subjects, that the opinion of Sir Dudley Ryder had related rather to a question of *administration,* than to one of *succession.* He must have been conversant with the cases which had been decided by Lord Hardwicke upon this subject so recently before; and he could scarcely have given an opinion contrary to the law so clearly laid down in those cases.

But whatever the opinion of Sir Dudley Ryder may have been, it must be admitted that there was some degree of supineness in taking a matter of this importance for granted upon so slender an authority, when the point, as will appear afterwards, had been repeatedly considered and decided in the English courts. If the cases of *Pipon,* and of *Thorne* and *Watkins* (to be immediately mentioned) had been then distinctly known, a great deal of litigation would probably have been prevented in Scotland, in regard to the cases in that country; as well those noticed above, as those to be afterwards stated.

CHAP. VII.

OF THE CASES UPON INTERNATIONAL SUCCESSION DECIDED IN
THE ENGLISH COURTS BEFORE THE TIME OF THE CASE OF
BRUCE *v.* BRUCE.

As far as has been seen, it is only in modern times, that questions of international succession have attracted attention in England.

The earliest case that appears to have occurred connected with this branch of the law, was one relating to a conflicting rule of succession in the customs of the city of London and of the province of York. This was the case of *Cholmley v. Cholmley* (1688.) (*a*) The custom of London was held to prevail over the custom of the province of York. A freeman of London died within the province of York, leaving a widow, and issue, two sons and a daughter. An estate of the father of about 50*l.* a year, within the province of York, descended to the elder son; and if the custom of the province of York should prevail, he would thereby have been excluded from having any share of the personalty, which was of the value of about 20,000*l.* A bill was filed in the Court of Chancery, for the direction of the Court how and in what manner the personal estate should be disposed of; and the Court was of opinion, that the deceased being a freeman of London, the custom of the city for the distribution of the personalty should prevail, and control the custom of the province of York; and that, notwithstanding the custom of the province to the contrary, the heir should come in for

_____

(*a*) 2 Vern. 47. 82.

a share of the personal estate; " for that the custom of the province was only local, and circumscribed to a certain place, but that the custom of London followed the person, though never so remote from the city." (b)

It does not distinctly appear in this case whether the deceased had fixed his domicil in the province of York or not; this point does not seem to have then attracted attention. From the words of the report, it might be inferred, that it was understood that the custom of York had merely operation in regard to effects and estates within the province. It is not unlikely that the doctrine, that personal estate had no locality or *situs*, was not brought forward in that case.

Another case occurred upon a similar question, *Webb* v. *Webb* and others, Mich. 1689. (c)   The custom of London was held to prevail over the law of the domicil. John Webb, late the husband of the plaintiff Elizabeth Webb, being a freeman of London, but having left town, *and living many years at Winchester*, in June 1684 made his will, and thereby devised a chattel lease to Nicholas Webb, and all his books to John Webb; and as to all the residue of his estate, he gave the yearly profits and benefits thereof to his wife for life by quarterly payments; and he directed his executors to pay his wife's funeral charges after her death, and gave her the use of his plate, &c. during her life, and directed that his stock and estate in the hands of one Cranmer should remain there during his wife's life, and the product be paid to her for her maintenance; and he gave several particular legacies; and, after the death of

---

(b) In the case of Somerville, to be afterwards noticed, it appears that a search had been made for cases arising out of the conflicting rules of decision in the province of York and city of London, and that this case of *Cholmley* was the only case which had been found.

(c) 2 Vern. 110.

his wife, he gave the residue and surplus of his estate to his brother, Nicholas Webb; and he made John Webb, William Cranmer, and others his executors. The testator died, leaving a widow, but no children.

The widow filed a bill in the Court of Chancery against the executors, claiming her *customary* rights as the widow of a freeman of London. The cause was first heard before the Master of the Rolls; and it was decreed that the plaintiff should have her widow's chamber, and one entire moiety of the personal estate, after debts paid, as well of the lease and books, which were specifically bequeathed, as of the rest and residue of the estate, by the custom of the city of London; and should have the benefit of the other moiety for life by the will; and an account was decreed accordingly. This decree was confirmed upon an appeal to the Lords Commissioners. (*d*)

In this cause a question was made, whether the legatees of the lease and books (a moiety of their legacies being taken by the widow by the custom of London) should have satisfaction made to them for what was evicted from them, against the legatees at large, or against the legatee of the residue. It was adjudged that they should not; for though the legatee of a specific legacy has a preference, and is not to abate in proportion with other legatees, when the estate falls short, as to the payment of debts, yet in any case he cannot have more than what the testator devised to him; and, as in this case the testator could only devise one moiety, nothing more passed by his will; and therefore the specific legatees must be contented with a moiety.

The case is also important, as showing that the custom of London in regard to the personal estate of a freeman

---

(*d*) This case was before the statute allowing freemen of London to give their whole estate by will; it shows the rule before that time.

prevailed over the law of the domicil.   Though, since the
statute 11 Geo. I. c. 18., this case could not occur upon
the will of a freeman of London, which would be effectual
against all claims of a widow or children; yet, in a case of
intestacy, according to this case (*e*), and the preceding
case of *Cholmley v. Cholmley*, the law of the domicil would
yield to that of the custom. (*f*)

(*e*) When inquiry was made in the case of Somerville as to conflicting cases between the customs of London and York and the law in
other places, this case does not appear to have been known.

(*f*) A case has recently occurred, showing, in a striking way, that
the custom of London not only controls the law of the domicil, but
that it does so, where the freedom was merely of an honorary nature.
That was the case of *Onslow* v. *Onslow* before the Vice-Chancellor
.(1 Sim. 18.), 1826.   In that case it appeared, that on the occasion of
Lord Rodney's victory in 1782, Sir Francis Samuel Drake, being an
admiral of the Royal Navy, was presented with the freedom of the city
of London, and in 1784 was made a liveryman of the Grocers' Company, and took the oaths.   In his marriage settlement of personal property on the wife this was expressed to be in lieu of all dower and
thirds, or other portion at common law, or otherwise, which the wife
might claim out of the freehold or copyhold lands, hereditaments, and
premises of the husband.

Sir Francis Samuel Drake having died intestate, and without issue,
his widow afterwards intermarried with Mr. Serjeant Onslow, and died
in 1822.   After her death, Mr. Serjeant Onslow having claimed that
the widow of Admiral Drake, as the widow of a freeman of London,
should take one half of the personal estate by the custom, and the half
of the residue by the statute, a bill was filed in the Court of Chancery
by the surviving trustee in the marriage settlement of Sir Francis
Samuel and Lady Drake against Mr. Serjeant Onslow and the personal
representative of Sir Francis Samuel Drake, for having those questions
decided.

The Lord Mayor and Aldermen, by the mouth of their Recorder,
certified to the Vice-Chancellor that the deceased was a freeman of the
city in the sense, meaning, and operation of the custom of the city,
relating to the distribution of the effects of freemen who die intestate,
and that the widow was not barred of her customary share by the clause
in the marriage settlement; and the Vice-Chancellor decided accordingly.

In the case of *Pipon v. Pipon*, Trin. 1744 (g), a bond
debt due in *London* to a resident in Jersey was, upon his
death intestate, distributable by the law of Jersey. Pipon
the intestate was resident in Jersey, and died there. At
the time of his death a bond debt of 500*l*. was due to him
in London. A question occurred in regard to this bond
debt. The representatives of certain deceased sisters of
the intestate filed a bill in the Court of Chancery against
the surviving sisters of the intestate for a distribution of
this 500*l*. bond, which was due in London, according to
the statute of distributions. The defendants, the surviving
sisters, according to the laws of Jersey, were personal representatives of the deceased, to the exclusion of the
plaintiffs, the representatives of the deceased sisters.
There were separate administrations in the province of
Canterbury, and in Jersey; and the question was, whether
this 500*l*. bond should be distributable according to the
law of England, it being found within the province of Canterbury; or whether it should be distributed according to
the laws of Jersey, where the intestate resided at the time
of his death. Lord Hardwicke said, on deciding this
cause, " I should be unwilling to go into the general
question, for it is very extensive. This is merely the case
of a debt. The question then is, whether the plaintiffs, as
next of kin, have a right to call for an account of this part
of the residue only; and I think there is not sufficient
ground for it. If I was to go into the general question,
the personal estate follows the person, and becomes distributable according to the law or custom of the place where
the intestate lived. As to the usage of taking out administration, that is only to give the party power to sue
within such a jurisdiction, and does not any way deter-

(g) Ambler, p. 25.

mine the equitable right which the party has to the effects.
This argument holds the same as to foreign countries, in
relation to this question. Though Jersey is under the
king's dominion as part of his duchy of Normandy, yet it
is governed by its own laws; and if the question was to be
determined now, I think the *locality* could not prevail, for
it would be extremely mischievous, and would affect our
commerce. No foreigner could deal in our funds, but at
the peril of his effects going according to our laws, and
not those of his own country. The words of the statute
are very particular, viz. the residue undisposed of is to be
distributed, &c. ; so that the plaintiffs are wrong in coming
into this court for an account of only part, for by the statute an account must be decreed of the whole, and the
general administration is not before the Court. If I was
to direct an account of the whole, the courts in Jersey
would act contrary, which would be to involve the people
in great difficulties. This case differs from where a specific part consists of chattels here in England — Bill dismissed with costs."

In the case of *Thorne v. Watkins,* 30th October 1750, a
similar decision was pronounced by Lord Hardwicke, in
the case of a Scotch personal succession, which was held to
be regulated by an English domicil. (*h*)

Richard Watkins, who resided in Scotland, died there,
and left the residue of his personal estate by his will among
his nephews and nieces. William Watkins, one of these
nephews, residing in England, died in that country, entitled
to a share of his uncle's residuary personal estate. The
defendant, who was one of the executors appointed by the
will of Richard Watkins, was also one of the next of kin
of William the nephew, and as such obtained letters of administration in England to William's estate.

(*h*) 2 Vesey sen. 35.

On a bill filed in the Court of Chancery by Thorne, another of the next of kin of *William* Watkins, against the defendant, his administrator, it was insisted for the defendant, that in accounting for William's personal estate, so much thereof as should arise and accrue to his share, from the personal estate of Richard, who resided and died in Scotland, should be accounted for in a different manner from the rest, viz. should be distributable according to the rule of the law of Scotland, where it was to be got in, *and where half blood was not regarded* (*i*) : and it was compared to cases where the subject of discussion arose abroad ; and he cited the case of *The Hans Towns v. Jacobson.* Lord Hardwicke, at giving judgment, said, " This is a strange imagination, for which there is no ground, either from the nature of the property, or the manner in which that property is to be recovered. These are two distinct rights ; for the estate of Richard must be sued in Scotland, and recovered in that right. William resided in England ; and, upon his dying intestate, the defendant takes out administration, and by virtue thereof gives a bond to distribute according to the statute of distribution here ; that is, every part of the personal estate which came to his hands. What ground is there for what is insisted upon ? First, as to that which is to be recovered : — If a man die here, and administration be taken out here, where he has left a personal estate ; and he have debts or part thereof abroad, in France, Holland, or the Plantations, that cannot be recovered abroad by virtue of the prerogative administration taken out here ; but he must invest himself with some right from the proper courts in that country, as administration must be from the Governor of the Plantations if it arise there, which

---

(*i*) Some of the parties appear to have been of the half blood only, which by the law of Scotland would have narrowed the division into fewer shares.

must be for form; and then it is generally granted on foundation of the administration granted here, and then it must be distributed as here. But the present case is not so strong as that now put, because the defendant would not want that, but must sue in the courts of Scotland to recover the personal estate of Richard; — as representative of Richard must recover it there. When it comes into the hands of the defendant, he will retain his own share of Richard's personal estate to his own use, and be accountable for that share thereof belonging to William. So it stands as to the recovery of it, and therefore not so strong, or liable to objection, as it would be, if necessary to sue as representative of William to get in any part of his personal estate. But that is not so material, as how it stands on the foot of *the right*. The person resided and died in England; all his effects in England, and letters of administration taken out of the Prerogative Court of Canterbury. He had no right to any specific part of the personal estate of Richard whatever; only a right to have that personal estate accounted for, and debts and legacies paid out of it; and so much as should be his share on the whole account paid to him, which is only a debt, or in nature of a *chose in action*, due to the estate of William. Then it comes to this: a subject of England, residing here, and administration of his personal estate taken out here, with debts due to him, or demands in nature of *choses in action* in Scotland, to be recovered by his administrator, whether that is to fall under a different rule of disposition from the rest of his personal estate. That never was thought of, and would create confusion. And this question relates not to the articles of union, which indeed preserve the laws of the different countries, the jurisdictions, *forums*, and tribunals of each country; but this question would be the same after as before the union of the two crowns, and would be the same on a question of this sort arising in France or Holland;

whether to be distributable according to the laws of those countries, or of England. The reason is, that all debts follow the person, not of the *debtor* in respect of the right or property, but of the *creditor* to whom due. Therefore, in the case of a freeman of London, debts due to him any where, are distributable according to the custom (otherwise it would be most mischievous if they were to follow the person of the debtor); and then, when got in, it is distributed; and of that opinion I was in *Pipon v. Pipon.* This also came in question in the House of Lords lately, in a case arising on the lunacy of Mr. Morison; for there the question was, whether the rule would be the same in the Courts of Scotland; and the opinion was that it would be the same; and it was taken that it would be the same on a question between a court of France and a court of England : it was the same; and different from the articles of union. This is just the same case in respect of that· As to the *Hans Towns v. Jacobson,* it was the case of merchants, subjects of England, going to reside at Hamburgh, and is different. It never was thought that, on the death of a person having those funds, a bill must be brought by the next of kin of a particular part of that personal estate; the rule must be, that a bill be brought for the whole, according to what I laid down in *Pipon v. Pipon,* otherwise it would destroy the credit of the funds; for no foreigner would put into them, if, because a title must be made up by administration or probate of the Prerogative Court of England, it was to be distributed different from the laws of his own country. The defendant therefore must account for the whole."

In these cases of *Pipon v. Pipon,* and *Thorne v. Watkins* the law is so clearly laid down by Lord Hardwicke, that it is to be regretted that they appear to have been totally unknown, during a considerable period, to the lawyers in Scotland, though the last of them reltead to property situated in that country.   He draws a clear distinction, between the right with which the executor or administrator was to be invested by the proper courts, within which the property was situated, and the right of succession or right in distribution; the first was to be regulated by the municipal laws of the country within which the property was situated, or was to be sued for; the other was to be regulated by the law of the domicil, or of the country within which the testator or intestate had his residence at the time of his death.   The doctrines now universally assented to, appear to have been familiar to that most eminent person.

One of the cases mentioned by Lord Hardwicke, that regarding *Morison*'s lunacy, appears to be of some difficulty in international law. (*k*)   George Morison, son to the late Morison of Prestongrange, was born and resided in England.   In July 1742 he lent 2100*l.* to his nephew, the Earl of Sutherland, then in London, who granted bond for it in the English form.   On a commission of lunacy in England, Mr. Morison was afterwards found to be a lunatic, and two grants were issued under the great seal; one by which the custody of the person of the lunatic was granted to Sir Nicholas Bayly; the other, by which the custody of the estate and effects of the lunatic was granted to Walter Baynes and Penelope his wife, the brother-in-law and sister of the lunatic.   These last, as such committees, brought an action upon the bond against the Earl of Sutherland, in the Court of Session.   In defence, he contended, that the lunacy had not been established in Scotland; that the law upon this subject was different in the two countries; and that the rules of distribution of the

---

(*k*) Reported by Elchies, Idiotcy, Morison, &c. *v.* Earl of Sutherland, 21st June, 1749.   Kilkerran, *voce* Foreign, 209.   In the House of Lords, Baynes *v.* Earl of Sutherland, 13th February, 1749–50.

personal estate of lunatics, within the same, were also different.

The question of title was argued several times before the Lord Ordinary. The defender contended, that the Lord Chancellor had no power to direct the management of any estate *extra territorium.* The pursuers answered, that *statuta personalia loci domicilii* must bind every where; and that *mobilia sequuntur personam,* and are regulated by the law of the place of domicil. The pursuers applied by petition to the Lord Chancellor, stating this process and defences; that the debt was in danger, and praying that the committees might have access to the lunatic, to obtain a power of attorney from him to authorise them to sue for this debt. This application the Lord Chancellor granted. The power of attorney was accordingly obtained, and the committees then insisted upon both titles. The Court of Session (21st June 1749) found, "that there was no sufficient title produced to carry on the action, and therefore sustained the defence, and decerned accordingly." But this judgment was reversed upon appeal to the House of Lords, and it was "declared, that there was a sufficient title in the appellant, George Morison, to carry on the action commenced by the appellants, and that the same be sustained at the instance of the said Morison."

In Lord Elchies's reports it appears, that he had understood that this case had been ultimately decided on the power of attorney; but in the above case of *Thorne* v. *Watkins* Lord Hardwicke puts it upon the broader ground of the general law. (*l*)

(*l*) This a very interesting case, though it be ambiguous upon what grounds it was decided. The doctrines of the civilians in regard to the different classes of statutes appear to have entered into the discussion in that case in Scotland. It was contended, on the one

The other case of the *Hans Towns* v. *Jacobson*, mentioned in *Thorne* v. *Watkins*, as far as has been observed, is not reported.

---

hand, 1st, That the inquisition in England was no legal evidence in Scotland; and, 2d, That the Lord Chancellor had no power to direct the management of any estate *extra territorium*. The other party insisted that *personal* statutes of the place of the domicil were of force every where; and that the powers of the committees of the lunatic extended to Scotland. The obtaining a power of attorney from the lunatic was but a *rude way* of solving this difficulty. Lord Elchies says (notes, p. 200.), " I reported the case, and the Lords unanimously found, that " neither the Chancellor's commission, nor the letter of attorney, gave " a sufficient title to carry on this suit. But this was reversed by the " House of Lords, and the title sustained to maintain the action in " Morison's name, 13th Feb. 1750, *which was founded on the letter of* " *attorney*, as I was told."

In the proceedings in this cause, it appears that English counsel had been consulted, and had given an opinion, " that an idiot's tutor appointed in Scotland could not, on that title, maintain an action in " England."

In the case of *Otto Lewis*, 2d August, 1749 (1 Vesey, senr. 298.), Lord Hardwicke acknowledged a proceeding before the senate of Hamburg, where the party resided, as establishing a lunacy in England.

In the well-known case of the lunacy of the Marquis of Annandale (*infra*), the proceedings took place in the two countries independently of each other. In 1747 a commission of lunacy was issued against him, under which he was found a lunatic, and Marchioness Charlotta, his mother, was appointed his committee in England. In 1757, he was cognosced a lunatic in Scotland, and the Earl of Hopetoun was appointed his curator. It does not appear that the English committee interfered with the property in Scotland; nor the Scotch curator with the property in England. The domicil of the Marquis was, as will afterwards be seen, extremely doubtful.

In another case in Scotland, *Leith* v. *Hay* (Fac. Coll. 17th January, 1811), the Court of Session sustained action in Scotland upon the bond granted to the King by the committee of an English lunatic and his sureties, such committee and sureties being domiciled in Scotland. In this action, decree was granted for payment of the bond, and the money was directed to be paid into the Bank of Scotland upon receipt, till, upon application to the Lord Chancellor, his Lordship should " direct " in what manner the money so to be paid shall be remitted to the " proper officer of the Court of Chancery, for the benefit of the estate

In 1787, a case occurred at the Rolls, *Kilpatrick* v. *Kilpatrick*, which was decided by Sir Lloyd Kenyon, then Master of the Rolls, upon the same principles of the law of the domicil, as in that of *Thorne* v. *Watkins*. *Kilpatrick* of Bengal, in 1781, made his will in India, bequeathing certain legacies, to be paid partly out of his effects in India, partly out of his effects in England, and, amongst others, 300*l.* to Archibald Fleming residing in Scotland. Fleming died in 1783, before this legacy was paid, having made a will disposing of his whole personal estate and effects. Fleming's widow (there being no children) put in her claim to half of her late husband's personal estate *jure relictæ*, and in particular to the half of the legacy given by Kilpatrick's will. A suit was depending in the Court of Chancery in regard to Kilpatrick's estate. Sir Ilay Campbell, then Lord Advocate, was consulted on a case relative to the rights of the widow, and gave his opinion, " That by the law of Scotland those effects which are called simply moveable, belonging either to husband or wife at the time of the marriage, fell under the communion of goods between the married parties, and in which also the children, if any existed, had an

---

" of the said lunatic." I see nothing in the report in regard to the domicile of this lunatic.

I observe that, in America, questions have occurred upon this point, of the effect of a commission of lunacy under a different jurisdiction. Dr. Story says of the case of *Morison* (Conflict of Laws, p. 414.), " Whether this decision has been since acted on in England does not " distinctly appear. It has certainly not received sanction in America " in the states acting under the jurisprudence of the common law. " The rights and powers of guardians are considered as strictly *local*, " and not entitling them to exercise any authority over the person or " personal property of their wards in other states, *upon the same general* " *reasoning and policy which has circumscribed the rights and authorities of* " *executors and administrators.*" And he cites as authorities the American cases of *Morrill* v. *Dickey*, 1 John. Ch. Rep. 153., and *Kraft* v. *Vickery*, 4 Gill. and John. Rep. 332.

interest; and that the husband *jure mariti* had the administration and disposal of them while the marriage subsisted, but upon the dissolution thereof a division took place, and the wife (if she was the survivor) took one third, and the children another third as their legitim in case a widow existed, and one half if no widow; and that the remaining share alone the husband could dispose of by testament, for that he could not by any testamentary deed exclude the children's *legitim* or the wife's *jus relictæ;* and that the *jus relictæ* might, however, be excluded by settlement, or provisions made upon the wife, with her own consent, before or after marriage; and that in Scotland there was no distinction between *choses in action* and effects actually recovered."

The Master therefore reported, " that the petitioner, Ann Fleming, the widow of the said defendant, Archibald Fleming, not having any settlement or provision made upon her by her husband, and he having died without issue, she was entitled to one moiety of the legacy in question and the interest thereof." This report was confirmed by the decree of the Master of the Rolls, who directed one moiety of the legacy and interest to be paid to the widow, and the other moiety to Archibald Farquharson, the executor of Archibald Fleming. (*m*)

(*m*) Appellant's case, *Bruce* v. *Bruce,* 15th April, 1790, p. 4.   Respondent's case, *Hog* v. *Lashley,* 17th May, 1792, p. 7.   The decree was printed at large in this last cause, from which the above abstract of it is taken.

CHAP. VIII.

OF THE DECISION GIVEN IN THE CASE OF *BRUCE v. BRUCE*, BY WHICH THE LAW OF PERSONAL SUCCESSION WAS FIXED UPON THE LAW OF THE DOMICIL ; AND OF THE SUBSEQUENT CASES UPON INTERNATIONAL SUCCESSION, IN ENGLAND AND IN SCOTLAND.

WE have now brought down our deduction of the subject to the case of *Bruce* v. *Bruce,* which has attracted equal notice in both countries, and which, according to universal assent, has established this branch of the law upon its proper basis, as part of the law of nations. In the further progress of our inquiries, the cases decided belong equally to both countries. They may be divided into two branches; one regarding the succession in personal estate alone; the other of a mixed nature, where questions in relation to the succession of real and personal estate were involved in the same decision.

SECT. I.

Cases regarding Personal Estate alone.

THE case of *Bruce* v. *Bruce* belongs to the first of these branches. (a) David Bruce of Kinnaird left issue, by his first wife, James Bruce (b); and, by his second wife, three sons, William, Robert, and Thomas, and two daughters, Elizabeth and Margaret.

(a) Fac. Coll., 25th June, 1788, Morrison, 4617. House of Lords, 15th April, 1790.

(b) This was Bruce the Abyssinian traveller.

William Bruce, the eldest son of the second marriage, went out to India, at first in the sea service; but afterwards, about 1767, he entered into the military service of the East India Company, on their Bengal establishment, in which he gradually rose to the rank of major. In his letters written home to his relations, from time to time, and particularly so late as the 18th of December 1782, he constantly expressed an anxious desire to return to his native country, to spend his last days there, as soon as his circumstances would permit.

Having acquired about 9000*l.*, he remitted 500*l.* to a friend in London; and his attorney at Calcutta, in January and February 1783, remitted to Messrs. Alexander Barclay and Son of Glasgow, bills on the East India Company for 5708*l.* 2*s.* 3*d.*, with a power of attorney from Mr. Bruce, and instructions to lay out the proceeds in securities on his behalf.

On the 30th of April 1783, Major Bruce died at Calcutta, a bachelor, and intestate; part of his property was then in London, part was invested in the Indian bills before mentioned, and on its way to Europe; and the remainder was in India. Disputes arose in the family in regard to this succession. James Bruce, the brother *consanguinean*, contended, that the succession was to be regulated by the law of England, which made no distinction between the full and half blood; and the children of the second marriage contended, that, as the deceased was a Scotsman by birth, as his residence in India was merely occasional, and as he had expressed his intention of returning home as soon as he had acquired a competent fortune, the law of Scotland ought to be the rule; and more particularly in regard to that part of his fortune which, at the time of Major Bruce's death, was on its passage home, and which could not be said to be in England more than in Scotland.

An action was accordingly brought in the Court of Session by James Bruce of Kinnaird, against his brothers and sisters of the second marriage; and against the agents to whom parts of the property had been remitted, Messrs. Alexander Barclay and Son of Glasgow, and Mr. David Erskine of Edinburgh, writer to the signet; concluding that the defenders should be ordained to pay to the pursuer 2000*l.*, as his share of the estate and effects of the deceased, or to render a just account thereof, and pay to him his rateable share.

In the Court of Session, this case does not appear to have excited much interest: it is reported very briefly in the Faculty Collection; almost without any statement of the argument. The Lord Monboddo, Ordinary, pronounced this judgment:—" Finds, 1st, that, as Major Bruce was in the service of the East India Company, and not in a regiment on the British establishment, which might have been in India only occasionally, and as he was not upon his way to Scotland, nor had declared any fixed and settled intention to return thither at any particular time, India must be considered as the place of his domicil (*c*); 2dly, that, as all his effects were either in India, or in the hands of the East India Company, or of others his debtors in England, though he had granted letters of attorney to some of his friends in Scotland, empowering them to uplift those debts, *his* RES SITÆ *must be considered to be in England:* Therefore finds, that the English law must be the rule in this case for determining the succession to Major

---

(*c*) In the case of Marsh *v.* Hutchinson (2 Bos. and Pull. 231.), Lord Eldon, speaking of this cause, says, " Lord Thurlow in his judg-" ment adopted this distinction, that if he had gone out in a King's " regiment, and died in the King's service, his domicil would not have " been changed; but that, having died in the service of the Company, " it was changed." It appears that this view *originated* with Lord Monboddo.

Bruce, and consequently that James Bruce of Kinnaird is entitled to succeed with the defenders, his brothers and sisters *consanguinean*, and decerns and declares accordingly." And, upon a reclaiming petition, the Court adhered.

Pending this cause, some of the parties had died; but the two sisters, and James Hamilton of Bangour, the husband of Margaret, brought their appeal against this judgment to the House of Lords. Then its great and leading importance as a question of international law came to be perceived; and the case for the appellants (*d*) entered into a statement, not only of all the cases which had been decided in Scotland upon this subject, but also of the *dicta* of the foreign jurists, and of the decisions which had been given in England upon similar questions.

The cause was argued at the bar by advocates of great celebrity (*e*), and the opinions delivered by Lord Thurlow, then Lord Chancellor, with the judgment pronounced in this cause, have ever since been held to have fixed the law of Scotland upon this subject, on the basis of the law of nations. Lord Thurlow, at the time of giving judgment in the appeal, spoke to the following effect:—

" As he had no doubt that the decree ought to be affirmed, he would not have troubled their Lordships by delivering his reasons, had it not been pressed, with some anxiety, from the bar, that, if there was to be an affirm-

---

(*d*) Prepared or revised by Mr. Alexander, afterwards Sir William Alexander and Lord Chief Baron. (This information was received from the late Mr. Chalmer, the agent in London for the appellants, a gentleman, during a very long life, distinguished for legal acuteness, for integrity, and for every good quality that belongs to the professional character.)

(*e*) For the appellants, by Sir John Scott and Mr. Alexander; for the respondent, by Sir Ilay Campbell and Charles Hope, both afterwards Presidents of the Court of Session.

ance, the grounds of the determination should be stated, to prevent its being understood that the whole doctrine laid down by the interlocutor appealed from, and particularly that on which, it was said, the judges of the Court of Session proceeded principally in this, and former cases similar to it, had the sanction of this House. It had been urged, that the judgment should contain a declaration of what was the law, and he had revolved in his own mind whether that would be expedient. It was not usual in this House, or in the courts of law, to decide more than the very case before them, and he had particular reluctance to go farther in the present case; because, as had been stated, with great propriety, by one of the respondent's counsel (Mr. Hope), various cases had been decided in Scotland upon principles which if this House were to condemn, a pretext might be afforded to disturb matters long at rest.

" But he could have no objection to declare what were the grounds of his own opinion, and how far he coincided with the rules laid down by the Court below. Two reasons were assigned for having declared that the distribution of Major Bruce's personal estate ought to be according to the law of England: First, that India, a country subject to that law, was to be held as the place of his *domicilium*, and certain circumstances from which that was inferred. These he considered only as circumstances in the case; that is, though these had been wanting, the same conclusion might have been inferred from other circumstances. In his mind, the whole circumstances of Major Bruce's life led to the same conclusion. The *second* reason assigned by the interlocutor was, that the property of the deceased, which was the subject of distribution, was, at the time of his death, in India or in England. As to this, he founded so little on it, that he professed he could not see how the property could be considered as in England; it consisted of debts owing to the deceased, or money in bills of exchange drawn on the India Company. Debts have no *situs*; they follow the person of the creditor; that proposition, therefore, in the interlocutor fails in fact.

" But the true ground upon which the cause turned was, the deceased being domiciled in India. He was born in Scotland, but he had no property there. A person's origin, in a question of where is his domicil, is to be reckoned as but one circumstance in evidence, which may aid other circumstances; but it is an erroneous proposition that a person is to be held domiciled where he drew his first breath, without adding something more unequivocal. A person's being at a place is, *primâ facie*, evidence that he is domiciled at that place, and it lies on those who say otherwise to rebut that evidence. It may be rebutted, no doubt. A person may be travelling; — on a visit; — he may be there for a time, on account of health or business; — a soldier may be ordered to Flanders, and be detained there for many months; — the case of ambassadors, &c.; and what will make a person's domicil or home, in contradistinction to these cases, must occur to every one. A British man settles as a merchant abroad — he enjoys the privileges of the place — he may mean to return when he has made his fortune; but if he die in the interval, will it be maintained that he had his domicil at home? In this case Major Bruce left Scotland in his early years; he went to India; returned to England, and remained there for two years, without so much as visiting Scotland, and then went to India, and lived there sixteen years, and died. He meant to return to his native country, it is said; and let it be granted: he then meant to change his domicil, but he died before actually changing it. These were the grounds of his opinion, though he would move a simple affirmance of the decree; but he would not hesitate, as from himself, to lay down for law generally, that personal property follows the person of the owner; and, in case of his decease, must go according to the law of the country where he had his domicil; for the actual *situs* of the goods has no influence. He observed, that some of the best writers in Scotland lay down this to be the law of that country, and he quoted Mr. Erskine's Institute as directly in point. In one case it was clearly so decided in the Court of Session; in the other cases, which had been relied on as favouring the doctrine of *lex loci rei sitæ*, he thought he saw ingredients which made the Court, as in the present case, join both *domicilium* and *situs*. But to say that the *lex loci rei sitæ* is to govern, though the *domicilium* of the deceased be without contradiction in a different country, is a gross misapplication of the rules of the civil law, and *jus gentium*, though the law of Scotland on this point is constantly asserted to be founded on them." (*f*)

(*f*) In this case the following references were made to foreign jurists : —

Vattel, lib. 1. c. 19. s. 218.; lib. 2. c. 8. s. 110.

Voet, Comment. ad Pandect., lib. 38. t. 17. s. 34.

Vinnius, Quest. sel., lib. 2. c. 19.

Van Leuwen, Censura Forensis, lib. 3. c. 12. s. ult.

Huber. Prælectiones Juris Civilis et Hodierni, pars i. lib. 3. tit. 13. s. 21.; pars ii. lib. 1. tit. 3. s. 15.

Denisart, *voce* Domicile, s. 3, 4.

It may be remarked here, that in this and other references to the foreign jurists, made in the different cases cited, it has not been deemed necessary to quote the passages referred to at large. The citations are generally insulated *dicta* of these writers, quoted on either side, as they appeared to bear on the arguments of parties; and often referred to in a way that rendered it difficult to trace the passages meant to be relied on. In no case have I seen the attempt made to go over the whole range of foreign authorities (often conflicting ones) upon any point. They frequently do not quote the passages referred to. The library of the British Museum, and the public law libraries in the metropolis, are very defective in regard to the writings of the foreign jurists.

The opinions thus given on the points of law entirely coincided with those given by Lord Hardwicke in the English cases already noticed.   The judgment was a simple affirmance of the decision which had been pronounced by the Court of Session.

Upon this point (the form of the judgment) it may admit of some doubt, if the views taken by the most eminent person who then presided in the House of Lords, were altogether free from objection.   The interlocutors of the Court of Session, *on the face of them*, appeared to be founded on two legal doctrines, as of equal weight; one, the domicil of Major Bruce in a country subject to the laws of England; the other, the *lex loci rei sitæ*.   It was meant that the judgment of the House of Lords should have affirmed one of these doctrines, and negatived the other; but, by a simple affirmance of the interlocutors, it appeared *upon the record* as if both members of the decision of the Court of Session had been affirmed. (g)   Happily the opinions delivered by the Lord Chancellor were preserved in an authentic shape (h), and were acted on in the other

---

Of ninety-one continental writers on the subject of the *conflict of laws*, quoted or referred to by the American jurists, Livermore and Story, a large proportion is not to be found in these libraries; but, except six, I see them all marked in the catalogue of that admirable repertory of books of law, the Library of the Faculty of Advocates in Edinburgh. Our present object is rather to see what has been done in our own courts, than to weigh the opinions of the continental writers.

The English cases cited were those of Pipon *v.* Pipon, Thorne *v.* Watkins, Kilpatrick *v.* Kilpatrick, noticed above; and the case of Burne *v.* Cole, to be afterwards noticed.

(g) In Morrison, 4618., when mentioning the affirmance, no notice whatever is taken of the grounds upon which the House of Lords proceeded in this cause.   Thus it stood on the face of the reported decisions in Scotland, as an affirmance founded upon both the grounds stated in the judgment of the Court of Session.

(h) The speech of Lord Thurlow is given in a note to the case of

cases which soon after followed this, and which also attracted great attention.

The first of these cases was that of *Hog* v. *Lashley* (*i*), which, for the variety and extent of the points decided in it, and in other cases arising out of it, is the most important which has occurred upon this branch of the law in either country. Roger Hog was a native of Scotland, and went to London at an early period of life, where he settled in business as a merchant and banker. In 1737 he married Rachel Missing, an English lady, in England. Previous to the marriage of the parties, articles were executed, by which, in consideration of the lady's fortune, amounting to 3500*l.* and upwards, Roger Hog covenanted to lay out a sum of 2500*l.*, part of the said sum of 3500*l.*, or any further sum, if the same should be wanting, in the purchase of messuages, lands, tenements, and hereditaments, of the clear yearly value of 100*l.*, in any county in England, and to settle the same to William Rickman and Thomas Missing, as trustees, for the use of Roger Hog for life; after the determination of that estate, to the trustees to preserve contingent remainders; " and from and after the decease of the said Roger Hog to the use and benefit of the said Rachel Missing his intended wife, for and during the course of her natural life; and from and after the several deceases of the said Roger Hog and Rachel Missing, his intended wife, then to the use and behoof of such child or children of the body of the said Rachel Missing by the said Roger Hog lawfully to be begotten, and for such uses, intents, and purposes only,

---

Marsh *v.* Hutchinson, 2 Bos. & Pull. 229. It is given above from the short-hand writer's notes.

(*i*) Fac. Coll., 7th June, 1791, Morrison, 4619. House of Lords, 7th May, 1792.

and for such estate or estates, either in fee simple, fee tail general, life, lives, for years, or other estate whatsoever, whether absolute or conditional, and charged with such yearly or other sum or sums of money, annuities, and rent charges, as the said Rachel Missing, the intended wife of the said Roger Hog, during her coverture with the said Roger Hog, and notwithstanding her coverture, whether she be sole or married, by any deed or deeds, writing or writings, under her hand and seal, testified by three or more credible witnesses, or by her last will and testament in writing, so attested as aforesaid, shall from time to time direct, limit, nominate, and appoint; and in default of such direction, limitation, nomination, or appointment, then to the use and behoof of all and every the children, if more than one, of the body of the said Rachel Missing by the said Roger Hog her intended husband lawfully to be begotten, to be equally divided between them, share and share alike; and for default of such issue to the use and behoof of the heirs and assigns of the said Rachel Missing, the intended wife of the said Roger Hog, for ever."

After the marriage certain premises were bought at Kingston in Surrey, for the purposes specified in the marriage articles, which were conveyed to the trustees of the articles. Of this marriage there were several children; and Mrs. Hog having conveyed the estate at Kingston to her eldest son Thomas, it was sold when he came of age, and the purchase money was received by the father.

In 1752, Mr. Hog, the father, who had acquired a considerable fortune in London, purchased the estate of Newliston in Scotland. From that period he began to reside during part of his time in Scotland. His residences in that country became longer by degrees; and, for a number of years before his death, he was clearly domiciled in Scotland.

In 1760, Mrs. Hog died at her husband's house of Newliston, in Scotland, leaving three sons, Thomas, Roger, and Alexander, and three daughters, Rebecca, Rachel, and Mary. At this period the bulk of Mr. Hog's personal estate was in England, where he continued to carry on business, and had a share in a banking house.

In 1766, Rebecca, the eldest daughter, intermarried with Mr. Thomas Lashley, a native of Barbadoes, and then a student of medicine at Edinburgh. No settlement was made at the time of this marriage; it was an imprudent match; but Mr. Hog signified his consent to give his daughter 2000*l.*, if the father of Mr. Lashley would settle an equal sum upon his son. This proposal did not take effect. Mr. Hog had advanced to Mr. Lashley 700*l.*, and in 1775 he executed a bond of provision for 1300*l.*, as the remainder of a portion of 2000*l.* intended for Mrs. Lashley, payable to her, and after her death to her children of the marriage, or, in the event of her predecease, to her heirs or assignees, at the first term of Whitsunday or Martinmas after the grantor's death. This bond excludes Mr. Lashley's *jus mariti,* and is declared to be " in full contentation to the said Rebecca Hog, my daughter, of all portion natural, legitim, bairns' part of gear, or other claim or demand from me, or from my heirs and executors, in and through my decease, or through the death of Mrs. Rachel Missing deceased, my spouse, excepting good will allenarly." At the same time Mr. Hog executed similar bonds of provision for 2000*l.* each to his two unmarried daughters.

On the subsequent marriages of these two daughters regular settlements were executed, in which they respectively acknowledged the receipt of the provisions settled upon them by their father at the time, which they " accepted in full satisfaction of all they could ask or demand by and through his decease, or the decease of their mother, in name of legitim or otherwise;" and released and discharged him of all claims and demands in respect of the same accordingly, his own good will only excepted.

It was stated by both parties in this cause, that the two younger sons, Roger and Alexander, when setting out in business, had accepted of certain provisions from their father, and had respectively released him of all claims for legitim or otherwise. This statement was not disputed in the cause, and it came to be decided without any question as to the rights of these younger brothers; but important questions afterwards arose, in regard to the import of the transactions which had actually taken place between Roger Hog the father and his son Alexander, which formed the subject of discussion in the Court of Session; and an appeal to the House of Lords. (k)

Roger Hog afterwards advanced 300*l.* further to Mr. and Mrs. Lashley in 1779, and in 1785 granted her an additional bond of provision for 200*l.*; and he also granted further bonds of provision for 500*l.* each to his two younger daughters. The bonds of provision granted for Mrs. Lashley's benefit appear to have remained in the hands of the father, but he had distinctly communicated his intentions to her and her husband. In 1770 he directed Mrs. Lashley to draw for 260*l.*, as four years' by gone interest on 1300*l.*, the then remainder of her 2000*l.*; and to draw annually on his house in London for 65*l.* of interest. This she did regularly down to the month of January before her father's death, her bills expressing that they were " to be placed to account of Roger Hog, Esquire, for one year's interest due to me to the 31st December last."

In 1787 he executed an entail of his estate of Newliston in Scotland, in favour of his eldest son, and a certain

---

(k) Infra, p. 133.

K

series of heirs; and by a general disposition and assignation, in the nature of a *mortis causa* instrument, he conveyed to his said eldest son all estates, real and personal,
debts and sums of money, stock in trade, money in the
funds, and all other effects belonging to him, subject to
the payment of his debts and donations, and directing the
son to lay out the same in the purchase of lands in Scotland, to be entailed and enjoyed with his entailed estate
of Newliston.

Mr. Hog, the father, died at Newliston on the 19th of
March 1789. At the time of his death his family stood
thus:—His eldest son, Thomas Hog, was married, and
had a large family; his second son, Roger, had died, leaving issue two daughters; his third son, Alexander, was
married; his eldest daughter, Mrs. Lashley, was married,
and had issue; his second daughter, Rachel, was married,
and had issue; his youngest daughter, Mary, had died,
leaving issue.

At the time of his death he had a real estate in Scotland
of very considerable value; his personal estate in that
country, remaining in his own possession, was nearly balanced by his debts; but he had a large sum invested in
the British funds, and some annuities in the funds of
France; and it became a question whether certain large
sums in Bank of Scotland stock, which he had transferred
to his eldest son, were still to be considered as part of the
personal estate of the father, or as belonging to the son.

The two bonds of provision in favour of Mrs. Lashley,
which were found in the possession of Mr. Hog's agent
after his death, were tendered to her, but she and her
husband refused to accept the same; and soon after these
parties brought an action against Thomas Hog, the eldest
son, the universal disponee and executor of his father,
concluding that he should account to the pursuers for one
half of his father's moveable or personal estate, in the

name of *legitim ;* and for Mrs. Lashley's proportion of one third of the goods in communion at the dissolution of the marriage by the death of Mrs. Hog in 1760, to which, it was contended, the children were entitled as next of kin to their mother; and the pursuers insisted, that as all the other younger children had released the father, Mrs. Lashley was entitled to share in the division, as if they had never existed.

The previous case of *Bruce* v. *Bruce* had shown the grounds upon which questions of this nature should be discussed; accordingly, in the printed pleadings in this cause, not only the dicta of the institutional writers, and the whole course of the decisions in Scotland, were minutely examined; but the doctrines of certain foreign jurists, and the cases decided in England, were also fully stated.

When the very important questions contained in this case came to be discussed in the Court of Session, the Court had difficulty in coming to a conclusion upon several of them. Upon these, conflicting decisions were pronounced, but they came ultimately to this judgment on the following points of the cause: 1st, That the pursuers were not barred from their present claims by any *homologation, acquiescence, or acceptance* on their part. 2dly, That these claims could not be excluded, or at all affected, by the trust disposition of the father, executed, but not delivered during his lifetime. 3dly, That the releases of the other children had the same effect as if those children were naturally dead, and operated not to increase the dead's part, but the shares of the children who did not renounce. (The Lord Ordinary had decided that these releases operated in favour of the defender; and, in his interlocutor, argued at considerable length for the policy of deciding in that way.) 4thly, That the *lex domicilii* was to regulate the succession, not only in regard to the effects situated in Scotland, but also as to personal estate situated in England; and they remitted to the Lord Ordinary, " to hear parties further with respect to the government annuities in France, and to do therein as he should see just." (The Court had at first decided, that the legitim " could in no degree affect the moveables not situated in Scotland at the father's death.") 5thly, That the pursuers were entitled to one half of the free personal estate, as at the death of the father, wherever situated; and it was remitted to the Lord Ordinary, " to hear parties further upon the pursuer's claim, in right of her mother, to a share of the goods in communion at the dissolution of the marriage, and to do and proceed as to his Lordship shall seem just."

Thomas Hog, the defender in the cause, appealed to the House of Lords against the above judgments given by the Court of Session.

His appeal was taken upon the following points :—

1. That there was in this case an implied renunciation on the part of Mrs. Lashley, which barred her claim for legitim.

2. That the right of the children to legitim was barred by the deed executed by Mr. Hog in his lifetime.

3. That the share of a child renouncing accrued to the father, so as to enable him to dispose of it by will.

4. That, even though the deed executed by Mr. Hog were ineffectual in Scotland, it operated as a will in England, so as to convey the personal property in that country according to the intentions of the deceased.

5. That the property in the English funds was to be considered as immoveable property, and descendible to the heir, like a fund in Scotland having a *tractus futuri temporis*.

The cause was pleaded on both sides by persons of great celebrity; by Mr. Grant (afterwards Sir William

Grant) and Mr. Anstruther (afterwards Sir John Anstruther) for the appellant, and by the Lord Advocate (Robert Dundas) and the Solicitor General of England (Sir John Scott) on the part of the respondent. The hearing was continued for four days. At the conclusion of the argument, on the 7th of May 1792, Lord Thurlow, according to his usual practice when he did not depart from the judgment, moved an affirmance, without delivering any opinion of his own upon these important questions. (*l*)

After the decision of the first cause, relative to the succession of Roger Hog, the parties returned to the Court of Session, to discuss the other points which remained undecided as between the original parties in that cause. These discussions lasted for several years in the Court of Session, and afterwards formed the subject of another appeal to the House of Lords. (*m*)

In the meantime a new question had arisen in regard to the succession of Roger Hog, the father, in respect of the legitim of Alexander Hog, one of the sons. This came before the Court in an action of multiplepoinding, at the instance of *Thomas Hog*, as executor of his father, Roger Hog, v. *William Thwaytes and others, assignees of Alexander Hog.* (*n*) During the proceedings in the original cause between Mrs. Lashley and Mr. Hog, and till the decision of the appeal therein on the 7th of May 1792, no claim had been made in regard to the legitim of Alexander Hog. During the pendency of these proceedings he had

---

(*l*) I am enabled to give in the Appendix a report of what passed in the House of Lords on this most important cause, taken by an eminent counsel (since long a judge upon the Bench), for the use of the respondent in the cause *Balfour* v. *Scott.*

(*m*) Infra, p. 139.

(*n*) This important cause is not reported. It was decided in the Court of Session, in 1795; in the House of Lords, 24th June, 1802.

become bankrupt, and William Thwaytes and others had been appointed his assignees.

Immediately after the decision in the first-mentioned appeal, these assignees made a claim upon Thomas Hog for a share of the legitim on behalf of Alexander Hog, the bankrupt, under the following circumstances : Alexander was born in February 1750; in 1768, when only eighteen years of age, he entered into business with Messrs. Farquhar and Cameron of London, grocers. On this occasion Roger, the father, advanced him 1500l., and 100l. for certain legacies which had been left to him.

On the 29th of November 1768, Roger Hog wrote to his son Alexander in these terms : " I intend now to trust and pay you off your patrimony, by advancing 1500l. without interest, which is the sum I always allotted to you ; and I owed you 90l. of legacies, which I make up to 100l.; so you have to grant me your bond for 400l. at five per cent., which I expect the profits of the house will enable you to pay off in a year or two, which profits I also generously give up to you to increase your capital, though I fancy most would think it my due during your nonage, as is the interest of your capital during my lifetime."

Alexander thus received 2000l. from his father at this period; it does not appear that he granted bond for the 400l. as mentioned in his father's letter, but he granted a special receipt, on the 31st of December 1768, for the 1500l. and 100l. before mentioned. The receipt was in these terms : " I, Alexander Hog, son to Roger Hog of Newliston, esquire, grant me to have received from the said Roger Hog, my father, the sum of 1500l. sterling money, *as portion bestowed upon me by him.*" (He also acknowledged receipt of the 100l. of legacies.) " And for both which sums of 1500l. and 100l. sterling so received by me I discharge the said Roger Hog, my father, and oblige myself to reiterate and renew these presents, after I arrive at the age of twenty-one years complete." This receipt Alexander transmitted to his father.

At the period when he made this payment to Alexander, the father made this entry in his journal: " 31st October 1768. Profit and loss 1500*l.*, for so much given him " (Alexander Hog) " as his portion or patrimony from me, and for which I have his discharge in full of all demand in my charter chest. 1500*l.*" On repeated occasions afterwards Alexander expressed his gratitude for what had been thus done for him.

In March 1779, Alexander borrowed from his father a sum of 2000*l.*; and, in September 1780, a further sum of 2000*l.* For these two sums Alexander granted bonds to his father in the English form.

Afterwards the father had formed the resolution of discharging these bonds to Alexander, in lieu of a provision of 4000*l.* which he had intended for him. Accordingly, on the 30th of December 1783, he executed a deed, in which, after reciting the bonds, he proceeded thus: " And now seeing, for the love, favour, and affection I have and bear to my said son, and for several other weighty causes and considerations moving me, I am resolved, in lieu of a provision of 4000*l.*, which I intended to have given the said Alexander Hog, my son, to discharge the foresaid two bonds granted by him to me for the sum of 2000*l.* sterling each, amounting together to the sum of 4000*l.* sterling, being equal to the foresaid provisions intended to have been given by me to my said son, and that besides what sum or sums of money I may have already given him, and also besides what provisions I may hereafter think proper to give or bequeath to him, by any deed or deeds to be hereafter granted by me: Therefore wit ye me to have exonered," &c. This deed contained a *power to alter*, a clause dispensing with the delivery, and a declaration that the money advanced should be in full of all *legitim, dead's* *part, portion natural,* or *bairn's part of gear.* It never was communicated to Alexander Hog, but remained in Mr. Roger Hog's repositories at the time of his death.

Alexander Hog's bankruptcy occurred after the date of the above deed, and his father proved upon his estate for the two 2000*l.* bonds and interest, and took his first dividend of 4*s.* in the pound, amounting to 818*l.* 1*s.* 4*d.*, upon the debt.

After the father's death, in March 1789, the above-mentioned discharge, having been found in his repositories, was, by the directions of Mr. Thomas Hog, the executor, delivered to Mr. Thwaytes, the acting assignee upon Alexander's estate, who granted a receipt for it, on a copy of the deed, in the following terms: " London, 30th April 1789. Received by me, assignee under the statute of bankruptcy of Alexander Hog, grocer, of London, from Thomas Hog esq., of Newliston, by the hands of Mr. John Robertson, writer in Edinburgh, a discharge granted by Roger Hog of Newliston, esq., to the said Alexander Hog, of which the three preceding pages is an exact copy." And Alexander Hog made and signed a memorandum at the bottom of the above receipt, in the following terms: " London, 30th April 1789. I approve of the above-mentioned discharge having been delivered to my assignees."

The assignees afterwards proceeded to divide the assets of the bankrupt, without paying or setting apart any dividend corresponding to the debt of 4000*l.*, to which the discharge related.

Soon after the decision in the appeal between Thomas Hog and Mrs. Lashley, Alexander Hog and his assignees brought an action in the Court of Session in Scotland against Thomas Hog, in which they claimed 15,000*l.*, for Alexander's share, as one of the nearest of kin of his mother, of the goods in communion between his father and mother at the time of her death, on 18th February 1760, and of the estate, heritable and moveable, to which she had right, as the same was intromitted with by her husband; and also the farther sum of 15,000l. for Alexander's share of the personal estate of his father, on the 19th of March 1789, or such other sums, less or more, as should be found to be due to Alexander, for his share of the estate of his father and mother, with interest on each sum from the date on which it should have been paid, till payment.

Mr. Thomas Hog thereupon raised a multiplepoinding in the same court, taking notice of the depending action at the instance of Mrs. Lashley and her husband, and concluding that the several parties claiming should have their preferences adjusted, and that the persons found best entitled should be preferred by decree of the court.

The Lord Ordinary pronounced the interlocutor which is usual in multiplepoindings, finding " the raiser of the multiple-poinding liable in once and single payment," and remitting the multiplepoinding to the previous process, to be discussed therein *ob contingentiam*.   The whole depending actions were then conjoined; and Mrs. Lashley and her husband on the one hand, and Alexander Hog and his assignees on the other, discussed two questions which appeared to be of chief importance between them; 1st, whether Alexander had released the father in his lifetime; 2d, whether the estate of the father had been released by any thing done after the father's death.

In the course of these proceedings Mrs. Lashley, at a hearing of the cause, advanced a new argument, namely, that she had right to the *whole legitim* by the judgment of the court, affirmed by the House of Lords ; that this judgment had proceeded upon the uniform averment made by Thomas Hog that Alexander had renounced; and that Thomas Hog might nevertheless be liable to the assignees of Alexander Hog for such share of the legitim as Alexander might have been entitled to, if he had not renounced.

The Court, after a discussion of these points, decided, " That Mr. Hog, the raiser of the multiplepoinding, was liable only in once and single payment; and that Alexander Hog's claim of legitim was not cut off during the life of his father, nor by what passed after his father's death; and therefore sustained his claim, and remitted to the Lord Ordinary to proceed accordingly, and to do further in the cause as he should see just."

Against this judgment, Mrs. Lashley and her husband brought their appeal, calling as parties only the assignees of Alexander Hog, he having died in the meantime. When the appeal came on to be heard in the House of Lords on the 5th of March 1802, it appeared to their Lordships that Mr. Hog ought to have been made a party, to defend that part of the interlocutor which found him liable in only once and single payment, as to which some doubts were expressed by the Lord Chancellor and Lord Thurlow. Leave was accordingly given to amend the appeal. Mr. Hog was made a party, and gave in a printed case upon his part; this he confined entirely to the question, whether or not he was liable only in once and single payment.

The cause came on to be argued in this amended shape on the 29th of April 1802, and counsel was also heard for Mr. Hog in support of that part of the interlocutor which found him liable in once and single payment.

After the cause had been fully argued, Lord Eldon, Lord Chancellor, on the 24th June 1802, made a speech in the cause, and on his motion the following judgment was pronounced: (o)

_____

(o) Notes of the Lord Chancellor's speech were preserved in this case, which are also given in the Appendix.

From a memorandum made by me at the hearing of this cause, I see the Lord Chancellor said, " I have always considered it a great defect

" Ordered and adjudged, That the interlocutors complained of, in so far as they found that Alexander Hog's claim of legitim was not cut off during the lifetime of his father, should be affirmed; and that the said interlocutors should be reversed in so far as they found that Alexander Hog's claim of legitim was not cut off by what passed after his father's death, and in so far as they sustained the said claim; and it was thereby declared and found, that the assignees of the bankruptcy of the said Alexander Hog were competent to release such claim, and that it appeared by facts proved in this cause that they had released it; and it was further ordered and adjudged, that, as to the rest, the said interlocutors should be affirmed, and the cause be remitted back to the Court of Session to proceed accordingly."

Simultaneously with this cause between the assignees of Alexander Hog and the other parties, the remaining questions in the important cause between *Mrs. Lashley and Mr. Hog* proceeded in the Court of Session. The following points were still to be discussed and decided between the parties in that cause:—1. In regard to the domicil of Mr. Roger Hog at the dissolution of the marriage by the death of Mrs. Hog in 1760; 2. Admitting that Mr. Hog had at that period a Scotch domicil, whether the rights of Mrs. Hog and her next of kin were to be regulated by the law of Scotland or by the law of England, she being an English woman, and having been married in England; 3. As to the effect of the marriage articles between Mr. and Mrs. Hog, and the provisions thereby covenanted to

---

in your legal practice that you do not take money into the hands of the court, as we do in this country." Apparently the appointment of an accountant-general, subject to the directions of the Scottish courts, would introduce a great improvement upon this branch of practice. In this way also immediate access might be had by litigants in Scotland to the public funds.

be settled upon her, and whether these excluded all legal provisions on the part of her, or her next of kin; 4. In regard to the legitim,—whether certain shares of Bank of Scotland stock, which Mr. Hog had transferred to his son many years before his death, but of which the father had continued to receive the dividends, belonged to the father's estate, or were vested absolutely in the son; and whether certain other shares which were transferred to the son a few months before his father's death, to be laid out in the purchase of land, belonged absolutely to him, or still remained part of his father's estate; 5. Whether the father was accountable to his eldest son for the price of the estate at Kingston, which was devised to the eldest son by his mother, and sold by him, and the price paid to the father; 6. Whether Mrs. Lashley should deduct from her claims what she had received from her father on account of the provision intended for her; 7. Whether Mrs. Lashley's claims were subject to deduction on account of the expence of the probate of her father's will in England, and the confirmation in Scotland.

The extent and variety of these questions, and their importance in regard to some of the most interesting doctrines connected with the present inquiry, were altogether unprecedented. (p)

(p) A very few of them are briefly noticed in the report of this case in the Faculty Collection, 16th June, 1795, Morrison, 4628. — In his appendix, voce Foreign, p. 12., he states, through mistake, that the judgment was affirmed on appeal to the House of Lords. It was reversed on one of the most important points stated in the Faculty Collection and in Morrison; namely, the effect of a marriage in England, and of the English marriage articles.

So, on the point of *legitim,* and the gratuitous deeds of the father *inter vivos,* Morrison does not appear to have known that the judgment was reversed. Dictionary *Legitim,* Appendix *hoc tit.* 2.

So also in *Brown's Synopsis,* voce *Legitim,* the decision of the Court of Session is mentioned, but its reversal is not stated.

The question of domicil was involved in a great variety of circumstances. Mr. Hog was a Scotsman born; as early as 1750 he had expressed his wish to fix his residence in Scotland, when he could retire from his business in London; in the end of 1752 he purchased the estate of Newliston in Scotland; from that period he resided sometimes at Newliston, and sometimes in London. In 1754 he assumed as a partner in his business Mr. Kinloch, whom he brought from Scotland; and in the articles of partnership for three years, executed between them, it was stated, that he intended " chiefly to reside in Scotland during the continuance of this copartnership;" but there was a provision for what was to be done if he came to London in the winters. In 1757 the contract of copartnership was renewed for four years more.

A great variety of circumstances of occasional residence, and expressions in Mr. Hog's letters, were founded on, on both sides, in the respective arguments of the parties. In July 1759, Mr. and Mrs. Hog left London for Newliston, and Mrs. Hog died at that place in February 1760. It appeared, in the investigation which took place, that, from the time when he purchased the estate of Newliston in 1752, till the period of Mrs. Hog's death, he had resided in London thirty-five months, and at Newliston fifty-three months. In October 1760, Mr. Hog brought his daughters to England, and placed them in schools in that country; he continued still occasionally to reside in London. In 1765 he renewed his copartnership with Mr. Kinloch, and then gave his second son, Roger Hog, half his stock in the company. In the articles of partnership, he still styled himself as " of London, merchant." In December 1772, he gave up the other half of his business to his son Roger; and (on the part of the defender Thomas Hog) it was contended, that not till then was his domicil fixed in Scotland.

Upon this branch of the cause, which related to the domicil at Mrs. Hog's death, and the right of her representatives to a share of the personal estate at that period, the Lord Ordinary at first decided, " that there were two domicils at the dissolution of the marriage, one in London and the other in Scotland, but that the last was the principal; and that when parties marry in one country, and afterwards remove to another, in which the legal rights of married persons are different, the change of domicil ought not to operate any change on any of the rights pre-established in them in the country where they married; and that all those rights ought to be preserved and enforced by the law of the country to which they have removed, unless they were incompatible with the morality or religion of that country."

The Court, however, altered the interlocutor of the Lord Ordinary in regard to the domicils, and "found that the deceased Mr. Hog, at the dissolution of the marriage, had his domicil in Scotland; and they found that Mrs. Lashley, in right of her mother, had no claim to any share of the moveable estate belonging to her father at the time of her mother's death."

In regard to the amount of the legitim as due at the death of the father, the Court found, " 1st, That the 120 shares of Bank of Scotland stock, which had been transferred to, and vested in the defender by his father, in the father's lifetime, were not subject to the pursuer's claim of legitim: 2d, That the late Roger Hog, by a general settlement of date 5th February 1787, disponed his estate, heritable and moveable, to the defender, his eldest son; and that he appears at one time to have vested his property in Bank of Scotland stock, in trust to be laid out in the purchase of lands to be entailed on the defender, though he afterwards changed his mind, and transferred the same directly and *inter vivos* to the defender; and therefore that, in the circumstances of this case, there was no room for the presumption of law *debitor non præsumitur donare ;* and that the defender, in competition with those claiming a right of legitim, was entitled, at the period of his father's death, to state himself a creditor upon the moveable estate left by his father for the price of the estate near Kingston in England, which belonged to the late Mrs. Hog, was left by her to the defender, and which price was uplifted and unaccounted for by the late Roger Hog; and that he was likewise a creditor at the period of his father's death for the principal sum of 1000*l.*, contained in a bond granted by Roger Hog to the defender and his wife Lady Mary Hog, in conjunct fee and liferent, and to the children of the marriage in fee, being the tocher which the defender received with his wife; and that those, as well as the other debts resting by the said Roger Hog at his death, must in the first place be deducted from the moveable estate of the said Roger Hog, and that the claim of legitim can only attach upon the remainder of the said moveable estate: 3d, That the ordinary expence of obtaining confirmation in Scotland, or of obtaining a probate in England by the defender, in order to carry into effect the late Roger Hog's will, being expences which arose subsequent to the existence of the pursuer's right of legitim, cannot be a deduction from, or burden upon, the late Roger Hog's moveable estate, in computing the extent of said claim: and they found, that the sums advanced to Mrs. Lashley and to Alexander Hog (*q*), with interest from the dates of advancing, must be considered as debts due to the moveable estate, subject to the legitim; and that the said sums due by them respectively were to be deducted out of their respective shares of legitim; but, of

(*q*) At this time Alexander's claims had not been decided on by the House of Lords.

consent, that interest was not be charged upon the annual payments of 65*l.* to Mrs. Lashley."

Mrs. Lashley and her husband brought their appeal against those parts of the interlocutors of the Court of Session, which related to her claim to a share of the personal estate at the dissolution of the marriage in right of her mother, and in regard to the amount of the funds of the father out of which legitim was due; and Mr. Hog brought his cross appeal against that part of the judgment which found that Roger Hog was domiciled in Scotland at the dissolution of the marriage, and which found that the ordinary expences of the confirmation in Scotland, and probate in England, were not to be a deduction from, or burden upon, the personal estate of Roger Hog.

These most important questions came on to be heard in the House of Lords on the 11th of May 1802. The cause was argued by the then Attorney General (Mr. Perceval) and Mr. Clerk (afterwards Lord Eldin) for the appellants, and by Mr. Romilly and Mr. Erskine (afterwards Sir Samuel Romilly and Lord Erskine) for the respondents. The hearing lasted for five days in that session, and two days in the following session, and concluded on the 9th of August 1803. An objection was taken to the cross appeal, that it had not been brought within the time limited by the standing order of the House of Lords of the 8th of March 1763, which ordered that a cross appeal should not be received unless it were presented within one week after an answer put into the original appeal.

After the pleadings had been finished the judgment was adjourned till the next session of Parliament 1804; nothing was done till towards the close of that session. At length, after a speech of two days by Lord Eldon, Lord Chancellor (*r*), judgment was given on the 16th of July 1804

(*r*) Notes of his Lordship's speech in this very important cause have been preserved, and are given in the Appendix.

in these terms : " It is declared, that the contract of marriage between the late Mr. Roger Hog and his wife is not so conceived as to bar a claim to legal provisions, and that the said Mr. Hog is to be considered as having his domicil in Scotland at the time of his wife's death ; and that the pursuer has therefore a claim in right of her mother, the wife of the said Mr. Roger Hog, who at the time of her death had his domicil in Scotland, to a share of the moveable estate of her father at the time of her mother's death : And it is further declared, that such shares of the stock of the Bank of Scotland, standing in the name of the respondent Thomas Hog at the death of the said Roger Hog, as shall appear to have been transferred to the said Thomas Hog, under any agreement or understanding that he would invest the same in land after the death of the said Roger Hog ; and also such shares, the dividends whereof shall appear, notwithstanding the transfer of the same to have been after such transfer ordinarily received for the account of, and applied for the use of, the said Roger Hog, ought to be considered as subject to the pursuer's claim of legitim : And it is therefore ordered and adjudged, that all such parts of the interlocutors complained of in the appeal as are inconsistent with those declarations be reversed ; and in so far as they are agreeable thereto, the same shall be affirmed : And it is further ordered, that the cause be remitted back to the Court of Session in Scotland, to ascertain whether any, and which of the shares in the Bank of Scotland, agreeably to the declarations aforesaid, are subject to the pursuer's claim of legitim ; and also to ascertain the interests of the pursuer in her father's estate at her mother's death and at his death, regard being had to this declaration : And it is further ordered and adjudged, that it is unnecessary to consider so much of the matter complained of in the cross appeal as relates to the domicil of the said

L

Roger Hog, touching which such declaration has been made, as is herein-before contained; and the said appeal also not having been presented in due time, it is further ordered and adjudged, that the same be dismissed this House." (s)

This appears to be in many respects the most important decision upon points of international law, connected with the subject of the present inquiry, which has been given in either country. Several of the questions discussed in this cause had not before been decided in the courts of England or of Scotland, particularly those in regard to the rights of the husband and wife under a marriage contracted under marriage articles, by parties then domiciled in one country, who afterwards removed into another country, where the rules of the law of succession were different. The opinions of the foreign jurists, which were conflicting opinions, were referred to as authorities by both parties.

On a review of the judgments ultimately pronounced in the different causes, it is difficult to challenge the decision given upon any of the points there decided, though persons of great eminence, when consulted as to some of the

---

(s) In these cases of Hog and Lashley the following foreign jurists were referred to : —

Voet, ad Pandectas, lib. 1. tit. 4. de Statutis, s. 11, 12.
—— lib. 23. tit. 2. s. 87.
—— lib. 28. tit. 3. s. 2. 12.
—— lib. 48. tit. 20. s. 7.
Vattel, lib. 2. c. 8. s. 109, 110, 111. 181.
Denisart voce Domicile, s. 3, 4.
Huber. Prælect. jur. civilis et hodierni, pars ii. lib. 1. tit. 3. s. 3. 13, 14.
—— lib. 3. s. 4. tit. 22, 23.
Rodenburg. tit. 1. c. 2. in fine, tit. 2. c. 2.
Christinæus, Leg. Mechlin. tit. 16. art. 39.
Grotius, lib. 2. c. 7. s. 3.
Puffendorf, lib. 4. c. 11. s. 1.
Peck. de Test. Conjug. lib. 4. c. 18.

points of law contained in the cause, were divided in opinion upon these at the time. (t)

(t) Sir William Grant, when consulted, at one time, gave his opinion, that in so far as not regulated by the marriage articles, the law of England, where the parties were domiciled at the time, ought to regulate the rights of husband and wife during the marriage, and at the dissolution thereof. There is no point which has been more discussed among foreign jurists than this, whether the *matrimonial* domicil, or the domicil at the time of the dissolution of the marriage (where the domicil has been changed) shall regulate the rights of the parties; and there is a great diversity of opinion among them upon this subject. In America this question has been much discussed, and a vast variety of learning has been brought out upon the subject. (See the point discussed, and the opinions of foreign jurists stated in Story's Commentaries on the Conflict of Laws, 143. et sequen.) The Supreme Court of Law of Louisiana, in the case of *Saul* v. *his Creditors*, 17 Martin's R. 571, 572., appears to have considered, " that the vast mass of learning which the " research of counsel can furnish, leaves the subject as much involved " in obscurity and doubt, as it would be if one were called upon to " decide, without the knowledge of what others had thought and " written upon it." In this case of *Saul* v. *his Creditors*, the court held, " that where a couple had removed from Virginia (their matri- " monial domicil) where no *community* exists, into Louisiana where a " community does exist, the acquests and gains *acquired after their* " *removal* were to be governed by the law of community in Louisiana." (Story's Comment. 153.)

The time of the acquisition was not discussed in the case of *Lashley* v. *Hog*. But it enters largely into the consideration of the foreign jurists (Story, 144.), and in this respect the American decision differs from ours; Mrs. Lashley's claims attached to the whole succession, whether acquired before or after the change of domicil. The point is curious, and has thus been decided differently in the two countries. It might lead to intricacy of inquiry to be obliged to trace the state of the property at the time of the change of domicil; but this might be done. In the case of *Lashley* v. *Hog* there must have been similar difficulty in tracing the state of the property at the dissolution of the marriage.

I regret that I have not yet seen this case of *Saul* v. *his Creditors*, at large. I could not find in London a copy of the book containing it (17 Martin's Rep.) From the reference made to it by Kent and Story, it appears to have been treated with great learning and research.

From the notes of Lord Eldon's speech it does not appear that the

What appears to have weighed with the House of Lords was, that there must have been innumerable cases of married persons changing their domicil from one country to the other, or from the province of York to the province of Canterbury, *et vice versâ;* yet that no question had ever occurred in regard to the law which was to regulate the succession in such cases; that the law of the domicil had, in these, by tacit consent, been allowed to rule universally; and that to lay down a contrary rule must be attended with strange consequences, and much inconvenience.

That part of the judgment of the Court of Session, by which the *ordinary expences of confirmation and probate* were found not to be a burden on the general estate of Roger Hog, was considered by Lord Eldon to have been totally erroneous. It was impossible in England to have got access to the funds in that country, except through a probate or administration granted by the proper Ecclesiastical Court; but, as these funds formed part of the legitim, there was no ground why those entitled to the legitim should not bear their due proportion of that necessary expence; and this could not be arranged otherwise than by taking such expences off the *præcipuum* of the whole estate; but, by reason of the irregularity in bringing the cross appeal too late, the House of Lords felt itself obliged to affirm this part of the judgment.

The following points appear to have been decided in these causes : 1st, That the succession in personal estate of every description, wherever situated, was to be regulated by the law of the domicil ; 2d, That personal estate, though situated in a country where there was an unlimited power of giving by will, could not be carried by an instrument of that nature, executed by a person having his

---

foreign jurists were much under consideration when the cause of *Lashley* v. *Hog* was decided.

domicil in Scotland, to the prejudice of the claims of his wife and children; 3d, That the discharges by the children of their legitim operated not in favour of the father, but in favour of the children who did not discharge; 4th, That conveyances *inter vivos* by the father, of part of his personal estate of which he continued to receive the dividends, did not bar the claims for legitim on such part of his estate; 5th, That a conveyance of personal estate to his eldest son, upon trust or confidence that it should be laid out in the purchase of land after the father's death, did not bar the claims of legitim of the younger children; 6th, That parties married in England, where they had their domicil, by removing to Scotland, and fixing their domicil in that country, changed their own rights and the rights of their children, and subjected these to the rules of succession of the law of Scotland; 7th, That the father's estate was accountable to his children, as in right of their mother, for one third of the goods in communion at the mother's death, the whole having remained with the father undivided. (*u*)

It must be admitted that this case was, in a popular view, one of very considerable hardship towards the testator. Up to the time of Mr. Hog's death, the *lex loci rei sitæ* was universally admitted by lawyers in Scotland to regulate in personal succession. While residing in Scotland, and carrying on an extensive business in England, he could have had no idea, that he was incurring a debt to his children as in right of their mother; and, when settling rational and competent provisions upon his other children, and taking their discharges, that he was acquiring such a

---

(*u*) Various questions might have been raised, under this branch of the judgment, in regard to the interests or profits to be accounted for by the father after the death of the mother. Upon inquiry, I found that, after the last judgment of the House of Lords, the parties had entered into a compromise in regard to all ulterior matters.

fortune for the only one of his children who had thwarted his wishes.

The situation of the eldest son was also, in these points of view, one of considerable hardship, particularly when he was called upon to defend the judgment in the multiplepoinding, which found that he was only liable in once and single payment. If it had not been found that Alexander and his assignees had discharged his claims after his father's death (a question attended with some difficulty), the consequences must have been very serious to the eldest son. (x)

It was deemed expedient not to interrupt the preceding statement of these questions in the affairs of Mr. Hog, but while they were in progress other questions of great importance upon points of international law had also arisen. To these we must now recur.

The principles as to the effect of the law of the *domicil* having been fixed in the cases before stated, the chief difficulty with the courts in both countries has since been to apply this doctrine to the facts of each particular case. Upon this subject there has been often a good deal of difficulty in fixing the domicil; and in some cases the circumstances have been so nicely balanced, that the parties deemed it better to settle the questions by compromise,

---

(x) Mr. Erskine (afterwards Lord Erskine and Lord Chancellor), who was of counsel for Mr. Hog in the two last appeals, often expressed his surprise to the parties that the law of Scotland, as connected with these questions, should have remained unaltered till that time. Other cases of the same nature may at this moment be coming forward for discussion, upon similar questions. Curious questions might also have occurred if Mr. Hog had been a freeman of London: I see no allusion to the fact, whether he was so or not. According to other cases, if he had been a freeman of London, he might have disposed of his whole personal estate by his will or testamentary disposition under the statute of 11 George I.

than to take a decision of the courts of law upon them. The cases upon questions of international succession; though sometimes occurring in one country, sometimes in the other, equally belong to both: they may, therefore, be stated in the order of their dates.

In the case of *Macdonald* v. *Laing* (27th November 1794), a question arose in the court of session in Scotland, as to the domicil of the party deceased (*y*), under the following circumstances, which are not stated very distinctly in the report. " William Macdonald, a native of Scotland, acquired a considerable plantation in Jamaica, where he had resided about fifteen years. In 1779, he was appointed a lieutenant in the 79th regiment of foot, at that time. quartered in the island; he also got the command of a fort in it. In 1783 he obtained leave of absence for a year, that he might return to Scotland for the recovery of his health. He died a few months after his arrival in Scotland. The 79th regiment was by this time reduced. He had no effects in Scotland, and his only property in England was two bills of exchange, which he had transmitted from Jamaica before he left it, in order, as was said, to purchase various articles for his plantation. His father intromitted with his funds in England."

The sisters of the deceased brought an action against their father to account for their brother's executry, the father claiming the whole as coming to him by the law of Jamaica. Pending the action the father died, having disponed to his grandson, Alexander Laing, his rights to the succession of his son.

The Lord Ordinary found, " that the succession was to be regulated by the law of Scotland, in respect that William Macdonald died in Scotland, his native country, where he had resided several months before his death."

(*y*) Fac. Coll., Morrison, 4627.

With a reclaiming petition, two letters of the deceased were produced, as showing an intention to return to Jamaica upon the recovery of his health. Some of the judges came to be of opinion that the domicil of the deceased was in Jamaica, but a considerable majority were of opinion with the Lord Ordinary, and his judgment was affirmed.

The circumstance of the deceased having been in the King's service as an officer in the army does not appear to have been founded on in this case, though a similar circumstance, and the difference between the service of the King, and the service of the East India Company, formed an important subject of discussion in the case of *Bruce* v. *Bruce.* (z) This is a case of difficulty; it appears to be doubtful whether the deceased, by coming to Scotland *for the recovery of his health,* and dying there, had abandoned his domicil in Jamaica. (a)

In the case of *Ommanney and another, executors of Sir Charles Douglas,* v. *Bingham,* the question of domicil was discussed and decided in the Court of Session and in the House of Lords. (b)

Sir Charles Douglas (c) was born in Scotland in 1729, being a younger son of Douglas of Finglassie, in Fifeshire. In 1741, when twelve years of age, he entered the British navy; from that time till 1748, his ship appears to have been his only home. In that year, after the peace of Aix la Chapelle, he was paid off. In the year following he

---

(z) Supra, p. 118.

(a) Apparently this case was not decided upon the same principles which were held to govern in the case of *Munro* v. *Douglas,* at the Rolls, *infra.*

(b) It does not appear that this case, though of considerable celebrity, is noticed in the Scotch Reports; it was decided in the House of Lords, 18th March, 1796.

(c) The celebrated person who was captain of Admiral Rodney's ship in the action of the 12th of April, 1782.

obtained a lieutenancy in the Dutch service, in which he continued for some years, residing sometimes on shipboard, sometimes at Amsterdam.

In 1754 he returned to the British service, and in 1759, after he had been made master and commander, he married a Dutch lady in Holland. After his marriage he had no fixed residence, but had lodgings in different parts of England, according to the station of his ship. In 1761 he obtained the rank of post-captain, and having been appointed to a foreign station, his wife, being pregnant, went to Amsterdam, where, in June, 1761, her first child, a son, was born; there the mother and child continued to reside till 1765.

In 1763 Captain Douglas accepted a flag in the Russian service. In the beginning of 1764 he went to Saint Petersburg, and commanded the Russian fleet during that summer. In 1765 he returned to England by the way of Holland, bringing his wife and child with him. But having given up the Russian service, in 1766 he got the command of the Emerald frigate, and was appointed to the Leith station. He took his family on board with him to Scotland, and they resided in a house on the shore at Leith.

About this time Lady Irvine dying, left him her residuary legatee, and her house and furniture at Kew. These he soon after disposed of. He continued on the Leith station till the beginning of 1769, and then went with Mrs. Douglas to London. He immediately sailed for the coast of Lapland. Mrs. Douglas returned to Amsterdam, where she bore a daughter (Mrs. Bingham) in April, and died in June, 1769.

On his return from Lapland he went to Amsterdam, and brought away his son, but left his daughter in Holland, where she continued till the death of her grandmother in 1786.

In 1771 he was appointed to the ship St. Alban's, and

sent to the Windward Islands station.   There he married Miss Wood, his second wife.   In 1772 he returned to Spithead.   He now took a house at Berry, near Gosport, in which he resided with his wife and family when not on shipboard.   He had two guard ships; one, the St. Alban's, at Portsmouth; the other, the Ardent, in the Medway. Mrs. Douglas, the second wife, bore her first child at their house at Berry, in February, 1774.

Soon after he carried his wife to Scotland, where they remained till the end of 1775 or beginning of 1776, Mrs. Douglas having in this interval had her second child.

In February, 1776, he sailed from the Nore to the relief of Quebec, in the command of the Isis.   He had taken the lease of a house at Gosport for his wife, in which she began to reside early in 1776, and continued there till she died in child-bed in August, 1779.   He was then at sea; he had in the interval commanded various ships, and had been created a baronet.

In September, 1779, he returned home, and in November sent his three children of his second marriage to Scotland, to his sister, Mrs. Baillie.   His eldest son of the first marriage was at the academy at Portsmouth; his daughter of that marriage was still at Amsterdam.   His family being thus disposed of, he let the house at Gosport, and lived on shipboard.   About a year after the death of his second wife, he married his third wife at Gosport, in 1780, and Admiral Evans quitting his house in that town, Lady Douglas went to reside in it.

After some time, Sir Charles accompanied Rodney to the West Indies, and was Captain of that Admiral's ship. He returned from the West Indies in July, 1783, to Lady Douglas, who was still residing at Gosport.

He was soon after appointed to the Halifax station; he gave up the house at Gosport, sent part of his household effects to Scotland, and carried the remainder with him on the voyage. Before he sailed he went to Scotland to see his children; he afterwards sailed from Portsmouth with his wife and her sister, in October, 1783. At Halifax he lived on shore in an official house.

On his return from Halifax in August, 1785, he carried his wife to Scotland. Returning from the north he lodged for some time in London; from thence, early in 1786, he went to Amsterdam, on the death of the mother of his first wife. He there rented and kept house for about half a year.

From Amsterdam he returned to London, bringing his eldest daughter with him, and a nephew, whose father had been in the Dutch service. He then went to Scotland, to the house of his sister, Mrs. Baillie. Before setting out, he wrote to her from London, on the 29th of November, 1786, in these terms: "On Tuesday the 14th three hair trunks, and a large round hat-case belonging to my ladies, went from the White Horse Inn at Cripplegate, in the Edinburgh waggon; and yesterday, from the same place, and by a similar conveyance, were sent to the northward a large Dutch basket with a lock hanging to it, two knife cases, and a middle-sized square mahogany case, belonging to the same owners, with whom, and *Charles* of *Venlo*, I set out on Saturday or Monday next, and shall not travel very fast. *Be pleased to observe that I do not engage to build my tabernacle in Scotland;* and that if it should some time hence prove convenient to me to establish myself elsewhere, because of service or otherwise, *I shall probably remove the whole of my family,* considering in such case my nephew aforesaid a very precious member thereof."

He remained in Scotland till September, 1787, when he was appointed an admiral, and called by the Admiralty to take an important command in the armament then forming. He carried his wife and daughter to London, where they all remained for a few weeks. Lady Douglas and his daughter then went down to Gosport, to obtain a house or lodgings. Lady Douglas's father gave up a house at Gosport to accommodate them for a while: another house at Gosport was afterwards taken for them, in which Lady Douglas and Miss Douglas resided great part of the year 1788. He himself was absent for some months in Scotland in that year. He returned in July. Soon after, on the prospect of being appointed to the command on the Halifax station, he gave notice that he should quit the Gosport house as at Lady Day, 1789, meaning to carry his wife and daughter to Halifax with him. In January, 1789, his appointment for Halifax took place, being for three years; and he hoisted his flag in the Downs. Meaning to go himself to Scotland, to see his children and friends before leaving Britain, he carried Lady Douglas and her sister to London, where they took lodgings in Titchfield Street.

In the beginning of March, 1789, Sir Charles went to Edinburgh alone by the mail, or some stage coach. On his arrival in that city he took furnished lodgings, where in two days he died in a fit of apoplexy.

In the year preceding his death, when he returned from Holland, it was communicated to him that the Rev. Richard Bingham, son of the Rev. Isaac Moody Bingham, had paid his addresses to his eldest daughter of the first marriage. For some weeks Sir Charles appears to have been not averse to the match; but having heard some reports to Mr. Richard Bingham's prejudice, he enjoined that his daughter should have no further intercourse with him, and did all he could to break off the match. On the 11th of October, 1788, Sir Charles added a codicil to his will, expressing his strong dislike to the marriage, and directing that if his daughter Lydia Mariana Douglas should intermarry with Mr. Richard Bingham, or any son of Mr. Moody Bingham (d), she, or such her husband, his

---

(d) In this codicil he is named *John* instead of *Isaac* by mistake.

or her heirs, executors, or administrators, should take no part of the testator's estate under his will, but that the same should be divided and distributed by the trustees thereby appointed, as if his daughter had died before her mariage, or attaining the age of twenty-one years, and without issue. At the same time he executed a disposition of some heritable and other property which he had in Scotland to his trustees, for the uses of his will.

The marriage, notwithstanding, took place between the parties in November, 1788. Sir Charles never saw his daughter afterwards.

After Sir Charles's death, Mr. and Mrs. Bingham brought their action in the Court of Session in Scotland, for reducing the codicil to Sir Charles's will, in so far as it related to the marriage between Mr. and Mrs. Bingham, as being *contra libertatem matrimonii.* The trustees met them upon this ground, and after a long discussion, the Court of Session, on 14th February, 1792, " sustained the reasons of reduction of the irritant condition contained in the codicil libelled; found the pursuer entitled to the whole provisions originally destined for her by her father's settlements; and that the defenders, as trustees under those settlements, were bound to account to her therefore, as if no such condition had ever been inserted in the said codicil, or as if she had married with their consent." This judgment was adhered to on 17th December, 1793.

It was found, that there was little of the property of the deceased in Scotland which could be affected by this judgment; and on consulting counsel, whether or not to apply to the Court of Chancery to make the same effectual, it was pointed out by the counsel who was consulted in England, that a very important point had not yet been considered;

Some argument was founded on this, but there was no doubt as to the identity.

namely, whether Sir Charles Douglas was domiciled in England or in Scotland at the time of his death. Of consent of parties, the question of the domicil of Sir Charles Douglas was then brought before the Court, in a reclaiming petition, by his trustees, and the several facts before mentioned were stated in minutes by the parties on both sides. The trustees contended, that he had an English domicil, and that by the law of England such codicil would be free from objection. On the other hand, Mr. and Mrs. Bingham contended, that Sir Charles's domicil was in Scotland at the time of his death. After the facts and arguments of parties had been discussed, the Court of Session, on the 17th of December, 1793, pronounced their first decision in these terms: "Upon report of Lord Dreghorn, and having advised the mutual informations for the parties, in respect Sir Charles Douglas was born in Scotland, and occasionally had a domicil there; that he died in Scotland, where some of his children were boarded; and that he had not at the time a domicil any where else, the Lords find his succession falls to be regulated by the law of Scotland, and remit to the Lord Ordinary to proceed accordingly."

On a reclaiming petition, and minutes given in by the parties, the Court, on 7th February, 1794, came to this further decision : " Having resumed consideration of the petition, and advised the same with the minutes given in by the parties, refuse the desire of the petition, and adhere to the interlocutor reclaimed against."

The trustees considered it to be their duty to appeal to the House of Lords against all these judgments. Under this appeal, the parties went into a discussion upon the several points before mentioned : 1st, Where the domicil of Sir Charles Douglas was at the time of his death : 2d, Whether the codicil was *contra libertatem matrimonii*, and whether this was a sound ground of reduction even in Scotland : 3d, Whether it could apply to Richard Bingham, the son of *Isaac* Moody Bingham, who had been described in the codicil as the son of *John* Moody Bingham.

The case attracted much attention at the time; it was argued by persons then of the highest eminence, who had been of counsel in the then recent cases.   Lord Thurlow assisted Lord Loughborough, then Lord Chancellor, at the hearing.   After hearing the cause, the House of Lords, on the 18th of March, 1796, came to this judgment: " Ordered and adjudged, that the interlocutors of 17th December 1793 and 7th February 1794 be reversed; and it is declared that the succession to the property of Sir Charles Douglas should be regulated by the law of England; and it is further ordered, that the interlocutor of the 14th February 1792 be also reversed."

Though the main ground of decision appears to have been, that Sir Charles Douglas had his domicil in England at the time of his death, and that the codicil, by the law of England, was not liable to objection, still the reversal of the interlocutor of the 14th February 1792 appears to infer, that the House of Lords did not coincide with the doctrine, that the codicil was contrary to the law of Scotland. (*e*)

In the case of *Bempde* v. *Johnstone*, in 1796, relative to the personal succession of the Marquis of Annandale, similar points received a decision in the Court of Chancery in England on the point of domicil. (*f*)

George Marquis of Annandale died in 1792, at an advanced age, at Turnham Green, near London, intestate, a

---

(*e*) The notes of the speech of Lord Loughborough, in this cause, have fortunately been preserved, and obtained from the agents in the cause: they are given in the Appendix.   These indicate that he was unfavourable to the doctrine, that this codicil was contrary to the law of Scotland; but, though he gave an opinion to that effect, he considered that the reversal of the first interlocutor was a necessary consequence of the reversal of the judgment in regard to the domicil.

(*f*) Hilary Term, 1796, 3 Vesey, 198.

bachelor and a lunatic. The question was, whether his personal estate, which was very considerable, arising from the accumulation of his rents during a long life, should be distributed by the law of Scotland or the law of England. Sir Richard Johnstone Vanden Bempde, and Charles Johnstone, half-brothers of the Marquis on the side of his mother, were his next of kin by the law of England; and Lady|Christian Graham, the only surviving issue of Henrietta Countess of Hopetoun, the Marquis's half-sister by the father's side, being his nearest agnate, was his next of kin by the law of Scotland.

The material facts were, that William Marquis of Annandale, the father of Marquis George, in 1718, married, for his second wife, the daughter of Mr. Vanden Bempde, in England. He was one of the sixteen peers elected to represent the peerage of Scotland. He never afterwards returned to Scotland, but lived at Whitehall, and at Ashted in Surrey, in houses which he rented. He died at Bath, in 1721.

He was succeeded by Marquis James, his eldest son of the first marriage, who died in 1730; and James was succeeded by Marquis George, the eldest son of the second marriage. George was born in 1720, at his father's house in London; he continued there till he went to Eton, and remained at that seminary till 1734, except in vacation time, when he was with his mother in London. Leaving Eton, he went abroad, and continued abroad in various places till 1738, when he returned to London. Thence, in a few days, he went to Scotland. He continued there little more than a month; returned to London, remained there two months, and then again went abroad. He remained abroad till December, 1739, when he returned to England. In April, 1740, he went to Scotland; he returned to England about the middle of July. In January, 1742, he again went abroad; in November he returned to England, and remained there, with a short exception of three weeks or a month at Paris, till December 1743. In December 1743 he went abroad. In April 1744 he returned to England, and remained there till his death. In 1747 a commission of lunacy was issued against him, and he was found to have been a lunatic from December 1744.

Under the will of Mr. Vanden Bempde, his maternal grandfather, Marquis George took, in strict settlement, certain estates in Yorkshire, and a house in Pall Mall. He did not get possession of the family estates in Scotland till 1733 or 1734, after a long litigation in regard to some settlements of those estates.

Marquis George went to Scotland also in 1741, to assist in his brother's election for the district of burghs which were near his estate. Upon the two other occasions of his going to that country, he went upon visits to his mother and others. He lived in lodgings, and ready-furnished houses, in England.

Much evidence was produced from the Marquis's letters to show his preference of one country over the other. The arguments took up the greater part of Hilary term, and (as stated in the report) "went very much at large into the learning of the civil law," as to the domicil of the Marquis and his father. The cases of *Bruce* v. *Bruce, Hog* v. *Lashley, Balfour* v. *Scott* (g), and *Ommanney* v. *Bingham,* were also cited.

The Lord Chancellor Loughborough spoke to this effect at giving judgment:—

" The great value of the property, and the consideration of the parties, produced in this case a large field of argument; and I am much obliged to the bar for their great ingenuity, and the great research they made. I do not recollect ever to have heard with more satisfaction an

(g) Infra.

M

argument carried on upon any point. I do not go into the detail of it, not from any disrespect to it, or any idea that the points do not deserve to be stated, and to receive such answer as might occur to me to give them; but all questions of succession are, in their nature, questions of positive law, and if the argument had raised a doubt in my mind, and I were not inclined to follow the rule that has prevailed in other cases, I am bound by repeated decisions in the House of Lords to make the decree I intend to make, that the Marquis had that domicil in England that decides upon the succession to his personal property, and carries the distribution according to the law of England. The point has been established in the cases in the House of Lords, which, if it was quite new and open, always appeared to me to be susceptible of a great deal of argument, whether, in the case of a person dying intestate, having property in different places and subject to different laws, the law of each place should not obtain in the distribution of the property situated there. Many foreign lawyers have held that proposition. There was a time when the courts of Scotland certainly held so. The judgments in the House of Lords have taken a contrary course; that there can be but one law; they must fix the place of the domicil; and the law of that country where the domicil is decides, wherever the property is situated. That, I take to be fixed law now. The Court of Session has conformed to those decisions, according to which the Courts of Great Britain, both of Scotland and England, are bound to act. The question, what was the domicil, has been, with regard to Lord Annandale, established upon a very few propositions. Born in this country, educated in this country, this country was the seat of his expectations for the greater part of his life, reckoning his life to terminate at the period of his lunacy. During the greater part of that period, he had no expectations of fortune, settlement, or establishment, any

where but in this country, according to the disposition his
maternal grandfather made in his favour. The habit of his
education carried him abroad at an early period. Returned, he never had a residence in Scotland. He never was
there at any period, with a fixed purpose of remaining.
His existence there was purely a purpose of either visit or
business, and both circumscribed and defined in their time.
Wherever he had a place of residence, which could not
be referred to an occasional and temporary purpose, that
is found in England, and nowhere else. I am not clear
that the period of his lunacy is totally to be discarded;
but I will take him to have died then. For the greater
part of the period previous to that, he was fixed in this
country; and fixed by all those ties that describe a settled
residence, and distinguish it from that which is temporary
and occasional. The argument, then, rests upon the domicil of his father. In the first place, that question, what
was the domicil of his father, is of itself a question I am
not called upon to decide; and I am by no means prepared
to adopt the proposition, that his father should be considered as having had a domicil in Scotland. In the latter
part of his life his domicil *de facto* was unquestionably in
England. During the latter part of it, and from an epoch
remarkable enough, when contracting a second marriage
and forming a new family, all the circumstances of his
family, at that period, point much more to England than
to Scotland. The question of domicil, *primâ facie*, is much
more a question of fact than of law. The actual place
where he is, is, *primâ facie*, to a great many given purposes
his domicil. You encounter that, if you show it is either
constrained, or from the necessity of his affairs, or transi-
tory, that he is a sojourner; and you take from it all
character of permanency. If, on the contrary, you show
that the place of his residence is the seat of his fortune; if
the place of his birth, upon which I lay the least stress;

but if the place of his education, where he acquired all
his early habits, friends, and connections, and all the links
that attach him to society are found there; if you add to
that, that he had no other fixed residence upon an establishment of his own, you answer the question, which
would be, where does he reside? In London. Is that
his domicil? It is; unless you show that is not the place
where he would be, if there were no particular circumstance to determine his position in some other place at that
period. In this case, every thing leads one to conclude,
that the place where Lord Annandale is found, is the place
where he would be, no occasion taking him to any other
place. When that is fixed, and you have found all the
circumstances that give a character of permanency to that
place where he really is, it is in vain to inquire where was
his father's domicil. The case last determined in the
House of Lords is the case of Sir Charles Douglas. I
particularly had the benefit of hearing all the arguments
so well pressed in this cause, and also at the bar of the
House in that. It fell to my share to pronounce the judgment; but it was much more formed by Lord Thurlow,
and settled in concert with him: the general course of the
reasoning he approved. It was one of the strongest cases;
for there was first a determination of the Court of Session
upon the point. Great respect was due to that. They
had determined the point. The judgment was reversed.
It came before the House with all the respect due to the
Court of Session upon the very point, and under circumstances that affected the feelings of every one; for the
consequences of the judgment the House of Lords found
themselves obliged to give, were harsh and cruel. If the
particular circumstances, raising very just sentiments in
every mind, could prevail against the uniformity of rule it
is so much the duty of courts of justice to establish, there
could be no case in which the feelings would have led one

farther. Lord Annandale's case is not near so strong. The habits of Sir Charles Douglas were military. He had no settled property. His life had been passed in different parts of the world. If the consideration of his original domicil could have had the weight that is attempted in this case, it would have had much more there; for there was less of positive fixed residence there, than in this case. At one time he was in Russia; at another in Holland; and in a fixed situation, as commander of a ship in the Russian and Dutch service. His activity rendered him not much settled anywhere. It was necessary to take him where he was found. The cause had this additional circumstance, that he happened to die in Scotland, the place of his birth; but undoubtedly he went there for a very temporary purpose, a mere visit to his family when going to take a command upon the American station. That is so strong a case that it makes it rather improper in me to have said so much. Dismiss the bill of Lady Graham; tax all the parties their costs; and let the distribution be according to the prayer of the other bill." (*h*)

It is to be remarked in this judgment, that something is said as if his Lordship had had a leaning to the doctrine of the *lex loci rei sitæ*, if the law had not been settled otherwise. In another case he delivered himself in strong terms against that doctrine. (*i*) .

(*h*) It is stated in the report, that the arguments " went very much at large into the learning of the civil law;" yet none of the foreign jurists are specially quoted in the report of the case.

(*i*) In the noted case of *Sill* v. *Worswick* (a case of bankruptcy), 1 Henry Blackstone, 665., Lord Loughborough says, " It is a clear proposition, not only of the law of England, *but of every country in the world where law has the semblance of science*, that personal property has no locality, but that it is subject to that law which governs the person of the owner. With respect to the disposition of it, with respect to the transmission of it, by succession, or the act of the party, it follows the law of the person. The owner in any country may dispose of his per-

In the case of *Colville* v. *Lauder* (15th January 1800, in
the Court of Session) (*k*), the succession of a Scotsman
dying abroad was regulated by the law of Scotland, when
he had not a fixed domicil elsewhere.

In 1793, David Lauder, a native of Scotland, went to
the island of St. Vincent's in the West Indies, to follow
his trade of a carpenter, leaving his wife Jean Colville
with her relations at Leith. On 21st July 1797 he wrote
thus to his father in Scotland, from St. Vincent's; " As I
never loved the West Indies, and as my health is very
much hurt by a long continuance in it, I have determined
to go off to America, in a ship that sails from this in a few
days, hoping my health may be re-established by a change
of climate. I have, during my stay in this part, made
shift to lay up some money, 200*l*. of which I have converted into a bill of exchange, which is sent you indorsed,
reserving to myself no more than will defray my necessary
expenses to New York, where, if it please God that I
arrive, you shall hear from me. But as a considerable
time will be necessary before I can fix upon any plan of
life, I will then be more explicit; for if I do not succeed
in America, I will return to my native country. I have
wrote three different times to our friends at Leith, but
have never been favoured with an answer. There must
be some very grave and important reasons for so very
extraordinary omission, but what they are I can't conceive.
However, be pleased to let them know that I have no

---

sonal property. If he dies, it is not the law of the country in which the
property is, but the law of the country of which he was a subject, that
will regulate the succession. For instance, if a foreigner, having property in the funds here, dies, that property is claimed according to the
right of representation given by the law of his own country."

Nothing can be more clear and explicit upon this point.

(*k*) Fac. Coll. Morrison, *Succession*, Appendix, No. 1.

desire to give them a fourth trouble. It may so happen, from the common incidents of life, that you may never hear from me again; the money is either at your or my dear mother's disposal."

He sailed to New York soon after, and remained there till spring 1798, when he went to Canada, where he was drowned in the September of that year. It appeared, from some memorandums found in his possession after his death, that he meant to have returned to Scotland in a few months.

His widow, in an action against the father, claimed one half of his funds, as *jus relictæ*. The father pleaded the above letter as excluding her right to any share of the 200*l.* bill. The Lord Ordinary repelled the defences.

In a reclaiming petition the defender pleaded—"When a Scotsman lives for years abroad, in prosecution of his employment, he acquires a domicil there, which must regulate his succession, though he may intend to return to Scotland at some future period. In this case, therefore, the law of England must prevail, according to which the letter in question would be held as a testament effectually excluding the claim of the widow. Blackstone, vol. ii. pp. 402. 434."

The widow answered—" In the whole circumstances of this case, the deceased cannot be considered abroad *animo remanendi*, or to have formed a domicil elsewhere, and therefore the law of his nativity must govern, Ersk. b. 3. t. 9. s. 4.; so that it is unnecessary to investigate the effect of the letter in question by the law of England."

The Court *adhered.* " Observed on the bench, when the deceased was in St. Vincent, his succession must have been regulated by the law of England ; but, after leaving that island, he must, in the whole circumstances, be considered as *in transitu* to Scotland."

Nothing further was done in this case: it was not of much importance in regard to the amount of the property;

but there appears to be reasonable ground to doubt whether the deceased had not acquired a domicil at St. Vincent, and died before acquiring another domicil. The reference to *Blackstone* appears to have no relation to either branch of this subject, but to the husband's interest in *choses in action* belonging to the wife. It seems not to have been made matter of dispute, on either side, that the letter was of a testamentary nature.

The next case of domicil in point of time was the well-known case of *Somerville* v. *Lord Somerville*, in Chancery, before the Master of the Rolls (January and February 1801). (*l*)   The question there was in regard to the distribution of the personal estate of James Lord Somerville, then lately deceased, who died at his house in London, in April 1796, a bachelor, and intestate, possessed of real estates in Scotland and in Gloucestershire, and of personal property in the funds to the amount of 50,000*l*. or 60,000*l*. He was described, in the books of the Bank, as of Henrietta Street, Cavendish Square. A question arose, whether this funded property should be distributed by the law of Scotland, or by the law of England. The claimants by the law of Scotland were his nephews and nieces of the whole blood, being the children of his brother, Colonel Somerville, and of his sister, Ann Whichnore Burgess (exclusive of his nephew, Lord Somerville, the heir at law of the real estates). Sir Edward Bayntun, brother uterine to the intestate (being the son of his mother by a former marriage), and certain nephews and nieces of the half blood (being the children of a deceased brother and sister of the intestate by another marriage of his father), claimed to participate in the distribution under the law of England. Lord Somerville, his nephew, and successor in the title,

---

(*l*) 5 Vesey, 750.

obtained letters of administration to his estate and effects, in the Prerogative Court of Canterbury.

The question came to be, what was the domicil of the intestate at the time of his death ? For, having this decided, bills were filed in the Court of Chancery by the parties, respectively claiming that his succession should be regulated by the law of Scotland, and by the law of England. In the course of the proceedings the facts of the case were stated in evidence. Some of these related to the domicil of his father; but there appears to have been no doubt that the father, who died at his family estate and mansion in Scotland, in 1765, had his domicil in that country at the time of his death.

James Lord Somerville, the intestate, was born in Scotland, on the 22d of June, 1727, either at the family house of *The Drum*, or at *Good Trees*, a house in the neighbourhood, which his father rented while *Drum* was rebuilding. He remained there till he went to school, first at Dalkeith, and afterwards at Edinburgh. At the age of nine or ten he went to England, to his relation Mr. Somerville, in Gloucestershire. In June 1742 he went to Westminster School, which he quitted at Christmas 1743. He then went to Caen in Normandy, for the purpose of education, where he remained till the age of eighteen.

In 1745 he was sent for by his father, on account of the then rebellion in Scotland. He entered the royal army as a volunteer, and he was present at the battles of Preston Pans and Culloden, at which he served as an aid-de-camp to Generals Cope and Hawley. He continued in the army till the peace of 1763, going with his regiment wherever it happened to be on service, in England, in Scotland, or in Germany. After quitting the army, in 1763, he went to Scotland, to Somerville House, where his father settled an annuity upon him. He then went abroad. In September 1765, on account of his father's illness, he returned to Scotland. He was present at the funeral in December in that year, and continued in Scotland about six months afterwards. He then went to London, and till 1778 or 1779 passed the winter in London, and the summer at Somerville House in Scotland. In 1779 he took the lease of a house in Henrietta Street, Cavendish Square, for twenty-one years, determinable at the end of the first seven or fourteen years, at a rent of 84*l.* a year. He continued to occupy this house as a winter residence till his death, going to *The Drum* in summer, and dividing the year nearly between that and his London house. The landlord of the house having purchased the ground lease, of which thirty-six years were unexpired, Lord Somerville endeavoured to get him to relinquish this for a premium, but did not succeed, and expressed regret at his refusal.

Being rated to the assessed taxes at 90*l.* per annum, he appealed, and was reduced to 84*l.* per annum. About ten years before his death he was elected one of the sixteen representative peers for Scotland, and attended his parliamentary duties every winter.

In Scotland Lord Somerville's establishment and style of living were suitable to his rank and fortune. In London he had only permanently two female servants; he brought two men servants with him when he came up from Scotland, taking them back with him, and using job horses occasionally. He kept his servants on board wages in London; he himself usually dined at a club, and saw no company. The house was out of repair, and furnished on a very limited scale. The furniture, on his death, (including coals and plate,) sold only for 66*l.* 7*s.* 1*d.*; the fixtures for 73*l.* 10*s.*

To some of his friends he declared repeatedly, that he considered his residence in London only as a lodging-house, and temporary residence, during the sitting of parliament; but he spoke of Scotland as his residence and home, where he was born, and with the warmth of a native. About a month before his death, Colonel Reading urged him to make a will, for the sake of his natural children; upon which, he said he meant to take care of them, and also of his brother's younger children. Soon after this conversation, he told Colonel Reading that he had seen his nephew, Sir James Bland Burgess, who had alarmed him by telling him that, if he died without a will, his personal estate would be divided among the several branches of his family, which he would much deplore; and afterwards he said that he should soon go to Scotland, and would then make his will. He died in about a month after this conversation.

Elizabeth Dewar, who had been housekeeper at Somerville House, in her depositions stated, that she had heard the intestate say he was an Englishman; that though he was born in Scotland he was educated in England; his connections were English; he had no friends in Scotland, and every thing he did was after the English fashion. The deponent had heard him say, that his reason for going to Scotland was that he might be at his estate; that he did not like it, but he had promised his father when dying, that he would live one half of the year in Scotland, and the other half in England; that he considered himself an Englishman; that his estate in England was preferable to that in Scotland; that he preferred England, and would never visit Scotland, except on account of the promise to his father; and that he did not care though Somerville House was burnt: and this he frequently said in conversation with the witness.

The cause was argued at the Rolls before Sir Richard Pepper Arden, Master of the Rolls, on the 24th, 26th, and 27th of January, and 23rd of February, 1801. (*m*)

_____

(*m*) The *Attorney General* (Sir John Mitford), the *Solicitor General* (Mr. Perceval), Mr. *Newbold*, and Mr. *M'Intosh*, were counsel for the

When the arguments of counsel had finished, the Master
of the Rolls spoke as follows : —

" This case has been extremely well argued on all sides,
and I have the satisfaction of thinking I have received every
information that either industry or abilities could furnish.
The question is, simply, as to the succession to the personal
estate of the late Lord Somerville.   It is in some respects
new, so far as it is a question between two acknowledged
domicils. 'In the late cases the question has been, whether
the first domicil was abandoned ; and where, at the time
of the death, the sole domicil was ? but here the question
is, which of two acknowledged domicils shall preponderate?
or rather, which is the domicil, according to which the
succession to the personal estate shall be regulated.   Questions upon the law of succession to personal estate have
been very frequent of late in this country, and unless the
Legislature interposes, which I sincerely hope they will,
to assimilate the law of the whole island upon this subject,
such questions may be expected very frequently to occur.
In the course of a few years there have been four cases in
the House of Lords, and one in this Court.   I have been
favoured with the opinions delivered by Lords Thurlow
and Loughborough, the former in *Bruce* v. *Bruce,* the latter
in *Ommanney* v. *Bingham,* the case of Sir Charles Douglas.
I have very fully considered all the cases, and the opinions

---

plaintiffs in the first cause ; Mr. *Mansfield,* Mr. *Adam,* and Mr. *Lockhart,* for the defendants in the same interest, claiming as next of kin of
the whole blood by the law of Scotland : Mr. *Piggott,* Mr. *Lloyd,* Mr.
Romilly, Mr. *Manners Sutton,* and Mr. *Steele,* for the defendants, claiming under the law of England.   In the course of the argument the reported cases in both countries are referred to.   Reference is also made
to a case of *Alexander* v. *M'Culloch,* before Lord Thurlow, in which,
upon the ground of the *animus revertendi,* and an establishment retained,
a party was held to be a Scotchman, and his will was construed according to the law of *Scotland,* notwithstanding his residence in Virginia.

of those two learned Lords, and the authorities referred to
in the printed cases, and also all the authorities referred to
by the foreign jurists, which were very properly brought
forward on this occasion.   It is unnecessary to enter into a
comment upon all these authorities.   It will be sufficient to
state the rules, which I am warranted to say result, with
the reasons for adopting them in this case.

" The first rule is that laid down by those learned
Lords, adopted in the House of Lords, and admitted in this
argument, to be the law by which the succession to personal
estate is now to be regulated, whatever might have been
the opinions of the courts of Scotland, which certainly at
one time took a different course.   That rule is, that the
succession to the personal estate of an intestate is to be regulated by the law of the country in which he was a domiciled inhabitant at the time of his death; without any
regard whatsoever to the place either of the birth or the
death, or the situation of the property at that time.   That
is the clear result of the opinion of the House of Lords in
all the cases I have alluded to, which have occurred within
the few last years.   This, I think, is not controverted by
the counsel on either side: but it was said, that that law
could prevail and be applied only where such domicil can
be ascertained; and that I admit.

" The next rule is, that though a man may have two
domicils for some purposes, he can have only one for the
purpose of succession.   That is laid down expressly in
Denisart under the title of Domicil, that only one domicil
can be acknowledged for the purpose of regulating the
succession to the personal estate.   I have taken this as a
maxim, and am warranted by the necessity of such a
maxim; for the absurdity would be monstrous, if it were
possible that there should be a competition between two
domicils, as to the distribution of the personal estate.   It
could never possibly be determined by the casual death of
the party at either.   That would be most whimsical and

capricious. It might depend upon the accident whether he died in winter or summer, and many circumstances not in his choice; and that never would regulate so important a subject as the succession to his personal estate.

" The third rule I shall extract is, that the original domicil, or, as it is called, the *forum originis* or the domicil of origin, is to prevail until the party has not only acquired another, but has manifested and carried into execution an intention of abandoning his former domicil, and taking another as his sole domicil. I speak of the domicil of origin rather than that of birth, for the mere accident of birth at any particular place cannot in any degree affect the domicil. I have found no authority or *dictum*, that gives, for the purpose of succession, any effect to the place of birth. If the son of an Englishman is born upon a journey in foreign parts, his domicil would follow that of his father. The domicil of origin is that arising from a man's birth and connections.

" To apply these rules to this case. It cannot be disputed, that Lord Somerville's father was a Scotchman. He married an English lady; returned to Scotland; repaired his family house, occupying another in the neighbourhood in the mean time; and he had apartments in Holyrood House. For the first part of his life after his marriage, he seems to have made Scotland almost his sole residence; nor was it contended that during that period he had acquired any other. The father being then without doubt a Scotchman, the son was born in Scotland, and at the age of nine or ten was sent into England for education, and from thence to Caen in Normandy. It cannot be contended, nor do I think it was, that during the state of pupillage he could acquire any domicil of his own. I have no difficulty in laying down, that no domicil can be acquired till the person is *sui juris*. During his continuance in the military profession, I have not heard it insisted that he acquired any

other domicil than he had before.   Upon his father's death
and his return to Scotland, a material fact occurs, upon
which great stress was laid on both sides.   It is said his
father's dying injunctions were, that he should not dissolve
his connection with Scotland.   In the subsequent part of
his life, he most religiously adhered to those injunctions.
But it is said, that in conversation he manifested his preference of England; and that if it had not been for those
injunctions of his father he would have quitted Scotland.
Admit it.   That, in my opinion, is the strongest argument
in favour of Scotland; for, whether willingly or reluctantly,
whether from piety or from choice, it is enough to say, he
determined to keep up his connection with that country; and
this makes not the least difference.

" Then see how, after his father's death, he proceeded
to establish himself in the world.   From that time, undoubtedly, he was capable of establishing another domicil.
Until that time, there could be no doubt that the surplus
of his personal estate must, if he had died, have been distributed according to the law of Scotland.   Then, to trace
him from that time; it appears, he had determined not to
abandon his mansion-house; so far from it, he made over-
tures with a view to get apartments in Holyrood House;
from which I conjecture, that if that application had been
granted he might have been induced to spend more time
than he did in Scotland.   He came to London.   I will not
inquire how soon he took a permanent habitation there;
but I admit, from that time he manifested an intention to
reside a considerable part of the year in London, but also
to keep up his establishment in Scotland, and to spend, as
nearly as possible, half of the year in each.   He took the
lease of a house, evidently with the intention to have a
house in London as long as he lived, with a manifest
intention to divide his time between them.   It is then said,

there are clearly two domicils alternately in each country. Admit it; then the question will arise, whether, in case of his death at either, that makes any difference? It was contended, in favour of the English domicil, that in such a case as that of two domicils, and to neither any preference, for it cannot be contended that the domicil in Scotland was not at least equal to that in England, except the *lex loci rei sitæ* is to have effect, the death should decide. There is not a single *dictum* from which it can be supposed that the place of the death, in such a case as that, shall make any difference. Many cases are cited in *Denisart* to show that the death can have no effect, and not one that that circumstance decides between two domicils. The question in those cases was, which of the two domicils was to regulate the succession, and without any regard to the place where he died. These cases seem to prove, and, if necessary, I think it may be collected, that those rules have prevailed in countries which, being divided into different provinces, frequently afford these questions. The fair inference from them is, that, as a general proposition, where there are two contemporary domicils, this distinction takes place, that a person not under an obligation of duty to live in the capital in a permanent manner, as a nobleman or gentleman having a mansion-house his residence in the country, and resorting to the metropolis for any particular purpose, or for the general purpose of residing in the metropolis, shall be considered domiciled in the country; on the other hand, a merchant, whose business lies in the metropolis, shall be considered as having his domicil there, and not at his country residence. It is not necessary to enter into that distinction, though I shall be inclined to concur in it. I therefore forbear entering into observations upon the cases of *Mademoiselle de Clermont de Sant Aignan* and the *Comte de Choiseul*, and the distinction as to the acts of the former, describing herself as of the place in the country. (*n*)

" The next consideration is, whether, with reference to the property or conduct of Lord Somerville, there is any thing showing he considered himself as an Englishman. It was said, for the purpose of introducing the definition of the domicil in the civil law, " *Ubi quis larem rerumque ac fortunarum suarum summam constituit,*" that the bulk of his fortune was in England : and the description in the Bank books was relied on. I lay no stress whatsoever on that description in those books, or in any other instrument; for he was of either place, and was most likely to make use of that to which the transaction in question referred. It was totally immaterial which description he used. It is hardly possible to contend, that money in the funds, however large, shall preponderate against his residence in the country and his family seat. It is hardly possible that that should be so annexed to his person, as to draw along with it this consequence. Upon nice distinctions, I think it might be proved, that his principal domicil must be considered as in Scotland. Great stress, and more than I think was necessary, was laid upon the manner in which he spent his time in each place. There is no doubt, the establishment

---

(*n*) The facts of the case of Mademoiselle de Clermont de Saint Aignan are not very clearly stated in Denisart. She had an estate in the province of Maine, to which she went every year during " le temps de la belle saison." During the rest of the year she resided in Paris, where she had an hotel, " un Suisse, tout son domestique, ses meubles, ses papiers; elle y fit ses Paques, y paya la capitation," &c. The Court of the Chatelet found that she had her domicil in Paris; but this was reversed in the Grand Chamber, and her domicil established in the province of Maine.

The case of the Comte de Choiseul had been referred to, in the above of Mademoiselle de Clermont de Saint Aignan ; he had died at Paris, but he was declared to have been domiciled in Burgundy : no other circumstances are mentioned.

N

in Scotland was much greater than that in London. In my opinion, *Bynkershoek* was very wise in not hazarding a definition. With respect to that to be found in the civil law, the words are very vague, and it is difficult to apply them. I am not under the necessity of making the application; for my opinion will not turn upon the point, which was the place where he kept the sum of his fortune. It is of no consequence, whether more or less money was spent at the one place or the other, living alternately at both. Some time before his death, he talked of making his will in Scotland. That circumstance is decisive that his death in England was merely casual, not from intention. The case then comes to this: — a Scotchman by birth and extraction, domiciled in Scotland, takes a house in London; lives there half the year, having an establishment at his family estate in Scotland, and money in the funds, and happens to die in England. I have no difficulty in pronouncing, that he never ceased to be a Scotchman; his original domicil continued. It is consistent with all the authorities and cases, that, where a man has two domicils, the domicil he originally had shall be considered his domicil for the purpose of succession to his personal estate, until that is abandoned, and another taken.

" It is surprising that questions of this sort have not arisen in this country, when we consider, that till a very late period, and even now for some purposes, a different succession prevails in the province of York. The custom is very analogous to the law of Scotland. Till a very late period, the inhabitants of York were restrained from disposing of their property by testament. The alteration may account for the very few cases occurring, for very few persons of fortune die intestate, though it has happened in this case. Before that power of disposing by testament, such cases must have been frequent; and the question then would have been, whether, during the time the custom and the restraint of disposing by testament were in full force, a gentleman of the county of York, coming to London for the winter, and dying there intestate, the disposition of his personal estate should be according to the custom or the general law. One should suppose it hardly possible that some such case had not occurred. I directed a search to be made in the spiritual court and the Court of Chancery, where it was most likely that such a case would be found; but I do not find that any such case has occurred. Some observations may arise upon that custom. It may be thought, there are some inaccuracies in the words of the statute (o) upon it. The custom (p), as it is stated to have existed, is thus expressed: that there is due to the widow and to the lawful children of every man, being an inhabitant or householder within the said province of York, and dying there or elsewhere intestate, being an inhabitant or householder within that province, a reasonable part of his clear moveable goods, unless such child be heir to his father deceased, or were advanced by his father in his lifetime, by which advancement it is to be understood, that the father, in his lifetime, bestowed upon his child a competent portion whereon to live. I observe, the statute giving the power of disposing by testament, after reciting the custom, directs, that it shall be lawful for any person inhabiting or residing, or who shall have any goods or chattels within the province of York, to give, bequeath, and dispose of all their goods, chattels, debts, and other personal estate. One would suppose from this, that the legislature had some reference to the *lex loci rei sitæ*, and that it was supposed the custom would attach upon any property locally situated there, though the party was not resident; and though it is now too late to doubt the law upon that, I have some

---

(o) 4 William 3. c. 2.   (p) 4 Burns's Ecc. Law, 457.

N 2

reason to think our spiritual courts inclined, as the courts of Scotland, to the *lex loci rei sitæ ;* and if the question had occurred in that court, and the authority of the House of Lords had not interfered, that would have been considered as the rule, and for this reason, that their jurisdiction is founded upon it: the distribution arising from the place where the property is situated, it is natural for the judge, who acquired his authority from the situation of the property, to suppose the rule should be that of the place where the property is; but that now certainly is not the case.

" I shall conclude with a few observations upon a question that might arise, and which I often suggested to the bar: What would be the case upon two contemporary and equal domicils, if ever there can be such a case? I think such a case can hardly happen, but it is possible to suppose it. A man born no one knows where, or having had a domicil that he has completely abandoned, might acquire in the same or different countries two domicils at the same instant, and occupy both under exactly the same circumstances; both country houses, for instance, bought at the same time. It can hardly be said, that of which he took possession first is to prevail. Then, suppose he should die at one, shall the death have any effect? I think not, even in that case; and then, *ex necessitate,* the *lex loci rei sitæ* must prevail; for the country in which the property is, would not let it go out of that, until they know by what rule it is to be distributed. If it was in this country, they would not give it, until it was proved that he had a domicil somewhere.

" On these causes I am clearly of opinion, Lord Somerville was a Scotchman upon his birth, and continued so to the end of his days. He never ceased to be so; never having abandoned his Scotch domicil, or established another. The decree, therefore, must be, that the succession to his personal estate ought to be regulated according to the law of Scotland."

This appears to be the case which has received the greatest discussion, upon the subject of domicil, in either country. The Master of the Rolls, in his clear, and luminous, judgment expressed his opinion, that the law ought to be assimilated in the two countries; but upwards of thirty years have since elapsed, without any change of the law. It is impossible to say, that many cases like this of Lord *Somerville*, or like that of *Hog* v. *Lashley*, may not now be coming to maturity.

It is worthy of remark, that very few cases have occurred, on the customs of the province of York and city of London; and that of *Cholmley* v. *Cholmley* (*q*) was the only case which, after a search made, had then been discovered. Indeed, the Master of the Rolls does not appear to have been aware that any such case had been discovered. The case of *Onslow* v. *Onslow*, in regard to the custom of London, as prevailing over the law of the domicil noticed above (p. 107.), is of very recent date.(*r*)

(*q*) Supra, p. 104.

(*r*) The following foreign authorities were referred to in this case :— *Farnese, Decis. Rom.* (a case in the *Rota* on the domicil of a *legatus*); *Denisart*, article *Domicile*, cases of Mademoiselle *de Clermont Saint Aignan* and *Comte de Choiseul; D'Aguessau*, tom. v. f. 115., case of the Duc *de Guise*, tom. vii. f. 373.; Cochin, tom. ii. f. 1., Case of the Duchesse *de Holstein ;* tom. iii. f. 702., Case of M. *Courtagnon ;* tom. v. f. 1., Case of the Marquis *de St. Paterre ;* Vattel, lib 1. c. 19. s. 218.; *Howard's* Dict. of Norman Law, art. *Domicil;* Domat, tom. ii. lib. 1. tit. 5. s. 7. par. 13.; tit. 16. s. 3. par. 5.; *Pothier, Coutumes d'Orleans,* passim.; Bynkershoek, Quest. Jur. Priv., lib. 1. c. 16.; Huber, (a case in the Supreme Court of Friesland, 2d July, 1680); Voet, ad pandectas, lib. 5. tit. 1. s. 98.

Henry, in his appendix to the Demerara case (p. 206. in notis), re-marks it as singular, that the following law in the Digest was not founded on in this case :— " Senatores, licet in urbe domicilium habere " videantur, tamen et ibi unde oriundi sunt, habere domicilium intelli- " guntur, quia dignitas domicilii adjectionem potius dedisse, quam per-

In 1811, a question occurred in a cause before Sir William Grant, at the Rolls, *Margaret Chiene, widow,* v. *James Sykes and others* (s), in regard to the domicil of Robert Chiene, the late husband of the plaintiff. Robert Chiene had made a will, dated in November 1801, and a codicil thereto, dated 29th January 1802, by which, among other things, he gave his wife the interest of certain sums of money for her life, and named Sykes and others his executors. Sykes proved the will and codicil in the Prerogative Court of Canterbury in 1802, soon after the testator's death. The bill was filed by the widow against the acting executor and legatees of her husband's will, and prayed for an account of the testator's personal property, and that a moiety thereof might be paid to her ; but, if the Court should decree against such claim, that the will of her husband might be established.

The ground of the widow's claim was, that by the law of Scotland her late husband had not the power to make a will to her prejudice, and that she was therefore entitled to a moiety of the goods in communion. The Court, by decree dated 27th April 1787, referred it to the Master to inquire, among other things, where the testator Robert Chiene was domiciled at the time of his death. The Master, by his report, dated 11th February 1808, certified, " that by the deposition of William Brown, postmaster of the royal burgh of *Crail* in Scotland, the said William Brown made oath, that he knew Robert Chiene, the testator, from his infancy ; that the said Robert Chiene was born in the town

---

" mutasse videtur." (D. lib. 1. tit. 9. l. 11. de Senator.) This law appears to have been founded on, in an opinion given by Voet (noticed by Henry); he considers it as decisive of the question in a case like the present.

(s) This case is stated in a note to the case of *Munroe* v. *Douglas,* 5 *Maddock's* Reports, 394.

of Crail, and, as the deponent believed, in the house of his maternal grandfather, with whom his mother resided at that time; that the said Robert Chiene was a natural child of John Chiene, shipmaster in Crail, and Anne Brown, residing there; that the said Robert Chiene received his education at the school of Crail, during which time he resided with his mother, and when seventeen or eighteen years of age he entered into the seafaring line, and went abroad as a sailor; that he the said William Brown had particular occasion to know that the said Robert Chiene returned to Crail again in the year 1784, from the circumstance of his the said William Brown's being postmaster at that time; and having inspected the quarterly bills of the office, he found entries of letters to a Robert Chiene in that year; that he the said William Brown could not with precision say how long the said Robert Chiene remained at Crail at this time, but that he was certain he went again abroad in less than twelve months, and resumed his occupation as a seaman, he the said William Brown having reason to believe, from seeing letters addressed to him, that he was appointed master of the *Experiment* frigate; that the said Robert Chiene returned to Crail again in the year 1802, and resided there till his death, which happened in November in that year; that some years before his return he the said William Brown understood that a dwelling-house and garden, and some other subjects, in the burgh of Crail, were purchased for him and his brother jointly; that on his return to Crail last mentioned he rented a house, in which he resided for some months, till he got one, purchased for himself, repaired, when he went to reside in it, and continued to do so till his death; that the said William Brown was informed, in the year 1780, by Elizabeth Wilkinson, his brother's wife, that the said Robert Chiene was sometime previous married to Margaret Wilkinson at Philadelphia, where she, Elizabeth Wilkinson, was present at the time; and he received the same information from her husband, Patrick Brown, and the brother of him the said William Brown; that he had heard that it was the said Robert Chiene's intention to buy some land in the neighbourhood after his last return, and from which he, the said William Brown, inferred, that it was his the said Robert Chiene's intention to reside at Crail in future. And by the deposition of Andrew Whyte, town clerk of the royal burgh of Crail, the said Andrew Whyte made oath, that he knew the said testator, Robert Chiene, for about eighteen years previous to his death; that he understood the said Robert Chiene to have been a native of the burgh of Crail before named, but that he had left that place and gone abroad before he, the said Andrew Whyte, became acquainted with him, which happened in the year 1784, on his return from abroad to his native place; that on his aforesaid return he became tacksman of a rabbit warren in the neighbourhood of the burgh of Crail, which he held for one season under him the said Andrew Whyte, and again went abroad in the course of the following year; that he again entered into the seafaring line, to which he was originally bred, and did not return to his native place at Crail till the year 1802; that some years previous to his return last mentioned, he caused to be purchased, jointly with John Chiene his brother, a dwelling-house, granary, and two gardens, in the burgh of Crail, all which had previously belonged to their father, and were sold for behoof of his creditors; that on the said Robert Chiene's return to Crail last mentioned, he at first rented a house, in which he lived for some months, and thereafter removed to the one purchased by him and his brother, after the last had undergone some repairs, and lived in it till his death, which happened in the month of November following; that on his said last-mentioned return to Crail he informed him, the said Andrew Whyte, that he was married to a lady who resided in Philadelphia, and, with a view of settling an annuity on his wife, he employed him, the said Andrew Whyte, to purchase some land in the neighbourhood of Crail; and that the said Andrew Whyte made an offer for same accordingly, but did not obtain the purchase. And that by the deposition of Robert Murray, the said Robert Murray made oath, that he knew the said testator, Robert Chiene, for a period of thirty years before his death, and from the time he was a boy at school; that he had heard the said Robert Chiene was born at Crail, and that at the time the said Robert Murray knew him as at school, he resided with his mother, Anne Brown, at the town of Crail; that the said deponent, Robert Murray, went abroad himself early in life, and did not return to Crail till the year 1787, so that he knew not the early part of the said Robert Chiene's history intervening betwixt his leaving the school at Crail and his return to that place after mentioned; that he knew the said Robert Chiene returned to Crail in the year 1802, where he resided till his death, which happened in the month of November in the said year; that he understood, although he had no particular occasion to know the same, that some years previous to the said Robert Chiene's return to Crail, as before mentioned, a dwelling-house, with gardens, with some other property, was purchased on account of him and his brother jointly in that burgh; that on the said Robert Chiene's return he at first rented a house at Crail, in which he resided for some months, and afterwards removed to the one he had purchased, after it had undergone some repairs, and resided therein till his death; that he had heard the said Robert Chiene married a sister of the wife of Patrick Brown, deceased, sometime a captain of a merchant ship, and a native of Crail, a brother of Mr. William Brown, the then postmaster of Crail; and that he had heard the said Robert Chiene's wife had resided, and still resided, in America. And the said Master further certified, that three several letters, appearing to have been written by the testator to the plaintiff, bearing date respectively the 1st day of November, 1801; the 21st day of March, 1802; and the 25th of August, 1802, had been exhibited to him, and the handwriting of the said testator proved by an affidavit of William Penrose, made in the said cause, on the 12th day of December, 1807, the contents of which letters, inasmuch as they appeared to him to show the said testator's intentions as to residence, he had set forth in the third schedule annexed to his report. And the said Master was of opinion, that the said testator was domiciled in Scotland at the time of his decease."

The decree of the Master of the Rolls was, accordingly, that the testator was domiciled in Scotland at the time of his decease, and that his property should be distributed according to the law of Scotland. It does not appear that the question of bastardy entered into consideration in the Chancery proceedings; nor does it appear, whether the testator had received letters of legitimation or not.

In the case of *Munroe* v. *Douglas* a similar question occurred in the Court of Chancery, in regard to the domicil of *Dr. Munroe* (t), in June and July 1820. *Dr. Munroe* was born in Scotland, and educated there to the profession of a surgeon. At the age of nineteen he went out to Calcutta, and in 1771 he was appointed assistant surgeon in the East India Company's service. In 1811 he obtained the rank of surgeon in his Majesty's service; but this was only local rank.

In 1797 he was married in India to a lady who survived him. On 15th March 1813 he made his will in India, and added a codicil thereto on the 22d September 1814. In January 1815 he left India, and arrived in England

_____

(t) 5 *Maddock*, 379.

on the 15th of June following. He took a house in England, but, owing to ill-health, he became undetermined whether he should continue to reside in England, or spend, his days in Scotland. He continued in England till July 1816, when he went on a visit to Scotland, and died at Sir Robert Lawrie's seat there, without leaving issue, on the 8th of August 1816.

By his will the testator gave property to his wife to the amount of 1000*l.* a year and upwards. He gave legacies to his nephews and nieces; but he had not disposed of the remainder of his property, amounting nearly to 60,000*l.*

The widow filed a bill in Chancery against the executors of the will, contending that the testator had his domicil in Scotland at the time of his death, and that she was entitled, by the law of that country, to one half of the property. In his will the testator says, in regard to his undisposed property, " I will not dispose of the remainder of my property *till I come home*, when it is my intention to cultivate a more intimate acquaintance with the junior members of my family, in order that I may divide my property equally among them." Many letters were given in evidence, written by the testator while in India, to show that his determination was to spend his latter days in Scotland. Letters and conversations were also given in evidence to prove that, after the testator's return to England, his health was such that he became undetermined whether he should spend his days in England or in Scotland. Clear evidence was adduced to show, that when he went to Scotland in 1816 it was only on a visit, and without any intention of permanently residing there. The evidence was very voluminous.

In the pleadings, the decisions pronounced in the House of Lords, and in the Courts of England and Scotland, are specially referred to, commencing with the case of

Bruce v. *Bruce.* Various references were also made to the *Corpus Juris* (*u*), and to the writings of the foreign jurists. (*x*)

After the pleadings were finished the Vice-Chancellor (Sir John Leach) gave the following judgment on the cause : —

" It is settled by the case of Major Bruce, that a residence in India, for the purpose of following a profession there, in the service of the East India Company, creates a new domicil. It is not to be disputed, therefore, that Dr. Munroe acquired a domicil in India.

" It is said, that having afterwards quitted India, in the intention never to return thither, he abandoned his acquired domicil, and that the *forum originis* revived. As to this point, I can find no difference in principle between the original domicil and an acquired domicil; and such is clearly the understanding of Pothier in one of the passages which has been referred to.

" A domicil cannot be lost by mere abandonment. It is not to be defeated *animo* merely, but *animo et facto* (*y*) and necessarily remains until a subsequent domicil be acquired, unless the party die *in itinere* toward an intended domicil. It has been stated, that, in point of fact, the testator went to Scotland in the intention to fix his permanent residence there; but this statement is not supported by the evidence.

" It has also been stated, that the testator, knowing he was in a dying state, went to Scotland, in order to lay his bones with his ancestors; but this, too, is clearly disproved.

(*u*) The following texts in the Civil Law were quoted :—Cod. lib. 10. tit. 38. s. 4.; tit. 39. s. 1. 3. Dig. lib. 50. tit. 16. s. 203.

(*x*) The following foreign jurists were referred to : — Voet. ad pandectas, lib. 5. tit. 1. s. 92. 96, 97. 99. Pothier, Coutumes d'Orleans, Introd. c. 1. s. 1. No. 7. 9. Denisart, tit. Domicile. Cochin, tom. v. p. 5.

(*y*) See the preceding case of *Colville* v. *Lauder*, where a contrary rule appears to have been laid down in Scotland. *Supra,* 166.

It may be represented as the certain fact here, that when this gentleman left England, on his visit to Scotland, he had formed no settled purpose of permanent residence there or elsewhere; that he meant to remain a few months only in Scotland, and to winter in the south of France; and, with this fluctuation of mind on the subject of his future domicil, he was surprised by death, at the house of a relation in Scotland. I am of opinion, therefore, that Dr. Munroe acquired no new domicil after he quitted India, and that his Indian domicil subsisted at his death.

" A domicil in India is, in legal effect, a domicil in the province of Canterbury; and the law of England, and not the law of Scotland, is, therefore, to be applied to his personal property."

In the case of *Anstruther* v. *Chalmer*, in the Court of Chancery, in February 1825 and February 1826, a question occurred in regard to the construction of a testamentary instrument executed by Miss Catherine Anstruther, which was prepared in Scotland, but was construed by the law of her English domicil.

Miss Anstruther was a native of Scotland. In 1821, she came to reside in England, and was domiciled in London up to the time of her death. She, however, from time to time, occasionally visited Scotland; on one of these visits, in 1814, she employed a writer to the signet to prepare a testamentary instrument in regard to the disposition of her property. This was dated the 16th of December 1814, and was entirely in the Scotch form. (z) It commenced thus: " I Miss Catherine Anstruther, daughter of Sir Robert Anstruther of Balcaskie, Baronet, for the love and affection I have and bear to Sir Alexander Anstruther of Caplie,

---

(z) 2 Simons, 1. This was in the nature of what is termed a *settlement* in Scotland. (See *ante*, p. 98.).

Recorder of Bombay, my brother, and for other good causes and considerations me moving, do hereby, with and under the burdens, declarations, and reservations after specified, give, grant, alienate, assign, and dispone, to and in favour of the said *Sir Alexander Anstruther, and his heirs and assignees whomsoever*, heritably and irredeemably, all and sundry lands, tenements, annual rents, and other heritages, and all heritable and moveable means and estate of whatever nature or denomination, and wherever situated." The instrument then went on to convey all her bonds, securities for money, rights of action, &c. ; it also contained an obligation to invest *the said Sir Alexander Anstruther and his foresaids*, in all her lands and heritages, and power to him to call in and pursue for, uplift, receive, and discharge or assign the debts, goods, and effects thereby disponed and conveyed ; and it appointed him sole executor in the following terms : —

" And I hereby nominate and appoint the said Sir Alexander Anstruther to be my sole executor, and intrometter with my moveable estate, hereby excluding and debarring all others my nearest in kin from the said office." Then followed clauses reserving the granter's life rent, a power of revocation, and dispensing with the delivery and consenting to the registration in the books of the Court of Session, or others competent, in the form commonly used in Scotland.

Miss Anstruther deposited this instrument in the hands of the writer to the signet who prepared it. She afterwards returned to England, but continued occasionally to visit Scotland as formerly. In September 1820 she died at her home in London. She had never altered or revoked the instrument in question, and it remained at her death in the hands of the gentleman with whom she had deposited it : she left no real estate ; her personal estate was in England. The instrument was registered in Scotland after her death ;

but this was for preservation merely, and gave no additional validity to the instrument.

Sir Alexander Anstruther, the executor and legatee named in this instrument, had died in 1818, during the lifetime of Miss Anstruther, having made his will, and appointed his wife his executrix.

In March 1821 letters of administration, with the testamentary instrument of Miss Anstruther annexed, were granted by the Prerogative Court of Canterbury to James Chalmer and Alexander Fraser, the attornies of Elizabeth Campbell, the sister and only next of kin of Miss Anstruther.

A bill was filed in the Court of Chancery, by the executrix of Sir Alexander Anstruther, against Mr. Chalmer and Mr. Fraser, and their constituent Mrs. Campbell, charging, that according to the law of Scotland the disposition to Sir Alexander Anstruther was absolute, and did not lapse by his death in the lifetime of Miss Anstruther, but subsisted for the benefit of his child or children; and that it had been intended that the disposition ought to be construed by the law of Scotland.

It was admitted that this was the true construction of the instrument by the law of Scotland, if the instrument were to be construed by that law. It was also admitted that Miss Anstruther was domiciled in England at the time of her death.

In the course of the argument it was contended for the plaintiff, that though the law of the domicil regulated succession as well in a case of testacy as of intestacy, still this was entirely a Scotch instrument; and it contained technical phrases which were totally unintelligible unless the Scotch law was applied to it.

The defendants insisted, that, as the testatrix was domiciled in England, there was not enough to prevent the court from construing the will according to the law of England.

At pronouncing judgment, the Vice Chancellor (Sir John

Leach) gave this opinion: — " In this case, Miss Anstruther, who was born in Scotland, but was domiciled in England, being on a visit in Scotland, caused her will to be prepared there by a writer to the signet, who made it in the Scotch form, so as to give an absolute interest in all her real and personal estate to Sir Alexander Anstruther, who afterwards died in her lifetime. This will, after the death of Miss Anstruther, was proved in England. Miss Anstruther, at her death, had no ~~personal~~ estate; and it being admitted that by the law of Scotland the gift to Sir Alexander Anstruther was not lapsed by his death in the lifetime of Miss Anstruther, the question in this cause is, whether Miss Anstruther's personal property would, under this instrument, belong to the representative of Sir Alexander Anstruther, or to the next of kin of Miss Anstruther, as in the case of a failure by lapse.

" By the law of England, where an absolute interest in personal property is given by a testamentary instrument, there the gift fails if the donee die in the lifetime of the testator; and, Miss Anstruther being domiciled in this country, the law of England must prevail in this case. The next of kin are therefore entitled." The bill was therefore dismissed. (a)

In the case of *Brown's Trustees* v. *Mary Brown* (b) a

(a) In this case a reference was made to Vattel (lib. 2. c. 8. p. 175.), in which it is said, " As to the form or solemnities appointed to settle the validity of a will, it appears that the testator ought to observe those that are established in the country where he makes it, unless it be otherwise ordained by the law of the state of which he is a member;" and he adds, " I speak here of a will which is to be opened in a place where a person dies." The doctrines involved in this case appear to have been much considered by the continental writers; but these do not appear to have entered much into the discussion on this case. This case appears to be in opposition to that of *Machargs* v. *Blain,* decided by the Court of Session. (Supra, p. 95.).

(b) 4 Shaw & Dunlop, 42. 4 Wilson & Shaw's Appeal Cases, 28.

question occurred in regard to the mode of construing a will made in Virginia by William Brown, a native of Scotland, but domiciled in the state of Virginia, in America. By this will, dated in 1805, he gave the following directions in regard to the residue of his property: — " The re-" mainder of my estate, after deducting therefrom the above " legacies, is to be divided in the following manner; viz., " to my father and mother, James and Mary Brown, of " Kirkcudbright, North Britain, I leave one fourth of the " balance of my estate; to them or the survivor of them. " To my sister, Jean Muir, Kirkcormick, in Galloway, Scot-" land, I leave one fourth share of the balance of my estate, " at her death to be equally divided between her children. " To my sister Isabella Black, of Castle Douglas, Scotland, " I leave one fourth of the remainder of my estate, to be " at her death equally divided between her children. To " my sister, Mary Brown, Kirkcudbright, North Britain, " I leave the remaining one fourth share of the balance of " my estate, at her death to be equally divided between " her children, *should she have any*." The testator died in Virginia, in 1811. All the above-mentioned parties survived him. The will was proved by the executors in America, and the father and mother took administration in England with the will annexed, in regard to certain funds of the testator in that country.

Mary, the only unmarried sister, was well advanced in life at the testator's death; she had no prospect of issue. Mary and her sister, Jean Muir, and the husband of the latter, about 1815, filed a bill in the Court of Chancery of the State of Virginia against the local executors, in regard to their rights under this will. The Court, by their decree on the 24th of May, 1816, ordered the executors to " *pay to the said Mary Brown one fourth of the residuary* " *estate of the testator*," and to the husbands of the other two sisters each one fourth of the residuum, " upon their

o

" severally executing in person, or by their attorney, bond
" to be deposited with the clerk of this court, payable to
" the said surviving executors, in the penalty each of
" 70,000 dollars; with condition that, at the deaths of their
" said wives, their said legacies shall be divided amongst
" their children, as provided by the will of the said
" testator." (c)

Disputes afterwards arose among the parties in regard to
the rights of Mary in her share of the residue; it was contended that she had only a right of life-rent therein. Upon
this subject Sir Arthur Pigott was consulted in England,
and gave his opinion, " that Mary Brown took only the
" interest for her life; if she never had, and will not now
" have, any children, the share of which she took only the
" interest for her life is now undisposed of, and seems,
" therefore, vested in the testator's father, subject to being
" divested in the contingency of the birth of a child or
" children of Mary Brown, at any time during her life."(d)

Mary was a person of a facile disposition, and had, upon
certain inadequate terms, granted a release of her rights;
but she afterwards brought an action in the Court of Session against John Brown, a nephew of the testator, who
had received her share of the money as her attorney. John
Brown had obtained right to the shares and interests of
the father and mother of the testator, under the will made
in Virginia. Various defences were pleaded, and, amongst
others, that Mary had only a right of life-rent in her

(c) This last part of the judgment is said to have been altered, but
what alteration was made does not appear. In England, if the funds
had been taken out of the hands of the executors, they would have
been paid over to the Accountant-General, to be invested till the
children became of age.

(d) It does not appear upon what facts Sir Arthur Pigott was consulted; nor whether the law of the State of Virginia, as to the succession in personal estate, had been before him.

fourth of the residue; and the opinion of Sir Arthur Pigott was founded on. There were many other points in the cause; but, upon the construction of the will, the Court found, " that by the plain import and meaning of the " words of the testament, as well as by the judgment of " the competent court in Virginia, where the testator died " (obtained to regulate the conduct of the executors), and " which stands unchallenged and unaltered, the fee of the " legacy in question is vested in Mary Brown, who, by the " assent of both parties, is long past the period of having " children : that the construction of this American will " cannot be affected by the opinion of any English counsel, " as it must be judged of solely by the laws of America."

An appeal was brought against the judgment of the Court of Session, consisting of many different points, and amongst others, that regarding the construction of the will. But the judgment was affirmed with costs. At pronouncing judgment in the House of Lords, the Lord Chancellor (e) said : — " It was further urged, and a petition was pre- " sented for that purpose, that the opinions of American " lawyers of that particular district of America should be " taken, for the purpose of guiding the consideration of the " case. The Court, however, rejected that petition, and I " think they were right in doing so, under the circumstances " of this case. The question with respect to the con- " struction of the will had been before the court in America. " In the year 1816, they had pronounced in effect a judg- " ment as to the construction of that will, for they had " decreed that Mary Brown was entitled absolutely to this " property ; they had directed that property to be paid to " her, and it was paid accordingly to her agent, appointed " by her to receive what she was entitled to under the

---

(e) Lord Lyndhurst.

" will. It seemed, therefore, under these circumstances,
" and after so long an interval of time, not right again to
" postpone the cause for the purpose of taking further
" evidence as to the real and proper construction of the
" will."

The import of this part of the judgment was, that the
estator's will was to be construed according to the law of
his domicil ; and having been construed by a court of competent jurisdiction in the State of Virginia, such construction was not to be challenged in a foreign country.

All the cases of domicil which have been hitherto noticed,
have related to the domicils of persons who were adults,
and of age sufficient to fix their own places of residence.
The following case of *Potinger* v. *Wightman*, at the Rolls,
in July 1817 (*f*), belongs to a different class, namely, to
that of infant children, who, after the death of their father,
followed their mother into a different domicil.

In December 1805, Thomas Potinger, a native of England, died in Guernsey, the place of his domicil, intestate,
leaving seven children living at his decease, four by a
former wife, and three by his wife Harriet (afterwards
Harriet Wightman), who was then pregnant of a fourth
child, afterwards born.

Shortly after the decease of the intestate, the Royal
Court in Guernsey, on the nomination of the nearest relations of the children, appointed *Daniel de Lisle Brock*
guardian for the children of the first marriage, and the
widow guardian for her own children ; and, by permission
of the Royal Court, Daniel de Lisle Brock and the widow,
in their character of guardians, sold the real and personal
estate of the intestate in the island of Guernsey, and vested
he produce in the English funds. In September 1806,

(*f*)   Merivale, p. 67.

the widow quitted the island of Guernsey, and came to England, bringing with her her four infant children, and from that time established her domicil in England. In May 1809, Henry James Potinger, one of her children, died at the age of six years; and in April 1812, John Lockman Potinger, another of her children, died at the age of ten years.

A bill was filed in the Court of Chancery, on behalf of the infant children of the second marriage, by Richard Potinger their next friend, against the mother and her second husband Robert Wightman, the infant children of the first marriage by Irving Brock, their guardian Daniel de Lisle Brock, and others, praying for the usual accounts of the real and personal estate of the intestate. The decree directed an inquiry, " Whether the intestate was domiciled in the island of Guernsey; and if the Master should find that he was domiciled there at the time of his death, he was to inquire and state who was or were his heir or heirs at law at the time of his death, and what was the law of the island with respect to real and personal estates, and who was or were, and are, according to the law of the said island, entitled to the intestate's real and personal estate therein, and in what shares and proportions ? "

The Master, by his report dated 8th April 1816, stated that the intestate was domiciled in Guernsey at the time of his death; and he also stated the law of Guernsey respecting the descent of the real estate, and the distribution of the personal estate, of persons dying intestate there. (g)

(g) The law is of considerable intricacy, as well in regard to the real as to the personal estate; it is stated in the report of the case, but this does not enter into the present question: among other things it is mentioned, that " *no real estate in Guernsey can be devised by will.*" In this it resembles the law of Scotland.

After ascertaining the original shares of the respective parties in the intestate's personal estate, the Master proceeded to certify, that, in consequence of the deaths of John Lockman Potinger and Henry James Potinger (two of the infant children of the second marriage of Thomas Potinger), their shares in the intestate's personal estate were by the law of Guernsey divisible in equal shares between Richard Potinger and William Potinger, the two sons of the first marriage.

When the cause came on to be heard for further directions, it was contended, on the part of the widow and daughters, that the shares of the deceased children were distributable by the law of England. It being admitted that the personal property was regulated by the law of the domicil of the proprietor, the question was, Whether the deceased children retained their paternal domicil in Guernsey, or acquired a new derivative domicil from their mother in England?

It was referred back to the Master to report on the domicil of the children at the time of their death; by his report, dated 8th March 1817, the Master gave his opinion, that the children, at the time of their deaths, were domiciled in England. The cause coming on to be again heard, this question was argued before the Master of the Rolls.

It was admitted that no authority existed upon this case in the English law. A *dictum* of Lord Alvanley in *Somerville* v. *Somerville* (h), that a minor cannot during his state of pupillage acquire a domicil of his own, was stated obviously to refer to that domicil which a minor could acquire by his own acts, or, according to the expression cited from *Bynkershoek*, "*proprio marte.*" But it was contended, that

---

(h) *Supra*, p. 174.

the domicil of the widow, combining (during her widow-hood) the characters of guardian and head of the family, was communicated to her minor children.

In the absence of English authorities, the following foreign jurists were referred to, to shew that it was the right of the surviving parent, whether father or mother, to transfer the domicil of the minor children, if this were done fairly, and without any fraudulent intention: *Voet. Comm. ad Pand. lib. 5. t. 1. s.* 100.; *Rodenburg. de Jure Conj. tit.* 2. *cap.* 1. *s.* 4. *cap.* 2. *ss.* 2, 3.; *Bynkershoek, Quest. Jur. Priv. lib.* 1. *c.* 16.; *Denisart, voce Domicile, ss.* 9. 14. 37.; *Pothier, Coutumes d'Orleans ; Introd. Générale, chap.* 1. *s.* 1. *no.* 16. 20.; *Mornac, Obs. in Cod. lib.* 3. *tit.* 20. *p.* 129.; *Decisiones Celeberrimi Sequanorum Senatus Dolani, authore Joanne Grivello, Dec.* 11. *pp.* 21. 24.; *Code Civ. liv.* 1. *tit.* 3. *art.* 108.

Cases of settlement under the Poor Laws were also referred to. Where the mother removes with her infant children, and acquires a new settlement, that settlement is communicated to them, and supersedes their original paternal settlement: *Inhabitants of Woodend* v. *Inhabitants of Paulspury* (Raym. 1473. Stra. 746. S. C.); *Rex* v. *Inhabitants of Barton Turfe* (Burr. Sett. Ca. 49.); *Rex* v. *Inhabitants of Oulton* (Burr. Sett. Ca. 64.); Wooddeson's Lectures, 278, 279.; 1 Nolan's Poor Laws, 236, et seq. to 276.

After the conclusion of the argument, the Master of the Rolls (Sir William Grant) said : —

" On the subject of domicil there is so little to be found in our own law, that we are obliged to resort to the writings of foreign jurists for the decision of most of the questions that arise concerning it. The *dictum* of Lord Alvanley in *Somerville* v. *Somerville* (*i*) has no relation to the point

---

(*i*) 5 Ves. 787.

now in dispute. He is speaking of the power of a minor to acquire a domicil by his own acts. Here the question is, Whether, after the death of the father, children remaining under the care of the mother follow the domicil which she may acquire, or retain that which their father had at his death, until they are capable of gaining one by acts of their own? The weight of authority is certainly in favour of the former proposition; it has the sanction both of Voet and Bynkershoek; the former, however, qualifying it by a condition, that the domicil shall not have been changed, for the fraudulent purpose of obtaining an advantage by altering the rule of succession. Pothier, whose authority is equal to that of either, maintains the proposition as thus qualified. There is an introductory chapter to his treatise on the Custom of Orleans, in which he considers several points that are common to all the customs of France, and, among others, the law of domicil. He holds, in opposition to the opinion of some jurists, that a tutor cannot change the domicil of his pupil; but he considers it as clear that the domicil of the surviving mother is also the domicil of the children, provided it be not with a fraudulent view to their succession, that she shifts the place of her abode : and he says, that such fraud would be presumed, if no reasonable motive could be assigned for the change.

" There never was a case in which there could be less suspicion of fraud than the present. The father and mother were both natives of England ; they had no long residence in Guernsey; and, after the father's death, there was an end of the only tie which connected the family with that island. That the mother should return to this country, and bring her children with her, was so much a matter of course, that the fact of her doing so can excite no suspicion of an improper motive ; and I think, therefore, the Master has rightly found the deceased children to have been domiciled in England. It is, conse-

quently, by the law of this country that the succession to
their personal property must be regulated." (*k*)

(*k*) Hitherto this is understood to be the only reported case upon
this branch of the law, relative to a change of domicil during infancy or
minority.   In 1827, a case occurred in the Court of Session in Scotland,
in regard to the domicil of *Robert Alexander Paterson Wallace*, connected
with this point.   He was born in Scotland: his father, Captain Wallace,
was by birth a Scotchman, and an officer in the army, who had married
Miss Oliver, an English lady, in England.   The father named guardians
to his child, one of whom (the maternal grandfather, Mr. Oliver) resided
in England; and another (Mr. Hathorn) resided in Scotland; but the
father dying when the infant was of tender years, he was carried by his
mother into England.   She also dying when the child was in infancy,
he continued in England under the charge of his maternal grandfather,
who was one of his guardians, and went to English schools, and an English university.   The bulk of the property consisted in stock of the
Bank of Scotland.   He occasionally visited that country, as well before
as after he came of age.   He purchased a small landed estate in Scotland
after he attained majority.   He died at Hastings, in England, on the
29th of May, 1824, at the age of 22 years and 7 months, a bachelor and
intestate.

His personal property was claimed in the Court of Session in Scotland by his maternal grandfather, as his next of kin, according to the
law of England; and by his uncle and aunt by the father's side as his
next of kin, according to the law of Scotland.   The law as to change
of domicil during minority was much discussed in that case.   The Lord
Ordinary (Cringletie) held, that after the age of puberty the minor had
a right to choose his own domicil; that *tutor datur personæ, curator rei;*
and he was inclined to the English domicil.

He gave out the following note on the cause, when he pronounced
an interlocutor thereon:—" 3d December 1827.   The Lord Ordinary
regrets that the parties have thought it necessary to detail the circumstances of Capt. Wallace's marriage with Miss Oliver in England, and
the terms of his contract of marriage with that lady; as, to the Lord
Ordinary, they appear not to have the least bearing on the cause.   A
man, by marrying in England an Englishwoman, does not thereby become
domiciled there; nor is it necessary that he should reside a day there
for that purpose; far less does he make his children domiciled there by
the mere act of marrying in England.   The lady must reside in a certain parish for a specified time, to enable her to be married in the
church of it, and an oath must be made that such has been her residence and domicil; otherwise she requires a special licence to be
married.   Of this the Lord Ordinary can inform the parties, for he

SECT. II.

Cases in which the Succession to real or heritable, and also as to personal Estate, was involved in the same Decision.

THE first of these mixed cases, in point of date, which

---

knows it personally; he married a lady born under English law, and who had resided all her life in and near London: he had to make oath that she had lived in the parish of Acton for a certain time, and he entered into a contract of marriage in the English form; but that had no more effect in fixing his domicil than the winds of heaven. Capt. Wallace, having been a Scotchman in the army, did not acquire any domicil by marrying there, but returned to Edinburgh, where he sold out of the army, lived here for some time, and died here. There can therefore be no doubt that he died here, domiciled as a Scotchman.

" As to his son Robert Alexander Paterson Wallace, it is admitted that he was born in Edinburgh, and went to England with his mother. Even had there been no contract made before he was permitted to accompany her, the Lord Ordinary could have no doubt that, had he died in pupilarity, his legal domicil of Scotland could not have been changed by his residence in England; a pupil has no *persona standi*, has no will in law, and he cannot act for himself — could not fix his domicil — cannot make a will. But the matter is quite changed when he passes the years of pupilarity. *As a domiciled Scotchman* he is entitled to act for himself, with the consent of his curators; *he is entitled to live where he pleases;* for *curators have no controul over his person.* ' Hence,' says Erskine (b. i. tit. 7. s. 14.), ' also, though the natural person of a pupil is under the power either of his tutor or next cognate, *yet a curator cannot claim the custody of a minor's person,* who hath attained the age of puberty, *or prescribe to him where he must reside.* A minor can make a will disposing of his personal succession, and of course can do so by change of domicil.' The defenders seem totally to have lost sight of this principle. They state their case as if Mr. Hathorn could have prevented Robert Alexander Wallace from living in England; as if he placed him there, and was at the expense of his education there; when it is quite plain, that it was Mr. Hathorn's indispensable duty to advance the minor's own funds to him, for a suitable and reasonable maintenance and education. Still, residence merely for education may be questionable how far it constitutes a domicil to govern succession. But when education is over, when a man attains majority, and still resides in England, making only short visits to Scotland; having no house of his own in which he lives in Scotland, and dies in England in a house of his own; — the Lord Ordinary confesses that he thinks that there is

occurred after the decision in the case of *Bruce* v. *Bruce*, was the important case of *Balfour* v. *Scott*. (*l*)

David Scott, of Scotstarvet, was a Scotsman born, and proprietor of the estate of Scotstarvet in Scotland. This estate had been strictly entailed by his father, but David Scott had reduced this entail by an action in the Court of Session, as *in fraudem* of his father's marriage settlement, by which the estate was destined to him without being entailed. He had succeeded to this estate in 1767; in 1774 he removed to London, where he took the lease of a house, and also a lease of chambers in Gray's Inn. Before he left Scotland he had sold off the chief part of the

---

little room for doubting what must be held to be his domicil. From the admitted facts in this case, the question appears to have been fairly tried in a competent court in England; and a question may arise, how far it is proper or competent to try it again here; and whether an appeal against the English judgment would not be the mode to obtain redress.

" Perhaps, as there has been a confirmation here, and no reduction of it has been brought, the decree of the English court is to be considered as a foreign decree, to which effect is not to be given if it can be shown to be wrong. But this is a doubtful and difficult matter, where the error lies entirely on a point of law. Was the confirmation here posterior to the English decree? Neither the one nor the other has been transmitted to the Lord Ordinary.

" 3d December, 1827. The Lord Ordinary appoints the cause to be inrolled in his note of motions, and parties to attend by counsel to close the record."

The proceedings in England to which Lord Cringletie referred, were those in the Prerogative Court of Canterbury, relative to the granting of letters of administration to the effects of the deceased situated in England. These were granted to the maternal grandfather. The questions made in that court are noticed in a subsequent chapter. The paternal aunt had obtained a *confirmation* in Scotland, without any contest.

The matters in dispute between the parties were settled by compromise, and the proceedings in the Court of Session were withdrawn; so that no final judgment was pronounced on this important case.

(*l*) Fac. Coll., 15th Nov. 1787, Morrison, 2379. 4617. House of Lords, 11th April, 1793.

furniture in his mansion house in that country. He continued in London till the time of his death, having visited Scotland only once or twice during the last seven or eight years of his life; occupying himself chiefly in attending to his property in the public funds, which was considerable. He held a public office in Scotland (m), but this was a sinecure office, and managed by a deputy. He died in London, in February 1785, a bachelor and intestate.

At the time of his death his property consisted of his estate of Scotstarvet, of the annual value of about 1500l.; some personal estate of inconsiderable value in Scotland; and personal estate in England, chiefly vested in the public funds and in government securities, to the amount of 60,000l. and upwards. His next of kin at the time of his death were Henrietta, Lucy, and Joanna Scott (n), daughters of his brother, General John Scott, deceased; and John Hay Balfour, Mrs. Lucy Moncrieff, and Mrs. Butler, children of his sister, Mrs. Elizabeth Hay, deceased.

Henrietta, the eldest Miss Scott, succeeded to the estate in Scotland, which was settled upon the eldest heir female *without division* by a deed of her grandfather, the father of the last David Scott of Scotstarvet; and it came to be a question, whether she, taking this estate in Scotland, could also claim a share of the personal estate of her late uncle, David Scott, as one of his next of kin.

All parties had joined in granting a power of attorney to John Way, esquire, by virtue of which he obtained letters of administration of the personal estate of the late David Scott, in the Prerogative Court of Canterbury; and, in this character, paid certain sums of money to Henrietta Scott. Mr. Hay Balfour, Mrs. Moncrieff, and

---

(m) It is understood that he was *director of the Chancery*.

(n) Afterwards respectively Duchess of Portland, Lady Doune, and Viscountess Canning.

Mrs. Butler, the children of David Scott's sister, thereupon brought an action in the Court of Session against Miss Scott and her guardians, concluding to have it found that she could take no part of the personal estate, either in Scotland or in England, without collating the heritage.

Miss Scott contended, 1st, That the doctrine of collation did not rule in *collateral* succession, but was confined to the case of the succession of descendants: 2d, That, as she took the real estate in Scotland under the deed of her grandfather, she was not obliged in such case to collate it, to enable her to take a share of the personal estate of her uncle: 3d, That the personal estate, being situated in England, was subject to distribution by the law of that country, where collation did not take place.

The pursuers contended, on the other hand, 1st, That according to the opinions of the institutional writers, and repeated decisions of the courts, it was clear that *collation* took place as well in collateral succession, as in the succession of descendants: 2d, That Miss Scott was heir *alioqui successura* to her uncle, as to one third of the real estate, and therefore bound to collate, though she took under the deed of her grandfather: And, 3d, That the law of the domicil must regulate in this matter, and that Mr. Scott was to be considered as having had his domicil in Scotland at the time of his death.

The Court, on the 16th November 1787, and 17th June 1788, found, " that Miss Henrietta Scott was not entitled to claim any part of the executry of her uncle, David Scott of Scotstarvet, without collating his heritable estates to which she succeeded as heir; and that the succession to the said David Scott's personal estate in England fell to be regulated by the law of England; and therefore, in so far as respected it, assoilzied the defender." At the time when this decision was given, it was universally understood by Scotch lawyers (o), that the *lex loci rei sitæ* was to regulate in personal succession. The Court thus meant to hold, that the succession of Mr. Scott was to be regulated universally by the *lex loci rei sitæ*. They had considered also, that this was a case in which collation should take place according to the law of Scotland, though Miss Scott took the real estate under the deed of her grandfather, not of her uncle.

Against this judgment Mr. Hay Balfour, Mrs. Moncrieff, and Mrs. Butler, brought their original appeal to the House of Lords; and Miss Scott brought her cross appeal against that part of the judgment which respected the collation of the real estate. The case came on to be argued in the House of Lords, soon after Lord Loughborough had received the great seal. At this period the cases of *Bruce* v. *Bruce*, and the first case of *Hog* v. *Lashley*, had been recently decided. This cause of *Balfour* v. *Scott*, which excited much interest, was pleaded by several of the eminent persons who had been of counsel in the former causes. Lord Thurlow, the late Lord Chancellor, also attended the hearing; and, after a speech on the cause, his Lordship moved the following judgment, on the 11th April 1793 : —

" Ordered and adjudged, that the original appeal be dismissed, and that so much of the interlocutors as complained of by the cross appeal be reversed ; and it is declared, that the said Henrietta Scott is entitled to claim her distributive share in the whole personal estate of her said uncle, David Scott of Scotstarvet in Scotland, without collating his heritable estate, to which she succeeded as heir, in so much as she claimed the said share of the said

---

(o) *Antè*, p. 101.

personal estate by the law of England, where the said David had his domicil at the time of his death." (p)

The judgment of the Court of Session finding that Miss Scott was not entitled to any part of the personal estate without collation was reversed in general terms, without noticing in the judgment the opinion of their Lordships upon the very important questions involved in it, namely, whether Miss Scott, taking the estate under a deed of destination of her grandfather, could be obliged to collate before claiming a share of the personal estate of her uncle. This belongs to another branch of the law of Scotland. The important questions involved in it were discussed in the printed cases; but the words of the judgment leave it uncertain whether the House of Lords meant to decide any thing upon this point. (q)

In the case of *Durie* v. *Coutts*, it appears to have been then clearly understood, that the succession to personal estate was to be regulated by the law of the domicil of the party deceased. (r)   Thomas Durie, a resident in the Isle of Man, had some heritable securities, besides personal property, in Scotland.   By an instrument in the Scotch form he conveyed these to trustees, for the use and benefit, in the first place, of the heirs of his body; failing them, of David Durie; and failing him, of Jane Durie and Margaret Durie.   Thomas Durie died domiciled in the Isle of Man; the succession under his deed, by failure of those called before them, devolved to Jane and Margaret Durie, who

---

(p) The following references were made to Voet. in this case : —
Voet. ad Pandectas, lib. 5. t. 1. sec. 91. et sequen. sec. 97.
————————, lib. 37. t. 6. sec. 27.

(q) There is reason to fear that no note has been preserved of the opinion delivered by Lord Thurlow in this very important case. Inquiry has been made for it in several quarters, but hitherto without success.

(r) Fac. Coll. 10 November, 1791. — Morrison, 4624.

also resided in the Isle of Man. Jane, having been the survivor, made a nuncupative will in favour of her mother. Two questions, therefore, arose in the Court of Session, between the mother on the one hand, and Alexander Coutts, the heir and personal representative of Jane according to the law of Scotland:—1. In regard to the heritable securities formerly belonging to Thomas Durie; 2. In regard to his personal property. The mother contended that the whole had become personal estate, by having been conveyed to trustees for the use and benefit of her daughters, and that all the personal estate belonged to her by the law of the *domicil*. The then recent case of *Hog* v. *Lashley* was referred to, as superseding all further argument upon this part of the case, namely, that personal estate was to be regulated as to succession, by the law of the domicil.

The Lord Ordinary decided, that " in virtue of the trust disposition by Thomas Durie, the persons for whose behoof that disposition was granted had not a *pro indiviso* share of the subjects conveyed to the trustees, but only a personal claim or ground of action against them, to account; and that the moveable succession of Thomas Durie must be regulated by the law of the Isle of Man, not that of Scotland."

The Court, however, altered the first part of the interlocutor, and " preferred Coutts to the sums *in medio* due by the heritable security," but adhered to the last part of the Lord Ordinary's interlocutor. Thus the heir at law took the real securities, notwithstanding the allegation that the trust-deed had made them personal; and the mother took the personal estate, as entitled to it by the law of the Isle of Man. It is to be remarked in this case, that the mother appears to have been admitted to claim under a *nuncupative* will, in which it differs from the former case of *Shaw* v. *Lewins* (s), though the point was not argued.

(s) Shaw v. Lewins, *suprà*, p. 89.

The mother was also next of kin by the law of the domicil to both her daughters. It does not appear, that the mother had been called upon to make up any title by confirmation, or otherwise, in Scotland.

In the case of *Drummond* v. *Drummonds* a very important decision was given in regard to the proper fund out of which a heritable bond, which was a charge upon the Scotch estate of a person domiciled in England, should be paid, and whether the law of Scotland, or the law of England, was to regulate in such case. (*t*)

David Drummond, a native of Scotland, became domiciled in England, having carried on the business of a wine-merchant in London for many years. In 1788, he succeeded to certain landed estates in Perthshire, termed *Duchally* and *Pittentian*, in virtue of a disposition and settlement of Mr. James Clow, late professor of logic in the University of Glasgow. This disposition and settlement contained a destination of these lands, failing David, to his next brother, James, and other heirs; but there was no limitation in the deed, in the nature of a strict entail according to the law of Scotland. Accordingly, when David succeeded to the lands, he took them as unlimited proprietor. He was infeft upon Mr. Clow's disposition on 30th August 1788, and the instrument of sasine was duly registered on the 16th of October thereafter.

In February 1789, David Drummond borrowed 2000*l.* from George Birrell, formerly in the service of the East India Company, then residing at Kirkcaldy in Scotland, for which he granted a heritable bond over his lands of Duchally and Pittentian in Perthshire. This bond was dated the 6th of February in that year; the sasine was

---

(*t*) Fac. Coll. 7th June, 1798.   Morrison, 4478.   House of Lords, 20th Feb. 1799.   No notice is taken in Morrison that this important case was appealed.

taken thereon on the 26th of February, and registered on the 27th of the same month.

This loan was applied by David Drummond to repay a similar loan which he had obtained from Messrs. Newnham and Company, his bankers in London. He had, in his books of account kept in his business, stated his stock in trade as debtor for the sum due to the bankers; and when he effected this heritable loan from Birrell, he noticed it in his books in the same way as a debt of his stock in trade. David Drummond died at his house in Sackville Street, London, on the 27th of July 1791, a bachelor and intestate. His mother survived him, as did his brother James Drummond and several sisters; these were his next of kin according to the law of England. James Drummond succeeded him as heir to the estates of Duchally and Pittentian, under the disposition of Mr. Clow.

The mother, residing in Scotland, renounced the right of administration in favour of her son James, and he thereupon obtained letters of administration of the estate and effects of his late brother in the Prerogative Court of Canterbury. He thus came to hold the two characters of heir and administrator to his brother.

Soon after David Drummond's death, James Drummond sold the estate of Duchally at the price of 3800*l.*, and in May 1792, he paid Mr. Birrell the principal sum of 2000*l* with 128*l.* of interest out of the price of these lands. Birrell thereupon granted his discharge of the heritable security, proceeding upon this narrative: " And now, seeing that James Drummond, merchant in London, brother-german of the said deceased David Drummond, and heir of provision in the foresaid lands of Duchally, &c. has, upon the 16th day of May last past, made payment to me of the foresaid principal sum of 2000*l.*, &c. Therefore I have exonered and discharged, and hereby exoner, quit claim, and *simpliciter* for ever discharge the said James

Drummond, his heirs, executors, and successors, and all others whomsoever, the heirs and representatives of the said David Drummond;" and he renounced his right to the lands. This discharge was registered on the 29th of June 1792.

James Drummond having failed to account to the other next of kin for the personal estate, a suit was commenced against him in the Prerogative Court of Canterbury to oblige him to exhibit an inventory of the effects of the deceased, and to render a true, just, and faithful account of his administration thereof; and also to make distribution according to the statute.

In consequence of this proceeding, an account was exhibited by James Drummond of his administration, and among other items he claimed deduction of the 2000*l.* of principal, and interest, paid to Mr. Birrell in satisfaction of the heritable security which he held over the real estate. In exception, it was pleaded by the other next of kin, that this, being a heritable debt, according to the law of Scotland fell to be paid out of the heritable estate in that country; and that though the creditor might have proceeded against the whole estate of the deceased, real or personal, still Birrell had used no diligence on the personal estate, and had in fact been paid out of the price of the lands of Duchally which had been sold; they claimed, therefore, that this payment should be disallowed in the discharge of the administrator.

The Judge, Sir William Wynne, on delivering his opinion on this case, said, " That, by the law of England, a mortgage is a clear charge on the personal estate. In this case it was pleaded, that there was no English bond, only a security on a foreign real estate. This Court will sometimes interfere in foreign transactions; but this is completely an English transaction. The deceased was an Englishman, and the administrator an Englishman; also the transaction was in England; the money was received in England and applied in England; and it seems so admitted by the other side, this being an application in an English court for the distribution of English property. The payment was made as administrator; he had a right to make it; his conduct as administrator was fair and honourable, and his account is a regular account, against which there does not appear any objection." And the Judge refused to make any reservation of an action for relief of the next of kin in Scotland. (*u*)

This judgment was not brought under review in any English court; but the next of kin raised an action in the Court of Session in Scotland, against James Drummond, concluding that he, as heir in the heritable property, should be decerned to pay to them from his own proper money six sevenths (he being entitled to the other seventh himself) of the sum of 2000*l.* of principal, and the interest thereof, paid to Birrell, as before mentioned. James Drummond made defences, insisting that he had a right to deduct these sums from the personal estate; and he also pleaded the judgment of the Prerogative Court in his favour.

The Lord Justice Clerk Ordinary (*x*) at first decided, "In respect that David Drummond died domiciled in England, and that letters of administration were taken out from the Prerogative Court of Canterbury by the defender, James Drummond, that the personal estate of the said David Drummond was to be administered according to the law of England; and, in respect that this question had already been tried, and received the decision of the Judge

---

(*u*) Case of the appellants in the House of Lords, p. 3. This still justifies the remark of Sir R. P. Arden, Master of the Rolls, in the case of *Somerville*, that the judges of the ecclesiastical courts had a leaning to the *lex loci rei sitæ*. (Supra, p. 180.)

(*x*) Lord Braxfield.

of the Prerogative Court, found the action not competent in that court, and therefore sustained the defences, assoilzied the defender, and decerned."

But upon a representation, which was followed with answers, the Lord Ordinary altered his opinion, and found, " that when a sum of money is secured upon lands by a heritable bond and infeftment, the lands are held to be the principal debtor; and in respect that the estate belonging to David Drummond, over which the heritable bond in question was granted, was taken up by James Drummond as heir to his brother, and that the same is of much greater value than the sum in the heritable bond, finds that James Drummond is ultimately liable for payment of that heritable bond, without relief against the personal estate of David Drummond; finds that the decree of the Prerogative Court of Canterbury went no further than to find, that the sum in the heritable bond being chargeable as a debt against the personal estate, so James Drummond, who paid the heritable bond, was entitled to take credit for the contents thereof, in accounting for the personal estate, but did not determine the question of relief competent to the *executors* (y) against the heir; therefore altered the former interlocutor, repelled the plea of *res judicata*, and found that James Drummond, the heir, was liable to the pursuers in payment of the contents of that heritable bond."

. On a reclaiming petition the Court decided, that " in respect the pursuers did only insist upon a decree for six seventh parts of the sums contained in the heritable bond, they, with this explanation, adhered to the interlocutor of the Lord Ordinary." And James Drummond being now dead, and succeeded by his son David, an infant, by a future interlocutor, the Court decerned against David Drummond and his tutrix, for payment to the pursuers of

---

(y) Meaning those entitled to the executry; the next of kin.

six seventh parts of the money paid to Birrell, the heritable creditor.

From these interlocutors David and his tutrix brought their appeal to the House of Lords. The same points appear to have been discussed in the appeal cases as in the Court of Session. After hearing counsel, the judgment of the Court was simply affirmed on the 20th of February 1799.

This is a very important case of *conflictus legum*; it shows that when an Englishman, or foreigner, succeeds to a real estate in Scotland, he takes it subject to those bur- thens which by the law of Scotland affect it at the time, to be discharged without relief from the English, or fo- reign, personal estate. It is remarkable on account of the conflicting decision in the English ecclesiastical court; it does not appear that the decision of the House of Lords in this case has since been matter of dispute. (z)

In *Wightman* v. *Delisle's Trustees* (16th June 1802) (a), a case occurred in the Court of Session on the point, whe- ther a will made in India, devising all the testator's "real and personal estate whatsoever and wheresoever," to trus- tees for certain purposes, was effectual in relation to a real estate in India, purchased after the will was executed.

In 1785, Philip Delisle, a native of Scotland, but settled in Calcutta as a merchant from an early period of life, made his will in India, giving and devising his "estate and effects, of whatever kind or nature soever, in India," to trustees in that country, for certain purposes. After giving certain legacies, he directed the trustees in India to trans- mit all the remainder of his estate and effects in India to trustees in Scotland, "to whom I do hereby give and de-

---

(z) This being a simple affirmance, it does not appear that any thing was said on moving the judgment. See the opinion of Sir William Grant upon this case, noticed in that of *Brodie* v. *Barry, infra.*

(a) Fac. Coll. Morrison, 4479.

vise the same, together with all my other real and personal estate whatsoever and wheresoever, upon and subject to the following trusts:" The trustees are then directed to pay certain legacies and annuities, particularly a legacy of 1500*l.* to his sister, Mrs. Ann Wightman, "and after payment thereof, then in trust as to the entire residue of my estate, of what kind or nature soever or wheresoever, for my three natural children, Mary Delisle, Thomas Delisle, and Philip Delisle, share and share alike," &c.

About ten months after the date of the will, the testator purchased a house in Calcutta, and soon after certain grounds and gardens at Similah. He died on 15th July 1788, without having altered or republished his will.

Ann Wightman, the testator's sister and heiress at law, brought an action before the Court of Session against his trustees, to have it found that she had right to the house, grounds, and gardens purchased by the testator, in preference to the trustees claiming under the will. The Lord Ordinary directed opinions of English counsel to be taken; and upon advising those with memorials for the parties, the Lord Ordinary found, "that by the law of England, as extended to the British settlements in India, in which the testator, Philip Delisle, at the time of making his last will and testament in August 1785, and at his death, in July 1788, had his domicil, the subjects in Calcutta, and at Similah, acquired by him after making said will, were not carried thereby, but devolved on the pursuer, Mrs. Wightman, as his heir *ab intestato*, and that she was entitled to take them up in that character, and at the same time to claim the legacy bequeathed to her by the said will. Likewise found it sufficiently instructed, that by the said law of England, the pursuer, by taking up the said subjects, did not become liable to relieve the rest of the testator's estate contained in said will of his debts, or any part thereof, although contracted for and on account of the subjects so taken up by her; but that, on the contrary, the funds conveyed by the will are primarily liable for all such debts. In respect of all which repelled the defences, and as the subjects in question had been sold, and the proceeds were in the hands of the defenders, the trustees under the will, found that the defenders must account for the same to the pursuer, and ordained them to account accordingly, and to produce the vouchers thereof."

The trustees reclaimed to the Court, pleading that this was a case of *approbate* and *reprobate*, and that Mrs. Wightman, after accepting the legacy in terms of the will, was barred from insisting in her claim. But the Court, being clearly of opinion that the law of England must decide the case, refused to listen to any argument founded on the law of Scotland, and adhered to the interlocutor of the Lord Ordinary. (b)

The difficulties in deciding these mixed cases were explained by Sir William Grant, in his judgment in the celebrated case of *Brodie* v. *Barry*, at the Rolls in July 1813. (c) In that case Alexander Brodie, a Scotsman by birth, but domiciled in England, by his will, attested so as to pass freehold estates in England, but not according to the forms of the law of Scotland, gave, devised, and bequeathed to certain trustees, their heirs, executors, &c. " all his freehold, leasehold, copyhold, and other estates whatever and wheresoever situated, in England, Scotland, and elsewhere, and all his personal estate whatsoever and wheresoever," upon trust to carry on his works for three years, and thereafter to sell the whole trust property, and to divide the residue among his nephews and nieces equally,

---

(b) It appears from a note to the report of the above case in the Faculty Collection, that a similar decision was given the same day in the case *Austin* v. *Austin*, concerning a will made in India, decided also according to the opinions of English counsel, agreeably to the doctrines laid down by the Court in this case.

(c) 2 Ves. & Beames, 127.

share and share alike, with remainder to their respective children. The testator's heiress at law in Scotland was Betty Cock, one of his married nieces. This heiress claimed his real estate in Scotland, as not duly carried to the trustees by the English will; and also her share of the personal estate, which was of considerable value. A bill was filed in the Court of Chancery by the other nephews and nieces; and the question came to be, whether Betty Cock could take the real estate in Scotland, and also her share of the other trust estate of the testator; or whether she was to be put to her election.

In the speech of Sir William Grant, at giving judgment on this cause, he enters into an account of several of the cases here previously noticed, particularly those of *Balfour* v. *Scott*, and *Drummond* v. *Drummond*. (*d*)

He says, " Where land and personal property are situated in different countries, governed by different laws, and a question arises upon the combined effect of those laws, it is often very difficult to determine what portion of each law is to enter into the decision of the question. It is not easy to say, how much is to be considered as depending on the law of real property, which must be taken from the country where the land lies; and how much upon the law of personal property, which must be taken from the country of the domicil; and to blend both together, so as to form a rule applicable to the mixed question, which neither law separately furnishes sufficient materials to decide.

" I have argued in the House of Lords cases in which difficulties of this kind occurred. Two of the most remarkable were those of *Balfour* v. *Scott*, and *Drummond* v. *Drummond*. In the former a person domiciled in England died intestate, leaving real estate in Scotland. The heir was one of the next of kin, and claimed a share of the

_____

(*d*) Ante, pp. 203. 209.

personal estate. To this claim it was objected, that by the law of Scotland the heir cannot share in the personal property with the other next of kin, except on condition of collating the real estate, that is, bringing it into a mass with the personal estate, to form one common subject of division. It was determined, however, that he was to take his share without complying with that obligation. There the English law decided the question.

"In *Drummond* v. *Drummond*, a person domiciled in England had real estate in Scotland, upon which he granted a heritable bond to secure a debt contracted in England. He died intestate, and the question was, by which of the estates this debt was to be borne. It was clear that, by the English law, the personal estate was the primary fund for the payment of debts; it was equally clear that, by the law of Scotland, the real estate was the primary fund for the payment of the heritable bond. Here was a direct *conflictus legum*. It was said for the heir, that the personal estate must be distributed according to the law of England, and must bear all the burthens to which it is by that law subject. On the other hand, it was said that the real estate must go according to the law of Scotland, and bear all the burthens to which it is by that law subject. It was determined that the law of Scotland should prevail, and that the real estate must bear the burthen.

"In the first case, the disability of the heir did not follow him to England, and the personal estate was distributed as if both the domicil and the real estate had been in England. In the second, the disability to claim exoneration out of the personalty did follow him into England, and the personal estate was distributed as if both the domicil and the real estate had been in Scotland."

In that case of *Brodie* v. *Barry*, Sir William Grant was of opinion that the will of the Scotch estates might be read against the heir at law; and the decree was, that the

heir must make her *election*.   In coming to this conclusion he appears to have considered that great weight was
due to the case of *Cunyngham* v. *Gainer*, in which a similar
doctrine had been laid down by Lord Hardwicke in the
Court of Chancery; and the doctrine of *approbate and
reprobate* had been applied between the same parties, by
the Court of Session in Scotland (*e*).

(*e*) This case of *Cunyngham* v. *Gainer*, in the Court of Chancery, is
fully stated in a note to the case of *Ker* v. *Wauchope*, 1 Bligh, p. 27.

The case between the same parties in Scotland is reported in Fol.
Dic. v. 3. p. 34., in Fac. Coll., 17th January, 1758, and in Morrison,
p. 617.   In that case the testator, by a will executed according to the
English forms only, devised a real estate in the Island of St. Christopher to his son; and a real estate in Scotland to his wife.   It was
found that the son, who took the estate in St. Christopher's by the
will, was barred from challenging the settlement of the Scotch estate,
made to the wife in the same instrument.

Three cases have also been decided in Scotland, upon points connected with the questions which arose in the case of *Brodie* v. *Barry ;*
but in these the heirs were not put to their election, but took the real
estates, and also the interests in the personal estates given to them by
the respective testators.   These were the cases of *Robertson* v. *Robertson* (Fac. Coll., 16th February, 1816).   *Trotters* v. *Trotters* (Fac. Coll.,
5th December, 1826, 3 Wilson and Shaw, 407., affirmed in the House
of Lords, 10th June, 1829); and *Murray* v. *Smith* (4th March, 1828,
6 Shaw and Dunlop, 690.).   In the two first cases, the wills had been
made in India by persons natives of Scotland, but domiciled in India.
In the last, the will was made in England by a person domiciled in that
country.   The testators in all these cases had heritable estates in Scotland.   In all of them, the instruments were not conceived according
to the forms of the law of that country, so as to carry heritable estate ;
and it was matter of ambiguity and discussion, whether the terms of
those instruments *imported*, that the testators meant to include their real
estates in Scotland, or otherwise.

The Court, considering that the wills were to be construed according
to the law of the domicils of the testators, in these cases, directed the
opinions of English counsel to be taken, for explaining the meaning and
import of the wills.   Counsel were of opinion, that the words did not
import devises of real estate. Accordingly, the decision in each of these
cases was, that the heir took the real estate in his own right, and also
his share of the personal estate under the will without collation.

But if the *import* of the words of the wills had been such as to have

In the case of *Robertson v. Macvean*, 18th Feb. 1817 (*f*), an important question was decided in the Court of Session, in regard to the heir, who took a real estate in Jamaica, claiming also a share of *legitim* in Scotland.

George Robertson, residing in Scotland, conveyed to his son and heir, James, all right that he had to a real estate in Jamaica. James, after his father's death, claimed a share of the personal succession of his father, in name of *legitim*. In this he was opposed by his sister Mrs. Macvean, who contended that he could take no part of the *legitim* without collating the real estate, whether situated in Scotland or elsewhere. There was some intricacy in regard to the title to the real estate in Jamaica, whether it came to James Robertson from George his father, or from his uncle James; but Mrs. Macvean restricted her claim to the collation of that part of the Jamaica estate which James took from his father George.

At first the Lord Ordinary decided, that " the Court of Session had no jurisdiction over the heritable estate in Jamaica, and that the heir was entitled to enjoy the estate in Jamaica, with all the privileges, and free from any burthen not imposed upon the heir in that country."

But on a reclaiming petition, the Court " altered the Lord Ordinary's interlocutor; found that James Robertson was not entitled to claim *legitim*, unless he collated such right as he had to the estate situated in the Island of Jamaica, as well as the other provisions and possessions received by him, as devolving upon him by the death of his father."

---

included real estate in Scotland, there appears no room to doubt, that the decision of these cases would have been the same as in the cases of *Cunyngham* v. *Gainer*, and *Brodie* v. *Barry*, to put the heir to his election.

(*f*) Fac. Coll.

The opinion of the Court as expressed in the report was, " that the heir could not claim a share of the moveables, without collating his right to the heritage. He lay under no compulsitor to take along with the *executors* (g); but if he chose to avail himself of this privilege, which may be regarded as a *prætorian* interposition to soften the rigour of the law, he must fulfil the condition annexed. There is no interference with the law of succession in a foreign country. Indeed this is not a question of succession at all; it is a question of right of parties *inter se.* The claimant comes forward, as a Scotch heir, to avail himself of a Scotch privilege, and to take something from the executors; and they are entitled to insist that equality shall be preserved, by throwing the heritage into the common fund. The petitioner has no more right to retain the Jamaica estate, and at the same time interfere with the executry, than a bankrupt, who claimed the benefit of the Scotch bankrupt law, could insist upon reserving free from his creditors heritable property which he happened to possess abroad." (h).

In the case of *Newland's Executors v. Chalmers' Trustees,* 22d November 1832 (i), questions occurred between the

---

(g) So the report terms them, meaning " next of kin."

(h) This case involves a very important point; it was not carried further. If the action had arisen in the courts of Jamaica, after the heir had received a share of the personal estate in Scotland, would the courts in Jamaica have ordered him to collate? It appears to be very questionable if they would. *Collation* appears to be introduced into the Scotch law, as between the Scotch heir and the Scotch next of kin. The foreign heir may, and must, have obligations unknown to the law of Scotland. It seems to differ in principle from the *Scotstarvet* case, and the case of *Drummond (supra,* pp. 203. 209). In the first of these cases the heir in Scotland took the English personal estate without collation; in the other the personal estate in England was held not to be liable for the debts due by the real estate in Scotland.

(i) Fac. Coll., 11 Shaw, Dunlop, and Bell, p. 65.

representatives of a wife and the trustees appointed by her husband, in regard to certain foreign bonds bearing interest, to which the wife had succeeded on the death of her brother, who died domiciled in Jamaica. The husband and wife were domiciled in Scotland; and, according to the law of Scotland, as between husband and wife, Scotch bonds bearing interest would have been deemed heritable, and would have formed no part of the goods in communion.

John Newland, a native of Scotland, died in Jamaica, leaving real and personal estates of considerable value in that island, where he had long been domiciled. He left a will indistinctly expressed, naming trustees for endowing a free school in the parish of Bathgate in Scotland. He was succeeded by his nephew Patrick Newland his heir at law, and Margaret Newland his sister and next of kin. The will became the subject of a suit, first in the Court of Chancery in Jamaica, and afterwards, by appeal, in the Privy Council. In 1815, it was finally adjudged by the Privy Council that the whole estate, for a period of ten years, belonged to the trustees for the purposes of the charity; " and that, so subject, the real estate has descended to the said Patrick Newland, heir at law of the testator; and the personal estate belongs to the said Margaret Newland, as the sole next of kin of the said testator John Newland at the time of his death."

Margaret Newland was married in Scotland to John Chalmers, butcher in Alloa; and powers of attorney were granted by them to persons in Jamaica, to recover and remit to Great Britain that portion of the succession which had been found to belong to her. Considerable remittances were made, and ultimately invested in the names of trustees appointed in a post-nuptial contract, executed by Chalmers and his wife, but which was afterwards set aside on the head of facility on the part of the husband. No part of the remittances was ever received by Chalmers or his wife, except some small annuities paid to them by their trustees.

Margaret and her husband died without issue in Scotland, where they had constantly resided, the former in 1818, the latter in 1826.

Thereafter John Newland's personal property, to which his sister had succeeded, became the subject of competition between her nearest of kin, and certain trust disponees of her husband; the former claiming, besides her share of the goods in communion at the dissolution of the marriage, an exclusive right to the bonds bearing interest, and to certain securities termed *island certificates*, and *island paper*, of which John Newland's personal estate in Jamaica in part consisted; and the latter claiming the whole of that personal estate, including these securities, as having passed to the husband by the law of England.

By the direction of the Lord Ordinary, English counsel were consulted on these three points:—1. Whether bonds bearing interest, island certificates, and island paper, of the island of Jamaica, are to be held, according to the law of England, as having, on the opening of the succession to Margaret Newland, fallen under the marital rights of John Chalmers? 2. Whether, if they did not at first, they ultimately, by the law of England, fell under such rights, in consequence of the proceedings in Jamaica, and the remitting the money to this country under the powers of attorney granted by Chalmers and his wife? 3. Whether, on the death of Margaret Newland (domiciled at the time in Scotland), her representatives would by the law of England have been entitled to succeed to the funds above specified, or to any of them, independently of the marital rights of Chalmers?

To these questions the counsel (*k*) answered,—" The

(*k*) Messrs. Bickersteth and Burge.

law of England, in relation to the right of the wife by survivorship to her *choses in action*, not reduced into possession by her husband, has no application to this case, because the husband survived the wife. By the law of England the husband is entitled to letters of administration of the wife's personal estate, and (in the absence of any settlement or trust affecting his right) to receive the whole of his wife's personal estate for his own benefit. If he died without having possessed the whole of her personal estate, and without taking out letters of administration, his personal representative is nevertheless entitled to the whole of her personal estate remaining unrecovered; and if her next of kin should obtain administration of her personal estate, and thereupon, as her legal representatives, collect her outstanding personal estate, they would hold it only as trustees for her husband's personal representative. 1. With reference to the facts of this case we are of opinion, that the particulars enumerated, viz. bonds bearing interest, island certificates, and island paper, are to be held, according to the law of England, as having, on the opening of the succession to Margaret Newland, fallen under the marital rights of John Chalmers. 2. It is immaterial, in any question betwixt the representatives of the husband and the next of kin of the wife, whether the personal estate of the husband was actually received by the husband in his lifetime or not. 3. The property in question having come to the wife by the intestacy of her brother, and not being affected by any settlement or trust, cannot be considered independently of the right of the husband surviving her. We are therefore of opinion, that, on the death of Margaret Newland (*domiciled in Scotland*), *her next of kin were not entitled to succeed to the funds above specified, or any of them.*"

The Lord Ordinary pronounced this interlocutor :—
" Having heard parties procurators as to the goods in

communion, finds that bonds bearing interest, island certificates, and island paper, fall to be reckoned as part of
the goods in communion, and that the fund *in medio*, including these bonds, certificates, and paper, fell under the
jus mariti of the now deceased John Chalmers, the husband of the said Margaret Newland or Chalmers, also deceased: finds the trustees of the said John Newland entitled to be ranked on the said fund *in medio, quoad* one
half of the goods in communion accordingly, and decerns;
sustains the decree-dative of date the 15th day of January
1830, in favour of William Newland (and others), cousins
and executors *qua* nearest in kin of the said deceased Margaret Newland: finds them entitled in virtue thereof to be
ranked on the said fund *quoad* the other half of the said
goods in communion accordingly; and decerns in the preference, and for payment accordingly."

This interlocutor was submitted to review, but it was
unanimously adhered to by the Court (Second Division).

Apparently this decision was given upon principles more
sound than those suggested in the conclusion of the opinion of the English counsel.   They had not been aware of
the doctrines of the law of Scotland, in regard to the right
of succession to the goods in communion on the death of a
husband and wife.   The question, whether the funds *in
medio* were to be considered as heritable or moveable, belonged to the *lex loci rei sitæ*.   As by that law they appeared to be clearly moveable, they were then to be dealt
with as moveable estate, to which Margaret Newland had
succeeded by her brother's death, and which had fallen
under the *communion* of goods between Chalmers and her.
According to the law of Scotland, one half of the goods
in communion devolved to the next of kin of Margaret
Newland, upon the event of her death.   Some question
appears to have been made as to whether she succeeded

to the property before or after her marriage. This was not distinctly ascertained, but it seems to be immaterial.

Another case upon this subject was also recently decided in the Court of Session and in the House of Lords, *Dundas* v. *Dundas* and others, 14th January 1829, House of Lords, 22d December 1830. (*l*)   In this case General Francis Dundas, domiciled in Scotland, by a *mortis causâ* instrument, executed in the Scotch form, and before two witnesses conveyed all his property, heritable and moveable, real and personal, including a freehold estate known by the name of *Sansonseal,* lying within the liberties of Berwick-upon-Tweed, subject to the law of England, to trustees, to be sold and converted into money; and, after paying an annuity of 800*l.* to his widow, the proceeds were to be distributed equally among his children. His whole property was valued at 51,000*l., Sansonseal* being valued at 14,000*l.*

His children were minors. On behalf of the heir a claim was made that he was entitled to take the estate of *Sansonseal* in his own right, and also his share of the trust estate, which had been duly conveyed to the trustees by the instrument in the Scotch form; and proceedings were had in Scotland to have this question tried in a multiple-poinding raised by the trustees for that purpose.

The Court decided, that if the heir should " ultimately take the estate situated in England, without surrendering the same to the purposes of the trust, he could not be entitled to claim under the trust deed any share of the heritable and moveable estates in Scotland thereby conveyed to the trustees." On an appeal to the House of Lords their Lordships simply affirmed the judgment.

Apparently this decision was given upon the same principles as those in the case of *Brodie* v. *Barry,* and the

---

(*l*) Fac. Coll., 7 Shaw and Dunlop, 241.; 4 Wilson and Shaw 460.

other cases of the same class. The words of the instrument interpreted, according to the law of Scotland, where the testator had his domicil, *clearly imported* that he meant to give his whole property to the same uses. As the heir could not both *approbate* and *reprobate* these, he was put to his election.

They thus avoided the great subtlety that attaches to that branch of the law of England which regards the devises by will of freehold estate in that country, which are not to be read against the heir unless attested according to the *statute of frauds (m)*.

A decision of similar import was come to in the case of *Bennett* v. *Bennett's trustees* (Fac. Coll. and Shaw and Dunlop 1st July 1829), in regard to an estate in the Isle of Man. John Bennett a Scotchman, then domiciled in Scotland in 1821, executed a trust disposition, and settlement, of his whole lands, heritages, heritable bonds, tacks, debts, and sums of money, belonging or owing to him, *or which should belong and be owing to him at the time of his death*, for certain purposes and *inter alia* for payment of a life-rent provision to his wife, in the event of her surviving him; it being declared that this provision should be in full of all that she could ask or claim from his estate, or by his death.

Shortly after this Bennett went to the Isle of Man, where he purchased a small landed estate, and died there in 1824.

Mrs. Bennett, his widow, claimed one half of this estate in the Isle of Man, as belonging to a widow by the law of that island, and also her annuity under the Scotch disposition or settlement: but the Court of Session held, that she could not claim the annuity unless she approbated the trust deed by consenting to pay over to the trustees, for

---

(*m*) *Habergham* v. *Vincent*, 2 Ves. 204., and the cases there cited.

the purposes of the trust, the property in the Isle of Man falling to her by the law of that island.

It does not appear from the report of this case, whether the deceased had his domicil in the Isle of Man or in Scotland at the time of his death; nor whether the law of that island has the same rule in regard to a will of *acquirenda* in real estate as obtains in England, where it would be entirely inoperative. The court construed the instrument according to its import and effect in the law of Scotland. (n)

SECT. III.

On the Rules of International Law regarding Bankruptcy.

The rules of international law which obtain in regard to the succession in personal estate, are so clearly and firmly

---

(n) In the case of *Anstruther* v. *Chalmer* (ante, p. 189.), Sir John Leach held, that a settlement made in Scotland was to be construed by the law of the domicil: perhaps the above case of Bennett was too little sifted upon this subject, though it was decided on equitable grounds.

It would be out of place here to enter into that class of cases, by which it appears now to be fixed, that when a trust disposition in the forms of the Scotch law has been executed of heritable estate in Scotland, for purposes to be afterwards declared, these purposes may be declared by an English will, or other instrument not tested according to the forms of the law of Scotland. It was so held in the case of *Willocks* v. *Auckterlony* (Morrison, 5539.); affirmed in the House of Lords, 14th December, 1769, in the case of *Brack* v. *Hogg* (Fac. Coll., 23d November, 1827, Shaw and Dunlop), affirmed in the House of Lords, 25th February, 1831, and in the case of *Ker* v. *Lady Essex Ker's Trustees*, 24th February, 1829 (Fac. Coll., and Shaw and Dunlop), affirmed in the House of Lords, 1st October, 1831; and in the case of *Cameron and others* v. *Mackie*, 19th May, 1831, (Fac. Coll., and Shaw and Dunlop), affirmed in the House of Lords, 29th August, 1833. These cases relate to *heritable* estate only, and do not belong to the objects of the present treatise. Apparently they have now fixed a very important point of international law upon grounds at least convenient to the community, if not entirely consonant to these strict principles which apply to real estate, and require that it shall be entirely governed by the *lex loci rei sitæ*.

established in the cases which we have already stated, that it is almost unnecessary to adduce in support of them, any thing that has been done or decided in regard to other branches of the law.

But in one of these, regarding *bankruptcy*, the British Courts have proceeded upon grounds so closely connected with those which regulate in matters of personal succession, that it would be improper to pass it over in silence, though to enter into it at large would open a field too extensive for our present views. A long class of cases has now been decided in the British courts, in questions of international law respecting bankruptcy, in which it has been clearly recognised and laid down, that personal estate has no *situs;* and that it follows the law of the domicil of the owner; but that real estate follows the law of the country in which it is situated.

The law of bankruptcy in England had its origin in an act of Parliament in the reign of Henry VIII. (*o*), and has undergone numerous modifications by different statutes, passed from time to time down to the present day, and some of these at a very recent period. (*p*)

The bankrupt laws were unknown in Ireland till a period comparatively recent. By an Act of the Parliament of Ireland, in the 11th and 12th of George III. (*q*), they were introduced into that country, by adopting, with some variations, the provisions of the acts in regard to bankruptcy which had up to that time been passed, and were then in force in England: thus the laws in regard to bankruptcy were established nearly upon the same footing in the two countries. The first-mentioned act has been altered and new rules and provisions have been introduced in

---

(*o*) 34 & 35 Hen. 8. c. 5.
(*p*) 6 Geo. 4. c. 16.; 1 & 2 W. 4. c. 56.
(*q*) 11 & 12 Geo. 3. c. 8. Irish statute.

different statutes of the Irish Parliament, down to the period of the Irish union; and of the United Kingdom, since that period. It would also be foreign to our present purpose to examine in what respects the bankrupt laws in Ireland concur with those in England, and in what those laws differ at the present day.

In Scotland there are two different kinds of bankruptcy; one under the act of the Scottish Parliament of 1696 (r), which extends to persons of every description, whether traders or not; the other under those statutes by which *sequestration* of the estate and effects is awarded against persons in trade, and the other descriptions of persons therein pointed out. Under the first species of bankruptcy all deeds of preference granted by the bankrupt " either " at, or after his becoming bankrupt, or in the space of sixty " days of before, in favour of his creditor, either for his " satisfaction or further security in preference to other " creditors," are declared to be null and void. But no general conveyance is directed to be made for the benefit of creditors, and this species of bankruptcy is of no effect or operation out of Scotland.

It is only to the other species of bankruptcy, namely that under the statutes for awarding sequestration, that the rules of international bankruptcy apply. The first of these statutes in regard to Scotland was passed in 1772 (s), which has been continued from time to time, with various alterations and improvements to the present time; thus the law of Scotland in regard to the sequestration of the estates of bankrupts, is also of very recent origin. (t)

There are several particulars, in which bankruptcy in England and in Ireland differs from a sequestration under the statutes in Scotland; but they are clearly held by all

---

(r) 1696. c. 5.　　　　　　　　(s) 12 Geo. 3. c. 73.

(t) The laws in regard to Bankruptcy were introduced into Ireland and into Scotland, nearly at the same period.

the British Courts to coincide in this, that a commission of bankrupt in England, or in Ireland, or a sequestration in Scotland, with the assignments and conveyances respectively following upon these, have the effect of transferring to the assignees, or to the trustee, the whole personal estate of the bankrupt, and of defeating all preferences attempted to be obtained by the diligence of the law of the country where the property happens to be placed, or by any voluntary conveyance of the bankrupt, after the period when the effect of the proceedings under the bankruptcy attaches to the funds. (u)

Towards the beginning of the last century, it appears that questions of international law respecting bankruptcy had attracted attention in England. Several of the most celebrated English lawyers at that time having been consulted as to the international effects of a bankruptcy in England and in Holland, appear to have been of opinion, than an English commission of bankrupt would carry the effects of the bankrupt wherever situated; but that the law of England paid no attention to a bankruptcy in Holland, and that such bankruptcy would not protect the effects of the Dutch bankrupt from any attaching creditor in England (x); and Lord Talbot, when at the bar, appears to have given a similar opinion in 1723, that the statutes of bankruptcy did not extend to the plantations, but that the personal property of an English bankrupt in the plantations passed to the assignees. (y)

(u) 2 Bell's Comment., 682.

(x) These opinions, including those of Lord Raymond, and Sir Joseph Jekyll when at the Bar, are given in Henry's Demerara Case, Appendix D., from a Dutch work, *Barel's Advysen over den Koophandel and Zeevaart*, vol. ii. p. 291.

(y) Beawe's Lex Mercat. 543. Thus at this period the English lawyers did not admit the *comity*, that a foreign bankruptcy carried effects in England, as was claimed for an English bankruptcy in foreign countries.

The first case of international law regarding bankruptcy which appears to have attracted attention in the courts, was that which arose out of the bankruptcy of Captain *Wilson*, a banker and agent in London, who had personal property also in Scotland. In that case the import and effect of an English bankruptcy came to be considered in both countries, in the Court of Chancery (in the time of Lord Hardwicke) in England, and in the Court of Session in Scotland. What was done in the Court of Chancery does not very distinctly appear. Three different sets of creditors claimed under this bankruptcy, one who had assignments of debts in Scotland due to *Wilson*, executed and duly intimated before the bankruptcy; another, who had such assignments executed, but not intimated before the bankruptcy; and a third set, who had arrested debts due to the bankrupt in Scotland after the bankruptcy. Lord Hardwicke appears to have given preference to the first and second classes as to mortgagees; but he decided, that if they claimed under the commission, they must account for what they received under their assignments; and he preferred the assignees under the commission to the arresting creditors. His Lordship appears to have been of opinion, that the bankruptcy carried the property in Scotland to the assignees, in so far as this was not subject to prior remembrances at the time of the bankruptcy. (z)

The same question appears to have been much considered in the Court of Session in Scotland under the same bankruptcy. (a) The decisions upon all the points do not very distinctly appear in the Reports. Lord Loughborough (in the case of *Sill* v. *Worswick*, to be afterwards men-

---

(z) 1 H. Black. 691.

(a) Fac. Coll., 1st Feb. 1755. This appears in the report of only one decision, but the cause appears to have been in court and discussed from 1754 downwards till 1758. 5 Brown's Supp. 280. 821. 988.

tioned), states that " the determination of Lord Hard-
" wicke and that of the Court of Session entirely con-
" curred." It appears to be doubtful if they concurred on
all the points decided in the two countries. We see*
from the Report in the Faculty Collection, that " the
" Court of Session preferred the assignees under the com-
" mission of bankruptcy *with respect to the English debts,*
" *that is to the debts contracted in the English form,* or pay-
" *able in England."* They also, according to Lord Monboddo's note, " preferred the voluntary assignees (which
" were prior in date to the bankruptcy, but not intimated)
" upon seeing the opinion of English lawyers." (*b*)

(*b*) This decision does not seem to have given satisfaction at the
time to that distinguished lawyer, Lord Kilkerran; nor to Lord Monboddo. Lord Kilkerran's notes on this case are given in 5 Brown's
Supp. 283. He appears to have held the opinion, " that the preference
" of creditors was to be determined, not by the laws of the country
" where the creditor had his residence, but by the laws of the country
" *ubi res fuit sita,* be they *mobilia* or *immobilia,* and that in this respect
" there was no difference of opinion between *nomina* and other *mobilia,*
" as by all the lawyers who have wrote on this subject, these *loco mo-*
" *bilium habentur;* and that the brocard *mobilia non habent sequelam* is
" an abstract notion, not founded in reason, nor in the nature of the
" thing."

He considered that it was almost ridiculous to talk of *comitas* in this
case, that there could be no *comitas* where it was not mutual, and that
the English allowed no such *comitas* to us. He adds, " if any man
" should argue in any of the courts in England for a preference by a
" judgment in Scotland, on effects in England, he would be laughed at;
" and really I can hardly keep my countenance when I see and hear it
" pled, that we should show them a good example."

In the argument as given by Lord Monboddo (5 Brown's Sup.,
p. 821.), it is stated, " that the maxim that *mobilia non habent situm* is
" only founded upon the authority of *some Dutch doctors,* and takes
" place no where else, except among the little states of Holland, which
" are so much mixed and interwoven one with another; but did never
" take place in separate and distinct states, such as France and Holland,
" France and Britain, or even England and Scotland, which are as
" much distinct, as to their laws and jurisdictions, as any two kingdoms
" in Europe: that this law does not hold even with respect to succes-

This case is curious, as showing the opinions of distinguished persons in both countries upon the state of the law connected, as well with succession as with bankruptcy at that period.   Already that eminent man Lord Hardwicke appears to have matured those doctrines, which in more recent times have obtained universal assent in the British courts; while Lord Kilkerran and Lord Monboddo appear to have considered, that even if the courts of Scotland decided upon enlarged views upon this subject, it was in vain to expect a reciprocity of decision in England.   That they were mistaken upon this subject, has been made apparent by the judgments which have since been given thereon in the English and Irish courts. (c)

It is not necessary here to do more than give a short sketch of these.   The first was the case of *Neale and Others*, assignees of Grattan, an English bankrupt v. *Cottingham*, who had attached effects of the bankrupt in Ireland. (d) Upon a bill filed by the assignees in the Court of Chancery in Ireland, to recover the property from the attaching creditor, Lord Lifford called in the assistance of several of the Judges; and, after great consideration in 1764, he pronounced a decree in favour of the plaintiffs, the assignees.

The same thing was done in the Court of Chancery in England, in regard to two cases of Dutch bankruptcy, *Solomons* v. *Ross*, before Mr. Justice Bathurst, sitting for

---

" sion; *and a man dying intestate has as many separate heirs as he has*
" *estates in different countries;* and so it was decided in this country in
" the case of *Duncan.*"

(c) It is to be remarked, that there was then no law in Scotland for the sequestration of the effects of a bankrupt, this having been first introduced in 1772, by the act of 12 G. 3. c. 72.   Thus, when the discussions took place in Wilson's case, the creditor in Scotland took nothing under which he could make a reciprocal claim against an attachment in England.

(d) 1 H. Black. 131., note to *Folliott* v. *Ogden*. It is to be remarked that at this period the bankrupt law had not been introduced into Ireland.

Lord Northington, in 1764, and *Jollet* v. *Deponthieu,* before Lord Camden, in 1769. (*e*) In both of these cases, creditors of the bankrupts had, after the bankruptcy in Holland, attached effects of the bankrupts in London; but *the curators of the desolate estates* in Holland having filed bills in the Court of Chancery in England against the attaching creditors, were preferred to them in regard to the funds which had been thus attached. (*f*)

Next came these well-known cases in England, of *Hunter* v. *Potts,* before Lord Kenyon, in the King's Bench, in 1791 (*g*) ; of *Sill* v. *Worswick,* before Lord Loughborough, in the Common Pleas, in the same year (*h*); and of *Phillips and others* v. *Hunter and others,* before Lord Kenyon, in the King's Bench, in 1795. (*i*) In all of those cases

---

(*e*) Ibid.

(*f*) At one time there appears to have been some uncertainty as to the rules of decision in England in questions of this nature. In the case of *Waring* v. *Knight,* before Lord Mansfield, in 1765 (Cooke's Bankrupt Law, 325.), his Lordship is said to have held the opinion, that the assignees of a bankrupt could not recover against a creditor of the bankrupt who after the bankruptcy had attached the effects of the bankrupt abroad, and thereby received payment of his debt; but in *Ballantine* v. *Golding* (Cook, 520.), his Lordship afterwards held, that a bankrupt who had obtained his certificate in Ireland could not be sued in England for debts incurred by him in Ireland previous to the bankruptcy.

It does not appear that the Court of Chancery, in the cases of Solomons v. Ross, and Jollet v. Deponthieu, made any inquiry whether the courts in Holland would have exercised similar *comity* in favour of assignees under an English bankruptcy, if arrestments had been laid in Holland on the effects of an English bankrupt. In the case of Wilson, the lawyers in Scotland appeared to have considered, that a comity of this kind should be reciprocal.

(*g*) 4 Term. Rep., 182.

(*h*) 1 H. Black., 665.

(*i*) 2 H. Black., 402. 405. 409. The last case was affirmed in the Court of Exchequer Chamber, Chief Justice Eyre alone dissenting. His difficulties appear to be important; he considered that we might thus be putting the foreign creditor into a better position than our own subjects; and he thought that inquiry should be made what the *comity of the* foreign country would have done in such case.

it was decided, that where creditors had, after the date of
the bankruptcy, attached the effects of the bankrupt
abroad, and had recovered and remitted the proceeds to
England, the assignees of the bankrupts were entitled to
receive back the value of those effects as against the
attaching creditors. In all of them the elaborate arguments of counsel, and the opinions of the judges, enter
fully also into the doctrines of international law in regard
to succession. In every one of them it is distinctly laid
down, that personal property followed the law of the domicil; and that real estate was governed by the *lex loci rei
sitæ*.

An important case next occurred in Scotland upon this
branch of the law, which was at last decided upon principles
which have now been universally recognised in both countries. Since the case of the creditors of Wilson had been decided by the Court of Session, as already noticed(*k*), several
cases had occurred in that Court, which (as a distinguished
writer observes) " exhibited a very distressing versatility
of opinion."(*l*)   But when the decisions had been given in
Bruce v. *Bruce*, *Hog* v. *Lashley and others*, establishing
that moveables had no *situs*, and that cases of succession
were to be regulated by the law of the domicil, the Court of
Session applied a similar rule of decision in cases of bankruptcy. Thus in the case of *Strothers* v. *Reid*(*m*), the Court
of Session pronounced a decision similar to those which had

(*k*) Supra, p. 232.

(*l*) 2 Bell's Commentaries, p. 683. He instances the following as of
this nature, among others : — *Thomson* v. *Tabor*, 1762 (Morrison,
4561.); *Pewtress* v. *Thorold*, 1768 (Ibid.) ; *Parish* v. *Rhones*, 1775, and
Vasie v. *Glover*, 1776 (5 Brown's Sup., 451.). Of these cases it is to
be remarked, that only the two last occurred after bankruptcy by sequestration had been introduced into Scotland ; and these were both decided
upon the principles now recognised in the British courts.

(*m*) Fac. Coll., 1st July, 1803. Morrison, *Forum Competens*, App. 4.

already been given in the above mentioned cases of *Neale* v. *Cottingham*, *Hunter* v. *Potts*, *Sill* v. *Worswick*, and *Phillips* v. *Hunter*, in the English courts. In the case of *Strothers* v. *Reid*, the English creditor of an English bankrupt Company had arrested some of their effects in Scotland, after the commission of bankrupt had been issued, and the assignment executed. Upon an action brought by the assignees against the arresting creditors, the Court of Session preferred the assignees; and though this only involved the case of an English creditor, it is mentioned in the report, that the Court by a great majority proceeded on the general ground, that the bankruptcy carried to the assignees all the effects of the bankrupt wherever situated.

This case was in bankruptcy in Scotland nearly what the case of *Bruce* v. *Bruce* was in personal succession. It fixed upon a certain basis the principles, which were to be acted upon in cases of this nature, and which have since been repeatedly recognised in similar cases, which have attracted general attention in both countries.

In the case of *Potter* v. *Brown* before Lord Ellenborough, in the Court of King's Bench, in 1804 (*n*), it was found, that a person who had become bankrupt in America, and had obtained his certificate in Maryland, and who had afterwards come to England, could not be sued in the latter country, for a bill which he had drawn in America before his bankruptcy upon a house in England, and which had been refused acceptance, and had gone back to America. (*o*)

(*n*) 5 East's T. R., 124.

(*o*) The Court of Session appears to have come to an opposite conclusion upon this subject, in the case of *Armour* v. *Campbell* (Fac. Coll. 21st January, 1792.) Campbell, settled at New York, drew a bill in favour of Armour, also settled there, upon Campbell's father in Greenock. This bill was not accepted. Soon after Campbell became bankrupt at New York, and received his discharge. Being afterwards sued

In the case of *Maitland* v. *Hoffman,* 4th of March, 1807 (*p*), it was decided in the Court of Session, that the assignees of an American bankrupt were preferable to a Scotch creditor arresting in Scotland, where the creditor had used arrestment after the date of the commission, but before the date of the assignment. In that case, the commission was issued on the 2d of February, 1802; the party was declared bankrupt on the 5th of February, and the assignment to Hoffman the assignee was executed on the 2d of March. In the mean time the arrestment had been used in Scotland on the 24th of February.

In the case of *The Creditors of Fairholme* v. *The Assignees* under the English commission against *Samuel Garbett* (*q*), the question formerly decided in the case of *Strothers* v. *Reid,* in regard to an arrestment in Scotland by an English creditor was again tried in regard to an arrestment by a Scotch creditor; and the Court of Session found, that the assignees of the bankrupt were to be preferred also to a Scotch creditor, who had arrested in Scotland after the date of the commission; they approved of the decision in

---

upon this bill in Scotland, to which country he had removed, he brought a suspension on the ground of his bankruptcy and certificate at New York; the Lord Ordinary sustained the reasons of suspension, but the Court altered this interlocutor, and " found that the statutory dis- " charge obtained at New York cannot bar the charger from recovering " the sums due to him in this country by the ordinary diligence of the " law of Scotland." I do not see this case mentioned in Bell's Commentaries; but it is important, though contrary to the principles laid down in modern cases.

(*p*) Fac. Coll. Another case of the same kind was decided on the same day, *Morrison's assignees* v. *Watt.* It does not appear to have been doubted in these cases that there would have been an entire reciprocity of decision in the American courts if the case had occurred in them; but vide *infra,* p. 244.

(*q*) 2 Dow 330.; 2 Rose's Bank. Cases, 291. It is singular that this very important case was not reported in Scotland.

Strothers's case, and held that the assignees were to be preferred to the Scotch arresting creditor. The judgment was affirmed upon an appeal to the House of Lords.

In the case of *the Royal Bank of Scotland* v. *Scott, Smith, Stein and Co.* 20th January 1813 (r), commonly called *Stein*'s case, a question occurred in regard to conflicting bankruptcies in the two countries, which should be preferred. Thomas Smith, John Stein, James Stein, Robert Stein, Robert Smith, and William Scott were Bankers and Insurance Brokers in Edinburgh, under the firm of Scott, Smith, Stein and Co. The same parties carried on business in London, under the firm of Stein, Smith, and Co.

The Scottish firm became insolvent in July 1812; the English house was also insolvent. On the 11th of August 1812, a Commission of Bankrupt was issued against the English house. A provisional assignment was executed by the Commissioners on the same day. On the 1st of September assignees were named. On the same day deeds in the English form, and on the 7th and 8th deeds in the Scotch form were executed, making over the whole property of the bankrupt, heritable and moveable, in Scotland, to the assignees. In the mean time the Royal Bank of Scotland had used diligence against the Scotch house: on the 28th of August 1812, they were rendered bankrupt in Scotland; and on the 29th of August, the bank presented a petition to the Lord Ordinary on the bills, praying in common form for a sequestration of all the estates of the Company, and of the Partners as individuals, wherever situated.

The English assignees appeared and opposed the sequestration in Scotland. The question was, whether or not the

---

(r) Fac. Coll. Buchanan's Cases, 320.; 1 Rose's Bank. Cases, 462. Appendix.

English Commission stopped the proceeding in the Scotch sequestration; and the Court decided that it was not competent to award a sequestration under the bankrupt statutes in Scotland, after a Commission of Bankrupt had been issued in England.

In a case of the same date (s), between the *Royal Bank of Scotland,* and *Scott, Smith, Stein and Co.,* it was decided that a bill drawn by a creditor in Scotland, and accepted by the bankrupts in London, was an English debt; but it was held, on the general question, that a certificate under a Commission of Bankrupt, operated as a discharge of all claims, though the creditor was resident and domiciled in Scotland.

In the case of *Odwin and the Orphan Chamber* of the Colonies of Demerara and Essequibo, v. *Forbes,* 10th of May, 1814, affirmed on appeal at the Cockpit, 31st of May 1817, (t) similar doctrines were recognised. Odwin and his partner Schweitzer, settled at Demerara, shipped produce from thence to Turnbull, Forbes and Co. of London; and on the strength of such shipments drew bills on that house payable in London. All those bills were accepted except two; but Turnbull, Forbes and Co. becoming bankrupt, all the bills were dishonoured. Forbes having gone out to Demerara, was sued in that Colony for payment of these bills. Previous to this action, the defendant and his partners took two several objections to the action; the first of *tibi adversus me non competit hæc actio,* contending that the certificate obtained in England was a legal and equitable bar to the action; the other of *incompetency and renvoi,* by which the competency of the Court in Demerara

---

(s) Fac. Coll., 20th January, 1813.

(t) Reported by Mr. Henry, the presiding judge. This report and the treatise annexed to it, contain much curious information heretofore almost unknown to the British lawyer.

to entertain the suit, after the certificate and discharge obtained in England, was denied.

The judgment of the Court (affirmed on appeal) was to admit the exception of *tibi adversus me non competit hæc actio;* but to reject the exception of *incompetency* and *renvoi.*

It would be out of place here to enter into the great variety of questions which have arisen in the two countries, on the subject of international law as applied to bankruptcy. It may be remarked, however, that the *retrospective* consequences of a commission, and of a sequestration, are not held to be of equal effect in the two countries; and that there is not an entire reciprocity in both, in regard to such consequences.

Thus in the case of *Hunter and Company* v. *Palmer and Wilson,* in the Court of Session, on the 25th of February 1825 (*u*), a question was decided, in some degree militating against the law of the domicil. By the English law, prior to the 49th Geo. 3. c. 121. (commonly known as Sir Samuel Romilly's act), a commission of bankrupt had a retrospective effect, so as to cut down all diligences against the bankrupt's estate, subsequent to any act of bankruptcy, however secretly committed. By that statute it was enacted, that all executions or attachments, at the instance of creditors, executed more than two months before the issuing of a commission of bankrupt, should be valid and effectual, provided the creditor was not in the knowledge of any prior act of bankruptcy committed by the bankrupt. But it was expressly provided in the act, that it should not extend to Scotland.

A commission of bankrupt was issued against Forster, a merchant in Berwick-upon-Tweed, on the 8th of July 1819; the assignment was made on the 13th of August thereafter.

_____

(*u*) Fac. Coll.; 3 Shaw and Dunlop, 586.

R

It was alleged that, in February preceding, he had committed certain secret acts of bankruptcy; that he had become notoriously insolvent on the 29th of April, and that on the 6th of June he had granted an assignment of all his effects to certain persons for the benefit of his creditors.

On the 3d, 5th, 6th, 8th, and 13th of May in that year, Hunter and Company, merchants in Greenock, used arrestments in the hands of Messrs. Galloway, of Glasgow, and others, debtors of the bankrupt *ad fundandam jurisdictionem;* and, on the 8th of July, the day on which the commission bore date, they obtained decree in their favour in the Court of Admiralty in Scotland. The arrestees having brought a multiplepoinding in that court, the arresting creditors, and the assignees of the bankrupt, appeared for their respective interests. The assignees pleaded that the law of the domicil was to regulate, and that the commission should have the same retrospective effects in Scotland that it would have in England; and consequently that the arrestments used on and subsequently to the 8th of May, being two months before the date of the commission (the bankrupt having committed prior acts of bankruptcy), were null by the statute. The arrestees pleaded that the courts in Scotland had gone as far as *comity* required; but that it would be giving bankruptcy too large an effect, to give it a retrospect in Scotland: that the act in question did not extend to Scotland, and that thus the case would be thrown into the law of England, as it was before the statute, if the assignees were well founded in their claims. The Judge Admiral found, " That all the arrestments founded on, which " were executed against the moveable estate of Forster in " Scotland, prior to the 8th of May, are effectual, unless " evidence shall be brought of acts of bankruptcy having " been committed by Forster prior to the said 8th of May, " and that the creditors were in the knowledge of these " acts of bankruptcy, or knew that the bankrupt was in-

" solvent, or had stopped payment ; and, *e contrario*, that
" all arrestments executed upon the said 8th of May, and
" subsequent, are struck at, not merely by the commission
" of bankrupt, but by all acts of bankruptcy committed
" prior to the date thereof."

But upon bills of advocation presented to the Court of
Session by the arresting creditors, the Lord Eldin Ordinary
remitted to the Judge Admiral to recall the interlocutors
against the arresters, " and to find that the arrestments
" were not affected by the Commission of Bankrupt, and
" to prefer the complainers to the fund *in medio :*" (x) and
on a reclaiming petition the Court unanimously adhered to
the Lord Ordinary's interlocutor.

This is a case of considerable intricacy ; the exclusion of
Scotland from the operation of the Act of Parliament was
considered to be of importance. It evidently superseded
the law of the domicil. Lord Glenlee's opinion upon this
subject is highly worthy of notice. He says, " It is no
" doubt an indisputed point of international law, that
" moveable property in Scotland, belonging to a bank-
" rupt in England, is transferred by an English Com-
" mission of Bankrupt; but to give the Commission the
" effect here contended for, would be more than any
" international principle of *comity* requires. International
" law means international justice; but supposing that,
" by the law of a foreign country, *the natives should be*
" *preferable to all creditors, inhabitants of other countries,*
" it certainly would not be incumbent on our courts to
" give effect to such a law, because it would not be inter-
" national justice to do so. The present case is something
" similar. The English law says, all diligences are
" voided by a prior Act of Bankruptcy. This rule is, how-

(x) Yet some of the arrestments were subsequent to the date of the
Commission.

" ever, restricted by the statute as to English diligences,
" if not executed within two months of the Commission.
" But Scotland is excluded by this Act, so that English
" creditors would be on a more favourable footing than
" Scotch creditors; and, consequently, to give effect to this,
" would not be international justice. Besides, it would
" appear, that it was the understanding of the legislature,
" that the retrospective effects of a Commission of Bank-
" ruptcy could not operate in Scotland, and that it was in
" consequence of this understanding that the above statute
" was declared not to apply to Scotland, as being unneces-
" sary there."

Some of these observations of Lord Glenlee appear to
be very important in regard to the law upon this subject.
The rules which the Courts have adopted in questions of
this nature, have been founded upon the principles, which,
it is understood, should regulate the *comity* of nations; but
if any country chooses to adopt different views upon this
subject, and if those shall be sanctioned by a long train of
decisions in their courts of law, shall we persist in observing
towards that country the same course of decision, or shall
we make an exception in regard to such nation? This is
an important question in international law.

It is understood, that, in the American states, the nation,
next to our own, the most commercial now in existence,
though there be a difference of opinion among the lawyers
of that country, as to the effects of international law regarding bankruptcy, and though there are decisions of
weight in favour of the more liberal system, the prepon-
derating authority now is, that the creditor attaching the
goods of a foreign bankrupt in America, is to be preferred
to the foreign assignee. (y)   It appears, however, to be ad-

(y) In Dr. Story's Commentaries on the Conflict of Laws (346.), the
arguments on both sides on this important subject, are stated and
weighed.

In Kent's Commentaries on American Law, that distinguished per-

·mitted in most of the cases in which assignments under foreign bankrupt laws have been denied to give a title against attaching creditors, that the foreign assignees might maintain suits in America for the property of the bankrupt. (*x*)

It is understood that the practice of Holland and of France, in questions of this nature, is similar to our own (*a*), and that equal comity upon this subject prevails in those

---

son clearly lays down, that the weight of American authority is in direct opposition to the doctrines recognised in the British courts upon this subject. His own opinion had been otherwise.

In Lect. 37. vol. ii. p. 406., after stating the case of Holmes *v*. Remsen (4 Johnson's Chancery Rep. 460.), by which the assignees of a bankrupt, being first appointed in England, were held prior in point of right, and passed a debt in the state of New York to the English assignees of the Bankrupt, in bar of a claim by the trustees under the Absconding Act of that state; he adds, " But whatever consideration might " otherwise have been due to the opinion in that case, and to the " reasons and decisions on which it rested, the weight of American " authority is decidedly the other way ; and it may now be considered " as part of the *settled jurisprudence of this country* that personal pro- " perty as against creditors has *locality*, and the *lex loci rei sitæ* prevails " over the law of the domicil with regard to the rule of preference in " the case of insolvents' estates. The laws of other governments have " no force beyond their territorial limits ; and if permitted to operate " in other states, it is upon a principle of comity, and only when neither " the state nor its citizens would suffer any inconvenience from the ap- " plication of the foreign law. A prior assignment in bankruptcy under " a foreign law will not be permitted to prevail against a subsequent " attachment *by an American creditor* of the bankrupt's effects found " here, *and our courts will not subject our citizens* to the inconvenience " of seeking their dividends abroad, when they have the means to " satisfy them under their own control."   And, after mentioning various cases decided in the American courts, he adds, " and still more " recently in the Supreme Court of the United States" (in the case of Ogden *v.* Saunders, 12 Wheat. Rep. 213.), " the English doctrine (for " it is there admitted to be the established English doctrine) was per- " emptorily disclaimed in the opinion delivered on behalf of the majority " of the Court."

(*x*) Story's Conflict of Laws, 354.

(*a*) Ibid. 350. Hitherto this has been little inquired into in this country.

countries as in ours. But the American courts appear to have adopted their own rule with a full knowledge of this, as well as of what had been done in the British courts. On future occasions, if American assignees shall (as they did in the cases of *Maitland* and *Hoffman,* and *Morrison's Assignees* v. *Watt,* before mentioned) (*b*), claim in the British courts a preference over the British attaching creditor (which, in those cases, was granted to them without inquiry), apparently they may be fairly met by this, that their own courts deny a similar comity in their country; and that therefore their subjects cannot ask for such indulgence here. (*c*)

But whatever intricacy or want of unanimity there may be in the intricate questions of foreign bankruptcy, there is none, as we have already seen, in regard to the doctrines of personal succession. In every country it appears now to be admitted, that the law of the domicil shall regulate (*d*); but it is equally clear, that a title must be made up by probate, by administration, or by conformation in the country in which the property is situated.

(*b*) *Supra,* p. 238.

(*c*) There can be no doubt that under the 3d Axiom of Huber, noticed above (p. 77.), the American courts were entitled to lay down this rule for themselves.

(*d*) There has always appeared to me to be this difficulty in regard to foreign bankruptcy, that, in recognising a foreign commission, and the assignment made under its authority, the decree of a foreign court is, in such cases, admitted to have effect *extra territorium.* In all cases of the administration of the property of deceased persons, it is necessary to have recourse to the courts of the country in which the property is locally situated, to make up a title to it. I see this difficulty noticed in support of the American doctrine. (Story, 349.)

While this treatise is in the press, I am much pleased to see, that a new edition of Dr. Story's valuable work has been published by **Mr. Clark** of Edinburgh.

CHAP. IX.

OF CONFIRMATIONS IN SCOTLAND, AND OF PROBATES AND LETTERS OF ADMINISTRATION IN ENGLAND, IN CASES INVOLVING QUESTIONS OF INTERNATIONAL LAW.

ALTHOUGH it is now clearly and universally understood that the *lex domicilii* is to rule in cases of intestate succession in both countries, it is equally well understood that in making up a title to administer the personal estate of a party deceased, it is necessary to have recourse to those courts which have local jurisdiction in respect of the *situs* of the property. When a title is once made up, the executor or administrator holds the property as a trustee for the use and benefit of those to whom the will, in a case of testate succession, or the law of the domicil, in a case of intestate succession, gives the beneficial right; whether this should be to strangers, or to the executor or administrator himself.

We have seen in a former part of this treatise that, in both countries, the clergy formerly claimed right to decide in all matters of this sort in their proper ecclesiastical courts. Before the Reformation, it is to be presumed that the practice in England and in Scotland was regulated very much in the same way.

At the Reformation in Scotland, this part of the ecclesiastical jurisdiction was settled by the establishment of consistory or commissary courts. One superior consistory or commissary court, with four judges, was established in Edinburgh, by Queen Mary, in 1563. (a) This court had

---

(a) Balfour's Practics, p. 670.

R 4

a local jurisdiction of its own within certain limits, and a right of reviewing the proceedings of all inferior commissaries. The Court of Session had the right of review of the decrees of the commissaries of Edinburgh. Upon the restoration of episcopacy it was enacted, by the act of the Scottish parliament of 1609, c. 6., that, of the commissaries, of Edinburgh, two should be named by the Archbishop of St. Andrews, two by the Archbishop of Glasgow; and the other bishops had the power of appointing commissaries within their respective dioceses. At the Revolution, the patronage of these offices devolved to the crown.

Confirmations of testaments, and appointments of executors dative, were to be granted by the commissary *ubi defunctus habuit domicilium*. When a person resided abroad, the commissaries of Edinburgh had jurisdiction in regard to the confirmation of his personal estate in Scotland. The person obtaining confirmation in any of these respective courts, whether the executor *nominate*, the executor *dative*, or the executor *creditor*, had, by obtaining such confirmation, the universal right of administration throughout Scotland conferred upon him, and as such could sue in any of the courts of law of that country (*b*).

Thus the jurisdiction of the commissaries remained down to a recent period. But by an act of the 4 Geo. IV. c. 97, the whole constitution of these courts was altered; the commissariot of Edinburgh was declared to extend over the sheriffdoms of Edinburgh, Haddington, and Linlithgow; the inferior commissariots were abolished; every county and stewartry in Scotland was to form a commissariot, with the sheriff or stewart for judge; and the right of review of the proceedings of all the inferior courts was taken from the commissaries of Edinburgh, and vested in the

---

(*b*) Erskine, b. 3. tit. 9. s. 29. Hall *v.* Macaulay, 19th Jan. **1753**, Fac. Coll.

Court of Session. By another recent act of the 11 G. IV.
and 1 W. IV. c. 69, this matter was further regulated.
The commissariot of Edinburgh was restricted to the
sheriffdom of Edinburgh, and every jurisdiction of a more
extensive nature, heretofore possessed by the commissaries
of Edinburgh, was entirely to cease, save and except such
as regarded the confirmation of testaments of persons
dying out of Scotland, having personal property in that
country, which jurisdiction was reserved to this court. All
the other jurisdiction of the commissaries of Edinburgh,
was devolved upon the Court of Session. Vacancies occurring in the offices of the judges of the Commissary Court
of Edinburgh were not to be filled up; and as soon as
vacancies should take place in the whole of such offices,
the powers and jurisdiction of the court were to be vested
in the sheriff of Edinburgh.

In England, probates of wills and administrations of intestates' effects have been in use to be granted by a very
great variety of courts:—1. Where a person dying had
bona notabilia, or goods to the extent of *5l.*, in more dioceses than one, wills were to be proved and administrations
granted in the *Prerogative* Court of the Archbishop respectively, within whose province the person dying had
such *bona notabilia*. Of these prerogative courts, that of
chief importance, and by far the greatest magnitude in
point of business, has been the Prerogative Court of the
Archbishop of Canterbury, sitting in Doctors' Commons
in London. The Prerogative Court of the other archbishop is held at York. 2. Probates and administrations
were generally granted in the Consistory Court of the
Bishop, within whose diocese the deceased had his residence. 3. But they were also granted by the judges of
a vast variety of *peculiar* jurisdictions, of deans, archdea-
cons, prebendaries, rectors, vicars, lords of manors, and
others, exercising ecclesiastical jurisdiction by prescription,

composition, or other special title (c). It is astonishing that this diversity of courts should have been found tolerable in England for such a length of time. It is to be remarked, that though these courts were tenacious of their jurisdictions, yet nothing done by one of them was of any avail out of that jurisdiction in which it was granted; and this limitation extended, not only to the inferior courts, but also to the Consistory Courts of the bishops, and the Prerogative Courts of the two archbishops. In this respect the law appears to have always been more conveniently regulated in Scotland, where a confirmation in any commissary court appears to have completed the grant. Happily these numerous jurisdictions are now in the course of being regulated; it is to be hoped that they will be arranged in such a way, that every just cause of grievance may be obviated in future.

The *ad valorem* fees payable to the judges and officers of court upon confirmations in Scotland, have been the subject of many statutory regulations. In addition to all the other fees of court in Scotland, in the times of episcopacy, the bishop was entitled to a twentieth part of the moveables of a person deceased, termed the *Quot*, because it was the proportion or *quota* to which the bishop was entitled for his own use at confirming; and, for a long period, debts were not to be deducted in estimating the quot. At last, by the act of 1641, c. 61, quots were declared to be a grievance, and prohibited in future. This act was revived after the restoration by the act of 1661, c. 28; and though quots were restored to bishops the year after, by the act of 1662, c. 1, they were by a posterior

---

(c) The *peculiar* jurisdictions in England and Wales, with the manorial courts exercising such jurisdiction, amount in number to nearly 300. (Report made to his Majesty on the practice and jurisdiction of ecclesiastical courts, 15th February, 1832.)

act of 1669, c. 19, ordained to be paid only out of the *free gear* or *deductis debitis*. By an act of 1701, c. 14, the act of 1661, c. 28, was revived, and quots were thereby prohibited, with a clause saving the *dues of court* payable to the commissaries and their clerks; and this clause was so explained in practice as to justify the demand, not only of a reasonable fee to the clerks, *but a composition to the judges in proportion to the amount of the property* (*d*). This very indefinite right remained down to a very recent period, and was only entirely abolished by the act of 4 G. IV. c. 97, s. 1.

In England, the fees payable upon the granting of probates and administrations have attracted much attention from time to time. In a former part of this treatise, we have noticed the statutes and regulations made upon this subject in England down to the 21st of Henry VIII. (*e*)

Some partial regulations were subsequently introduced in regard to the probates of the wills or administrations of the effects of persons dying in the naval service of the country, by the statute of the 31 G. II. c. 10. (*f*)

It is not proposed here to enter into any particular inquiry how or by whom confirmations may be obtained in Scotland, or probates and administrations in England, in common cases. This always has been, and always must

---

(*d*) Erskine, b. 3. tit. 9. s. 28.

(*e*) *Supra*, p. 27. *et sequen.*

(*f*) The most extravagant fees which have been the subject of regulation in either country, appear to have been those which were claimed within the archdeaconry of Richmond in the province of York. By a statute of 26 Henry VIII. c. 15., it appears that certain " parsons, vicars, and others" within that archdeaconry had been in use to take " of every person when he dieth, in name of a *pension* or of a *portion* sometime the *ninth part* of all his goods, and sometime the *third part*, to their open impoverishment." This was abolished by that act under the pain of a *præmunire*, and the fees were restricted to those which could be demanded under the act of the 21st of H. VIII. c. 5.

remain, subject to the regulations to be observed in the courts having jurisdiction in such matters in the two countries respectively. Our purpose is merely to inquire what has been done when questions of *international law* have occurred in either country in regard to the grants of such confirmations, and of probates or administrations; namely, where the grant was claimed by those who considered that they had the right of administration according to the law of the domicil of the deceased, and opposed by those who claimed such right, according to the *lex loci rei sitæ.*

SECT. I.

Of Confirmations in Scotland in cases of Foreign and International Succession; and on the Effect in Scotland of Titles made up in other Countries by Executors and Administrators.

IN Scotland, down to a very recent period, confirmations were required for two purposes: 1. To *vest* the succession. 2. To give an *active title* to the personal representative. If the person having the right of personal representation in a case of intestacy died before confirmation, nothing was vested in the person having the right; but the same devolved to and became vested in the other next of kin, who obtained confirmation, to the exclusion of those who died before confirming. (g) But this did not extend to the *jus relictæ* of a wife, or the *legitim* of children, which were vested without confirmation, as falling under the law of the communion of goods in the married state. (h)

(g) Probably this rule may have been to enforce confirmations, and with an eye to the *quots;* it has always been unknown in England, where the right vests *ipso jure;* and probates and administrations were only required to give an active title.

(h) Erskine, b. 3. tit. 9. s. 30.

Several cases have occurred in Scotland, upon points of international law, in regard to the effect of the titles made up by executors or administrators in England, or Ireland, or in foreign countries; but no rule appears to have been laid down in Scotland to meet the case of one party claiming confirmation as having right to such confirmation according to the law of the domicil, in opposition to another claiming such right according to the law of Scotland.

There exist no reports of what has been decided in the ecclesiastical or consistoral courts in Scotland, in cases that may have been disputed before them in regard to the granting of confirmations *either* in cases of testate or intestate succession. It is to be presumed, that during the length of time that these courts existed, important questions of international law must have occurred before them upon these subjects. Probably these are now to be consigned to oblivion.

It is only in the common law courts in Scotland that we find any thing connected with our present subject of inquiry. In these there are cases reported from time to time, in regard to the effect of probates or administrations taken out in England or in Ireland, and the titles made up by executors or administrators in foreign countries, when founded upon, in the courts of common law in Scotland.

The earliest case which appears to have occurred in the Court of Session connected with this subject, was that of *Lawson* v. *Kello*, 16th February 1627. (*i*) Anna Lawson, an Englishwoman, was the executrix named in the will of her husband, Alexander Lawson, *indweller* in London. After his death she obtained probate of the will in London, and thereupon sued Bartel Kello, who was indebted to her late husband upon bond, in the Court of Session in Scotland.

(*i*) Durie, p. 277.   Morrison, 4497.

. A defence was made to this action, that no special inventory was given up nor contained in the probate. According to the report, " the Lords sustained the action at the instance of the said executrix, and her procurators constituted by her, to pursue upon that bond and testament, albeit there was no special inventory given up, nor contained in the said testament; the pursuer proving that the form of England was to confirm testaments in that manner, and that the same would furnish actions to the executors of the defunct against their debtors, albeit no special inventory, nor particular mention of the debt acclaimed, were in that testament; the pursuer showing the bond to qualify the debt, and that she was confirmed executrix to the defunct; which the Lords found sufficient, this being proven; or otherwise they sustained this pursuit, the pursuer finding caution to warrant the defender of the debt at all hands, who might claim the same from him; the option of the which two, viz. either to prove the custom or to find the caution, they gave to the pursuer, and that one of them should suffice to maintain the action; and this English testament was sustained to produce this action, at an English woman's instance in this realm; albeit it was alleged, that no writ could produce action in this realm, which dissented from the form of writs allowed and required by the law of the kingdom where the pursuit was made, which was repelled; caution being found *ut supra.*"

But the litigation upon this small matter did not end here. (*k*) Alison Lawson, sister of the deceased, was confirmed executrix-dative to her late brother for the same debt; and she also claimed it from Kello the debtor. He raised a double poinding against the two claimants in the Court of Session; and the question as to the preference

---

(*k*) The bond of Kello appears to have been only for 20*l. sterling.*

between the widow suing under the English probate, and the executrix-dative, came to be decided in the Court of Session on the 15th of January, 1629. (*l*)

" The two executrices coming to dispute which of them should be preferred, the first obtruded her nomination approved in the Prerogative Court of Canterbury; in respect whereof *non locus erat dativo ;* like as she offered to confirm the same debt here at home.   The other alleged that she, being executrix confirmed, should be preferred ; and for the nomination, no respect should be had to it withal, it having been done in England ; and for her offer to confirm, let her do it ; but she must reduce the other dative.   The Lords preferred the executrix-dative, she finding caution to refund it back again to the executrix-nominate, if she should happen to reduce the dative hereafter."

It is difficult to see upon what grounds this case was decided, in either instance.   The executrix-nominate apparently was entitled at once to have had the decree-dative superseded, as granted *per incuriam.*   But still a confirmation in Scotland would be necessary upon her part; and the English probate was not of itself held a sufficient title to sue.

In the case of *Rob* v. *French*, 25th of February, 1637 (*m*), Thomas French, a servitor to the King's Majesty in England, made his testament in Scotland, and took it with him to England, where he died.   His testament contained legacies to John Rob and others.   The testament was proved in the Prerogative Court of Canterbury by Robert

---

(*l*) Reported by Spottiswoode, Brown's Supplement, vol. i. p. 162. The case as here reported, for which we are indebted to Mr. Brown at a very recent period, totally does away the import of the former report, which alone had been previously known.

(*m*) Durie, p. 831.   Morrison, 4497.

French, clerk of Kirkcaldy, the executor-nominate; "but" (as is noticed in the Report) " no inventory given up or contained therein."

Upon this testament so proved in England, the legatees sued the executor in Scotland for payment: but " the Lords would not sustain process upon this testament confirmed in England, until the time the legatees should confirm a testament in Scotland, seeing the executor was here compearing and renouncing to be executor."

This appears also to be a case of some difficulty; but it was found that a title must be made up in Scotland, before the Courts would sustain the action.

In the case of *Brown and Duff* v. *Bisset*, 18th of July, 1666 (*n*), a question occurred in regard to the personal estate of Andrew Duff, a native of Scotland, who had died resident as a merchant in Poland. A debt of 600 guilders was due on bond to the deceased by James Brown, burgess of Aberdeen; and the widow and daughter of the deceased having assigned this bond to William Bisset, he raised an action upon it in the Court of Session in Scotland against the representatives of Brown the debtor; and produced his assignation, and a certificate under the common seal *Civitatis Pucensis*, certifying that the parties assigning were the wife and daughter of the deceased, and that as such they had a right to his moveables by the law of that place.

The pursuer contended, that there was a sufficient right without a confirmation in Scotland; and referred to the act of 1426. c. 88. (*o*), and to the previous case of *Lawson*

(*n*) Stair's Dec., vol. i. p. 398. Dirleton, No. 21. p. 10. Newbyth MS. Morrison, 4498. There is some confusion in the names, in the different reports.

(*o*) *Supra*, p. 78.

v. *Kello.* (p)　The defender answered that it was otherwise decided in the case of *Rob* v. *French ;* and that " there was no reason that those that lived out of the country *animo remanendi,* should be in better condition than those who resided in the same, and behoved to confirm *and pay the quot.*"

According to Stair, " the Lords found that the testament behoved to be confirmed by the commissaries of Edinburgh ; for having considered the old act of parliament, they found that the point there ordered was, to what judicatures the merchants going abroad to trade should be liable, and that such as went abroad not *animo remanendi* should be subject to the jurisdiction of that place where their testament would be confirmed (viz. where they had their domicils), but those that went out of the country to remain are excepted ; but nothing expressed where their testaments should be confirmed; and for the *decision* (*q*), the point in question was not, whether a confirmation in England was valid, but whether a confirmation without an inventory was valid; and, therefore, seeing nothing was objected against the confirmation itself, the Lords did justly find, that the wanting of an inventory in an English confirmation, where that was the custom, did not prejudge it ; neither is the case determined by the decision betwixt Rob and French, in respect that the executor having confirmed in England, and *rather being confirmed by the legators,* would not own the confirmation, but renounced the same ; and, therefore, the Lords found no consuetude or decision in the case, but determined the same *ex bono et æquo.*"

(*p*) This must have been to the case of *Lawson and Kello,* as first noticed and reported by *Durie, supra,* p. 253.; not the posterior case reported by *Spottiswoode.* There is an error in printing the report in Stair ; apparently the words " rather being confirmed by the legators," should have been " *after being sued by the legators.*"

(*q*) *Lawson* v. *Kello, supra,* 253.

s

The report in *Dirleton* merely notices the import of the decision: — " It was found, *nemine contradicente,* that a stranger residing in *Holland* (*r*) *animo morandi,* or elsewhere, though by the law of the place his nearest of kin without confirmation has right to all goods or debts belonging to him; yet if the debtor's goods be due by Scotsmen, or be in Scotland, they cannot pursue for the same, unless the right thereof be settled upon them according to the laws of Scotland, by confirmation if they be moveables, or by a service if they be heritable."

This case appears to have been decided upon sound principles.

In the case of *Trent and Brown* v. *Duff,* 11th of November 1692 (*s*), an English probate was held to be a sufficient title to receive a debt due in Scotland. The circumstances are briefly and very indistinctly stated by the reporter. William Duff, in Inverness, owed a sum on bond to Colonel Man. After Man's death, Duff paid the debt to Man's daughter, who had taken probate of his will in England, but there had been no confirmation in Scotland. Trent and Brown (who had some interest in this bond, the nature of which does not appear,) sued Duff, the debtor, in the Court of Session. Duff pleaded in defence the payment to the English executrix, and her discharge.

The pursuers insisted that an English probate was not a sufficient title to uplift sums lying in Scotland, for " both *mobilia et immobilia sequuntur legem istius loci ubi sunt.* The Court assoilzied Duff, but in regard the payment was after the intimation of the right made to James Brown, they modified 4*l.* sterling to be paid to him for his expenses in this process."

(*r*) Apparently a mistake for Poland.
(*s*) Fountainhall Decisions, Brown's Supplement, p. 2.

The case is so indistinctly stated in the report, that little can be made of it, and it can scarcely be founded on as an authority.

Another case occurred upon this subject, *Wardlaw* v. *Maxwell*, 21st of January 1715. (*t*)   Jean Wardlaw, at her marriage with Maxwell of Coull, got an obligement from Maxwell of Orchardton, and another from her husband, to pay her 20*l.* a-piece yearly after her husband's death.   She surviving him, made her testament in Ireland, leaving the by-gones of these annuities to Catherine Wardlaw.   This will was proved in Ireland; and the probate bore, that the will was subscribed in the presence of three witnesses, whereof two were women, and one subscribed by initial letters only.

Catherine pursuing the representatives of Orchardton and Coull, various defences were made: — 1. That the testament was null, because women could not be sustained as witnesses in Scotland, "yea, *non constat*, that they are sustained in England;" 2. Because the original testament was not produced, but only an *Irish writ of administration* (*u*), which was not subscribed by any person.

The pursuers answered, 1. That the law and custom of each place must regulate as to the solemnities requisite on subscribing wills; at least, with respect to moveables; and that such was the custom of England was notour, and needed no probation.   2. That the testament produced was authentic from the records of the diocese where the principal testament was *probated;* "that the principal testament behoved to be probated in Ireland, and must remain as the warrant for this probate;" and that the probate produced, having the office seal appended, and

(*t*) Bruce, No. 36. p. 45.   Morrison, 4500.

(*u*) I have repeatedly observed that down to this day the difference between probates and administrations is not, in general, distinctly known in Scotland.   This appears frequently in the proceedings of the courts in that country.

being attested by the clerk, had all the requisites " *of a formal probated writ.*"

The defenders replied, that though it were probative, it could not be a title in Scotland, unless the pursuers had applied for a confirmation in Scotland, as was found in *Rob* v. *French.* (x)

The pursuers duplied, that though this were true as to administrations *ab intestato,* which can, indeed, " go no further than the jurisdiction of the granter; yet the administration here proceeding upon the defunct's testament, it may be confirmed in any judicature, with respect to all the defunct's goods ; " and they referred to the decision in *Lawson* v. *Kello* (y), where the Court sustained action at the suit of the executrix on an English probate. As to the case of *Rob* v. *French,* they stated that the specialty there was that the executor, confirmed in England, was competing, and renounced to be executor; and, therefore, the Court found a confirmation in Scotland to be necessary.

" The Lords sustained the title libelled on, as a sufficient title in this process, the pursuers confirming before extract."

In the case of the *Earl of Breadalbane* v. *Innes and others,* Court of Session 1734 and 1735, House of Lords, 11th of February 1736 (z), it was decided that an executor creditor, confirmed in Scotland to a person deceased, could not in that country recover a debt due to that person, there having been already a probate of his will granted by the Prerogative Court of Canterbury to an executor named in the will.

Major Sinclair by his last will and testament appointed Ann Tibo his sole executrix: he died in London in 1718,

---

(x) *Supra,* p. 255.   (y) *Supra,* p. 253.
(z) 1 Craigie and Stewart, 181.

and the executrix duly proved the will in the Prerogative Court of Canterbury. (a)

William Innes being a creditor of Major Sinclair to a considerable amount, was afterwards confirmed *executor creditor* in Scotland, and thereupon raised an action against the Earl of Breadalbane, for payment of a sum of 100*l.* and interest, as contained in a bond granted by his Lordship to the deceased. The money had been lent in London, and the bond was granted there.

The Earl pleaded in defence, that by Major Sinclair's will Ann Tibo was named his executrix; that she had proved the will in the proper court in England; and, therefore, that he could not be compelled to pay the contents of the bond to the pursuers, until Ann Tibo the English executrix was made a party to the suit; for, as the bond itself was not produced, or ready to be delivered upon payment, he might be sued anew by her in England, where he sometimes resided, and compelled to pay the debt over again.

It was answered that, as the executrix resided in England, she could not be compelled to become a party to the suit; and that the pursuer was willing to grant a discharge with absolute warrandice.

The Court repelled the defences, and decerned the pursuer, upon payment, to grant a discharge to the Earl with absolute warrandice. But upon appeal to the House of Lords, it was ordered and adjudged, that the interlocutors should be reversed, and that the appellant should be absolved from the instance or libel.

It does not appear upon what grounds this case was decided: it was probably upon this, that where there was

---

(a) The domicil in this case does not appear to have been inquired into.

an *executor nominate*, as in this case, a confirmation to a creditor without making her a party was inept.

In the case of *Clerk* v. *Brebner*, 20th December 1759 (*b*), a question arose in regard to the effect of English letters of administration as a warrant to sue in Scotland. In 1755 Brebner and Co. purchased six hogsheads of vinegar from Fletcher, a merchant in London.

On the death of Fletcher, Mrs. Pott, his sister, obtained letters of administration of his estate and effects from the Prerogative Court of Canterbury, and granted a power of attorney to John Pott, her husband.

Pott drew a bill upon Brebner and Co. for 12*l*. 4*s*., as the price of this vinegar, payable to John Clerk. This was protested for non-acceptance, and a process was there-upon brought against Brebner (his partner having failed) before the Sheriff of Aberdeen, who gave decree against Brebner.

Brebner suspended, insisting that the process had been brought before the sheriff, without the pursuer's instructing a sufficient title, as the letters of administration had been at no time produced: 1. That such letters of administration, though they may have been sustained *ad inchoandum litem*, had not hitherto been sustained as a sufficient title to recover payment in Scotland, or to grant a valid discharge of the Scotch debt. It was answered, that there had been no objection to the title in the inferior court; and that, therefore, such objection came too late. 2. That the debt was contracted in England; and, therefore, that the administration formed a good title. 3. That Fletcher had in a letter agreed to pay the debt to Pott. The Court " found " the letters orderly proceeded, and expenses due; but " ordained the charger to confirm before extract."

(*b*) Fac. Coll.

In this case, the Court apparently decided in terms of the previous case of *Wardlaw*, sustaining the suit on the foreign title, but directing the title to be made up in Scotland, before the decree was extracted.

For a very considerable period no further cases connected with this branch of the law appear in the reported decisions of the courts in Scotland. The important case of *Mrs. Mary Wardlaw Cuming Egerton* v. *Duncan George Forbes*, however, occurred in 1812. (*c*) It arose out of the following circumstances:—

In January 1803, Lady Cuming, widow of Sir John Cuming, died at Bath; but her domicil, at the time of her death, was in Scotland. She was then possessed of moveable property, partly in Scotland, partly in England, and, *inter alia*, of 5333*l*. stock in the 3 per cents.; and, as she died intestate, the whole devolved on her six children, one of whom (afterwards Mrs. Egerton) was at that time married to Arthur Forbes of Culloden, and resided with him in Inverness-shire.

Colonel Cuming, another of Lady Cuming's children, was in England at the time of his mother's death. He took out letters of administration to the deceased in the Prerogative Court of Canterbury, as one of her next of kin. In virtue of these he took the management of the property in England, on behalf of all who were interested in the succession. He drew half a year's dividends on the stock, and granted a power of attorney to a house in London to turn the property in England into money.

About four months after the death of Lady Cuming, Mr. Forbes of Culloden, Mrs. Egerton's first husband, died, without any further steps taken for making up a title to Lady Cuming's succession, or obtaining actual posses-

---

(*c*) Fac. Coll., Nov. 27. 1812.

sion of any part of her funds.   He was succeeded by his
son Duncan George Forbes, as his heir and executor.
His widow was afterwards married to Mr. Egerton of
London.

In these circumstances a question arose between Mrs.
Egerton and Duncan George Forbes, concerning the right
to that share of Lady Cuming's fortune which had devolved
to Mrs. Egerton in right of her mother.   Mrs. Egerton
insisted, that during the lifetime of her first husband a
proper title had not been made up to vest her share in him;
and that this share, of consequence, belonged to her in her
own right.   It was maintained, on the other hand, by
Duncan George Forbes, that this share fell under the *jus
mariti* of his father, and devolved upon him as his father's
representative.

Mrs. Egerton thereupon brought her action in the Court
of Session, containing a declaratory conclusion of her right
to this share, and concluding against Colonel Cuming for
payment thereof to her.   In this action Mr. Forbes and
Colonel Cuming appeared as defenders.

The Lord Robertson Ordinary, in June 1809, found,
" that the proper domicil of the late Lady Cuming, the pursuer's mother, was in Scotland; that as Lady Cuming died
intestate, the succession to her moveable estate, wherever
situated, must be regulated by the law of Scotland; and
that the pursuer, as one of the nearest of kin to her
deceased mother, has right to an equal share with the other
nearest in kin of her free moveable estate."   (In so far
there appeared to have been no doubt between the parties.)
But he also found, " that the pursuer had not made up
titles to her share of her mother's moveable estate by confirmation, nor had obtained possession of any part thereof
prior to the decease of the late Arthur Forbes; therefore
he repelled the defences of Duncan George Forbes, and
decerned against the other defender, Lieutenant-Colonel

Henry John Cuming, for payment as libelled upon, the pursuer completing her title by confirmation."

But, upon a representation to the Lord Ordinary, he reported the cause to the Court; and the Court ordered memorials upon this question, "whether the letters of administration taken out by Colonel Cuming had the effect of vesting in his sister, Mrs. Forbes, her share in the moveable estate of her mother, recoverable in England, so as to take the same out of the *hæreditas jacens* of her mother, and subject it to the legal assignation by her marriage in favour of Mr. Forbes." At the desire of the Court, the opinions of English counsel were taken upon the law of England, as applicable to this case.

Sir Samuel Romilly and Mr. Bell gave a clear opinion that, by the law of England, the shares of the next of kin in the personal estate of a person dying intestate were vested before administration taken, and were transmissible by assignment or will of such next of kin, and, in case of their dying intestate, would pass to their representatives: but they noticed a peculiarity of the English law in this case, namely, that Mrs. Forbes's interest in the stock in England was a *chose in action*, which, although transmissible to representatives, did not vest in a husband *jure mariti*, not being reduced into his possession in his lifetime.

The Court, upon advising the memorials and the opinions of English counsel, decided that Mrs. Egerton's share of the stock in the funds did fall and belong to her late husband Mr. Forbes; and remitted to the Lord Ordinary to consider further as to her share of the personal estate in Scotland.

In a reclaiming petition and answers, the matter was again fully brought before the Court, and the Judges delivered their opinions *seriatim* in this case, as one of very considerable importance. The Lord Ordinary continued of his former opinion, and Lord Bannatyne concurred with him; the other four Judges, including the Lord Justice Clerk, were of a contrary opinion; and on the 27th of November 1812, the Court found, " that the pursuer, Mary Wardlaw, during her marriage with the late Arthur Forbes, did acquire right to a share of the moveable estate of the late Lady Cuming, her mother, situated in England, as one of the children; that the same did vest in her; and by virtue of her marriage did fall and belong to the late Arthur Forbes."

This was a case of considerable intricacy. At that time, according to the law of Scotland, personal estate in that country, in a case of intestacy, did not vest without confirmation (d); but confirmation as an active title was only necessary in regard to the personal estate in Scotland; nor could it have been of any avail in England, in regard to the stocks in that country. Here was a direct *conflictus legum* upon two points:—1. The non-vesting of personal estate by the law of Scotland before confirmation; 2. The doctrine of the law of England as to *choses in action* of the wife not being vested in the predeceasing husband, unless reduced into possession. Apparently, the Court decided rightly as to the vesting of the share of the stock in Mrs. Egerton in the lifetime of her first husband; and also in rejecting the English law as to a *chose in action*, as not having operation in her case. The question, whether this property being vested in the wife during marriage, passed to her husband or not, was not one of succession, but related to the right which, by the law of Scotland, a husband acquired in the personal estate of his wife.

Lord Robertson remarked, that Mr. Forbes was put in a better situation than he had right to, either by the law of

---

(d) Altered by tr. rt 4 Geo 4 c 9P. (*Supra*, p. 65.)

England, or the law of Scotland; that, according to the opinions of English counsel, the property in that country did not transmit to him, but to the next of kin: in Scotland, again, he would have been told that the right not having been vested could not be claimed by him; but "by a jumble of the laws of both countries, the Court was about to give him what he could not have obtained either by the one law or the other."

Apparently the administration obtained by Colonel Cuming was of great weight in this case; the representation to the deceased was thereby full in England; and he, as administrator, was trustee for himself and the next of kin. (e)

Several of the same questions occurred a few years afterwards in the case of *Craigie* v. *Gardner* in 1817. (*f*) The facts were these:—Mrs. Janet Anderson, widow of Wil-

---

(e) Several of the questions which arose in this case of *Egerton* appear to have been discussed in two former cases mentioned by Fountainhall (*Burnet* v. *Burntfield*, 8th March, 1683; 3 Brown's Supplement, 459.; *Veitch* v. *Irving*, 25th July, 1700; 4 Brown's Supplement, 495.); but in neither is the judgment given. In the first of these cases Burnet, the commissary of Peebles, insisted against Burntfield that he should confirm in Scotland money due to a defunct in England. Answered, the commissaries' jurisdiction did not extend beyond Scotland; and what locally lay in England, the Englishmen, ere they would pay it, would have it confirmed in their prerogative court; and there cannot be an instance given of any money lying in England that ever was confirmed by a Scotch commissary. Yet we say *mobilia sequuntur personam* where he dwells; but Sir George Lockhart said, " our law could not force money abroad to be confirmed here."

The other case related to a cargo belonging to one Johnston, which had been freighted for Dumfries, but had put into Whitehaven. Administration as to these was obtained by Veitch before the official of the county palatine of Chester. Irving was confirmed executor creditor to the deceased in Scotland. A competition thereupon arose between the English administration and the confirmation in Scotland; but it does not appear that any decision was given thereon.

(*f*) Fac. Coll., June 12. 1817.

liam Anderson, writer to the signet, died intestate in December 1813, leaving, amongst other personal property, stock in the public funds. George Anderson, her only child, in regard to the stock in the public funds obtained letters of administration to the deceased in the Prerogative Court of Canterbury; these were entered in the usual way at the Bank of England. He died in May 1814, intestate, and without having taken any steps by confirmation or otherwise in Scotland with regard to the property in the funds; and at his death the stock still stood in the name of his mother.

Disputes having arisen as to the succession of this part of the property, mutual actions of declarator were brought by Mrs. Dorothea Craigie, the sister of Mrs. Janet Anderson, who contended that the property had never been vested in George Anderson, but remained *in bonis* of his mother Mrs. Janet Anderson, and descended to Mrs. Craigie as her next of kin; and by Mrs. Margaret Gardner, the sister of William Anderson, the father of George, on the ground that the property vested in George Anderson, *ipso jure*, without confirmation, and, therefore, must descend to her as his next of kin. The whole parties were domiciled in Scotland.

The opinion of English counsel was taken on a joint case for the parties (g); and the Lord Pitmilly Ordinary,

---

(g) This was the opinion of Sir Samuel Romilly: he merely explains the law of England on the state of the parties. According to that law, the property vested in George Anderson, the next in kin; he had properly obtained letters of administration to his mother's estate; and as the stock still stood in her name, it could only be obtained by the next of kin of the son obtaining letters of administration *de bonis non* to the mother. He mentioned that the paternal and maternal aunts were, by the law of England, in equal degree to the son, and would be jointly entitled to the administration; but that still the granting of administration was not conclusive in the English courts, as to the beneficial interest in the residue. He gave no opinion upon the question then at issue on the law of Scotland.

on the 18th of November 1815, found "that the late Mrs. Janet Anderson, having been domiciled in Scotland at the time of her death, and having died intestate, the legal right to the government stock which belonged to her fell to be determined by the law of Scotland, the *lex domicilii*; but that the form or legal process by which that right was to be vested in and rendered effectual to him to whom it by law belonged, fell to be regulated by the law of England, as being the law of the place in which the moveable property was situated; that George Anderson, the son of Mrs. Janet Anderson, and who survived his mother a few months, had a right, by the *lex domicilii*, to succeed to her moveable property wherever situated; and that the form of confirmation, though necessary (unless possession had been obtained) to vest in him that right to such parts of the property as were situated in Scotland, was not necessary either to vest the property of the government stock situated in England, or as the means of obtaining letters of administration from the Prerogative Court of Canterbury, to the effect of entitling the administrator to sue for and acquire possession of the stock, and of rendering him accountable for it to all having interest; and in respect it appears from the opinion of English counsel referred to by both parties, to be the rule of the law of England, that no form of law whatever is required, as in this country, to vest the beneficial interest in the personal property of an intestate, after payment of debts, in the person having the legal right of succession; but that the property vests immediately and *ipso jure*, without any form of law, on the death of the intestate, only that the person succeeding is not entitled to recover, except

---

It is not noticed in this opinion, that by the English law two administrations would have been necessary in this case; one to the son, and the other to the effects *de bonis non* of the mother.

through the means of letters of administration obtained either in his name or that of another; that the legal right of succession to the government stock accrued to George Anderson, and was also effectually vested in him: and of consequence that the stock now belongs to the pursuer, Mrs. Margaret Gardner, his nearest in kin."

A reclaiming petition was presented for Mrs. Craigie, in which, and in answers thereto, the whole point was fully argued. In this reclaiming petition there appears to have been a statement in regard to the practice of the English Ecclesiastical Courts, which was not entirely well founded; it is there stated, — " The English Ecclesiastical Courts do not, in granting letters of administration, pay the least regard to the *lex domicilii*, but prefer the person who would have had the beneficial interest by the law of England; but the administrator is a trustee, acting for behoof of the person who may, by the law of the domicil, have the beneficial interest."

On the 12th of June 1817 the Court adhered to the interlocutor of the Lord Ordinary.

This case also involved a *conflictus legum:* apparently it was decided upon sound principles, though now of less importance since the passing of the act 4 G. IV. c. 97. (*h*)

In the case of *Milligan* v. *Milligan*, 9th of February 1826 (*i*), a similar decision was pronounced. The facts were these:—William Milligan, a native of Scotland, died domiciled in South Carolina, leaving a considerable personal estate in Britain, consisting chiefly of stock in the public funds, but partly also of debts due to himself in Scotland. In his latter will he gave all his property to certain trustees for the payment of legacies and other purposes therein specified. To his eldest sister, Helen Irving,

---

(*h*) *Supra*, p. 65.   (*i*) Fac. Coll.; 4 Shaw & Dunlop, 432.

the testator left a legacy of 2000*l.*, and a share of the residue of his estate.

Helen died domiciled in Scotland in May 1818, leaving two children, Anne and James; and Dr. Milligan and John Keir were appointed curators to them, and took out letters of administration in England in their name.

In August 1818, Anne made a testamentary disposition in favour of her brother James; and, in October following, James made a testamentary disposition, nominating Dr. Milligan and Mr. Keir his executors. Both Anne and James died without expeding any confirmation to the mother, and the executors named by James entered upon a general intromission with the mother's estate.

Under these circumstances Elizabeth Milligan and her husband, and her brother Peter Milligan, claimed the succession of their sister Helen, as her nearest of kin, and brought an action of count and reckoning against the executors of James her son.

The property of Helen consisted of moveable funds both in Scotland and in England. With regard to the funds in Scotland, it was admitted ultimately by the defenders that those parts of them of which possession had not been taken by Helen's children, necessarily fell to her next of kin. The only question then was, as to the funds situated in England, and derived from William Milligan the brother.

The pursuers contended, that Helen being a domiciled Scotchwoman, the distribution and transmission of her property fell to be regulated by the law of Scotland; and that the children having died without confirmation, the property went to her next of kin, unless so far as possession had been obtained by her children.

The defence was, that though the *lex domicilii* does generally rule in the succession of moveable property, to the effect of determining who has right to succeed, the question of vesting was regulated by the *lex loci rei sitæ ;* and the former cases of *Egerton* and *Craigie* were referred to.

The Court was much divided in opinion: two of the judges, Lord Craigie and Lord Gillies, delivered opinions in favour of the pursuers; but the Lord President, Lord Hermand, and Lord Balgray, were in favour of the defenders, and of opinion that the funds in England vested without confirmation.

Accordingly, " the Court sustained the defences as to the funds situated in England;" and they afterwards adhered upon advising a petition and answers. (*k*)

This case, involving also a *conflictus legum,* was decided· after the passing of the act 4 G. IV. c. 97., but was not ruled by that act, as it related to a succession which had occurred before the act was passed.

The last case which has been observed upon this branch of the subject, is that of *Sir Henry Steuart* v. *Macdonald,* 21st November 1826. (*l*)

Sir Henry Steuart, as survivor of three executors of the will of the late Archibald Seton, who died in Calcutta,

---

(*k*) The reporter appears to have stated the opinion delivered by Lord Gillies in an erroneous way. According to that report, the law of the domicil ought to rule in every case, not only in regard to *succession,* but in regard to making up the *active title* to the property. In a subsequent case of *Robertson* v. *Gilchrist* (Fac. Coll. 25th Jan. 1828), upon the head of *service and confirmation,* Lord Alloway says, " he had the best information that the opinion of Lord Gillies, upon which the pursuer founded, is not correctly reported."

(*l*) 5 Shaw & Dunlop, 29. It may be remarked in this case, that the interlocutor of the Lord Ordinary mentions a *probate* and *letters of administration* as synonymous, though they are very different.

The counsel who pleaded the second preliminary defence for Macdonald, do not appear to have been aware that the law of England was clearly against him on this point. The executors named by Mr. Seton took as *joint tenants,* and all their rights survived to the survivor without the necessity of any clause of devolution. (Williams on Executors, 897., and the cases there stated.)

having obtained probate in the Prerogative Court of Canterbury, raised action against Macdonald for the contents of a bill due to the deceased, payable in Edinburgh.

Macdonald pleaded as dilatory defences, 1st, That a probate from the Prerogative Court of Canterbury was no sufficient title to sue in Scotland; 2d, That, *by the law of England*, the survivor of three executors was not entitled to take out a probate, unless there had been a devolution on the survivors, which was not the case here.

The Lord Ordinary repelled these preliminary defences, and found that the " probate and *letters of administration* " produced by the pursuer afford a sufficient title to " pursue, the pursuer always, in case he shall be successful, " *confirming before extract*." And by a second decision, the Court, after hearing counsel for Macdonald, unanimously refused a reclaiming note for him. They considered that the question was settled by the previous cases of *Wardlaw* and *Clerk*, before noticed.

SECT. II.

Of Probates and Administrations in England, in cases of Foreign and International Succession.

IT is matter of regret that no reports have been published of the decisions of the ecclesiastical courts in England till a very recent period. For this reason, the information to be had upon the subject of our present inquiry is more scanty, and commencing at a later period, than it must otherwise have been (*o*). During the great length of time

---

(*o*) The earliest published ecclesiastical reports are those of Dr. Phillimore, commencing from Hilary Term 1809. Similar reports have been continued by Dr. Addams, and Dr. Haggard; and the latter has also published reports of the cases argued and decided in the Consistory Court of London, commencing in 1789. These reports, with the reports of the decisions in the High Court of Admiralty, have fortunately pre-

that these courts have subsisted, numerous questions must have come before them, the knowledge of which would not only have been interesting to the professional inquirer; but must have tended to illustrate the history and state of the law in our own country, and in the other countries of Europe.

In England it is a general rule in the ecclesiastical courts, that, in cases of intestacy, and in construing the statutes of the 31 Edw. III. c. 11. and 21 Hen. VIII. c. 5. the grant of administration shall conform to the beneficial right.

There appears to have been an exception to this rule in modern times in regard to the granting an administration of the goods of a deceased wife, who had been survived by her husband also deceased. In such case, though the beneficial interest was in the representatives of the husband, the practice had been to grant the administration to the representatives of the wife (p).

But in a recent case, in the Prerogative Court of Canterbury, *Fielder and Fielder* v. *Hanger* (in Hilary Term 1832 (q), administration *de bonis non* to a *feme covert* was granted to the representatives of the deceased husband, though an appearance was given, and administration prayed by the next of kin of the wife; and the Court directed that, though the modern practice had been otherwise, such grants should for the future pass to the husband's representatives, unless special cause to the contrary was shown.

According to the broad terms of the above general rule, it should appear to follow that, in case of intestate succession, where the law of the domicil of the person deceased, has laid down different rules in the succession of personal estate, from those of the law of England, in granting ad-

---

served to the world much of the judicial labours of Lord Stowell, — a name alike respected at home, and by all foreign nations.

(p) 1 Haggard, Eccles. Rep., 341.   Ibid. vol. ii. Appendix, 158. 170.

(q) 3 Haggard, Eccles. Rep., 769.

ministrations, the Courts should enquire into the *beneficial interest, according to the law of the domicil,* and grant the administration according to such beneficial interest; but it is not known that it has yet been so ruled in any case. (r)

(r) In the case of the next of kin of *Robert Alexander Paterson Wallace* (before referred to, p. 201.), a question arose in the Prerogative Court of Canterbury, whether he was domiciled in England, or in Scotland, at the time of his death. The succession was claimed by the *maternal* grandfather, John Bass Oliver, as his next of kin according to the law of England, on the one hand; and by his *paternal* uncle and aunt, Captain Wallace and Mrs. Rooke, as his next of kin, according to the law of Scotland, on the other. If the English domicil was established, Mr. Oliver, the grandfather, was admitted to be preferable to the uncle and aunt under the statute of distributions; while, by the law of the Scotch domicil, as a maternal relative, he would have been entirely excluded.

The uncle and aunt were advised to claim the grant of administration to the exclusion of the grandfather. A learned civilian (Dr. Phillimore) gave this opinion on the subject:— " But in deciding upon the " grant of administration, a question will arise upon the construction of " the 21 H. VIII. c. 5., which enacts that administration shall be granted " by the ordinary to the next of kin; and it will be contended, that " the Court is bound to grant it in this case to the maternal grandfather, " who is the next of kin by the law of England. In my judgment it " will be sufficient to state, in reply to this, that the uncle and aunt, " being next of kin according to the law of the country, which is to " regulate the succession to the effects of the intestate, are the next of " kin in the sense and meaning of the statute; *but the case is one, as* " *far as I can learn, entirely* primæ expressionis, *and it is impossible to* " *give any decided opinion as to the decision of the Court upon it.*"

In 1825, these parties respectively claimed administration in the Pferogative Court of Canterbury; the matter proceeded at first by act on petition, but afterwards upon plea and proof. Much evidence was taken on both sides, but the case was not argued by counsel. On the 4th of March, 1826, administration was decreed to the grandfather. At pronouncing judgment, the judge, Sir John Nicholl (according to a note taken and revised by counsel at the time), appears to have spoken as follows:— " The only question to be decided in this case is, to whom " administration should be granted : the statute decides this. I do not " state this ground of decision to avoid looking into the whole of this " case. I am aware that in the case of a residuary legatee, it has been " ruled that the statute did not cover that case; but that, on the con-

In matters of testate succession, it is now also clearly understood in England, that in the case of a will made by

---

" trary, it has been held, that the deceased in such a case intended that
" the residuary legatee should have the administration. The general
" principle is, that the administration and the beneficial interest should
" go together. But there is a case in which parties are excluded from
" the distribution, and yet are not excluded from the administration.
" This is the case of a woman dying intestate, being survived by her
" husband; and the husband afterwards dying also without taking out
" letters of administration to the deceased wife. In that case, adminis-
" tration is given to the representatives of the wife, though they become
" mere trustees for the representatives of the husband. I doubt very
" much the propriety of this rule; but such has long been the practice
" of this Court. Perhaps a case of foreign law is analogous to this.

   " In the present case, the only ground upon which I could exclude
" the grandfather from the administration, would be, that he had no
" beneficial interest. I think I am warranted in holding, that if it be
" even doubtful, whether or not the grandfather is entitled in distribu-
" tion, I cannot deny him administration, as that would be to exclude
" him also in distribution. I must be clearly of opinion that the grand-
" father is totally excluded by law in the distribution, before I can ex-
" clude him from the administration."

   But the judge in that case, after going over the facts, was inclined to
the opinion that, upon a review of the whole, the deceased was to be
held as domiciled in England. He concluded in these terms:—" Even
" if the matter were more doubtful, sufficient ground would not, in this
" case, have been established to exclude the next of kin by the law of
" England from the administration.

   " If I am wrong in this opinion, my error may be rectified by a
" superior court. If I am right as to granting administration, and wrong
" as to the domicil and distribution, the parties have it in their power
" to apply to another jurisdiction, to decide whether the administrator
" should not be held to be only a trustee for the other parties."

   The matter proceeded no further, the case having been settled by
compromise. In Scotland, where the bulk of the personal estate lay,
Mrs. Rooke, the paternal aunt, was confirmed executrix-dative *qua*
nearest in kin; Mr. Oliver, the maternal grandfather, not having opposed
this, but having proceeded afterwards in the Court of Session, as mentioned before (p. 201.). In the Prerogative Court, the point, whether
or not a domicil could be charged during infancy, was not stated by the
judge: he founded his opinion on this,— that the deceased had himself
selected an English domicil, after he had attained majority.

a person dying with a foreign domicil, inquiry should be made with regard to the validity of that will, by the law of the domicil; and that according to the result of such inquiry probate of the will should be granted or rejected in the English ecclesiastical courts. It is not without some conflicting decisions that the courts have arrived at these rules.

The cases which have occurred upon this branch of the law, whether in regard to testate or intestate succession as far as they are known, are few in number.

The earliest case which appears to have been under discussion was that of *Burn* v. *Cole*, at the Privy Council, 7th of April, 1763. (*s*)

Jacob Allin, having two legitimate children, Ann Burn and Sarah Whitcomb, made his will in Jamaica on the 1st of May, 1755, giving several legacies and annuities, and *inter alia* 50*l.* a year to Julia, the daughter of Mary

---

I see that in the recent case of *Stanley* v. *Bernes*, before the delegates (3 Haggard's Eccles. Rep., 462.), it is argued thus by the King's Advocate and Mr. Stephen: — " In granting administration to a domiciled " Scotsman, where the half blood do not succeed, the Court could not " exclude a brother by the half blood, in favour of an uncle by the " whole blood; nor could it exclude the mother, who, by the law of " Scotland, cannot succeed to her children in favour of a brother." They cited no authority for this: it is contrary to the opinion given by counsel in the case of Robert Alexander Paterson Wallace; and the principle of looking to the beneficial interest would induce us to form a different conclusion.

It has been already noticed, that the anomalous case of giving the administration to the next of kin of the wife, where the next of kin of the husband were beneficially entitled, has been altered in the case of *Fielder and Fielder* v. *Hanger.* When this matter shall come fairly before the Court, perhaps it may see fit, in granting administration in a case of foreign succession, to construe the statutes by the beneficial interest, as has been done in other cases.

(*s*) Ambler, 415. There is some obscurity in the report, as to whether Julia Cole was executrix, or administratrix with the English will annexed.

T 3

Cole, and the residue of his estate to his daughter Ann Burn, with remainders over, and made John Pool executor.

The testator afterwards came to England, and made another will in that country on the 11th of April, 1756, in favour of the said Julia Cole or Allin (who appears to have been a natural daughter of the deceased). He afterwards resided some time in England, and died there. In this last will no executor was named.

In Jamaica the original will of May, 1755, was set up by Ann Burn and the widow of the testator; and Pool, the executor, having renounced, and the widow declining to act, administration, with that will annexed, was granted in Jamaica to Ann Burn, the legitimate daughter, and her husband.

In the mean time, Julia Cole had obtained administration, with the will of April, 1756, annexed, in the Prerogative Court of Canterbury; and producing an exemplification thereof under the seal of the same court, applied to the judge of probate in Jamaica to have the administration which had been granted to Ann Burn and her husband re-called: she succeeded, and obtained administration to herself. The sentence was appealed to the Privy Council in England. The respondent, Julia Cole, making default, the appeal came on to be heard *exparte*.

Lord Chief Justice Mansfield, after having taken time to consider of it, delivered the opinion of the Lords: That the sentence should be affirmed, which he said went upon this foundation, that Jacob Allin was resident and died in England, and had assets here; and administration of his will had been granted by the Prerogative Court here: Whenever that is the case, and the residence of the party in England is not merely as a visiter, *the judge of the probate in the plantations is bound by the administration here, and ought to grant it to the same person:* That it would be very mischievous if it were otherwise; there would be great litigation, different sentences, and much confusion. His Lordship noticed the case of *Pipon* v. *Pipon* (t), where the distribution of an intestate's effects was held to be according to the laws of the country where the intestate resided and died.

He cited two cases before the Privy Council bearing upon this case. In the first of these, *Browne* v. *Phillips,* in December, 1739, " one died intestate in England; administration granted in England to A., a creditor. The attorney of A. applied in Jamaica for administration, but refused; and upon an appeal to the king in council, which was heard *exparte,* the sentence was affirmed, because, as none of the kin applied, it was *discretionary* in the judge to grant administration to a creditor." (u)

In the other, *Williams* v. ———, in 1747, one " resided and died intestate in England; administration in England was granted to his widow; in Jamaica, to his sisters and their husbands. Application by the widow to the judge in Jamaica for administration was refused. On appeal to the king in council the sentence was reversed. Lord Chief Justice Lee, who then attended in council, gave his reasons, that the plantations being within the diocese of London, are subordinate to the Prerogative (Court) of Canterbury, and, therefore, bound by the probate of that court: but Lord Mansfield declared himself dissatisfied with that reason; for the plantations are considered within the diocese of London for some purposes only, and not in every respect or point of jurisdiction. He said the better and more substantial reason for such determination is the residency."

A case which attracted a good deal of notice upon this

(t) *Antè,* p. 108.

(u) This appears rather to militate against the principle laid down in Burn *v.* Cole.

branch of the law was that of *Lashley* v. *Hog*, which has already received a large share of our attention, in another part of this treatise. (*x*)

Thomas Hog, in 1789, propounded for probate in the Prerogative Court of Canterbury the whole testamentary instruments executed by his late father, who died domiciled in Scotland, in which he was named sole executor. (*y*)

(*x*) Lashley *v.* Hog, *suprà*, p. 126.   3 Haggard, Eccles. Rep., 415. (*in notis*).

The Prerogative Court of Canterbury is usually resorted to in cases of probates and administrations from Scotland, particularly where the deceased had money in the British funds.   The Bank of England has always received, and acted on, such probates and administrations granted by the Prerogative Court of Canterbury.

In 1828, a question arose in regard to a will of Thomas Dickson, formerly of Drury Lane, but last of Northfield, in the county of Dumfries, deceased.   The testator had some leasehold property in Drury Lane, some bond and other debts in Westminster, and 10*l.* Long Annuity in the British funds, and his will was proved, on the 18th of March, 1828, in the *Consistory Court of the Bishop of London*, by James Scarth, the surviving executor.

When the probate was tendered at the Bank of England, they refused to transfer the Long Annuity belonging to the testator and standing in his name, on the authority of such probate.

Scarth, the executor, thereupon served the deputy registrar of the Consistory Court of the Bishop of London with a monition, to bring into and leave in the registry of the *Prerogative Court*, the probate obtained in the Bishop's Court.   The registrar appeared under protest, insisting that the probate so granted was legal and valid.

After argument in the Prerogative Court, the judge (Sir John Nicholl) holding the probate obtained in the Consistory Court to be legal and valid, allowed the protest, and dismissed the deputy registar from the monition. (*Scarth v. Bishop of London, Trinity,* 1828; 1 Hagg. Eccles. Rep., 625.)

The reporter adds, that after the judgment given in this case, the Bank of England acquiesced in the transfer of the 10*l.* Long Annuities, upon the original probate taken in the Consistory of London.

(*y*) In regard to testamentary instruments executed in Scotland, the practice generally is to register such wills or testamentary instruments in the books of the Court of Session, or of any court competent to the registration of such writings, in that country; and the ecclesiastical

This was opposed by Mrs. Lashley, the daughter, on the same grounds upon which she contended, in the Court of Session, and in the House of Lords, that these testamentary instruments were invalid, namely, that the testator had exceeded the powers which, according to the law of his domicil, he was entitled to exercise in these testamentary instruments; and that while he had attempted to dispose of his whole personal estate by these instruments, she was entitled to half of such personal estate in the name of *legitim*. But, notwithstanding this opposition, a general probate was granted by the judge, Sir William Wynne, to the executor, in Michaelmas Term 1789. This was before any decision had been pronounced in the causes in the Court of Session and House of Lords.

Mrs. Lashley appealed from this judgment to the Court of Delegates, and prayed the Court to reject the allegation, or to suspend the consideration of the admission thereof, till the proceedings still depending in the Court of Session were determined. But on the 4th of December, 1790, the Court of Delegates, without hearing the counsel for Mr. Hog, affirmed the decree of this Prerogative Court with the costs of the appeal, and retained the cause.

Witnesses having been examined by Mr. Hog, but no plea given in by Mrs. Lashley, the judges, after hearing counsel for Mr. Hog only, on the 8th of February, 1793, pronounced for the will; but, at Mrs. Lashley's prayer,

---

courts in England accept the office copy (termed an *extract* in the Scotch law) as evidence of the originals; and, retaining the office copy, they issue their probate thereof accordingly. No inquiry is made, in the common case, whether a confirmation has been previously obtained in Scotland or not. This practice has passed under my own observation for the last forty years.

In Scotland the probate, or an exemplification, or office copy of it, where the original will cannot be had, is held sufficient for the purposes of obtaining confirmation in that country.

directed an act on petition to be entered into, as to whether a general or limited probate should issue.

Mrs. Lashley in her petition stated, that by decisions in the Court of Session, affirmed in the House of Lords (z), she was entitled to a moiety of the whole personal estate of her father in her own right; and that any disposition of such moiety by her father was null; and that he had no power to appoint an executor in respect thereto, but that he must be considered, in point of law, to have died intestate as to the same. She, therefore, prayed that the probate might be limited to one moiety of the personal estate of the deceased within the province; and that administration might be granted of the other moiety to Mr. and Mrs. Lashley, on security to pay a proportionate share of such debts as might be legally chargeable thereon.

On the other side the decrees of the Court of Session and judgment of the House of Lords were admitted; but it was contended that, by law, the respondent was entitled to a general probate as sole executor, whatever might be the effect or operation of the will, in regard to the duty or office of the executor so appointed. *The judges delegates having heard counsel on both sides, on the 14th of June, 1796, condemned Mrs. Lashley in the costs, and decreed a general probate to Mr. Hog.*

It appears to be doubtful, whether this be consonant to the principles, which have been since adopted in the ecclesiastical courts in England. The Prerogative Court and the judges delegates appear to have considered, that Mrs.

(z) On the 7th of June, 1791, the Lord Ordinary, in Scotland, decided in favour of Mrs. Lashley on the *lex domicilii,* and on her right to *legitim;* on the 29th of November, and 23d of December, 1791, the interlocutor of the Lord Ordinary was adhered to by the Court; and on the 7th of May, 1792, these decrees were affirmed in the House of Lords.

Lashley's claim for *legitim,* as forming part of the estate of her deceased father, could only be obtained through a representation to him, and therefore granted a general probate to Mr. Hog. In this case of *Lashley* v. *Hog,* a discussion appears to have occurred as to the form of the instruments: it was contended that these were not of a testamentary nature, but in the form of deeds *inter vivos.* This argument was founded on a misapprehension as to the practice in Scotland in cases of this nature. The *will simply* has almost been banished from Scottish conveyancing, and is superseded by the testamentary disposition in the form of a deed *inter vivos,* and reserving the grantor's liferent and powers to him to alter.

Cases of this kind are of rare occurrence, and the next in point of date was that of *Nasmyth* v. *Hare and others,* in the Prerogative in Court of Canterbury, in Michaelmas term 1821. (*a*) In that case a question arose in regard to the validity of the testamentary writings of the deceased. Dr. James Nasmyth was a native of Scotland. He went in early life to India: he returned to Scotland in 1798, and from that time till 1812, he usually resided at Hope Park, near Edinburgh. In 1812 he came to London; and, though he intended from time to time to return to Scotland, he remained in London till his death, which took place on the 7th of December, 1813.

The deceased had large personal property within the province of Canterbury: his testamentary writings were propounded for probate, by the asserted executors, in Hilary term 1815. Sir John Nicholl expressed himself as

---

(*a*) 2 Addams, 25. (*in notis*). The only matter connected with this important case, which is reported in the Scotch decisions, is that regarding the right of the executors-nominate in Scotland to appropriate one-third of a residue undisposed of under the act of 1617, c. 14.: this was found not to be in *desuetude.* (Fac. Coll., 17th Feb. 1819.)

inclined to think that the papers had not legal validity according to the English law. But it appearing, on the face of these, that the deceased was a domiciled Scotsman, and that an action was depending in the Court of Session in Scotland, in regard to the validity of the same instruments, the Court suggested the propriety of suspending proceedings till that action was decided, intimating that it might feel it its duty to pronounce for the validity of the testamentary papers, or that the deceased had died intestate, *according as the courts of Scotland should determine that question, either upon general principles, or upon principles applicable to the subject, if any, peculiar to Scotch jurisprudence.*

Proceedings in the Prerogative Court were accordingly suspended. But the validity of the will and codicils having been pronounced for, by three interlocutors of the Lord Ordinary in Scotland of the 18th of May, the 9th of June, and the 14th of November, 1815, and an interlocutor of the second division of the Court of Session of the 7th of June, 1816, the next of kin declined to make any further opposition to the probate in England, and the same was thereupon decreed by the Prerogative Court to the executors, in the second session of Michaelmas term 1816.

Subsequently to this, the next of kin appealed to the House of Lords from the judgments of the Court of Session; and their appeal came to a hearing on the 27th of June, 1821, when the interlocutors of the Court of Session were reversed, and it was found that the asserted will and codicils were of no effect or avail in law, as testamentary dispositions.

A proctor for the executors thereupon brought into the Prerogative Court the probate formerly obtained, and consented to the same being revoked; and the Court, in the fourth session of Michaelmas term 1821, proceeded to revoke the probate obtained in 1816; and, finally, to decree administration of the goods of the deceased as intestate (according to its own original impression) to certain next of kin.

The Ecclesiastical Court, in this case, apparently proceeded upon principles, which have put the law upon a clear footing. They had originally doubts as to the validity of the instruments; but as the deceased was domiciled in Scotland, and as the validity of the instruments was questioned in the Scotch courts, they suspended proceedings till in that action a decision had been given for the validity of the instruments. Thereupon the Prerogative Court, deferring to the court of competent jurisdiction, granted probate of the same. But when the House of Lords had finally decided against their validity, then the probate formerly obtained was brought in and revoked.

When the previous case of *Lashley* v. *Hog* was decided, apparently the principles which ought to govern in a case of this kind had been less maturely weighed: as already noticed, in that case general probate had been decreed, although the will was only good to a certain extent, and void as to the remainder, and had been so decided by the competent courts in Scotland, and in the House of Lords.

In the matter of *Sidy Hamet Benamor Beggia*, a Moorish subject, Michaelmas, 1822 (*b*), a question arose, in the Prerogative Court of Canterbury, as to the administration to be granted to his effects. The deceased was a native of Larache in Fez, and thus a natural-born subject of the Emperor of Morocco. He died at Gibraltar, while consul of Morocco, in that place, in 1821, intestate. He died a bachelor, without father, mother, brothers, sons, daughters,

---

(*b*) 1 Addams, 340.

uncles, aunts, sons of the aunts (*by the father*), or any other *proper* heir by the Mahomedan law, leaving effects at Gibraltar, and in England. The Emperor *Muley Soliman,* under the circumstances, became entitled to the effects of the deceased, under the Mahomedan law.

These facts having been authenticated to the courts of Tangier and Rabal, they issued decrees declaratory of the law as above, and the emperor granted commission to two of his subjects (Haggi Thaer al Kial Rebati, and Haggi l'Arbi Mahanino) to proceed to Gibraltar, *and act there* on his behalf, by taking possession of the estate and effects of the deceased, appointing at the same time Mr. Judah Benoliel (the successor of the deceased in the consulate at Gibraltar) his attorney *to receive the deceased's estate,* in the first instance, and deliver it to the said commissioners.

In July, 1821, administration of the estate of the deceased was granted by decree of his Majesty's Court of Civil Pleas at Gibraltar, to the said two commissioners of the Emperor of Morocco, security being directed to be taken (and which was taken accordingly), to meet any claim of creditors or others, upon the estate of the deceased, which might be made within a year and day from that time.

These two commissioners, afterwards, delegated to Mr. Judah Benoliel all the powers vested in them by the said decree, and *all other powers and authorities which they possessed, as the commissioners of his said Imperial Majesty,* to receive and take possession of the effects of the deceased; to appear before any court ecclesiastical or secular, and to do all acts, matters, and things necessary or expedient touching and relating to the estate and effects of the deceased *in all places, countries, dominions, or jurisdictions whatsoever.*

Under these circumstances, Mr. Benoliel applied to the Prerogative Court of Canterbury for administration of the estate and effects of the deceased in England (on giving

sufficient security), for the use and benefit of the Emperor
of Morocco, he being also the only public functionary of
the emperor in the British dominions.

The Court considered the facts to be sufficiently verified,
but suspended the grant of administration till a specific
power was granted to some person to take administration
on the part of the Emperor of Morocco, the commission
granted to the two commissioners having been limited in
express terms to act *at Gibraltar.*

Afterwards, in February, 1824, administration was
granted to Mr. Judah Benoliel, " the Consul-General, and
" sole public functionary in the British dominions, of His
" Imperial Majesty *Muley Abderahman Ben Hisham,* Em-
" peror of Morocco, as a person for that purpose named
" and appointed on behalf of the Emperor, and for his use
" and benefit." (c)   .

In the case of *Curling* v. *Thornton,* in Michaelmas term
1823, the Prerogative Court of Canterbury had to decide a
case of considerable intricacy in regard to the will of a British born subject, who had resided for some time in France,
and died in that country.   Colonel Thomas Thornton (d)
went to France in 1815, and resided there for some time.
Towards the end of 1816, he removed the greater part of
his moveable goods to France: in January 1817, he obtained a royal *ordonnance,* allowing him to establish his
domicil in France for all civil rights; and in July 1817,
he purchased a considerable landed estate in that country,
and assumed the title of Marquis de Ponté, attached to

(e) This case appears to be almost a decision on the point, that in
the case of a foreign intestacy, administration is to be granted to the
person having the beneficial interest, without regard to the statutes of
31 Edw. III. c. 11. & 28.; and 21 Henry VIII. c. 5.'(See *ante,* p. 275.)

(d) 2 Addams, 6.   This was the will of the gentleman well known as
Colonel Thornton, of the sporting world, having been Lieutenant-Colonel
of the second regiment of York Militia.

that estate. In September or October 1818, he was in England, and there made and executed his will according to the English forms. It begins as follows : — " This is the last will and testament of me Thomas Thornton, of Falconer's Hall, and Boythorp in the East Riding of Yorkshire; and of the principality of Chambord, near Blois, and Pont le Roi, department de St. Aube, in the kingdom of France, Esq." This instrument gives and bequeaths all the testator's real and personal property to his executors, in trust for the payment of his funeral expenses, debts, and legacies. It directs that Priscilla Duins should be allowed to select for her residence whichsoever of his houses in France or England she thought fit, with all the household furniture, plate, and effects in such house for life, and with an annuity of 500*l.* It provides for the maintenance and education of Thornvillia Diana Rockingham Thornton, his natural daughter by the said Priscilla Duins, till she attained the age of twenty-one; and gives her a life-interest in all his property (with the exception of a few pecuniary legacies), which it strictly entails, first on her issue, and in failure thereof, then successively on different branches of his own family.

It authorises the trustees to sell any part of the real estate in England or in France; but, estates to be purchased, or exchanged, were to be in England only. It directs that the personal property should be sold and invested in the purchase of estates, but in England only. Certain parts of the personal estate, plate, books, paintings, and drawings, were made heir-looms, to go to the tenant in tail of the entailed estates. This will was very long, occupying twenty-eight sheets of paper; it was drawn in England, with reference to English forms and to the English law; it was executed by the deceased in England, so as to pass real estate in England, in the presence of, and attested by, three witnesses.

Immediately after executing this will, Colonel Thornton returned to France, and resided there till his death, which took place in France in March 1823. He left a lawful widow, and a lawful son by her. In the will no provision was made for the widow; a legacy of 100*l.* was given to the son, who is described in the will as " the son of Mrs. Thornton."

The will having been propounded by the executor for probate in the Prerogative Court of Canterbury, this was opposed by his widow and relict. She pleaded that the deceased had acquired a domicil in France, and that his will was to be judged of by the law of that country; that, by the law of France, the will made in favour of his adulterous offspring and her mother, while the lawful widow and the natural and lawful son were "almost wholly excluded" from any share of the property, was null and void; and that the property in question devolved by succession upon the widow and lawful child, the same as if the deceased had died intestate.

She stated also, that in June 1823, she had applied to the civil tribunal of First Resort for the department of the Seine, at Paris, for letters of administration of the goods of the deceased, as dying intestate, by the laws of France; and, though opposed by the executor, in August 1823 the president of that tribunal adjudged the possession to her, and constituted her administratrix provisionally, during the pendency of the suit, which was still not concluded.

This cause came on for argument in the Prerogative Court of Canterbury, in Michaelmas term 1823; and by the judgment of the Court, the will was admitted to probate. Sir John Nicholl, the judge of the Court, in delivering his opinion, appears to have proceeded upon this, that the facts of the case negatived the *voluntary total abandonment* by the deceased of his native country, and that he never had ceased to be an Englishman: he also doubted, " whether this can be; whether a British subject is entitled so far *exuere patriam* (e) as to select a foreign domicil in complete derogation of his British; which he must at all events do, in order to render his property in this country liable to distribution according to any *foreign law.*" (f)

It is to be remarked, that subsequently to the sentence in the Prerogative Court of Canterbury, the Court of First Instance at Paris came to a decision totally different from that of the English court, pronouncing the will *null and void*, and condemning the executor in costs. Thus in the two countries the courts of competent jurisdiction came to decisions directly opposed to each other.

The decision of the Prerogative Court in this case appears not to be free from difficulty. It was not carried by appeal to the Court of Delegates. Some proceedings were afterwards had between the parties in the Court of Chancery in England, but no decision was pronounced in

---

(e) He alluded to the maxim of Lord Coke, Co. Litt. 198., *nemo potest exuere patriam*.

(f) 2 Addams's Reports, p. 17. This appears to be set at rest; and there can now be no doubt that a person may so *exuere patriam*, as to establish a foreign domicil for all purposes of succession. See the case of *Stanley* v. *Bernes*, *postea*, p. 297. In the argument in that case of *Stanley* v. *Bernes* (3 Haggard's Eccles. Rep., p. 452.), it is stated that no such distinction was ever adverted to by any court, till thrown out in *Curling* v. *Thornton*. In Lord Thurlow's judgment in *Bruce* v. *Bruce* (*supra*, p. 121.), it appears that he had no difficulty of this kind.

In the case of *Curling* v. *Thornton*, Sir John Nicholl also noticed the case of *the Duchess of Kingston's will*, which had been made in Paris in 1786, and which, according to the *then* custom of Paris, was null and void. It was admitted to probate in England, after some opposition of the next of kin (*non constat*, upon what grounds) had been withdrawn. *Monsieur Target*, a French lawyer, had given his opinion that the will was valid. (See *Collectanea Juridica*, vol. i. pp. 323. 331.)

that court, the parties, as is understood, having made some arrangement by way of compromise.

In the goods of the *Countess da Cunha*, a Portuguese lady, in Hilary term 1828 (g), respect was had to the law of Portugal in granting a limited administration to the person entitled by the law of that country. The Countess da Cunha had 14,911*l*. 16*s*. three per cents. in her own name, in the books of the Governor and Company of the Bank of England; she was described in the Bank books as " now the wife of His Excellency Don Joze Maria Vasques da Cunha, Count da Cunha."

This lady, by her will, dated 8th of September 1824, appointed her daughter Donna Maria da Carmo (a minor) residuary legatee. The will was established in Portugal, and a judge administrator assigned, who, in that character, had the entire management and control of the minor's property.

On the marriage of the minor to the Count Da Viana, under the licence of the Prince Regent of Portugal, her disability as a minor ceased, and the appointment of the administrator was thereby at an end. The husband was also a minor, but it appeared that, by the laws of Portugal, by reason of his holding a commission in the army, and of his marriage, he was considered as of full age, and was legally authorized to do all acts, as if he had attained the age of twenty-one. On this account, therefore, a guardian could not be appointed.

To establish these facts, the sentence of the Court confirming the Countess da Cunha's will, the will therein embodied, the appointment of the judge administrator, an affidavit as to the existence of the stock, and certificates of

---

(g) 1 Haggard's Eccles. Rep., 237.

four Portuguese advocates as to the law of that country, were laid before the Court.

It appeared also, that by the law of Portugal the Countess Da Viana, under her dotal contract, was entitled to the dividends on this stock during her life. It was therefore moved, that a limited grant of administration should be made to the Countess Da Viana, who, though a minor by the law of England, was, by the law of Portugal, competent to act as administratrix.

The Court, considering that the Countess Da Viana was entitled to the dividends, and that no possible inconvenience could arise from the limited grant, allowed it to pass as prayed.

In the case of *Larpent* v. *Sindry* (in the goods of Thomas Barnes, of the Honourable East India Company's service, deceased), in Easter term 1828 (*h*), a question occurred, whether the Prerogative Court, in granting administration, should be be governed by the decision of the Court of Probate, where the deceased was domiciled.

Thomas Barnes had left two testamentary papers, both written with his own hand, bearing date respectively the 12th of April 1825, and 6th of May 1826, both beginning in the same formal manner, and both disposing of the *whole* of his property, though differently. By the first will five executors were appointed; but, by the second, no executor was named, though it contained a reference in one place to "the executors hereinafter mentioned;" and the paper thus concluded, "I feel too fatigued to write more."

The last paper bequeathed the residue to the testator's natural son, who, in 1824, had been sent to England for

---

(*h*) 1 Haggard's Eccles. Rep., 382.

his education; the paper was subscribed, but not witnessed. The testator died in India in May 1826.

Of both these instruments probate had been granted, by the Supreme Court of Judicature at Calcutta, to John Palmer, one of the executors of the will of 1825, with the ordinary power reserved to the other executors to come in and prove the will. An exemplification of the Indian probate having been transmitted to England, administration, with the will annexed, was prayed to be granted to Mr. Larpent, partner in the house of Cockerell and Company, the attornies of John Palmer, the executor. The property within the province of Canterbury amounted to nearly 2000*l.*

The Court was of opinion that the grant in India was not exactly according to their practice. In this country the two papers would have been proved, as together containing the will of the deceased; but the court in India, where the deceased died domiciled, and which was the court of competent jurisdiction, considered them as a will and codicil. The Judge added, " The question how far this and other courts of probate are to be governed by the decision of the court of probate where the deceased was domiciled, has never been expressly determined (*i*); but I should not feel inclined to depart from what has been the general practice, unless a strong case of inconvenience were brought under my consideration. I have, on the present occasion, the less difficulty in following the Indian grant, because I am not aware that there will be

(*i*) Apparently it was decided in the case of *Burn* v. *Cole*, at the privy council (Ambler, 415.; *ante*, p. 277.): there it was determined that when a testator, resident in England, died, the judge of probate in the plantations was bound by the probate granted here, where the testator resided.

much difference in the ultimate results, whichever way the decree passes."

The administration was therefore granted to Mr. Larpent, as prayed for.

This rule of law or practice was soon afterwards, in Easter term 1828, again considered, in the matter of the goods of *Lieutenant-Colonel Read.* (k) He was deputy quarter-master-general of the forces in India, and died there, in 1827, leaving a widow, and two daughters of a former marriage. He left a testamentary writing, which contained these passages:—" The little property I possess being in household goods, plate, carriages, horses, &c., I give, after all my just debts in Madras are paid, to my dearly beloved wife, Lydia, to apply and dispose of as she may think proper." It concludes in these terms :—" I refrain from separating into small parcels the little property that may arise from the sale of my effects, but wish my dear and affectionate wife may enjoy the whole, after, as I before said, my just debts in Madras are paid." This instrument was written by the testator, but not signed, nor was the date filled up, except that of the year (1827); blanks were left in some places; there was also, at the end, the word " witnesses," but it was not attested.

On the 17th of September 1827, probate of this instrument was granted at Madras to his widow, as *sole legatee and constructive executrix.*

Some time after, the Prerogative Court of Canterbury was moved that probate should be granted in this country, as granted at Madras. This would have given the widow the control of the property in England, without finding surety. But the Court was of opinion, that it was very doubtful whether, according to the due construction of the

---

(k) 1 Haggard's Eccles. Rep., 474.

will, the widow was " sole legatee and constructive executrix." The Judge added, " That the deceased, when
he wrote this will, was not, as it seems, apprised that he
had any property in England to dispose of; whereas he
had 380*l.* in his agent's hands. It is possible that the wife
may yet be called upon at Madras to prove this will in
solemn form of law ; or that, from the decree already made
there, an appeal to the King and Council may be prose-
cuted by the daughters of the former marriage. My difficulty, therefore, in granting probate to the widow as *constructive executrix* is, that she would, in that character, be
exempted from giving security. But I see no objection to
allow administration, with the paper annexed, to pass to
her as *relict and principal legatee,* on her giving security.
There is some difficulty in varying the form of the grant,
but yet there is still greater difficulty the other way."

Administration was accordingly decreed to Mrs. Read, as
the relict and the principal legatee, the usual security being
given. The case shows, that the Court did not hold itself
bound by the Indian probate, but entitled still to decide
as appeared to be just and expedient in the circumstances
of the case. It is not stated in the Report, whether the
deceased was in the military service of the East India Company, or of the public; this would have ruled his domicil.
In the case of *Burne* v. *Cole* (*supra,* p. 277.), the domicil
appears to have formed an important feature in the cause.

In the goods of *Donna Maria de Vera Maraver,* a case
occurred, in Easter term 1828, similar to that of the *Countess
Da Cunha.* (*l*) In this case of *Donna Maria de Vera Maraver* (*m*), it appeared that the deceased, a native of Spain,
had made her last will and testament on the 22d of No-

(*l*) *Ante,* p. 291.

(*m*) 1 Haggard's Eccles. Rep., p. 498.

vember 1815, and named her husband and her sons executors. She died at Seville, in November 1820.

In April 1821, the surviving husband, Don Martin Saravia, accepted and formalised the will of his late wife,
and ratified her appointment of executors. He died in
August 1827. A sum of stock in the British funds (consisting of upwards of 3000*l.* new 4 per cent. annuities)
stood in the name of Donna Maria de Maraver, wife of
Don Saravia. On the death of the husband a power of
attorney, held by Messrs. Mastermans for receipt of dividends, ceased. In order to sell out the stock and receive
the dividends which had accrued since the death of the
father, Don Cayetano Saravia, one of the sons, and a
surviving executor, came to England for the purpose of
proving his mother's will.

He made affidavit (through a sworn interpreter), that
by the law of Spain " the fortune or property of a Spanish
lady on the occasion of her marriage (unless she expressly
declines having any settlement) is inventorised and valued,
and such inventory and valuation is signed by her intended
husband, and the amount thereof remains vested in the
wife, and must, at her decease, be made up and paid by
the husband to her executors or heirs ; that the husband
and wife, during their joint lives, are, with respect to their
property, in a state of copartnership, and the husband, in
case of his wife's decease, is answerable to her executors
or heirs for a moiety of such profits, or increase of their
joint property (called *Gananciales*) as may have arisen
during their cohabitation (*n*) ; that the wife has full power
of authority to make her will as a feme sole," &c. That
in this case all that the surviving husband could have done

(*n*) This goes much further, than the law of Scotland does ; no claim
would arise there till after the wife's death. (*Lashley* v. *Hog, ante,*
p. 138.

would have been to alter or revoke so much of the will as related to one fifth of the property; but that, instead of revoking, he had declared and formalised the will.

The Court, after satisfying itself by other evidence as to the identity of Don Cayetano Saravia, granted him a general probate of his mother's will.

Very important questions occurred in regard to the law on this subject, in the case of *Stanley* v. *Bernes*, in the High Court of Delegates, upon appeal from the Prerogative Court of Canterbury, in Hilary term 1830. (*o*)

The points there discussed involved the question, whether a British subject could acquire a domicil in a foreign country, so as to bring him under the rules of the law of that foreign country in relation to his testamentary acts (*p*); and what should be done when such testamentary acts, though valid according to the English laws, were invalid according to the law of the domicil.

· John Stanley, a native of Ireland, died in the island of Madeira on the 15th of November 1826, being then upwards of eighty years old, leaving Helena Stanley, his widow, and John Stanley, his only legitimate child, him surviving. The deceased had left Ireland prior to 1770, and settled at Lisbon. In January 1770 the deceased, by a public act, had abjured the Protestant religion, and professed that of the Catholic church : this was in order to enable him to contract a marriage with a Catholic. In the same month he married Helena Doran, of Irish extraction, but a natural-born Portuguese subject, without any marriage articles.

In 1798 the deceased obtained an act of naturalisation from the Queen of Portugal; and on the 6th of March

---

(*o*) 3 Haggard's Eccles. Rep., 373.
(*p*) This had been made matter of doubt in the case of *Curling* v. *Thornton, ante,* p. 287.

1801, he signed a bond of allegiance to the Crown of Portugal. The French, on their occupation of Portugal in 1808, first treated him as a British subject, and put him in prison, but afterwards released him. It was thus matter of dispute in this cause, whether the French considered him as a British subject or not. On his release by the French he removed to and settled in Madeira. In 1823 the deceased, then resident at Madeira, authorised his son to take, at Lisbon, on his father's behalf, an oath of observance of the constitution under the Portuguese monarchy. The deceased at that time received a pension from the Portuguese government.

The deceased had had four children by his wife, but only one son, John Stanley, survived him. His wife having become insane, went or was removed from Portugal to Ireland, where the connections of both resided: there she remained at the death of her husband: she was supported in Ireland by an allowance out of the husband's property. From the time that the deceased went to Madeira, he resided in that island, within the dominion, and subject to the laws, of Portugal, till his death in 1826.

Besides his legitimate son John Stanley, the deceased left a natural son Joze Maria Bernes. This natural son was married, and at the time of the death of the deceased had five children, whom the deceased treated as his grandchildren.

On the 21st of June 1820, the deceased made his will at Funchal in Madeira. In that will he declared that he was brought up in the religion of the church of England, and that he intended to die in that religion, and requested to be buried in the English burial ground. He gave to the natural son and his children, and to Joaquina, the grandaunt of these children, who resided in family with the testator, legacies to a considerable amount; he gave the residue of his property to his legitimate son John Stanley, jun.;

and he appointed executors to his will. By a first codicil, dated at Funchal, the 4th of July 1820, he gave further legacies to his natural son and his family, and he named another executor. By a second codicil, dated at Funchal, the 11th of July 1820, he gave a farther legacy to the natural son, and to Joaquina the grand-aunt.

This will, and the first two codicils, the deceased declared, in the presence of a notary and five witnesses, to be his solemn will and testament, and desired that they might be considered as good, firm, and valid; and he requested the notary to draw up an act thereon, which being done, the deceased approved and signed such act; the notary attested it, and the five witnesses subscribed their names thereto.

By a third codicil, dated at Funchal the 24th, and an addition to it, dated the 31st of October 1822, he merely changed some of the executors. By a fourth codicil, dated at Funchal, the 29th of October 1825, he bequeathed various sums of stock, which he had in the English funds, to and for the use of his natural grandchildren, to the exclusion of his lawful son John Stanley; and, of the same date, he made an addition to this fourth codicil. The third codicil and the addition thereto, and the fourth codicil, were each published and declared in the presence of three witnesses, who attested them. The addition to the fourth codicil was signed by the testator, but not attested. The whole of the testamentary writings of the deceased were in the handwriting of the testator.

After the testator's death, the will and codicils were deposited at the British consul's office at Madeira, and authenticated copies were sent to England.

It was understood, that all the executors had renounced, and these testamentary writings were propounded for administration, with these writings annexed, by Bernes the natural son. This was opposed by John Stanley junior, the lawful son, who claimed administration as in case of total intestacy.   He alleged, 1st, that his father was a Portuguese subject, domiciled in Madeira at the time of his death; 2d, that by the laws of Portugal, a Portuguese subject leaving a widow, not endowed, and issue, cannot dispose by will of more than one sixth of his whole property, the widow taking a moiety (to two thirds of which moiety the issue necessarily succeeds as heir at her decease), and the issue two thirds of the other moiety, or the whole of the moiety if the father does not dispose by will of his third thereof; 3d, that though the will and two first codicils were executed with the forms required by the Portuguese law, yet the whole were repugnant to the Portuguese law, and therefore invalid; 4th, that there was this further invalidity in regard to the third and fourth codicils, that they were not executed according to the forms of the Portuguese law.

Upon the counter-allegations of the parties, a great deal of evidence was adduced on the subject of the domicil of the deceased, and in regard to the law of Portugal.   It appeared, that the evidence did not support the allegation of John Stanley in regard to the total invalidity of these instruments according to the Portuguese law.   He therefore afterwards admitted the validity of the will and two first codicils, which were executed and attested according to the Portuguese forms, and restricted his opposition to the two last codicils, which regarded the property in the British funds, and which were not executed according to the Portuguese forms, though they were valid according to the forms of the English law.

The Prerogative Court does not appear to have had any difficulty as to the domicil : but stated, that " the true question was, whether a British subject who has acquired a foreign domicil was deprived of the right of disposing of his British property according to the forms of the British law." It was admitted that this point had not yet received a distinct decision in that court; and thus the case became one of great importance.

In the course of the argument, the cases which had hitherto occurred in England and in Scotland upon points connected with the questions made in this cause, and various authorities from the foreign jurists, are stated and commented on. No case of this kind in the Ecclesiastical Court had been previously treated with the same extent of discussion. In Easter term 1830, the Prerogative Court decreed, that administration should be granted to Bernes with the whole testamentary writings annexed, and the costs were given out of the estate. The ground of the decision was stated thus in the note of the judge (q) :—
" What then is the Court called upon by the opposer of the codicil to decide? That the codicil is invalid, contrary to the manifest intention of the testator, that intention being expressed in an instrument duly executed, according, and with reference, to the law of this country, in his own handwriting, and attested by three witnesses. The Court is called upon to extend disqualification, and to deprive of privilege; to disqualify a British subject, because he is resident in a foreign country, from giving effect to his wishes in the disposition of his property at his death; and to deprive him of the testamentary privilege, which is so highly favoured by the general law of this, and of most other countries. Without some more direct authority than any which has been quoted, or with which this Court is acquainted, I do not feel warranted to proceed to such a length. I am the less disposed so to do, because in one way the decision of the Court of Probate would be conclusive; in the other it would not. If the codicil be pronounced against, and probate be refused, the legatee could not resort to any other jurisdiction; if pronounced

---

(q) 3 Haggard's Eccles. Rep., 443.

for, this Court would merely decide on the *factum*, and the residuary legatee might resort to a Court of Equity, to take its decision upon the question of construction."

Against the decision of the Prerogative Court an appeal was taken to the High Court of Delegates; the cause was again very fully argued before them. In the course of that argument, the difficulty stated by Sir John Nicholl in the case of *Curling* v. *Thornton* (r), — whether a British subject was " entitled so far *exuere patriam* as to select a foreign domicil in complete derogation of his British," and thereby to render his property in England liable to distribution according to any foreign law ? — was adverted to and considered. It was said, that " no such distinction was ever adverted to by any court till thrown out in *Curling* v. *Thornton*." On the 11th of February, 1831, the Judges reversed so much of the decree of the Prerogative Court as pronounced for the third and fourth codicils, and the addition to the third codicil, and decreed letters of administration, with the will and first two codicils annexed, to John Stanley, the residuary legatee, and directed the costs to be paid out of the estate.

This appears to have been a most important case: it decided that a British-born subject might so *exuere patriam*, that his testamentary acts should be subject, as to their validity in regard to his property in England, to the laws of the adopted country; that the will of such British-born subject, when domiciled in a foreign country, if invalid by the laws of that country, though valid according to the English forms, should not be admitted to probate in England.

It would appear, that the Prerogative Court, in this case of *Stanley* v. *Bernes*, proceeded on the same principle

---

(r) Curling *v.* Thornton, *ante*, p. 287.

as the Prerogative Court and Court of Delegates had done before on the case of *Lashley* v. *Hog.* (s) In that case, it seems to have been considered, that the decision of the Scotch courts ought to make no difference in their sentence, and that the testamentary papers should be admitted to probate in England, regarding property in England, because not repugnant to the English law, whatever might be their character according to the law of Scotland. The Court appears to have considered also, in that case, that the *legitim* of Mrs. Lashley could only be obtained after a representation to the deceased ; and therefore that probate should be given to the executor named, leaving Mrs. Lashley to make good her claims against the executor in the courts of competent jurisdiction.

In the case of *Stanley* v. *Bernes,* the Court of Delegates (t), in moving the decree of the Prerogative Court, appears to have adopted the true principle, by inquiring into and deciding according to the law of the domicil ; and this, notwithstanding the ground which appears to have weighed with the Prerogative Court, namely, that by deciding against the codicils, parties could go no further ; whereas, if they were admitted to probate, parties might still discuss their beneficial rights in the Court of Chancery. (u)

(s) *Ante,* p. 280.

(t) The Court of Delegates consisted of

Justice Parke, K. B.	Burnaby,
Baron Bolland,	Daubeny, } LL. D.
Justice Bosanquet,	Chapman,
	Curteis,

(u) The following foreign jurists appear to have been referred to in the case of Stanley *v.* Bernes : —

Denisart, tit. Domicile, s. 11.; Vattel, lib. 2. c. 8. s. 111.; Voet. lib. 1. t. 4. pars 2. lib. 5. t. 1. lib. 28. t. 1. s. 3.; Huber. de Conf. Leg. lib. 1. t. 1.; Argentrie de la Coutume de Bretagne, art. 449.; Maillaire, Dict. de Droit Canonique, tom. ii. p. 220.; Huberi Prælect. tom. ii, lib. 1. t. 3. s. 5.; Grotius de Jure Belli, lib. 11. c. 6. s. 14.; Heinec. Recitat. lib. 11. t. 10. s. 492.

In the goods of *Anne Dormoy*, (in Hilary term 1832,) (*x*) inquiry was made into the law of the domicil, and administration granted to a person having beneficial interest, though an executor had been named.

Anne Dormoy, a widow, died in November 1818, in the West Indies, in that part of the island of St. Martin which was subject to the laws of France. She left four children, and of her will appointed Cremony, her son-in-law, sole executor; but by this will she made no disposition of her property, except as to bequeathing to several of her slaves their freedom. Cremony assigned over all his interest in Mrs. Dormoy's estate to her eldest son, and administration was, in 1828, granted by the Prerogative Court of Canterbury, to the son's attorney. The attorney became bankrupt, and brought in the administration; and the son prayed that it might be granted of new to himself. It was objected in the Registry, that the residue being undisposed of, Cremony, as nude executor, was entitled to the grant. To meet this objection, the son made an affidavit, " that, by the 913th article of the French Code, no person, leaving three or more children at his death, can dispose by will of more than a fourth part of his effects; and by the 1025th and 1026th articles, a testator may name testamentary executors, and may give them the possession of his moveables, but that such possession cannot continue beyond a year and day from his decease:" that the will of the deceased was executed according to the French law; and by that law Cremony ceased to be executor at the expiration of the year and day, and could no longer interfere with the estate.

After some inquiry into the law of France, the administration was granted to the son, as prayed for. (*y*)

(*x*) 3 Haggard's Eccles. Rep. 767.

(*y*) The French Consul in London certified, that the French part of he Island of St. Martin was effectively governed by the French laws;

It does not appear that there is any class of cases in England, where effect, as a title to sue, has been given in that country to a confirmation obtained in Scotland, or, to what is equivalent to a probate or administration obtained in any foreign country. The general rule in England is, that letters testamentary, or administrations granted abroad, give no authority to sue in that country, though they may be sufficient ground for obtaining new authority in the proper Ecclesiastical Courts in England to the same parties. (z)

According to the law of England, an executor may perform many acts appertaining to his office, before obtaining probate. Such probate is rather the authentic evidence than the foundation of the executor's title; for he derives all his interest from the will itself, and the property of the deceased vests in him from the moment of the testator's death. (a)

The executor may *commence* actions before obtaining probate; but he cannot advance in them beyond that step when the production of the probate becomes necessary, till probate be obtained. The rule appears to be different in different kinds of actions: in some, the executor must declare before probate; in others, it is sufficient if the probate be produced at the trial. (b)

---

and that the affidavit set forth the law with perfect accuracy. Sir John Nicholl appears to have had some doubt if the certificate of the consul-general was sufficient; and if the ambassador should not have certified in this case. Under all the circumstances, the administration was granted, but the sureties were made to justify.

(z) Tourton v. Flower, 3 P. Wms. 369. Lee v. Bank of England, 8 Vesey, 44. It has been seen that, to a certain extent, a different rule obtains in Scotland. (*Supra*, pp. 259. 262. 273.)

(a) Hensloe's case, 9 Co. 38 a.; Graysbrook v. Fox, Plowden, 281.; Comber's case, P. Wms. 767.; Smith v. Milles, 1 T. R. 480.; Woolley v. Clark, 5 B. & A. 744. 1 Dowl. & Ryl. 409.; Williams on Executors, 159.

(b) Williams on Executors, 163, 164.

In regard to the administrator, inasmuch as he derives his authority entirely from the appointment of the ordinary, the general rule is, that the party entitled to administration can do nothing as administrator till letters of administration are granted to him. Thus the letters of administration must issue before the commencement of a suit at law by the administrator; for he has no right of action till he has obtained them. (c)

He may, however, file a bill in Chancery before he has taken out letters of administration, and it will be sufficient to have them at the hearing; but the bill must allege that they are already obtained. (d)

But as there appears to be no difference between the powers of the English, or of the foreign executor or administrator, before obtaining probate or letters of administration respectively, it would be out of place to enter minutely into their respective powers here. As far as has appeared, there is no instance where, in the English courts of common law or courts of equity, an executor or administrator has placed any reliance upon a probate or administration granted in a foreign country, or upon a confirmation granted in Scotland, as being of any force or validity *extra territorium*.

Thus there appears to be no class of cases similar to that which we have already stated as having occurred in Scotland, in regard to the effect of foreign probates and administrations.

(c) Williams on Executors, 239.

(d) Ibid. A recent case, however, in regard to an executor, would appear to militate against this rule. In Simons v. Milman, it was pleaded against a bill filed by a person in the character of executor, that the probate had not been obtained, and this plea was allowed. (2 Sim. 241.)

CHAP. X.

OF THE RULES OF LAW AT PRESENT IN FORCE IN REGARD
TO THE SUCCESSION IN, AND DISTRIBUTION OF, PERSONAL
OR MOVEABLE ESTATE, IN THE DIFFERENT PARTS OF THE
UNITED KINGDOM.

UNDER this division of the subject, it is not proposed to
enter into the wide field which would be opened to us were
we to treat, in detail, of all that has been done and decided
in the courts of the different parts of the kingdom, under
their respective laws, in questions connected with personal
succession. It is our object to confine this part of the
treatise to matters explanatory of our international law;
and to exhibit, as far as may be, in one view, in what
particulars the laws of the several countries, or of the
different parts of the same country, coincide, and in what
they disagree, in regard to the succession in, and distribution of, moveable or personal estate. (a)

It is important to notice, in commencing this branch of
the inquiry, that the terms *personal estate*, or *personalty*, in
the law of England; and *moveables*, or *moveable property*, in
the law of Scotland; though they coincide in regard to
many particulars, are by no means synonymous in their
extent and application. It would not be expedient to
enter at present into a minute inquiry as to all the particulars in which these coincide, or in which they differ, in

---

(a) It has, in general, been deemed sufficient to refer, under the
different heads, to those books of authority in both countries in which
the points are discussed and the relative cases stated in detail; yet, in
some instances, we have referred to the cases themselves.

the two countries; but there are some important points in which they differ so materially, that it is proper briefly to notice them.

1. In regard to leases. According to the general law of England, these, of whatever length of duration, are termed *chattels real*, and are of the nature of personal estate ; and, upon the decease of the lessee, devolve to the personal representative. (*b*)   In Scotland, on the other hand, leases are held to be property of a *mixed* nature.   In regard to succession, they are accounted heritable, and descend to the heir ; but they are still moveable in the case of the single *escheat* of the lessee, and would in such event fall to the Crown as moveable estate.   They are thus (in the language of the law of Scotland) *heritable* as to *succession*, but *moveable* as to the *fisc*. (*c*)

2. Mortgages and securities for money affecting lands or real estate in England, and bonds of all kinds, are of the nature of personal estate, and belong to the personal representative (*d*) : while, in Scotland, all securities for money affecting lands or heritable property are themselves heritable, and descend to the heir.   Formerly a large class of bonds, containing covenants for the payment of interest, were held to be heritable in that country ; but by the act of the Scottish parliament, 1661, c. 32. (re-enacting the rescinded act of 1641, c. 57.), these were rendered moveable as to succession ; though they neither fall to the Crown in a case of single *escheat*, nor go to a widow *jure relictæ*.   Thus such bonds are also of a mixed nature : in so far as regards the children and nearest of kin, they are moveable ; but in so far as regards the *fisc*, and the *jus*

(*b*) 2 Blacks. Com. 386.
(*c*) Erskine, b. ii. t. 2. s. 6.
(*d*) 2 Blacks. Com. 156.

relictæ, they remain heritable, as they were before the making of the statute. (*e*)

It may be remarked also, that in both countries, certain parts of the chattels or personal estate of a person deceased go to the heir, and not to the personal representative. These are termed heirlooms in England, and heirship moveables in Scotland. These resemble each other in many particulars: the law as to both has been transmitted from a remote antiquity. It has been matter of much discussion in both countries, what articles go to the heir under these respective denominations; it would be foreign to our present inquiry to enter into these questions here. (*f*)

The rules of a general nature which relate to the objects of our present inquiry, and which have equal application in the two countries, appear to be very few in number. These may be comprehended under the following heads: —

SECT. I.

Rules of Succession common to the Law of both Countries.

1. THE succession to, and distribution of, the personal estate of the deceased is to be governed by the law of that country in which the residence or legal *domicil* of the deceased was fixed at the time of his or her death.

This is clearly laid down as a general rule in the cases of *Pipon* v. *Pipon* (*g*), *Thorne* v. *Watkins* (*h*), *Bruce* v.

(*e*) Erskine, b. ii. t. 2. s. 5.

(*f*) As to heirlooms in England, see 2 Blacks. Com. 427.; Williams on Executors, 461. et sequen., and the cases there quoted.

As to heirship moveables in Scotland, see Leg. Burg. c. 125. 1474. c. 53. Erskine, b. iii. t. 8. s. 17., and Brown's Synopsis, *hoc verb.*

(*g*) Supra, p. 108.   (*h*) Supra, p. 109.

Bruce (*i*), and the other cases of that class already fully noticed; but it appears to be a rule not without exception. It does not extend to the personal estate of a freeman of London, which, according to the cases of *Cholmley* v. *Cholmley* (*k*), *Webb* v. *Webb* (*l*), *Onslow* v. *Onslow* (*m*), and other authorities, is held, in a case of intestacy, to be distributable by the custom of London, wherever such freeman may have fixed his domicil, and wherever such personal estate may be situated.

> 2. Though the rights of succession and distribution be to be regulated by the law of the domicil of the person deceased, yet the party entitled to the administration of the estate of the deceased, whether as executor, or other personal representative, must invest himself with such right of administration under authority of the proper courts, or according to the law of the country, within which the personal estate is locally situated.

This also is clearly laid down in the above-mentioned cases of *Pipon* v. *Pipon*, and *Thorne* v. *Watkins*. It is, indeed, founded upon principles so clear, that it scarcely needs authority to support it.

Though the practice is less fixed in Scotland, it appears that, in England, the courts having jurisdiction in regard to probates of wills, have respect to the law of the domicil of the deceased, in deciding as to what testamentary instruments shall be admitted to probate. The cases of *Nasmyth* v. *Hare* (*n*), *Stanley* v. *Bernes* (*o*), and others of that class before mentioned, clearly go to this extent: when the matter shall come to be the subject of special discussion in

---

(*i*) Supra, p. 118.   (*k*) Supra, p. 104.

(*l*) Supra, p. 105.   (*m*) Supra, p. 107.

(*n*) Supra, p. 283.   (*o*) Supra, p. 297.

Scotland, it is likely that it must there be decided in a similar way. Though the point has not yet undergone similar discussion in England in cases of intestacy, by parity of reason, in the grant of administrations, inquiry should be made into the beneficial right of the party, according to the law of the domicil of the deceased, or other law or custom regulating his succession. (*p*)

      3. All persons in either country, having attained the age of *discretion*, and being unmarried and without children, if of sound mind, may dispose of their whole personal estate by will, or other testamentary instrument.

It does not appear to have been clearly settled in England what shall be the lowest age at which a person shall be allowed to make a will of personal estate. The rule of the civil law is, that the age at which a party has the power of making a testament, and the age of *puberty* coincide, namely, fourteen in males, and twelve in females. (*q*) Some of the English cases appear to fix the age of discretion at fourteen in both sexes. (*r*) Blackstone appears to incline to the opinion, that the age of puberty in both should be held to be the age of capacity. (*s*)

(*p*) Supra, p. 274.

(*q*) Institut. lib. ii. tit. 12. s. 1. D. lib. xxviii. tit. 1. c. 5.

(*r*) See the various cases upon this subject in 4 Burn's Eccles. Law, p. 44. et sequen.

(*s*) 2 Blacks. Com. 496. While this treatise is in the press, a bill has been introduced into the House of Commons, *for the Amendment of the Law with respect to Wills.* It is meant that this shall extend to England and Ireland. By one of the clauses of this bill, no person under the age of seventeen is to be capable of making a will of personal estate; but any person of that age may make a will as well of *real* as of personal estate: and it is proposed to establish certain rules in regard to the attestation of wills, as well of personal as of real estate.

In Scotland there does not appear to be any doubt that, as in the civil law, the *testamentary* age agrees with the age of *puberty*. (*t*)

But to this universal power of making a will, there is one clear exception in England; namely, that regarding the *orphanage part* of the children of a freeman of the city of London: this, as shall be afterwards noticed (*u*), cannot be given by will or other testamentary instrument, made by the child of a freeman, till he or she shall attain twenty-one years of age; but, in case of the death of one of these children unmarried, his or her share descends to the other or others of them among whom the orphanage part is to be divided.

There is also a clear exception in Scotland; namely, that of *bastardy*. According to the law of Scotland, it is held that a bastard, before receiving letters of legitimation from the Crown, can make no valid will or testamentary disposition, unless he have lawful issue, in which case he possesses the *testamenti factionem*, like other inhabitants of Scotland. (*x*) This matter was discussed in the case of *Purvis* v. *Chisholm*, before stated (*y*); and important inquiries suggest themselves upon that case. The bastard there was born in Scotland, but died in England: his will was admitted to probate in the English Ecclesiastical Courts, but his personal estate fell under escheat to the Crown in Scotland. In that case the domicil appears to have been little, if at all, inquired into. Even at the present day, a question might be raised as to the personal estate of an English bastard which might be situated in Scotland, or of a Scotch bastard which might be situated in England; in either case, a direct *conflictus legum* might be pleaded, which the courts of law would have to deal with as they best could. In any arrangement that may

---

(*t*) Erskine, b. i. tit. 7. s. 33.   (*u*) Infra.
(*x*) Erskine, b. iii. t. 10. s. 6.   (*y*) Supra, p. 85.

be made in regard to the international rules of succession
in personal estate, this point of bastardy cannot be overlooked.

But the other rules of the law of the two countries upon
these subjects differ widely; and it is necessary to treat of
them in detail, in regard to the one country and the other.

It has been an advantage on the part of Scotland, that,
as far back as our knowledge of the Scottish law distinctly
extends, there has been but one general rule of law in
regard to the succession in personal estate, common to
every part of that country; and any alterations in the law
which may from time to time have been made, have been regulations of a general, not a local, nature.   It has also been
an important advantage, that a confirmation obtained in any
of the courts established in Scotland for granting confirmations, is of force in the whole of that country. (z)   It has
long, also, been in the power of parties residing in Scotland,
when entering into contracts of marriage, to make special
covenants and stipulations in regard to the rights of the
husband and wife, and of their issue, in the personal
estate of the parties contractors.   This must have tended
to render the present state of the law less felt, and less the
subject of observation, in that country, than it otherwise
must have been. (a)

In England, on the other hand, besides the general
law under the statutes of distribution, there always have
existed, and still exist, local customs of great intricacy, in
regard to the succession in personal estate.   These have
been already traced to their present state.   They may
be controlled by the deeds of settlement between a
husband and wife, in so far as the rights of the husband
and wife are concerned; and now, by the several statutes
before mentioned, by the last will and testament of

(z) Erskine, b. iii. t. 9. s. 29.
(a) Ibid. b. iii. t. 3. s. 30., t. 9. s. 23.

the father: but in so far as the succession is left to be regulated by law, these local customs still take effect in their full vigour. (*b*)

It has also been a source of much inconvenience in England, that probates and administrations have been granted in that country by a vast variety of courts; and that such probates and administrations were only effectual within the limited range of these local jurisdictions. (*c*)   But this inconvenience is now, probably, in the course of receiving an effectual remedy.

Thus it happens, that there are few general rules in the law of succession in personal estate which apply to every part of England.   The following rules, however, are of a general nature in that country, and apply as well to the general law under the statutes of distribution, as to the local customs reserved from the operation of these statutes.

SECT. II.

Rules applicable to England generally.

1. EVERY husband and father, in every part of England, may dispose of his whole personal estate by his will, or other testamentary disposition, in the same manner as, before the statutes enabling him in that behalf, he could have disposed of any part of such personal estate. (*d*)

It has been seen that the same power was extended to Ireland, by the Irish statute of the 7th of W. III. before referred to. (*e*)   Some of these alterations in the law of England were not made without much consideration. (*f*)

(*b*) Supra, p. 53.   (*c*) Supra, p. 250.

(*d*) Statutes 4 W. 3. c. 2., 2 & 3 Ann. c. 5., 11 G. 1. c. 18.

(*e*) Supra, p. 57.

(*f*) Protests on 11 G. 1. c. 18.   Supra, p. 50.

As far as is known, they have never been objected to as inconvenient; and, except for this power, the anomalies in the rules of distribution which still exist in different parts of England, must have been attended with inconveniences altogether intolerable. It will be for consideration, whether a similar power should not also be extended to Scotland, in any alteration to be made in the law of succession in that country. Already this power is competent to all husbands and fathers in Scotland, in those cases in which the rights of the wife and children are fixed with reasonable provisions, in lieu of their legal provisions under contracts made before marriage; and the assimilation of the law of Scotland to the law of England, in this respect, would merely be an extention of the law which the parties can at present lay down for themselves by contract for the regulation of their own properties. (g)

(g) Infra. In Swinburne we find the arguments for and against the universal power of testing, nicely balanced. He lived in the latter end of the reign of Elizabeth, and was judge of the Prerogative Court of York. In his time the customs were in their full vigour, and the power of making a will of the whole personal estate extended only to the province of Canterbury. He says, " In the opinion of some, the law of this land, which " leaveth all the residue to the disposition of the testator, funerals and " debts deducted, seemeth to have better ground in reason, than the " custom whereby he is forced either to leave two parts of three, or at " least the one half, to his wife and children ; for what if the son be " an unthrift or naughty person ? what if the wife be not only a sharp " shrew, but of worse conditions? Is it not hard that the testator " must leave either the one half of his goods to that wife or child, or " more; for the which, also, peradventure, he had laboured full sore all " his life ? Were it not more reason that it should be in the liberty of " the father or husband to dispose thereof at his own pleasure? which, " when the wife and children understood it, might be a means whereby " they might become more obedient, live more virtuously, and content " with good desert to win the good will and favour of the testator. " Those reasons make for the testator, and for the equity of the *common law*, which leaveth the whole residue to his disposition.

" But the *custom* whereby this liberty of the testator is restrained, is

2. A married woman, or female under coverture, can make no will or testamentary disposition of personal estate, unless thereto specially empowered by her marriage settlement, by the consent of her husband, or by the deed or will of some other person giving her such power in regard to some special property. (*h*)

In this respect, the law of England appears to differ from the laws of those countries which recognise a *communion of goods* between persons in a state of marriage, and particularly from the law of Scotland. (*i*) In England, the rights of the married pair, in regard to personal estate, during the subsistence of the marriage, are totally merged in the husband.

3. Upon the dissolution of a marriage by the predecease of the wife, the whole rights in the per-

---

" not without reason also : for when it is asked, What if the child be an
" unthrift, the wife worse than a shrew ? so it may be demanded, with like
" facility, What if the child be no unthrift, but frugal and virtuous ?
" what if the wife be an honest and modest woman ? which thing is
" rather to be presumed ; but, if it be not amiss to fear the worst, then,
" on the contrary, What if the testator be an unnatural father or un-
" kind husband ? perhaps, also, greatly enriched by his wife, whereas
" before he was but poor. Standeth it not with as great reason, that
" such a wife and children should be provided for, and that it should
" not be in the power of such a testator to give all from them, or to
" bestow it upon such as had not so well deserved it, and by that means
" set his wife and children a begging ? Surely the custom hath as good
" ground in reason against lewd husbands and unkind fathers, as hath
" the law in meeting with disobedient wives and unthrifty children."
(Swinburne, p. 303.)

It is to be remarked that, in addition to the arguments in Swinburne in favour of the universal power of bequeathing, we have, in its favour, the experience of the long period that has elapsed since the enabling statutes were passed in England.

(*h*) 4 Burn's Eccles. Law, p. 50. et sequen.

(*i*) Infra.

sonal estate of the husband remain vested in him as before her death, without any right or claim accruing thereby to the next of kin of the predeceasing wife. (*k*)

It does not appear that this has ever been otherwise in England. The contrary rule, in Scotland and other countries, has resulted from the doctrines incident to the *communion of goods* between husband and wife, established in the laws of Scotland and of those other countries.

4. In such case, also, where the wife dies possessed of personal property not vested in the husband, the husband surviving is entitled to obtain letters of administration to such personal property; and, under such letters of administration, to apply the same wholly to his own use. (*l*)

After the statute of distributions was passed, doubts were raised whether, in the case of a surviving husband, administrator to his wife, he was not bound by the statute to distribute her property to her next of kin. To obviate these, it is provided by a clause in the *statute of frauds* (29 Car. II. c. 3. s. 25.), that neither the statute of distributions, nor any thing therein contained, " shall be construed to extend to the estates of *feme coverts* that shall die intestate; but that their husbands may demand and have administration of their rights, credits, and other personal estates, and recover and enjoy the same as they might have done before the making of the said act." This was made perpetual by 1 Jac. II. c. 17. s. 5. (*m*)

(*k*) 2 Blacks. Com., 434.
(*l*) 4 Burn's Eccles. Law, 278., with Tyrwhitt's note.
(*m*) Supra, p. 37.

If, after the death of the wife, the husband shall die without having taken out administration to her, the ecclesiastical courts formerly found themselves bound by the statute 21 Hen. VIII. c. 5. to grant administration to the next of kin of the wife, and not to the representatives of the husband; and in such case the administrator was considered, in equity, with respect to the residue, as a trustee for the representatives of the husband. (n)   But now, as it has been already seen, the practice of the Ecclesiastical Court has been altered, and administration is granted to the representatives of the husband. (o)

5. But if the marriage be dissolved by the predecease of the husband, the *chattels real* of the wife, of which the husband had made no disposition in his lifetime; and the *choses in action* of the wife, not recovered or reduced into possession by the husband, shall survive to the wife as her own, and shall not go by will to the executors, or, in case of intestacy, to the personal representatives of the husband. (p)

Thus, in regard to two species of the personal property of the wife, her *chattels real* (such as leases for years), and her *choses in action* (such as bonds and other securities for money), the dissolution of the marriage by the predecease of the husband operates a change in the rights of the parties. The chattels real were vested in the husband, not absolutely, but *sub modo ;* they were vested in the husband and wife by a species of joint-tenancy, and as such

---

(n) Williams on Executors and Administrators, 910.
(o) Supra, p. 274.
(p) Popham, 5.; Co. Litt. 351.; 2 Blacks. Com. 434.

accrued to the survivor absolutely, as the surviving joint-tenant. (*q*)

As to the *choses in action* of the wife, these were not carried absolutely by the marriage ; they might have been recovered or reduced into possession by the husband, but if the wife survived would again belong to her. The distinction, however, is now unimportant if the husband survive ; for the before-mentioned statutes of 29 Car. II. c. 3. s. 25. and 1 Jac. II. c. 17. s. 5. have given to the husband the administration of all the personal property of the wife for his own benefit ; and, supposing him to die after her, and before he has recovered or reduced her *choses in action* into possession, his personal representatives will be entitled to them, and not the next of kin of the wife. (*r*)

In other respects, the law of succession and distribution in England, as laid down in the statutes of distribution, is modified by the local rules established in the different parts of that country. It is necessary, therefore, to see how the law is fixed, taking these local rules also into consideration.

The statutes of distribution apply generally to the province of Canterbury (*s*) ; and they apply to the principality of Wales, the province of York, and to the city of London, where not controlled by the customs established in those parts of the kingdom, which were reserved by the statutes, in so far as these customs are still in force. We shall, therefore, consider, first, how the law of succession is regulated generally under the statutes of distribution ; and,

---

(*q*) 2 Blacks. Com. 434.

(*r*) 4 Burn's Eccles. Law, 420. ; 2 Blackstone, 434. ; *in notis* of Coleridge's edition.

(*s*) The same rules obtain in Ireland, in British India, in the West Indies, and in other British colonies, so far as these are subject to the laws of England.

next, how this is controlled by the local customs of the principality of Wales, of the province of York, and of the city of London.

SECT. III.

Of the Rules of Distribution under the Statutes of Distribution in England.

THE statutes of distribution apply only to cases of *intestacy;* and it has been held, in repeated instances, that the Ecclesiastical Courts have no power to compel an executor to make distribution of the surplus undisposed of in a case of testate succession. (*t*)

According to the older authorities of the ecclesiastical law, the appointment of an executor was essential to a testament (*u*); and in the case of *Woodward* v. *Lord Darcy,* the common-law judges laid down, that without an executor a will is null and void. (*x*) Thus, there may be a *legal* intestacy where there is a will, if no executor be appointed: but this strictness has long ceased to exist, except in regard to the power of the Ecclesiastical Courts to make distribution; and the Court of Chancery has long held that, where the testator made his will, but named no executor, still the will was good in equity. (*y*) Courts of equity have also compelled the distribution of a residue not disposed of in a case of *quasi* or *partial* intestacy, in such manner as it would be distributed under the statutes. Where no executor was appointed, there was less of dif-

---

(*t*) Petit *v.* Smith, L Raym. 86. Rex *v.* Raines, L. Raym. 363. Hatton *v.* Hatton, Strange, 865. 4 Burn's Eccles. Law, 395.

(*u*) Swinburne, pt. i. s. 3. pl. 19. Godolphin, pt. i. c. 1. s. 2.

(*x*) Plowd. 185.

(*y*) Wyrall *v.* Hall, 2 Chanc. Rep. 112.; Swin. 7th ed. p. 15. *in notis.* Williams on Executors, pp. 7. 54.

ficulty upon this subject; but where an executor was named, a question in many cases arose, whether the executor was to distribute the residue, or if he was entitled to take it to himself. Down to a very recent period, the executor was the testator's residuary legatee appointed by law, and, as such, was entitled to the personal estate (except lapsed legacies) which the testator had not otherwise disposed of; but notwithstanding their *legal* title, courts of equity deemed executors to be trustees for the testator's personal representatives in all cases, where the intention of the testator was apparent, that the executors should not take beneficially by virtue of their office. Upon this subject many cases of great intricacy, in regard to the intention of testators, occurred in the courts of equity. (z)

But all difficulty upon this subject is done away by the recent statute (11 G. IV. and 1 W. IV. c. 40.), and now executors are to be "deemed, by courts of equity, trustees for the person or persons (if any) who would be entitled to the estate under the statute of distribution, in respect of any residue not expressly disposed of, unless it shall appear by the will, or any codicil thereto, the person or persons so appointed executor or executors was or were intended to take such residue beneficially."

Thus, in every case, the rules of the statute are now to be applied, as well by the administrator in a case of *pure intestacy*, as by the executor, or administrator with the will annexed, in a case of *quasi* or *partial* intestacy.

1. On the dissolution of a marriage by the death of a husband intestate, leaving a widow, and a child

---

(z) 2 Roper on Legacies (by White), 590. *et sequen.*, and 640. *et sequen.*

or children, one-third of the clear personal estate (after all debts, funerals, and just expenses of every sort first allowed and deducted) shall go to the widow, and the residue to the child or children, or their lineal descendants; if no children, or lineal descendants of them, then one moiety shall go to the widow, and the other moiety to the next of kindred. (*a*)

The widow's title under the statute may be barred by a settlement before marriage, excluding her from her distributive share of her husband's personal estate; and even a female infant may be barred of her right by such a settlement made before marriage, with the approbation of her parents or guardians. (*b*)

Various questions have occurred in the courts in regard to the meaning and interpretation of settlements, as affecting the rights of the wife in the distribution of her husband's personal estate. (*c*) These do not affect the general rule, but only show how this is to be applied in special cases, and it would be out of place to enter into them here.

2. In case there be no wife, the child, if only one, or, if more than one, the children, or such persons as shall legally represent them, in case any of the said children be then dead, shall take the clear personal estate of the deceased under the statutes of distribution. (*d*)

Though the expression *distribution* does not strictly apply in the case of one child, yet, where there is only one

---

(*a*) 4 Burn's Eccles. Law, 392.
(*b*) Williams on Executors and Administrators, 912. *et sequen.*
(*c*) Ibid.
(*d*) 4 Burn's Eccles. Law, 411.

person that can take, the statute vests the right in that person. (*e*)

Also, in cases regarding the distribution of personal estate, an infant in *ventre sa mere* shall be held to be entitled to a share by the statute. (*f*)

By the words of the statute, " such as shall legally represent such children," their lineal descendants to the remotest degree are called, to the exclusion of the collateral next of kin, and the widows of such descendants. (*g*)

3. If all the children, where there are more than one, be alive, the distribution among them shall be *per capita*, share and share alike; but if some of the children be alive, and others or other be dead, leaving descendants, each surviving child shall take one share; and the descendants of each child deceased shall take the share of such child by representation, under similar rules of succession. (*h*)

4. If all the children be dead, leaving only grandchildren, the succession shall also be divided among such grandchildren, *per capita*, share and share alike, and not by way of representation : but, in such case, if some of the grandchildren be alive, and others or other be dead, leaving descendants, a similar rule shall obtain, as above stated, in the case of children ; and the same rule shall take place if there be *only* remote descendants. (*i*)

Thus, while there are descendants, these exclude every other species of kindred. In the descending line, repre-

---

(*e*) Davers *v.* Dewes, *in notis*, 3 P. Will. 50.; Palmer *v.* Garard, H. 1690, Pre. Ch. 21.; 4 Burn's Eccles. Law, 396.

(*f*) Ball *v.* Smith, Freeman, 230.; 4 Burn's Eccles. Law, 396.

(*g*) Williams on Executors and Administrators, 915.

(*h*) 4 Burn's Eccles. Law, 411.   (*i*) Ibid. 412.

sentation is admitted to the remotest degree. When the descendants are all equal in degree, whether nearer or more remote, the distribution is *per capita.* Where there are descendants in different degrees entitled to share, the descendants in the remotest degree take *per stirpes.*

In this the law of England differs from the civil law, as laid down in the 118th novel of Justinian. According to it, in the succession of grandchildren, or other descendants, these took *per stirpes* in every case, being entitled to the same share of the intestate's estate, which their parents would have had, if such parents had lived. (*k*)

5. The descendant being the heir of the deceased ancestor shall take a share of the personal estate with the other children, or descendants, according to the above rules of distribution, without any abatement, in respect of the land or real estate, which he hath, by descent or otherwise, from the ancestor. Yet, if such heir have had any advancement from his father in his lifetime, otherwise than by land or real estate as aforesaid, if there be other children, or descendants of them, he shall abate for such advancement in like manner as the other children shall abate for advancements made to them. (*l*)

In like manner it seems that coheiresses shall bring together into hotchpot such advancement (not being lands) as they shall respectively have received from their father, before they shall be entitled to receive their distributive shares, agreeably to the general purport of the act, which is, evidently, to promote an equality as much as may be. (*m*)

(*k*) Novel, 118. c. 1.   (*l*) 4 Burn's Eccles. Law, 397.
(*m*) Ibid.

It has been matter of question whether the heir in lands held by the tenure of borough English (being the youngest son), should abate for these lands, or should be considered as an heir-at-law, who by the statute is to have a distributive share, without any allowance for lands by descent. In the case of *Pratt v. Pratt*, in E. 5 G. II., it was ruled by Sir Joseph Jekyll, Master of the Rolls, that the heir should allow for those lands; for he said the statute only intended to provide for the heir of the family, who is the common law heir, and not for one who is only heir by custom in some particular places. (*n*)

But in the case of *Lutwyche* v. *Lutwyche*, E. 1733, where a similar question occurred, whether the youngest son, who took a copyhold estate of the tenure of borough English, should have an equal share of the personal estate with the other children, or only so much as, with that copyhold, should make his portion equal to that of the other children; By Talbot Lord Chancellor, — " The heir at law is the eldest son, and not the heir in borough English, and the exception in the statute extends only to the eldest son; yet, nevertheless, the youngest son, who is heir in borough English, shall not bring the borough English estate into *hotchpot*. There is no law to oblige him to do this, but only the statute; and there are no words in the statute which require it; for the statute speaketh only of such estate as a child hath by settlement, or by the advancement of the intestate during his lifetime." And it was decreed that the youngest son should have an equal share with the other children, without regard to the borough English estate.

And the case of *Pratt* v. *Pratt* having come afterwards before Lord Chancellor Talbot, he reversed the decree of

---

(*n*) 2 Strange, 935.; 4 Burn's Eccles. Law, 397.

the Master of the Rolls, and decreed agreeably to this case. (*o*)

> 6. In case of the intestacy of the father, if any child other than the heir-at-law have received an advancement from the father in his lifetime, either of lands or personal estate, by settlement or otherwise, such child shall bring this advancement, or the value thereof, into *hotchpot* (or collation) with the other children, before he or she shall be entitled to receive his or her distributive share of the father's personal estate. And the same rule shall obtain in the case of the advancement of a child, when his or her descendants claim a distributive share by representation in the personal estate of the ancestor. (*p*)

The questions which have occurred in regard to the advancement of children, and what shall or shall not be deemed an advancement, are numerous and of considerable intricacy; it would not be profitable to enter into these in this place.

It is important to remark, however, that the rule obliging children to pay their advancements into hotchpot, applies only in a case of *actual* intestacy; for where there is a will, and a residuary estate, not disposed of by that will, is to be distributed by the executor, in such case a child, advanced by a father in his lifetime, cannot be called upon to bring his or her advancement into hotchpot, in claiming a share of the residuary estate. (*q*)

(*o*) Cas. temp. Talb. 276.; 4 Burn's Eccles. Law, 398.

(*p*) 4 Burn's Eccles. Law, 398. *et sequen.*

(*q*) Walton *v.* Walton (M. 1807.), 14 Ves. 324. If no executors were appointed, would the same rule apply in the case of an administrator with the will annexed?

It is also to be remarked, that a child advanced in part shall bring in his or her advancement only among the other children; and that no benefit shall accrue from it to the widow. (r)

The rules in regard to the advancement of children, are extended to grandchildren claiming their parent's distributive share *per stirpes* in the succession of the grandfather, where the parent had been advanced; in such case, the grandchildren are to bring their father's advancement into hotchpot. (s) But it does not appear to have been decided whether the same rule would obtain where grandchildren were claiming *per capita;* nor whether advancements to grandchildren, or other more remote descendants, should or should not be brought into hotchpot before such grandchildren, or other more remote descendants, should be entitled to share in the succession. (t)

Nor has it been decided whether grandchildren advanced, some more, some less, by their father in his lifetime, shall bring their several advancements into hotchpot, one with the other, before they shall distribute their deceased father's share of their grandfather's personal estate. (u)

But whatever a child receives out of the *mother's* estate, it is said, shall not be brought into hotchpot in taking a distributive share of that mother's estate. So it was decided by Lord Chancellor King, in the case of *Holt* v. *Frederick,* T. 1726. (x)

7. In case there be no children, or legal representatives of them, a moiety of the intestate estate

---

(r) Ward v. Lant, Prec. Chanc. 182. 184.; Kirkcudbright v. Kirkcudbright, 8 Ves. 51. 64.; 4 Burn's Eccles. Law, 402.

(s) 4 Burn's Eccles. Law, 403.

(t) Ibid.   (u) 4 Burn's Eccles. Law, 403.

(x) 2 P. Will. 356.; 4 Burn's Eccles. Law, 402.

shall belong to the wife, and the other half thereof shall go to the next of kindred of the deceased who are in equal degree, and to those who legally represent them. But in case there be no widow or children, or representatives of such children, the personal estate of the intestate shall go wholly to the next of kindred of the deceased in equal degree, and those who legally represent them. (*y*)

Kindred are distinguished either by the *right* line or by the *collateral;* the *right* line is of parents and children, computing by *ascendants* and *descendants*. The collateral line is between brothers and sisters, and the rest of the kindred.

Those of the right line are reckoned upwards, as parents or ascendants; or downwards, as children or descendants. Those of the collateral line are reckoned *ex transverso* or sidewise, as brothers and sisters, uncles and aunts, or the like, and such as are born from them. (*z*)

It appears that under the statutes of distribution, in case of a total intestacy, or in the distribution of a surplusage under a will, kindred is reckoned in England, in accordance with the rules of the *civil* law, and rejecting the rules of the *canon* law, where these differ from those of the civil law. (*a*)

In the right or ascending and descending lines, there is no difference between the rules of the *civil* and *canon* law; but every generation, whether ascending or descending, constitutes a different degree. Thus, the father of *John* is related to him in the first degree; so likewise is his son. His grandfather and grandson are related to him in the

---

(*y*) 4 Burn's Eccles. Law, 394.

(*z*) 4 Burn's Eccles. Law, 404.

(*a*) 2 Blacks. Com. 504.

second degree; and his great-grandfather and great grandson in the third degree, and so on.

But in reckoning the collateral line, there is a difference between the rules of the *civil,* and those of the *canon* law. In the *civil* law, the computation is made by reckoning upwards from the one of the parties to the person from whom both are branched, and then descending downwards to the other, with whom the degree of kindred is to be traced. Thus, a brother is in the second degree of kindred, as having the same common father; an uncle and nephew are in the third degree; a great uncle and a cousin-german are in the fourth degree, and so on.

By the *canon* law there is another mode of computation among collaterals. The canonists always commence with the stock or common ancestor, and reckon the degree of kindred downwards from him alone, without also reckoning the line of ascent upwards to that common ancestor. Thus, in regard to two brothers (who by the civil law would be in the second degree of kindred), by the canon law they are accounted in the first degree. In this case the father was the common ancestor; from him to the son was one degree. Thus, also, cousins-german, by the canon law, are accounted in the second degree between themselves; the grandfather was the common ancestor; from him to his son was one degree; to his grandson was the second degree. But if the parties proposed be not equally distant from the common stock, the most remote fixes the degree of kindred between them: thus, an uncle is in the second degree of kindred to his nephew; the grandfather was the common ancestor; from him to his son, the uncle, was one degree, but to the nephew, the son of another son, was a second degree; and he being the most remote from the common stock, they are distant among themselves in the same degree: and the son of a cousin-german is by the canon law reckoned of the third degree; he was one degree further from the common stock than the cousin-german. (*b*) This is illustrated by the annexed diagram.

> 8. If a person die intestate in whole or in part, without wife, or descendants in the lifetime of his father, the father shall take the personal estate of the party dying intestate as aforesaid, to the exclusion of all the other kindred. (*c*)

According to the rules both of the *civil* and *canon* law, the father and mother would in such case be in the first degree of kindred to the deceased. But as, during marriage, the rights of the mother were totally merged in those of her husband, the father alone would take. This rule is not in accordance with that of the Roman law. By it brothers and sisters of the full blood are made to share with parents. (*d*)

> 9. If the person intestate as aforesaid die without wife or descendants, or a father him surviving, in the lifetime of his mother, every brother and sister of the deceased, and *the representatives of them*, shall have an equal share with the *mother;* but if there be no brother or sister, or legal representatives of them, the mother in such case shall take the whole personal estate. (*e*)

This rule as to brothers and sisters sharing with a mother was introduced by the statute of 1 James II. c. 17. According to the prior statutes, the mother in such case would have taken the whole personal estate, as next of

---

(*b*) 4 Burn's Eccles. Law, 404. *et sequen.*
(*c*) 2 Blacks. Com. p. 515.; 4 Burn's Eccles. Law, 413.
(*d*) Novel, 118. c. 2.   (*e*) 4 Burn's Eccles. Law, 394.

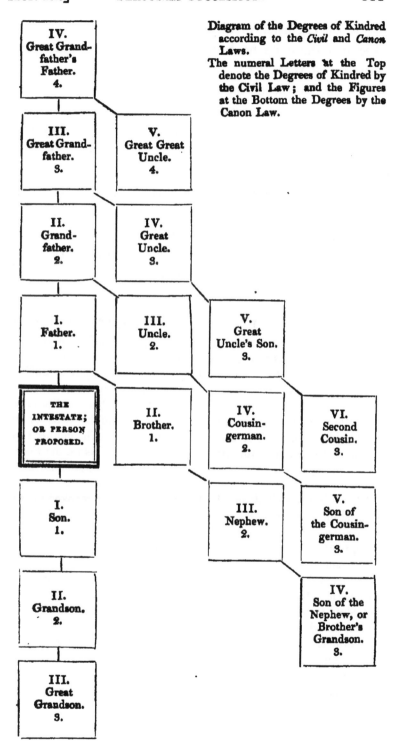

Diagram of the Degrees of Kindred according to the *Civil* and *Canon* Laws.

The numeral Letters at the Top denote the Degrees of Kindred by the Civil Law; and the Figures at the Bottom the Degrees by the Canon Law.

kin, to the exclusion of all the other kindred, and she still takes it if there be no brothers or sisters, or legal representatives of them. (ƒ)

The succession of the mother, however, in such case, even when it was universal in other parts of England, was always controlled by the custom of the city of London, in regard to the orphanage part of the children of a freeman. (g)

Questions have arisen under this statute of James II. what should be done if the deceased also left a *wife*, which was out of the *words* of the statute. This statute, as well as the statute of distribution, is incorrectly penned (h); and it has been found necessary, in several cases, to consider

---

(ƒ) 4 Burn's Eccles. Law, 427. At one time, and for a short period, the succession of the mother was rejected by the English courts. In the *Duchess of Suffolk's case*, it was held that the mother was *not of kin to her child*. In the reign of Edward VI. Charles Duke of Suffolk, having issue by one venter a son, and by another a daughter, by his will devised goods to his son, and died. After his death his son died intestate, without wife and without issue; his mother, and his sister by the father's side, born of the former venter, then living. The mother took the administration; but the sister commenced a suit before the Ecclesiastical judge, claiming that it might be revoked, and the administration granted to her. The most learned as well in the common law as in the civil law, were consulted, and the Ecclesiastical Court revoked the administration granted to the mother, and granted a new administration to the sister, albeit she were of the half-blood to the deceased. (Swinburne, p. 912.) But he adds (p. 918.), " True it is, that, in those days, " this example did so much prevail, that many judgments passed accord- " ingly upon the like case; but yet, in process of time, the truth pre- " vailed (for what is stronger than truth), and the mother was every where " adjudged to be of kin to her child, who, dying intestate and without " issue, the administration of his goods may be committed unto her (if " the ordinary in discretion so think good), as next of kin according to " the statute."

(g) Infrà.

(h) Lord Hardwicke in Stanley *v.* Stanley, 1739; 1 Atkyns, 458.

points, as to which the statutes were silent. In *Keylway* v. *Keylway* (T. 12 Geo. II.) (*i*), where a person died without issue, leaving a *wife*, several brothers and sisters, and a mother, him surviving; the wife took a moiety; and upon a bill filed in the Court of Chancery, in regard to the other moiety, it was decided that the mother in such case did not take the whole, but only a share with the brothers and sisters of the intestate. In *Stanley* v. *Stanley* (May, 1739) a person died intestate, leaving a wife, a mother, and children of a brother deceased: the wife took her moiety; the children of the brother contended that the mother, under the statute, took only an equal share with each of them: but upon a bill filed in the Court of Chancery, Lord Hardwicke decreed, that the residue of the estate should be divided into four parts; two-fourths to go to the wife, one-fourth to the mother, and the other fourth to the representatives of the brother deceased. (*k*)

10. No representation shall be admitted among collaterals after brothers' and sisters' children. (*l*)

This rule was also the creation of the statute, introduced from the third chapter of the 118th Novel of Justinian. It is expedient that the right of representation should stop somewhere. A similar rule is embodied in the *Code Civil* of the French law. (*m*)

Under this rule questions have occurred, whether the words of the statute are to be intended of brothers and sisters to the *intestate*; or whether when distribution falls

---

(*i*) 2 Strange, 710., 2 P. Wms. 344.; Gilb. Eq. Cas. 189.; 2 Eq. Cas. Abr. 441, 442.; 4 Burn's Eccles. Law, 428.

(*k*) 1 Atkyns, 458.; 4 Burn's Eccles. Law, 428.

(*l*) 4 Burn's Eccles. Law, 423.

(*m*) Code Civil, No. 742.

out amongst brothers and sisters, though remote relations to the intestate, representation shall also be admitted amongst them. But it has been settled, that the representation should be only between the brothers and sisters to the intestate. (*n*)

11. In reckoning the degrees of kindred, in the succession of personal estate, no distinction shall be made between kindred of the full, and those of the half-blood; and propinquity, or kindred, is to be deduced as well from the mother, and the maternal relations, as from the father and the paternal relations. (*o*)

After the statute there were several precedents of judgments given, allowing only half a share to the half-blood; but the law in this particular has now become fixed and certain, since the judgment of the House of Lords, in the case of *Crooke* v. *Watt*, upon an appeal from a decree in Chancery, which had been given in favour of the half-blood, and was affirmed in the House of Lords. (*p*)

This is regulated otherwise in the Novel of Justinian. (*q*) It appears to be doubtful if the rule adopted in the case of *Crooke* v. *Watt* has fixed this matter upon its just basis. Great hardship may often occur from this rule.

12. Affinity, or relationship by marriage, gives no right to a share of the property under the statute:

(*n*) Maw *v.* Harding, T. 1691, 2 Vern. 233.; Pett *v.* Pett, T. 1700, 1 P. Will. 25., 1 Salk. 250.; Bowers *v.* Littlewood, M. 1719, 1 P. Will. 594.; 4 Burn's Eccles. Law, 424.

(*o*) 4 Burn's Eccles. Law, 422.

(*p*) Strahan's Domat. 658.; 2 Vern. 124., S. C. Show. P. C. 108.; 4 Burn's Eccles. Law, 422.

(*q*) Novel, 118. c. 3.

therefore, if the intestate had a son and daughter, and they both die in the lifetime of the intestate, the former leaving a wife, and the latter a husband; upon the intestate's death afterwards, such wife and husband respectively have no claim on the intestate's estate. (r)

In questions of distribution between ascendants and collaterals, not provided for by the statutes, the following points have been decided : —

(1.) In questions between a brother and a grandfather, the brother is preferred to the whole succession. (s)   (2.) In a question between a grandmother and uncles and aunts, the grandmother will take in exclusion of the uncles and aunts. (t)   (3.) A grandfather by the father's side, and a grandmother by the mother's side, shall take in equal moieties. (u)   (4.) In competition between two aunts, and a nephew and niece, children of a brother deceased, Lord Chancellor Hardwicke ordered the surplus to be divided into four parts *per capita*, they being all in equal degree; but if the brother had been alive, he would have taken the whole. (x)   (5.) Great grandfathers, or great

---

(r) Toller, 386.

(s) Pool v. Wishaw, in Chancery, T. 1708. Norbury v. Richards, in Chancery, M. 1749, cited in Evelyn v. Evelyn, before Lord Hardwicke, Hil. 1754; 3 Atk. 762.; Ambl. 191.; 4 Burn's Eccles. Law, 416.

(t) Blackborough v. Davis, 1 Salk. 38. 251.; 12 Mod. 623.; 1 P. Will. 51.; Ld. Raym. 684.; Woodroffe v. Wickworth, Prec. Ch. 527.; 4 Burn's Eccles. Law, 415.

(u) Moor v. Barham, May, 1723; 1 P. Will. 53.; 4 Burn's Eccles. Law, 414.

(x) Durant v. Prestwood, June, 1738; 1 Atk. 454.; 4 Burn's Eccles. Law, 424. There would clearly have been a different mode of distribution under the 118th Novel, c. 3., but this appears to have been correct under the Statute of Distribution.

grandmothers, being in the third degree, take a distributive share with uncles and aunts. (*y*)

It appears that the only one of the above cases, which is not reducible to a preference of the nearest of kindred by the civil law, is the first; namely, that a brother shall take in preference to a grandfather, though these are both equal in degree. In all the other cases the nearest in degree has been preferred, and those equal in degree have taken equally. And so the rule is in all other remoter degrees of kindred, that the nearest in degree takes the whole, and those who are equal in degree take equally. (*z*)

       13. Where a person entitled to a distributive share of an intestate estate dies within a year after the intestate, though no distribution could be made till after one year be fully expired after the intestate's death, the share of the person deceased was an interest vested and transmissible to his executors or administrators. (*a*)

In this sense the statute made a will for the intestate; and it is as if a legacy was bequeathed payable a year hence, which would plainly be an interest vested presently. In the case of a distribution of an undisposed surplus under a will, *à fortiori*, the share thereof would be vested in any of the next of kin dying before distribution.

Sect. IV.

Rules of Distribution in the Principality of Wales.

We learn from the before mentioned statute of the

(*y*) Lloyd *v.* Tench, 2 Ves. sen. 215.

(*z*) 4 Burn's Eccles, Law, 404.

(*a*) Brown *v.* Farndell, Carth. 51, 52.; S. C. Comberb. 112.; Bac. Abr. Exor. I. 4.; Williams's Law of Executors, 936.

7 & 8 Will. III. c. 38., that the doctrine of the *pars ratio-nabilis* extends to the effects of intestates in that principality. It will be seen, however, that the above statute speaks very indistinctly of this custom. It states that " *in several counties and places* within the principality of Wales, and marches thereof, the widows and younger children of persons dying inhabitants therein *have often claimed and pretended* to be entitled to a part of the goods and chattels of their late husbands and fathers, called her and their reasonable part, by virtue or colour of a custom or other usage within the said principality and marches thereof."

Thus, at the time of making the statute, it does not appear that much had been distinctly known in regard to the local extent of this custom. It is singular, that no case in relation to it appears in the books which treat of matters of this nature. The writers concur in saying, that there is little to be gathered, in regard to this custom, except from the statute. (*b*)

SECT. V.

Rules of Distribution in the Province of York.

ACCORDING to the ancient custom of this province, " there is due to the widow and to the lawful children of every man being an inhabitant or an householder within the said province of York, and dying there or elsewhere intestate, being an inhabitant or householder within that province, a reasonable part of his clear moveable goods; unless such child be heir to his father, deceased, or were advanced by his father in his lifetime, by which advance-

---

(*b*) Toller on Executors, 403.; Off. Ex. 97. *in notis.;* Suppl. 72.; 4 Burn's Eccles. Law, 478.; Williams on Executors, 937.

ment it is to be understood, that the father in his lifetime bestowed upon his child a competent portion whereon to live." (c)

Thus the custom applies only to the personal estate of a person dying domiciled within the province; and in so far as such personal estate is not regulated by the custom, it is distributable by the statutes of distribution. (d)

Down to the time of passing the statutes which enabled an inhabitant of the province of York to make a will of his whole personal estate, under every circumstance (e), the custom must have ruled in every case of succession to the personal estate of a husband and father. From that period questions must have occurred in cases of partial intestacy in regard to the distribution of a surplusage under a will; whether such surplusage was to be distributed by the custom or under the statutes. Some of these, of very considerable intricacy, have been decided in regard to the custom of this province.

Where an inhabitant of the province of York makes a will, appointing an executor, but making no disposition of the residue of his estate, if such residue did not go to the executor (being a case of *equitable* intestacy), courts of equity have held that the residue was distributable by the statute, and not by the custom. (f)

It seems, however, that if the testator should die, leaving a will, *but without having appointed an executor* (being a case of *legal* intestacy), his personal estate undisposed of must be distributed subject to the custom, as if he had

---

(c) Swin. 233.; 4 Burn's Eccles. Law, 457.

(d) 4 Burn's Eccles. Law, 452.

(e) 4 W. 3. c. 2.; 2 & 3 Ann. c. 5.

(f) Wheeler v. Sheer, Moseley, 302.; Lawson v. Lawson, 4 Bro. P. C. 21.; Wilkinson v. Atkinson, 1 Turn. Chanc. Cas. 255.; Fitzgerald v. Field, 1 Rus. Chan. Cas. 416.

died actually intestate. (*g*)   Thus, a difference appears
to have been introduced by those decisions, between a
case of *equitable* and one of *legal* intestacy: under the
first, the residue undisposed of would be distributed by
the statute; but under the second by the custom.

Doubts, however, have been stated as to the principle
involved in the first class of these decisions, on the ground
that a residue undisposed of by the will of an inhabitant
of the province of York ought to be divided according to
that custom, which was the *lex loci.* (*h*)   But since the
recent statute of 11 G. IV. and 1 W. IV. c. 40. was passed,
this matter (though the statute was made for another purpose) appears to be settled in the case where a will has
been made appointing an executor, with a surplus undisposed of.   In such case, the executor is bound to dispose
of the surplus under the statute of distributions, in every
part of England. (*i*)

It has been already noticed, that this statute in its terms
only applies to the case where an executor has been appointed, and not to the case where there is no executor;
and it does not appear that any question has occurred
since the passing of this statute, in regard to the surplusage
under a will, where there was no executor.   In such case,
the residue might still be distributable under the custom.

The following rules appear to be established in regard
to the custom of the province of York.

> 1. The *custom* takes place only in regard to the
> rights of the widow, and of the child or children
> of an inhabitant or householder within the province;
> if there be no widow and no child, the whole per-

(*g*) Wheeler *v.* Sheer, Moseley, 303.

(*h*) 4 Burn's Eccles. Law, 470. *in notis.*

(*i*) Supra, p. 39.

sonal property is of the nature of deadman's part; and distribution thereof is made according to the statutes, without any interference of or reference to the custom. (*k*)

The widow is entitled to her customary share whether the children be of her or of a former wife, and a posthumous child shall come in for a customary share, as well as other children. (*l*)

2. In every case, where any part of the personal estate is distributable by the custom, the deadman's part is distributable solely under the statutes. (*m*)

3. On the dissolution of a marriage by the death of the husband intestate, leaving a wife and children, or other remoter descendants, after payment of debts and funeral expenses, according to the custom, the personal estate shall be distributable as follows: the wife is entitled by the custom, besides her apparel, the furniture of her bedchamber, and a coffer-box, containing her jewels, chains, and other ornaments of her person, to one third of the whole free personal estate of the intestate; the surviving children, not being the heir at law, or advanced by the father in his lifetime, are entitled to another third part thereof; the remaining third, being the *deadman's part*, shall be distributed by the statutes of distribution to the widow and children, including the heir (without regard to any shares taken by them under the custom), and to the descendants of children deceased, under similar

---

(*k*) Swinb. 299.; 4 Burn's Eccles. Law, 457.
(*l*) Williams on Execut. and Admistr. 946.
(*m*) Ibid. 938.

rules of distribution, with those which, under the statutes, obtain generally within the province of Canterbury in a case of intestacy. (*n*) Thus, if the property were divided into ninths, the widow takes four ninths (three under the custom, and one under the statute), and the children take the other five ninths.

When the act of 1 Jac. II. c. 17., settling the share to be taken by a mother in competition with the brothers and sisters of a party deceased, was passed, a case of *Stapleton* v. *Sherrard* was depending in the Court of Chancery of this nature :— Robert Stapleton died an inhabitant of the province of York, intestate, and without issue, leaving Dorothy his widow him surviving. Dorothy, the widow, took administration of his goods and effects, and intermarried with Bennet Sherrard. The next of kin of Robert Stapleton were his brothers and sisters, and their representatives; they filed a bill in Chancery against the administratrix for an account of the personal estate of the deceased, and to make full distribution of the same. The administratrix claimed one half of the personal estate under the custom, as the widow, and one half of the other moiety under the statutes of distribution. The cause was at first heard before the Lord Keeper of the Great Seal on the 24th of February, in the first year of the reign of James II., and his Lordship desired the then Archbishop of York to certify, — when a man dies intestate within the province of York (after his debts and funeral expenses paid), how the residue was to be divided by the custom of the province of York, and what part remained to the ordinary to be distributed. The Archbishop, on the 18th of March,

---

(*n*) Swinb. 300.; 4 Burn's Eccles. Law, 452.

1 Jac. II., certified that, in such cases aforesaid, the widow of the intestate, by the custom of the said province, had usually allotted to her one moiety of the clear personal estate, and that the other moiety had been distributed amongst the next of kin to the deceased intestate, and that this had been the constant practice of the Ecclesiastical Court at York. The Lord Keeper thereupon decided against the claim of the widow to the moiety of the deadman's part. But, upon a petition to the Lord Chancellor, and a rehearing of the cause, his Lordship declared, that he was fully satisfied that the administratrix ought to have the one moiety of her late husband's personal estate by the custom, and one half of the other moiety by virtue of the statutes of distribution, and made his decree accordingly; and, upon a rehearing before his Lordship, he confirmed this decree. (o)

It is singular that this intricacy in regard to the distribution of the deadman's part, which was under consideration thus early, has been allowed to exist till this day, in regard to the distribution of the estate of an intestate in the province of York; and the intricacy is not confined to the share of the widow, but extends also to the shares of children, or the representatives of them. (p)

4. The widow's title to a share of the personal estate under the custom may be barred by settlement, or agreement before marriage; and, being so barred, she shall be, in regard to the custom, as if she did not exist; but, unless such settlement or agreement extends also to bar her share under the statute, she will be entitled to share in the distribution of the deadman's part. (q)

(o) Hilary, 1684; 1 Vern. 305. 314. 482.; 4 Burn's Eccles. Law, 452.

(p) 4 Burn's Eccles. Law, 472.

(q) Williams on Executors and Administrators, 944, 945.

It is not necessary to notice here the cases which have occurred upon this subject; these relate chiefly to ambiguity and uncertainty in the meaning and intention of parties, and do not affect the general rules upon this subject.

> 5. The child being heir-at-law of his father in lands held in fee simple, or fee tail, or being heir in reversion, is barred from any filial portion under the custom; but being heir in lands of the tenure of borough English, or in copyhold or customary lands, is not so barred. (r)

Although the lands to which the heir succeeds be of very small revenue, " peradventure not past a *noble* yearly rent, and the goods very great in comparison of so small a rent," still the heir takes nothing according to the custom, and he has no power of *collation* as in the law of Scotland. (s)

That the heir in borough English, copyhold, or customary estate in lands, should not be barred of his filial portion of the personal estate under the custom, is laid down in the books treating of this matter (t); though this appears to be opposite in principle to what was decided as to the heir in lands of the tenure of borough English, and in copyhold or customary estate in the province of Canterbury. (u) In the cases last-mentioned, the heir in these was put upon the same footing with the heir in fee simple lands, both being entitled to share in the distribution of personal estate of their father; but in the province of York, a marked difference is made between the heir in freehold

---

(r) 4 Burn's Eccles. Law, 463.

(s) Swinb. 332.; 4 Burn's Eccles. Law, 463. If the heir takes nothing from his father in *that character*, I presume he is not excluded; but I have seen no direct authority for this.

(t) Ibid. 332.; 4 Burn's Eccles. Law, 464.   (u) Supra, p. 325.

estates, and the heir in the estates of the other tenures before mentioned. The heir in the first is barred from sharing; the heir in the other takes a share of the personal estate, with the other children.

> 6. If any child be fully advanced by the father in his lifetime, whether such advancement be by lands or hereditaments, or personal estate, such child is also barred from taking any filial portion under the custom. (*x*)

A good deal of intricacy appears to prevail upon this subject of advancement, in regard to what is a full, and what an imperfect advancement. It would not be profitable here to enter minutely into the cases which have been decided upon this subject. Swinburne (*y*) holds the opinion, that the gift of the father shall either be held to be an advancement, or no advancement; if it shall be found to be a preferment, then the child is excluded from receiving a filial portion; but if it shall be found to be no preferment, then the child is not barred from receiving a filial portion according to the custom. But the general opinion appears to be, that a short advancement is " to be brought into hotchpot with the children, but not with the widow." (*z*)

Again : a question hath arisen in case where a child hath received, in his father's lifetime, an advancement not only sufficient to debar him of his customary part, but so large as to extend into, or to overbalance, what would be his proportionable share also of the deadman's part; whether, in such case, the child shall receive any share of the deadman's part, unless he shall bring into hotchpot, in

---

(*x*) Swinb. 334.; 4 Burn's Eccles. Law, 459.

(*y*) Swinb. 338.

(*z*) 4 Burn's Eccles. Law, 468.

regard to the deadman's part, so much of his advancement as exceedeth his just proportion of the customary part. Upon this point various opinions have been held; and it does not appear to have been expressly decided; but in the case of *Gudgeon* v. *Ramsden*, Trin. 1692, it was decided, in a question between the heir, and a daughter (the only other child), who had a portion given her in marriage, in lieu and full satisfaction of what she might claim by the custom of the province, — that the daughter must not bring back her portion into hotchpot, for that came in lieu of the customary part, and was as the price the father thought fit to give her for the same. (*a*)

Burn, however, considers that if there had not in that case been a special contract or agreement, as a purchase by the father from his child of her right to the customary part; and if the advancement had been general, without any respect either to the customary or distributive share, the decision might have been otherwise, and so as best to answer the intent of the statute, which expresseth " that the estate of all the said children shall be made equal, as near as can be estimated." (*b*)

7. When a man dies leaving a widow and an only child, being his heir-at-law, as before mentioned (rule 5.), the division of the personal estate shall be bipartite; one moiety to the widow, the other to the deadman's part. So also, when he dies leaving a widow, a child being his heir-at-law, and another child or other children, which other child or other children have been advanced by the father in his lifetime, the division of the personal estate

---

(*a*) Gudgeon *v.* Ramsden, T. 1692; 2 Vern. 274.
(*b*) 4 Burn's Eccles. Law, 461.

shall be bipartite, one moiety to the widow and the other to the deadman's part. (c)

8. If a man leave no widow, but only children, the division of the personal estate shall also be bipartite; one moiety to the children excluding the heir, the other moiety to the deadman's part, distributable by the statute; but if the younger children shall be fully advanced by the father in his lifetime, the whole shall go, under the statute, to the child being the heir-at-law. (d)

9. In regard to leases, the wife and children cannot have any rateable part thereof within the province, unless they prove that, by special custom of that place (namely, of that city, county, deanery, or parish where the intestate dwelt and had such leases), the wife and children were accustomed to have their rateable part, as well of the leases as of the moveable goods of the intestate; but if such special custom be proved, they may receive the rateable part as before, but not by the general custom of the province. (e) In regard to *debts* due to the intestate, the wife and children take their rateable parts thereof, after the same shall have been received by the administrator, but not before (f); and in regard to estates *pur auter vie*, where not devised, these (in terms of the act 14 G. II. c. 20.) shall go and be distributed as the personal estate of the intestate would go and be distributed. Thus,

---

(c) 4 Burn's Eccles. Law, 472.
(d) Ibid. 471. 477.
(e) Swinb. 302.; Burn's Eccles. Law, 461.
(f) Swinb. 301.; Burn's Eccles. Law, 462.

part might go by the custom, and part by the statutes of distribution. (g)

10. If by settlement a jointure be limited to the wife in bar of her demands out of the personal estate of her husband under the custom, the division of the personal estate under the custom is bipartite as if no widow had existed, one half to the children, excluding the heir, the other half to the deadman's part. (h)

11. A child being of full age, for a valuable consideration may release his or her filial portion (i); and such release shall operate as if that child were dead, and his or her portion shall go to increase the shares of the other children. And the same thing shall result from the advancement of such child. If all the children release, or be advanced, and there be a widow, this also makes the division of the personal estate under the custom bipartite between the wife and the deadman's part; and if there be no widow, the whole shall be deadman's part. (k)

12. Grandchildren, or more remote decendants, take no share of the filial customary part; and thus, if an intestate leave a wife and only grandchildren, or more remote descendants, by the custom, the division of the personal estate is bipartite, one half to the widow, the other half to the deadman's part;

(g) 4 Burn's Eccles. Law, 463.

(h) 1 Vern. 15.; 4 Burn's Eccles. Law, 457.

(i) 4 Burn's Eccles. Law, 461. note.

(k) Ibid. 471.

but the wife takes not only one half as her share under the custom, but also of the deadman's part one third under the statute; the other two thirds of the deadman's part go to the grandchildren or other descendants under the statute; and if no widow, the whole is deadman's part. (*l*)

The intricacy of the distribution by the custom of the province of York, mixed with a distribution under the statute, is strongly marked in a case given by way of example by Burn (*m*) in the following terms : — " A man inhabiting within the province dieth intestate, leaving a clear personalty of 9000*l*., and leaving a widow and four children; the first being heir-at-law to freehold lands, and having received likewise of his father 400*l*. to set him up in trade; the second advanced by the amount of 3000*l*.; the third partly advanced to the amount of 600*l*.; and the fourth not at all advanced. The question is, how this personalty shall be distributed? First of all, the widow shall have one third part by the custom, as her widow's portion; to wit, 3000*l*. Another third part by the said custom shall be distributed among the children: of which the heir-at-law (as such) by the said custom is excluded from receiving any share; the second son also, as being fully advanced, is excluded; but hereunto the third son shall bring his partial advancement of 600*l*. into hotchpot, and then the third and fourth sons shall divide the 3600*l*. equally between them; but the real benefit thereof to the third son will be but 1200*l*., and to the fourth son 1800*l*. The remaining third part of the said personalty, which is the deadman's part, shall be distributed by the statute: of which, by the said statute, the widow shall have one third, to

---

wit, 1000*l.*; and the residue, being 2000*l.*, shall be distributed equally among the said three children; namely, the heir-at-law, and the third and fourth sons (the heir-at-law being let in for so much by the statute, and the second son being still excluded, as having more than his just proportion of his father's whole personal estate); but hereunto the heir-at-law shall first bring his partial advancement of 400*l.* into hotchpot, and so the said three children shall divide the whole 2400*l.* equally among them; but the real benefit thereof to the heir-at-law will be but 400*l.*, and to the said two youngest children 800*l.* each.   So that of the clear personalty of 9000*l.* —

" The widow shall receive	-	£ 4000
The heir-at-law	-	400
The second child	-	—
The third child	-	2000
The fourth child	-	2600
Total	-	£ 9000*l.*"

As already observed, except for the statutes enabling a will to be made of the whole personal estate, this intricacy must have been intolerable; and it would have been much increased if any of the above children had died leaving descendants, thereby introducing new classes of persons into the distribution of the *deadman's* part.

13. If a person leave no wife, but an heir-at-law, or an only child being advanced, or partly advanced, though such child might be barred by the custom, or obliged, if there were other children, to bring his or her advancement into hotchpot, such child shall take the whole personal estate. (*n*)

(*n*) 4 Burn's Eccles. Law, 471.

14. Every share to which a child is entitled, under the custom, becomes vested in such child, whether of age or not, on the death of the intestate; and on the death of such child, shall pass to the executors, or other legal representatives of such child. (o)

SECT. VI.

Of Distribution according to the Custom of London.

THERE is a marked difference betwixt the custom of London and that of the province of York in this respect: that in the latter (as we have seen) (p) the custom applies only to the personal estate of a person dying domiciled in the province of York; in the former the custom applies to the personal estate of a freeman of London, wherever situated, and wherever he may be domiciled, and controls the law of the domicil. (q)

The recent case of *Onslow* v. *Onslow* (r), in which the custom was found to rule, even in regard to the personal estate of an *honorary freeman*, leaves no room for doubt upon this subject. This matter has not yet attracted attention in Scotland; but from the principles laid down in the books of authority in regard to the custom of London, and the cases which have been decided upon this subject, there would, at least, be ground to contend that the custom should prevail against a domicil in Scotland, or a foreign domicil, as it has against a domicil in the province of York,

---

(o) 4 Burn's Eccles. Law, 477.; Blacks. Comm. 51.; Williams on Executors, 955.

(p) Supra, p. 338.

(q) Cholmley v. Cholmley, 2 Vern. 48. 82.; Webb v. Webb, 2 Vern. 110.; Onslow v. Onslow, 1 Sim. 18.

(r) Supra, p. 107.

or in the province of Canterbury. Thus, also, it might be contended, in terms of the before-mentioned statute of the 11 G. I. (s), enabling all freemen of London to dispose of their whole personal estate by their last wills, that a freeman of London dying domiciled in Scotland, might, notwithstanding the rules of succession in that country, make a testamentary disposition of his whole personal estate. (t)

As noticed in regard to the custom of the province of York, down to the time of passing the statute which enabled a freeman of London to make a will of his whole personal estate (u), the custom must have ruled in every case of the succession of a freeman leaving a widow and children. From that period questions have occurred in regard to the application of the custom in cases of partial intestacy, whether such intestacy were of a *legal* or of an *equitable* nature.

In one case, Lord Hardwicke appears to have held, in 1744, where a freeman of London had made a will appointing an executor, but leaving a residue undisposed of, that the executor was to distribute this under the custom (x); but subsequent cases appear to have fully established that courts of equity, in such case of *equitable* intestacy, distributed the residue under the statutes; and that the custom only applied in a case of *legal* intestacy, where a will had been made, and no executor appointed. (y) Thus the rule

---

(s) 11 G. I. c. 18. ss. 17, 18.

(t) I do not know if *Mr. Hog*, the testator in the noted case of Hog *v.* Lashley, was a freeman of London or not; but if he was, a new line of argument might have been introduced into that case. (Supra, p. 127.) And, according to the case of Onslow *v.* Onslow, it is to be presumed, that an honorary freeman would have the same power of bequeathing by will.

(u) 11 G. I. c. 18. ss. 17, 18.

(x) Beard *v.* Beard, 3 Atk. 73.; 4 Burn's Eccles. Law, 471.

(y) Williams on Executors and Administrators, 939.

laid down by courts of equity appears to have been the same, in such cases, as already noticed in regard to the custom of the province of York. (z)

The recent statute of 11 G. IV. & 1 W. IV. c. 40. has removed all doubt in regard to the mode of distribution in a case of *equitable* intestacy, as well in regard to the statutes of distribution generally, as in regard to the customs of London, and of the province of York.   In every case where there is an executor under a will, and a residue undisposed of, such residue must now be distributed by the executor under the statutes of distribution.

Since the making of this statute, it does not appear that any question has occurred, in regard to a surplus under a will in a case of *legal* intestacy, where no executor was appointed, and a residue undisposed of.   Such a case may still be regulated according to the train of decisions upon this subject (a), and the residue be distributable under the custom.

It was clearly understood in former times, that a freeman of London could not, by will or otherwise, devise the disposition of the body, or guardianship, of his child under age; and if he did, yet that the infant should remain in the custody of the mayor and aldermen, who were guardians to the children of all freemen of London under age at their father's death. (b)   Thus if a freeman or freewoman died, leaving orphans within age unmarried, the Court of Orphans of the city had the custody of their body and goods, and the executors and administrators were obliged to exhibit inventories before that court, and become bound to the chamberlain of the city to the use of the orphans, to make a true account upon oath; and if they refused, they

---

(z) Supra, p. 338.   (a) Ibid.
(b) Priv. Lon. 287, 288.; 4 Burn's Eccles. Law, 444.

might have been committed till they so became bound. (*c*)
And their being bound in the Spiritual Court did not
excuse them from this custom, as they might still have
been compelled to give other security to the Chamber of
London. (*d*)

The rights of the Orphan Chamber, and the powers of
the Court of Orphans, in these times, formed important
matter for consideration in the affairs of the freemen of the
city of London and their families. These are stated at
large in the books which treat of the custom of the city of
London. But the business of the Orphan Chamber, in
regard to the property of orphans, and of the Court of
Orphans, is now of much smaller importance.

It appears that the mayor, commonalty, and citizens of
the city of London had, by taking in the monies of orphans,
contracted a debt to the orphans, and other creditors, for
principal money and interest, much greater than they were
able to pay and satisfy without assistance. By an act of the
5th of W. III. (*e*), provision was made for the relief of the
orphans and other creditors of the city of London. It was
fixed that an interest of four per cent. should be paid upon
the money of the orphans; and it was specially provided
(§ 18.), that no person or persons should thenceforth be
compelled or obliged, " by virtue of any custom within the
said city, or any order or process of the Court of Orphans,
or otherwise howsoever, to pay or deliver into the chamber
of the said city of London any sum or sums of money, or
personal estate, due or to be due, or belonging to any
orphan or orphans, or any freeman of the said city, any
law or usage for enforcing the same notwithstanding." (*f*)

(*c*) Priv. Lon. 280—287.   (*d*) Law of Exec. p. 252.
(*e*) 5 W. 3. c. 10.

(*f*) There was a regular mode of proceeding, on the death of any
freeman, for calling the orphanage money into the chamber of the city.

A A

At the present day, the Court of Orphans and the Orphan Chamber, though they still subsist, and their powers have not been specially abolished, have neither the persons nor property of any orphans under their charge; neither do they interfere to call any executors or administrators of freemen to account to them, for the orphanage part of the children of freemen. This resulted from the embarrassments into which the city had fallen, and the clause in the act of William III. before recited, doing away the compulsory power of calling in the orphanage part of a freeman's personal estate into the chamber of the city. (g)

It sometimes happens (now less frequently than it was formerly) that before marriage an agreement is made, that the personal estate of the husband, a freeman of London, shall go, at his death, according to the custom. This is a good and binding agreement; and, in such case, notwithstanding his will, two thirds of the personal estate would go according to the custom; and he could only dispose of the other third, or deadman's part, by such will. (h)

The following rules appear to be still in force, in regard to the distribution of personal estate, in a case of intestacy, under the custom of London : —

On the death of a freeman leaving children under age, the clerk of his parish gave notice thereof to the common crier, who summoned the executor or administrator to appear before the court of aldermen, there to be bound to bring in an inventory of the estates of the deceased.— (Seymour's Survey of London, &c. vol. ii. p. 260.)

(g) In books treating of the custom, the powers of the Orphan Chamber and of the Court of Orphans are mentioned as if still in force. (Burn's Eccles. Law; Lovelass, Dow's edition, &c.; Foster on Executors; Williams on Executors and Administrators, &c., on this point.) Upon inquiry in the office of the chamberlain of the city of London, I learned, that though the powers of the Court of Orphans had not been exercised for the last eighty years, they were understood still to be in existence.

(h) Webb v. Webb, 2 Vern. 111.; 2 Roper on Husband and Wife, p. 3. 2d ed.

1. The custom takes place only in regard to the rights of the widow, and of the child or children of a freeman of London; under the custom, the widow and children have certain rights in the personal estate of the intestate; and the children, while under age, have certain rights among themselves to the orphanage part: but if there be no widow and no child, the whole personal property shall be distributable under the statutes of distribution, without any interference of, or reference to, the custom. (*i*)

The widow is entitled to her customary share, whether the children be of her or of a former wife; and the children are entitled to their customary share, though they were born out of the city, and though their father did not inhabit or die in London (*k*); and though the estate is not situated within the city, but elsewhere. (*l*)

2. If a freeman of London die intestate in London or elsewhere, leaving a widow and a child, or children, his personal estate (after his debts paid, and the customary allowance for his funeral and the widow's chamber, are deducted thereout), is by the custom of the city to be divided into three equal parts, and disposed of in the following manner; to wit,.one third part thereof to the widow, being her *pars rationabilis;* another third part to the children; and the other third part thereof is deadman's part, subject to the statutes of distribution. Thus in such case, dividing the whole into nine parts, four ninths belong to the wife, and five ninths to the

---

(*i*) 4 Burn's Eccles. Law, 442—444.
(*k*) Ibid.　　　　　　　(*l*) Priv. Lond. 288.

children. (*m*)   And if there be an after-born child, such child will be entitled to a share, or come in with the rest for the customary and statutory shares of the father's personal estate. (*n*)

The widow's apparel and furniture of her bed-chamber in London are called the widow's chamber.   (2 Blacks. Com. 518.)   In the case of *Biddle* v. *Biddle,* before Lord Parker, 18th of March, 1718, it was said that the widow was entitled to the furniture of her chamber; or in case the estate exceeded 2000*l.*, then to 50*l.* instead thereof. (*o*) Thus in the case of a widow and children, as part of the personal estate is distributable by the custom, and part by the statute, the same intricacy of distribution prevails, as already stated in regard to distribution under the custom of the province of York.

3. The wife of a freeman may be compounded with for, and barred of, her customary share, by a settlement before marriage, either by a jointure upon land, or out of personal estate. (*p*)

But the bar must be clearly made out: a jointure in bar of dower, or thirds, or other portion at common law or otherwise, will not bar the wife of her customary part. (*q*) And where the wife is barred, it is held as if there were

---

(*m*) 2 Salk. 426.; Redshaw *v.* Brasier, Ld. Raym. 1328.; Rutter *v.* Rutter, 1 Vern. 180.; 4 Burn's Eccles. Law, 442. 444.

(*n*) Walsam *v.* Skinner, Pre. Cha. 499.; Gilb. Eq. Rep. 153.; 4 Burn's Eccles. Law, 444.

(*o*) *Viner,* tit. Customs of London, b. 2.

(*p*) 4 Burn's Eccles. Law, 444.

(*q*) Babington *v.* Greenwood, 1 P. Wms. 530.; Cleaver *v.* Spurling, 2 P. Wms. 527.; Onslow *v.* Onslow, 1 Sim. 18.; 4 Burn's Eccles. Law, 444.

no wife, and the division is bipartite; one half to the children, the other half to the deadman's part. (r)

4. The heir-at-law is entitled to an orphanage share, along with the other children, notwithstanding of such heir taking any lands or real estate from the intestate by descent, by settlement, or otherwise. (s)

In this respect the custom agrees with the statutes of distribution, but differs totally from the custom of the province of York. (t)   In the establishment of the custom, the citizens of London appear to have had no regard to real property, on the supposition that a freeman would not purchase land, but employ his whole fortune in commerce. (u)

5. If any child be fully advanced by the father in his lifetime, such child is barred from taking any share of the orphanage part with the other children; but no grant or settlement of lands or real estate on a child, is to be held as an advancement within the custom. (x)   And when a freeman leaves a widow and an only child, no advancement by the father excludes such only child from the orphanage share. (y)

6. But where a child is not fully advanced, and

(r) Lewin v. Lewin, 3 P. Wms. 16.; Hancock v. Hancock, 2 Vern. 665.; 4 Burn's Eccles. Law, 444 445.

(s) Ci___ ich, 1 Vern. ___ ___   Law, 477.

(t) ___ 143.   ___les. Law, 446.

(___ ___ ich, 2 ___   Belitha, 2 P. Wms.

27___   ___ Eccles

___ Eccles

has received only a partial advance from the father, upon bringing such partial advance into hotchpot with the other children, such child may receive his or her customary share with them; and such advance is not to be brought into hotchpot with the widow, but only with the orphanage part. (z)

Here, as in regard to the rules of distribution in the province of Canterbury, and by the custom of the province of York, a good deal of uncertainty appears to prevail on the subject of advancements to children. Many cases have been decided upon this subject, into which it would not be profitable to enter minutely here. It may be noticed, however, that if a freeman hath advanced his child on marriage, this is to be taken as a full advancement, unless the father shall by writing under his hand not only declare that such child was not fully advanced, but likewise mention, in certain, how much the portion given in marriage did amount to, that so it may appear what sum is in such case to be brought into hotchpot; and then every child producing the writing of the father, and bringing the portion into hotchpot, shall have as much as will make up to the same a full child's part or portion of the customary estate; and no declaration of the father that the child was fully advanced, or not advanced, will be of any avail. (a)

In the case of *Annand* v. *Honeywood,* M. 1685, the question was whether *money* given by the father *to be laid out in land,* to be settled on a son and his intended wife for their lives, with remainders in tail, should be reckoned

---

(z) 4 Burn's Eccles. Law, 451.

(a) Jenks v. Holford, 1 Vern. 61.; Civil v. Rich, 1 Vern. 216.; Chace v. Box, Ld. Raym. 484.; Green's Priv. of Lond. 53.; Dean v. Lord Delaware; 2 Vern. 630.; Cleaver v. Spurling, 2 P. Will. 527.; 4 Burn's Eccles. Law, 446.

to be an advancement by part of the personal estate of the father; so as that the son ought to bring the same into hotchpot, to entitle him to a share of the personal estate: the Lord Chancellor said there was no colour to reckon this any part of the personal estate. (b)

Where the advancement shall have exceeded the child's share by the custom, it has been said that if it have been given and accepted expressly in satisfaction of the customary share, no respect shall be paid to such advancement in the distribution of the deadman's part; but that where there is no such special contract or agreement, and the advancement is general, it shall be applied either to the customary share only, or both to the customary and distributive share, according to the amount of the advancement. (c)

7. The child of a freeman of London, when of age, may, in consideration of a present fortune, bar himself or herself of all right to the customary part; and such release, or an advancement of that child, shall operate as if that child were dead, and go to increase the shares of the other children. If all the children release or are advanced, and there be a widow, this also shall make the division of the personal estate under the custom bipartite, between the wife and the deadman's part. If there be no widow, but only children, the division also shall be bipartite; one moiety to the children, the other to the deadman's part. (d)

But it has been held that a release by a child of a cus-

(b) 1 Vern. 345.

(c) Foster on Executors, 395.; Burn's Eccles. Law, 460.

(d) 4 Burn's Eccles. Law, 444, 445.

tomary share, without a valuable consideration, would not be good (e): and if a man, who is of age, marries a freeman's daughter, who is under age, he may bar himself of any future right to his wife's customary share. (f)

8. Grandchildren, or remoter descendants, take no share of the filial customary part; and thus, if an intestate leave a wife and grandchildren or remoter descendants, by the custom the division of the personal estate shall be bipartite; one half to the widow, the other half to the deadman's part: but the wife shall take not only one half of her share under the custom, but one third of the deadman's part under the statute; and the other two thirds of the deadman's part shall go to the grandchildren or other descendants under the statute. (g)

Thus there is a similar intricacy in the distribution of the personal estate of a freeman of London as of that of an inhabitant of the county of York. In regard to the former, however, the heir is entitled to a customary share with the other children, as in the province of Canterbury.

9. If a person leave no wife, but an only child, being advanced or partly advanced, though such child might be barred by the custom, or obliged, if there were other children, to bring his or her advancement into hotchpot, such only child shall take the whole personal estate, and may, if at the

---

(e) Morris v. Burroughs, 1 Atk. 401.; 4 Burn's Eccles. Law, 448.

(f) Cox v. Belitha, 2 P. Will. 272.; Ives v. Medcalfe, 1 Atk. 63.; 4 Burn's Eccles. Law, 449, 450.

(g) Fowke v. Hunt, 1 Vern. 397.; Northey v. Strange, 1 P. Will. 341.; 4 Burn's Eccles. Law, 451.

years of discretion (*h*), dispose of the same by will; and if such child shall die intestate, his or her rights to the personal estate shall devolve to the next of kin, according to the statutes of distribution. (*i*)

10. The customary share of the wife shall vest immediately upon the death of the husband; but the customary shares of the children, if more than one, are not vested till they respectively attain twenty-one years of age. (*k*)

There are several intricacies in regard to this rule. If an orphan die *unmarried* before attaining twenty-one years of age, his or her orphanage share shall accrue to the other or others of the orphans; and no orphan, till attaining such age, can make a will of his or her orphanage share. But the share which any child takes by accruer or survivorship in the orphanage share of a brother or sister deceased, is vested and becomes distributable by the statute of distributions. (*l*) It has been decided, however, that an orphan under age cannot devise by will what accrued by survivorship any more than his own original share. (*m*) On the other hand, the shares of the children in the deadman's part are vested immediately on the parent's death, and may be disposed of by will or otherwise, as they might be by the statutes in the province of Canterbury: and if there shall be only one child, the share of such child, whether under the custom or under the statute, shall be vested immediately on the death of such child, and will pass to his or her executors or other legal representatives. (*n*)

(*h*) Supra, p. 311.   (*i*) 4 Burn's Eccles. Law, 442—451.

(*k*) 4 Burn's Eccles. Law, 444.

(*l*) Anon. Prec. Chanc. 537.; 4 Burn's Eccles. Law, 444.

(*m*) Harvey *v.* Desbouverie, Cas. temp. Talb. 135.; Williams on Executors, 955.

(*n*) 4 Burn's Eccles. Law, 444.

Some of the rules of the custom of London, particularly those in regard to the accruer of the orphanage shares of children dying under age, are important, and may be worthy of consideration in any general revision of the law. Formerly the Court of Orphans had been accustomed to exercise a similar charge of the persons of their orphans, in respect to marriage, as is exercised by the Court of Chancery, in regard to the wards of that court. In the Court of Orphans marriage was discouraged till the orphans or wards should attain twenty-one years of age.

It appears to be uncertain, whether when a man marries an orphan, who dies under twenty-one, her orphanage share shall accrue to the other orphans, or go to her husband. In the case of *Fouke* and *Lewen*, M. 1682, it is said that if a man marries an orphan who dies under twenty-one, her orphanage part shall not survive to the other children, but shall go to the husband. (*o*)   But in *Merriweather* and *Hester*, T. 5 G. 1. (*p*), it is said that if a man marries an orphan, yet till twenty-one his right is not so vested, as to prevent his wife's share from surviving, in case she died before twenty-one; and Blackstone says, that if the children of a freeman die under the age of twenty-one, whether sole or *married*, their share shall survive to the other children. (*q*)

11. A wife divorced for adultery shall not have her customary share. (*r*)   So where a freeman husband was attainted of felony, and pardoned on

---

(*o*) Fouke *v.* Lewen, M. 1682, 1 Vern. 88, 89.; 4 Burn's Eccles. Law, 444.

(*p*) Anon. Prec. Cha. 537.; 4 Burn's Eccles. Law, 444.

(*q*) 2 Blacks. Com. 518.

(*r*) Bunb. 16.; 4 Burn's Eccles. Law, 444. This refers to a divorce in the Ecclesiastical Courts; a divorce *a vinculo matrimonii* would change them to single persons.

condition of transportation, and the wife afterwards became entitled to some personal estate, as orphan to a freeman of London, this was decreed to belong to the wife as to a *feme sole*. (*s*)

12. If the daughter of a freeman marry in his lifetime without his consent, unless the father be reconciled to her before his death, she shall not have her orphanage share of his personal estate. (*t*)

13. A lease for years to attend the inheritance of a freeman, is not assets within the custom. (*u*) So, also, if a freeman have the trust of a term to attend an inheritance and dies, the trust of the term shall not be subject to the custom (*x*); but a mortgage in fee shall be counted part of a freeman's personal estate, and subject to the custom. (*y*)

SECT. VII.

Of the Rules of Succession in Personal Estate by the Law of Scotland.

THERE is reason to conclude, that some of the rules of succession in personal estate in Scotland were not fixed till a period comparatively recent. It has been already seen, that in the opinion of Craig, maternal succession was not

(*s*) Newsome *v.* Bowyer, 3 P. Will. 37.; 4 Burn's Eccles. Law, 444.

(*t*) 1 Foden *v.* Howlett, 1 Vern. 354.: sed contra, Cha. Cas. Finch, 248.; 4 Burn's Eccles. Law, 450.

(*u*) Tiffin *v.* Tiffin, 1 Vern. 2.; Dowse *v.* Percival, 1 Vern. 104.; 4 Burn's Eccles. Law, 451.

(*x*) 2 Freem. 66.; 4 Burn's Eccles. Law, 452.

(*y*) Thornbrough *v.* Baker, 1 Cha. Cas. 285.; 4 Burn's Eccles. Law, 452.

excluded in the law of Scotland (*z*); and that Sir James Steuart was inclined to the same doctrine. (*a*)

In the *Minor Practicks* of *Hope*, it appears also, that his opinion did not coincide with the doctrines of the law, as these appear to be fixed in our day. He says (*b*): " In testaments, all those who are of a like degree are admitted to the office of executry; albeit some of them be *germani*, some of them *uterini tantum*, and some of them *consanguinei tantum*." (*c*) In this respect, he appears to have considered that the rules of the law of Scotland coincided with those of the law of England.

Even in the time of Stair, the whole rules of succession in moveables do not appear to have been clearly fixed; when treating of the succession of a father, in certain cases, he says (*d*): " As to the third degree of succession in moveables, failing descendants, and brothers and sisters, and their descendants, the question is whether the father surviving will exclude his own brother, or if there be any place for ascendants in the succession of moveables. Such cases occur rarely, and I have not observed it debated or decided. *It is but of late that the like case hath fallen in the succession of heirs and heritable rights* (*e*), wherein our custom hath, according to the course of the law of nature, found the father to be heir to his son, and not the father-brother, or any of his descendants; and in that we have differed from the custom of England. *And there is no reason why, if the question should occur, that the like should not be done in moveables.*" It appears here, as if we saw

---

(*z*) Supra, p. 67., on the doctrine of *paterna paternis, materna maternis.*   (*a*) Ibid.

(*b*) Hope's Minor Practicks, tit. 3. s. 16.

(*c*) This is noticed as an error, in Spottiswoode's notes to this passage of the Minor Practicks.

(*d*) Stair, b. iii. tit. 8. s. 32.

(*e*) He alludes to the case of Burnet contra Mauld, noticed b. iii. t. 4. s. 35.

in this the origin of the rule, by which certain classes of collaterals are preferred to ascendants in the law of succession to personal estate in Scotland. At that time the rule had not been clearly ascertained.

In later writers I have not observed that the rules of law have been made matter of any doubt or question. The following rules of succession appear to be assented to by all the writers of the present day : —

> 1. Upon a marriage, if there be no conventional provisions to the contrary, the personal estate of the married pair becomes *goods in communion*, remaining under the sole management and control of the husband by his *jus mariti* (*f*), subject to his power of disposition of the whole by acts or deeds *inter vivos*, made in *liege poustie*, provided these be not made or granted *in fraudem* of the legal rights of a wife and children; but his power of disposing of the personal estate in case of his death, by will or disposition *mortis causâ*, is limited to his own share thereof, termed the *dead's part*. (*g*)

If the marriage have not subsisted for a year and day, or produced a living child, it is not considered as a *permanent* marriage, and there is a restitution, as nearly as possible, to the state in which matters were before marriage; and the personal property then existing is to be restored to those to whom it originally belonged, the surviving party, and the representatives of the party deceasing. (*h*)

If a deed or disposition of a father be made fraudulently, or in order to disappoint the rights of children, without

---

(*f*) Erskine, b. i. tit. 6. s. 12.
(*g*) Ibid., b. iii. tit. 9. s. 18.
(*h*) Ibid. b. i. tit. 6. s. 38.

touching the father's own right during his life, this will be ineffectual, and will not disappoint the children of their claims of legitim. (*i*)

The same principles would apply to the case of deeds made fraudulently or in order to disappoint the rights of a widow.

If a person be not in a state of *liege poustie,* or have contracted a sickness which ends in death, he loses the *legitima potestas* of disposing of the goods in communion. All gratuitous deeds, therefore, executed by him after that period, tending to diminish the rights of the widow and children, are void, though they should not be fraudulent. Certain of his acts and deeds may also be challenged after his death by his heir on the head of *death-bed* (*k*), even though these regard moveables or personal estate. The following are of this nature: — 1. A disposition of heirship moveables. 2. An assignation of a moveable bond, secluding executors. 3. An alienation of any part of the conquest during a marriage, which, though moveable, may have been provided to the heir. 4. Bonds granted, or assignations executed of moveable debts, where the personal estate of the grantor is not sufficient for satisfying his own personal debts, as these would be raising charges against the heir. (*l*)

It has been seen that the father in England has the power of disposing of the whole personal estate by will.

(*i*) Hog *v.* Lashley, supra, p. 127. Millie *v.* Millie, Fac. Coll. 17th June, 1803; House of Lords, 18th March, 1807.

(*k*) The law of *death-bed* in Scotland has relation chiefly to real estate: all deeds granted to the prejudice of the heir after the grantor hath contracted the sickness of which he dies, may be set aside by the heir, *ex capite lecti,* unless, after executing such deeds, the grantor has gone to kirk or market unsupported, or shall have lived sixty days after the execution thereof. (Erskine, b. iii. tit. 8. s. 96, 97.)

(*l*) Erskine, b. iii. tit. 8. s. 98. tit. 9. s. 16.

If we often saw a father exercising this power by totally passing over children and descendants, and giving the whole estate from them to other favoured objects, we should be apt to regret the abrogation of the old law as to the *reasonable partition* of personal estate. But the law has been settled, as it now stands in England, in regard to the power of a father to make a will, upon principles consonant to the commercial feelings of that country. Nor does this power appear to operate with any general inconvenience.

　　2. Upon the dissolution of a marriage by the death of the husband, leaving a wife and a child or children, the free personal estate, after payment of debts and funeral expenses, receives a tripartite division; one third belongs to the wife, termed her *jus relictæ;* another third belongs to the child, or children, as *legitim* or *bairns' part of gear,* even though such child, or all such children, was or were of a former marriage; the remaining third is the *dead's part,* subject to the will or testamentary disposition of the father, if he made such will or testamentary disposition, or if he made none, then to go to his next of kin, according to the law of Scotland. (*m*)

This general rule of the law of succession appears to have existed in Scotland from the earliest period to which the knowledge of their legal history extends; it is the same in the province of Canterbury, and it was the same in the province of York and in the city of London before the statutes of distribution had introduced the intricacy al-

---

(*m*) Erskine, b. iii. tit. 9. ss. 15. 18.

ready noticed in regard to the distribution of the *dead's part* by the customs of those places. (*n*)

It now differs in an important way from the rules of distribution by the customs of the province of York and city of London, as controlled by the statutes of distribution; in these, as it has been already seen, the widow not only takes her *pars rationabilis* under the custom, but her distributive share of the *deadman's part* under the statutes. (*o*)

3. If he die leaving only a wife, and no child or children, the division becomes bipartite; one moiety of the free personal estate, in such case, being *jus relictæ*, shall go to the widow; the other is *dead's part*, subject as before to the will or testamentary disposition of the father, if he made such; or if he made none, to go to his next of kin, according to the law of Scotland. (*p*)

4. If he die, leaving only a child or children, and no wife, the division (subject to what may belong to those entitled in right of the predeceasing wife) shall also be bipartite; the child, or children, taking one moiety as *legitim;* the other, being *dead's part*, subject to the will or testamentary disposition of the father; and if he have made no will or testamentary disposition, then to go to such child or children as his next of kin. (*q*)

5. If the marriage be dissolved by the death of the wife, the share which would have formed her *jus relictæ*, if she had survived, shall go

---

(*n*) Supra, p. 340.   (*o*) Ibid. p. 355.

(*p*) Erskine, b. iii. tit. 9. s. 19.   (*q*) Ibid. b. iii. tit. 9. s. 19.

in such way as she may have directed by any will or testamentary disposition made by her, in relation to this share of the goods in communion, which she is empowered to make during the subsistence of the marriage without the husband's concurrence or consent (r); and in case of her death intestate, her said share shall descend as her absolute property to her children by her last or any former marriage; and if she have left no children, then to her other next of kin. (s)

In regard to the power of a wife to make a will during the subsistence of the marriage, the law of Scotland differs entirely from the law of England, as well the general law, as the local and customary law, of that country.

I see no limitation to this testing power of the wife: she could execute it to the prejudice of her children, or any of them, and in favour of strangers.

No legitim is due to children at the death of their mother out of her share of the goods in communion. Thus the whole is in the nature of dead's part in the mother, and entirely subject to her testing power. (t)

If the children or any of them shall be under age at the death of the mother, and if there be no will of hers to the contrary, the shares of such minor children shall remain with their father as administrator for them. (u)

The father is entitled to such administration for their behoof till they respectively attain to twenty-one years of age; but this power of administration cannot extend to the shares of children of the wife by a former marriage. (x) It has rarely happened that any question has been made in

---

(r) Erskine, b. i. tit. 6. s. 28.   (s) Ibid. b. iii. tit. 9. s. 21.

(t) Ibid. b. iii. tit. 9. s. 21.

(u) That is, *administrator* in the sense of the civil law, or *manager*.

(x) Erskine, b. iii. tit. 9. s. 21.

the courts of law in Scotland in regard to this right of administration in the father, or the obligations to which this would subject him in regard to his children.   It did occur, however, in the case of *Lashley* v. *Hog*, already stated (*y*); but various questions which might have arisen, upon that subject in that case, were settled extra-judicially, and by way of compromise between the parties.

It seldom occurs that any great succession falls to the collateral relations, as the next of kin, of a deceasing wife, for her share of the goods in communion.   But cases might be suggested where the present rule of law in Scotland would be attended with strange consequences: a wealthy capitalist might marry a person of inferior condition without a contract; or a person from England might fix his domicil in Scotland, without any provision, by ante-nuptial contract, in regard to the rights of a wife according to the law of the latter country; if in such case the wife should predecease the husband, *her* next of kin would be entitled to the half of the personal estate, or goods in communion, and would take the same from the surviving husband. (*z*)

There is an intricacy in the law in regard to the succession in *heirship moveables* (*a*), which may be here noticed. Where the husband predeceases, neither the widow nor younger children can claim a right in any part of the heirship moveables, because these then belong to the heir.

(*y*) Supra, p. 144.

(*z*) Some years ago, a case of this kind, from Scotland, which was under consideration at the legacy-duty office in London, excited the surprise of the then intelligent comptroller, Mr. Campbell; he had not been aware that such a rule of law existed.   The next of kin of the wife resided in Ireland, and upon her death, took half the personal estate of the husband living in Scotland.   There was no lawsuit as to this; it was settled by the opinions of counsel.

(*a*) Similar to heir-looms in England.   Supra, p. 309.

But where the wife predeceases the husband, her next of kin are entitled to a share of the whole moveables, without deducting any part as heirship, because heirship is a certain share of the moveable estate at the time of the death of the husband; and, therefore, while he is alive, he can have no heirship. (b)

6. There is no succession in the law of Scotland by affinity: thus a husband and wife never succeed to the personal estate of each other, nor can the separate relations of the one succeed to those of the other.   On the dissolution of a marriage, each takes that share of the goods in communion to which he or she is entitled; and the respective shares of the parties thus taken, in case of intestacy, devolve to their respective nearest in blood, or next in kin, according to the law of Scotland. (c)

It has been already seen, that very different rules upon this subject exist in the province of Canterbury, as well as in the province of York and city of London. (d)   In England, upon the death of a wife, the whole of the personal estate, which had fallen under the marital rights of the husband, remains with him as his own.   On the death of the husband, the wife has certain rights under the statutes in the province of Canterbury; and her customary rights, as well as her statutory rights, in the province of York and city of London.   The rights thus vested in the wife by the death of the husband, in case of intestacy, devolve to her next of kin, whether her children or other relations.   And there, as in Scotland, no kindred is to be deduced by affinity; and no part of the personal estate to

---

(b) Erskine, b. iii. tit. 9. s. 21.   (c) Bankton, b. iii. t it. 4. s. 28.
(d) Supra, p. 317.

which the wife has succeeded shall go to the next of kindred of the husband, except in regard to his children or descendants, who are also the children or descendants of the wife. (e)

7. Legitim is due only to children existing at the time of the father's death, and not to grandchildren, or other remoter descendants: thus, upon the death of a father leaving a wife, and only grandchildren or other remoter descendants, the division of the goods in communion shall be bipartite, one half to the wife, the other half *dead's part;* and if in such case there be no wife, the whole shall be dead's part. (f)

In this respect the rules of the law of Scotland appear to agree with the rules in England, in the province of York, and in the city of London, in regard to the customary and orphanage shares of children, and the division of the personal estate, where there are no children, but only grandchildren or remoter descendants. (g) In all of these the rules of distribution are less equitable than those which obtain in the province of Canterbury, and which allow the right of representation in every case of *descendants* of different degrees entitled to share. (h)

8. The rights of a widow to her *jus relictæ,* and of a child to *legitim,* were always *vested* on the death of the husband and father; these did not fall to them as rights of succession, but belonged to them of their proper right, as their respective shares

---

(e) Supra, p. 335.

(g) Supra, p. 347. 360.

(f) Erskine, b. iii. tit. 9. s. 17

(h) Supra, p. 321.

of the goods in communion; and as to them confirmation was not necessary to vest the rights of the parties, as it formerly was in all other cases of succession in personal estate by the law of Scotland. (*i*)

In England, in every case of succession in personal estate, a right accruing has become instantly vested, except in regard to the orphanage shares of children under age, according to the custom of London, which do not become vested in the minors, but go over to their brothers and sisters if they die under age. (*k*)

9. The rights of a widow to her *jus relictæ*, and of children to their legitim, may be barred by reasonable provisions settled upon the wife and children in an ante-nuptial contract of marriage, with an express exclusion of the legal rights of the widow to her *jus relictæ*, and of the children to their legitim or other legal rights. The parties in such case are respectively only entitled to their conventional provisions; and, after satisfying such conventional provisions, the remainder of the personal estate is of the nature of dead's part; and the *dead's part* shall comprehend the shares of the party or parties so barred (*l*).

This power of barring the legal rights of a wife and children, by an ante-nuptial contract of marriage, must have rendered the operation of the law of *reasonable partition* among the widow and children much less extensive in its operation than it otherwise would have been. Clauses

(*i*) Erskine, b. iii. tit. 9. s. 30.   (*k*) Supra, p. 361.
(*l*) Erskine, b. iii. tit. 9. s. 20. 23.

to this effect are of common style in contracts of marriage in Scotland. (m)   When such clauses are introduced into an ante-nuptial contract of marriage in Scotland, the father can make a will, or testamentary disposition, of his whole personal estate, subject to his debts and obligations; and, amongst other obligations, to the conventional provisions given to his wife and children.

10. In every case of moveable succession, the person taking any part of the heritable estate of the same ancestor or relation, the succession to whose moveable estate is in question, as heir of line or heir *alioqui successurus,* is excluded from any portion of such personal estate, unless such person be the sole next of kin of that degree; but it is the privilege of every heir, if he shall see fit, to *collate,* or bring the heritage into general account with others in the same degree, and thus to receive his share of the mixed estate. If the heir be the sole next of kin, such heir shall take the whole personal estate also. This rule as to collation applies to collateral, as well as to direct succession. The collateral heir is excluded from the personal estate of his kinsman, if there be any other in equal degree, unless such heir collate the heritage. (n)

This differs entirely from the rules of the province of Canterbury and those of the city of London; and it differs from those of the province of York in several particulars. (o)

(m) 1 Juridical Styles, p. 6.

(n) Erskine, b. iii. tit. 9. s. 3. While this treatise is in the press, important questions are under discussion (in the *Anstruther* and *Breadalbane* cases), whether the heir of line, or heir *alioqui successurus,* be called upon to collate more than what he takes exclusively in those characters.

(o) Supra, p. 343.

The disability of the heir in the last-mentioned province
extends only to the succession in the personal estate of the
father, and it has no place in regard to the succession to
any other ancestor, or in collateral succession. The heir
in that province has no power of collation, nor apparently
of rejecting a succession devolving upon him by the law.

It has been seen that in the province of Canterbury, and
by the custom of London, the heir, taking the real estate,
is entitled to his share of the personal estate, along with
the other children. (*p*)

11. The right to legitim may be released by the
express discharge of the child for an onerous consideration, or by the child's accepting a provision,
having a condition annexed to it, of renouncing the
legitim; and the discharge of legitim by a child has
the same effect towards the other children's rights
as if such child had never existed; and if all the
children discharge, the effect upon the rights of
the other parties, is as if no children had ever existed. (*q*)

12. For preserving an equality among the children in the distribution of the legitim, any child
who shall have received a provision of personal
estate from the father, not only by a *tocher* or
other provision in his or her marriage contract, but
by any sum of money actually advanced to this
child, or for his or her behoof, shall collate the
same with the other children, and impute it in part
of the legitim. But the father may, by any bond or
instrument, declare that such advances shall not
affect the right to legitim; and the right to legitim

(*p*) Supra, pp. 324. 357.   (*q*) Erskine, b. iii. tit. 9. s. 23.

shall not be diminished by any legacy of the father out of the dead's part; nor by any grant or settlement of real estate to a younger child; nor shall the expense of maintenance, education, apprenticeship, or the like, be deducted from the legitim. (r)

Apparently, the rules in regard to the collation of personal estate among children in Scotland, in cases of provisions given to them, do not materially differ from the rules obtaining in England, in regard to the bringing the advancements of personal estate given to children into hotchpot. But the law of Scotland differs from the rules in the province of Canterbury and in the province of York, in regard to the advancements by means of real estate to younger children. In the two latter, as has been already seen, a younger child may be advanced by the father out of his real estate, and such advancements must be brought into hotchpot. (s) But in Scotland, a grant or settlement of real estate on a younger child is not to be brought into collation; and in this respect the law agrees with the rules upon this subject under the custom of London. (t)

13. In case a father die intestate, leaving a widow and children, although the children may have renounced their legal provisions of legitim, they are still entitled to their shares of the dead's part as the next of kin of the father; and in the dead's part the widow, in such case, takes no share. (u)

(r) Stair, b. iii. tit. 8. s. 45.; Erskine, b. iii. tit. 9. s. 25.; Bell's Principles, 442, 443.

(s) Supra, pp. 326. 344.   (t) Supra, p. 357.

(u) Erskine, b. iii. tit. 9. s. 23.

In regard to this rule, there is this difference between the law of Scotland and the customary law in England, that the widow in England would take her own share by the custom, and would be further entitled to her share of the dead's part under the statutes of distribution. (*x*)

> 14. In every case of succession to personal estate, the same is divisible *per capita* to those who are next in degree of blood, or next in kin to the deceased according to the law of Scotland, and never *per stirpes;* and no right of representation is allowed in the succession to personal estate among descendants or collaterals, in competition with those who are nearer in degree. (*y*)

It is singular that this very inequitable rule should subsist in full force in Scotland at this day. In this way immediate children surviving, exclude grandchildren by a child predeceased; and where there is no issue of the deceased, if there be brothers or sisters surviving, and children by brothers or sisters deceased, the latter would be entirely excluded. This rule applies not only to legitim, but to every other share of personal estate in Scotland, coming from any ancestor or other relation.

In England, grandchildren also are excluded from the customary shares of their parents, according to the customs of the province of York and city of London; and in this respect these customs resemble the rules of the law of Scotland in regard to legitim. But according to the statutes of distribution (founded upon the 118th Novel of Justinian, c. 1.), *representation* is allowed in England among descendants to the remotest degree. Among collaterals, it

---

(*x*) Supra, pp. 340. 355. (*y*) Erskine, b. iii. tit. 9, s. 2.

was deemed necessary to stop somewhere; and thus, amongst them, representation does not extend beyond brothers' and sisters' children. This was adopted in England from c. 3. of the same Novel of Justinian. (z)

15. In every case of intestate succession among collaterals, the kindred of the full blood shall exclude those of the half-blood in the same line of succession. (a)

Thus brothers and sisters german, and their issue, exclude brothers and sisters consanguinean and their issue; but brothers or sisters consanguinean, and their issue, will bar the father, or his brothers and sisters, though of the full blood.

This, as has been already seen, totally differs from the rules of succession in England. In Scotland, kindred is to be deduced only through a father and paternal ancestors. But of the kindred through the father, some may be of the full blood, as brothers and sisters *german;* and some of the half-blood, as brothers and sisters *consanguinean.*

Upon this subject the doctrine, as laid down in Erskine, does not appear to go to the full extent of the present rule. He says (b), " Yet in questions between the full and the half-blood, *representation* is admitted even in moveables. Thus where one deceased leaves a sister consanguinean, or by the father only, and a nephew by a sister german, or full sister predeceased, the nephew, though more removed by one degree from his uncle than the sister by the half-

---

(z) I have observed some recent cases of great hardship in Scotland, arising from the present state of this law as excluding brothers' and sisters' children where a brother or sister survived.

(a) Bankton, b. iii. tit. 4. s. 17. 28.; Erskine, b. iii. tit. 9. s. 2. 4.; Bell's Principles, 672.

(b) B. iii. tit. 9. s. 2.

blood, shall take the whole movable succession, as representing his mother, who was sister to the deceased by the full blood." And for this he refers to the case of Gemmil, July 4. 1729, observed in Kames's Dict. II. p. 398.

With great respect for this learned author, the case to which he refers does not appear to be one of *representation*, but of a total exclusion of the half-blood in competition with the full blood *in the same line of succession*. Among those of different degrees of kindred, the right of representation would be excluded in all cases, as well in regard to the full blood as to the half-blood.

16. If the deceased have died intestate without a widow, or children, or other descendants, his personal estate shall go to those who are *next in degree of blood*, or *nearest in kin* to the deceased. (c)

Though this be laid down as a general rule by the institutional writers, it will be seen, in the sequel, that in regard to the succession in personal estate in Scotland, the degrees of kindred are reckoned very differently from those which are known in the civil or canon law, or in the law of England.

17. In reckoning such nearest in degree of blood, or next in kin, the mother of the deceased, and all the relations connected with the deceased through the mother only, are entirely excluded from the succession : thus, if a person deceased left only a mother, and maternal relations, the king would take the succession in preference to them. (d)

(c) Stair, b. iii. tit. 4. s. 24., tit. 8. s. 31.; Bankton, b. iii. tit. 4. s. 22.; Erskine, b. iii. tit. 9. s. 2.

(d) Erskine, b. iii. tit. 8. s. 9., tit. 9. s. 2.

It is singular that this rule of law should still obtain in Scotland, and it does not appear to have been so fixed from an early period. (e)   It is said to have been taken from the laws of the Twelve Tables (f); but in adopting the rules of the civil law, it is matter of some surprise that these obsolete rules of succession were taken instead of the more equitable rules of the *jus novissimum* of the Roman law.   In any alteration of the law it is scarcely possible that this can remain as at present.

18. Where the deceased shall die without wife or children, but shall leave a father, and brothers or sisters, or descendants of them, the brothers or sisters, or their descendants, shall take in preference to the father; and the father shall only take if there be no brothers or sisters of the deceased, or descendants of them. (g)

This also is a singular rule, which has been adopted in Scotland in the law of succession; it appears to militate

---

(e) Supra, p. 363.   It has been seen from the case of the Duchess of Suffolk (supra, p. 332.), that a similar rule for a short while prevailed in England.

(f) Bankton, b. iii. tit. 4. s. 20.

The law of the Twelve Tables is very obscure upon this subject. Tabula V., as restored by Jaques Godefroy, is in these terms : — " Ast si intestato moritur, cui suus hæres nec escit, agnatus proximus familiam habeto: si agnatus nec escit, Gentilis familiam nancetor." (Terasson, Histoire de la Jurisprudence Romaine, 1750, p. 126.)   An *agnate*, according to Terasson, differed from the *agnate* of· the law of Scotland; he describes him as " descendu d'un même tronc masculin, *et par des branches masculines*."   A *cognate* was any relation claiming through a female.   The *Gentiles* were those of the same *paternal* race.   (Heineccius, Antiq. Roman, l. 3. tit. 2.)

The above law is certainly silent as to the mother.

(g) Bankton, b. iii. tit. 4. s. 18.; Erskine, b. iii. tit. 8. s. 9., and tit. 9. s. 2.; Bell's Principles, 672.

against the terms of that general rule (No. 16.), which gives the succession to the *next in degree of blood,* or nearest in kin. By the civil law the father is in the first degree, and a brother or sister in the second degree. Although by the canon law a father, as well as a brother and sister, are in the first degree, this would not exclude the father; under both laws the descendants of such brother and sister, of course, are more remote.

It has been seen that in this case the law of England gives the whole succession to the father. (*h*)   Whether this rule of the English law be entirely equitable or not, may be matter of question.

> 19. In regard to the succession of remoter ascendants and their collaterals, where the deceased shall die without wife or children, and without brothers or sisters, or descendants of them, and without a father surviving, the rule is, that the collaterals of his father and their descendants shall take in the first place; and, failing them, that the remoter ascendants shall take. Thus uncles and aunts, and their descendants, are preferred to a grandfather; and so on in the ascending degrees and their collaterals. (*i*)

These rules also appear to be contrary to those of the civil and canon laws, and of the law of England. A grandfather, in the civil law, is nearer in degree than an uncle or aunt; by the canon law, they are equal, both being in the second degree. It has been seen that in England a grandfather has been preferred to an uncle or

---

(*h*) Supra, p. 330.
(*i*) Erskine, b. iii. tit. 8. s. 9., and tit. 9. s. 2.; Bell's Principles, 672.

aunt, though this was not specially provided for in the statute. (*k*) The grandfather is clearly nearer in degree, both by the civil and canon law, than the descendants of an uncle or aunt.

The same observations apply to this rule in regard to the succession of remoter ascendants. Such succession, however, must be of very rare occurrence. (*l*)

> 20. The right of *succession*, which formerly was not vested before *confirmation*, is now (apparently) put upon a similar footing as it is in England: by a recent statute, the right of the next of kin to obtain confirmation does not expire with the death of the party first having such right, but in case of the death of such party is transmitted to his or her representatives.

Till the making of a recent statute, if any relation who, at the time of the death of a party, was one of his or her next of kin, or sole next of kin, should die without having reduced into possession what such next of kin was or were presumptively entitled to, or before a confirmation obtained in the proper consistorial court, the rights of the next of kin so dying were totally lost, and accrued to those

---

(*k*) Supra, p. 335.

(*l*) I see that rules of succession somewhat similar existed in the custom of Normandy; thus we see in the *Coustumier:* —

" 241. Père et mère, aïeul et aïeule, ou autre ascendant, tant qu'il y a aucun descendu de lui vivant, ne peut succéder à l'un de ses enfans.

" 242. Les pères et mères excluent les oncles et tantes à la succession de leurs enfans; et les oncles et tantes excluent l'aïeul et l'aïeule en la succession de leurs neveux et nièces: ainsi des autres.

" 243. Les oncles et tantes excluent les cousins en la succession de leurs neveux et nièces. (La Coutume Reformée du Païs et Duché de Normandie. Rouen, 1694, p. 372.) But here the maternal succession was not excluded.

of the kindred who were next in the order of succession, and who obtained possession, or took confirmation. But by the act 1690, c. 26. special assignations, neither intimated nor made public during the life of the grantor, were declared to be sufficient without confirmation; and the courts extended this to special legacies (Jan. 1729. Gordon), though formerly neither such assignations nor legacies took the subject out of the executry of the deceased till confirmation was obtained. This rule never extended to *legitim* or *jus relictæ*, which were held to belong to the parties of their proper right, and in case of their death went to their own next of kin. A partial confirmation, however, was held to vest the whole executry in the persons confirmed, so as to be transmitted to their representatives. And the confirmation of an executor nominate, being a trust for the next of kin, had the effect of establishing their right to the subjects confirmed as effectually as if they themselves had confirmed them. (*m*)

But the rules of law upon this subject, which were often attended with great injustice, are (or were meant to be) done away by the act of the 6 G. IV. c. 98., by which it is enacted, " that in all cases of intestate succession, where any person or persons who, at the period of the death of the intestate, being next of kin, shall die before confirmation be expede, the right of such next of kin shall transmit to his or her representatives, so that confirmation may and shall be granted to such representatives in the same manner as confirmation might have been granted to such next of kin, immediately upon the death of such intestate."

This act of parliament was intended to place the law in Scotland as to the vesting of personal estate upon the same footing upon which it has always been in England.

(*m*) Erskine, b. iii. tit. 9. s. 30.

It is to be regretted that some doubts are entertained as to the efficacy of this most just statute, owing to the conciseness of its terms (Stair by Brodie, 597. *in notis*). (*n*)   It has been said that before confirmation nothing was *vested* in the next of kin, and that thus nothing could be *transmitted* to his or her representatives.   But the *right to obtain confirmation was vested* in the party dying, and the statute meant to *transmit such right* to his or her next of kin. (*o*)

In the law of Scotland there is no express rule to restrain the executor-dative from making distribution at any time after confirmation obtained, as there is in the English statute of distribution.   But as he is not entittled to pay debts, without decree till after the expiration of six months (Gardener and Pearson, 28th November, 1816, Fac. Coll.), *à fortiori*, he should not till then distribute the estate to the next of kindred. (*p*)

(*n*) I cannot mention this work, without adding my humble meed of praise to the great labour and research which the editor has applied to the illustration of the antient and modern law of Scotland.

(*o*) See also 1 Bell's Comment. 142.; and Erskine by Ovory, 894. *in notis*. If any doubt exist upon this most important point, *should it not be instantly removed?*

(*p*) There would be a great hardship in a strict enforcing of the law, that no executor could pay a debt but upon decree, as throwing great expense upon the estate of the deceased : the rule seems now to be much relaxed in practice.

CONCLUSION.

AFTER having considered this important subject at some length in the preceding treatise, the whole may be concluded with a few miscellaneous remarks.

There appears to be no room to doubt, that it would be highly advantageous, in many obvious respects, if one code were established for the succession in personal or moveable estate, in every part of the realm. The present state of the law is ill adapted to existing circumstances, and frequently gives rise to litigation upon questions of great difficulty and intricacy. It has tended to retard that unreserved communication between the different parts of the kingdom, which would, in a high degree, be most beneficial to all.

If the time be not yet come for the establishment of one uniform system, something might, perhaps, be done to remove those inconveniences in the law of personal succession, which are the most prominent in both countries. Even this would necessarily lead to a wide field of legislation, and ought not to be entered upon without the fullest and most mature consideration. (a)

It is owing to the rules of the law of Scotland, in regard

(a) The commissions of inquiry in both countries, for an examination into the state of their respective municipal laws, have already done much good : a similar mode of inquiry, in regard to matters of *international* law, might also tend to produce results highly beneficial.

to personal succession, that the chief inconveniences of an international kind have already arisen, and may be expected to arise in future. In the preceding pages we have shewn upon what points the principal questions connected with this subject have originated. Some of the most important of these may be briefly resumed here.

1. The limitation upon the power of a husband and father in Scotland of making a will, or testamentary disposition, of personal estate in that country, appears to require regulation and revision.

In England the power of the husband and father to dispose of his whole personal estate by his last will, grew up, by lapse of time, in the province of Canterbury, as an alteration of the ancient common law. This power was specially extended, by different statutes, to Ireland, to Wales, to the province and city of York, and to the city of London. This appears to have been consonant to the views and feelings of the country; and it has not been attended with any serious inconveniences.

May not the same power be with propriety extended to Scotland? It is obvious, that, but for this power, the operation of the local customs in England, in regard to the succession in personal estate, must ere now have become intolerable.

2. The succession of ascendants and collaterals in Scotland also requires regulation and revision: so (we have seen) their own writers admitted more than a century and a half ago. (*b*)

In regard to the father, it appears to be contrary to their own general rule of preferring " the nearest in blood," that brothers and sisters and their descendants should exclude him; that uncles and aunts and their descendants should

---

(*b*) Supra, p. 2.

exclude a grandfather; and so on, in the higher degrees of ascendants.

In regard to the mother, the rule that she can claim nothing in the succession of her child, appears to be both cruel and absurd. If a person were dying without issue, leaving a mother, every natural feeling would prompt him to leave to this mother a competent part of his substance: but the law upon this subject is opposed to every such natural feeling.

To what extent a mother should take, in competition with her own children and their descendants, may be matter for consideration: in England the statutes have regulated this apparently in an equitable way, by giving a third in such case to the mother.

3. The total exclusion of maternal relations from the succession, in any case, appears to require revision.

The succession of maternal relations is one deserving of much consideration: perhaps it is too much to put them precisely on the same footing, in all cases, with relations on the father's side (as is done in England); but it appears to be manifest that they ought not to be entirely excluded.

4. The total exclusion of *representation* in every case in Scotland, in regard to the succession in personal estate, appears also to be most inequitable. Why should not representation be admitted among descendants to the remotest degree; and among collaterals to a limited and reasonable extent? This is the rule of the civil law, and it is the same under the statutes in England.

5. The rights of the executors, or nearest in kin of a wife predeceasing her husband in Scotland, also appear to require revision. Great inconveniences might occur from the state of the law upon this subject, as it now is.

We have little to direct us in regard to the precise nature of the obligations which a father might incur to his children, in regard to their interests in the personal estate of a predeceasing mother. But unpleasant family disputes have arisen, and must arise in the present state of the law, upon this subject. We have seen that the rule of law, according to which the collateral relations of a wife, predeceasing without children, carry off the half of the goods in communion from a surviving husband, might be attended with strange consequences.

6. There appears to be no reason, why a person of illegitimate birth should in Scotland be unable to dispose of his personal estate by will or testamentary disposition, as he may so dispose of it according to the law of England. The habilitation of a bastard, by letters of legitimation from the King, is so easily obtained, that the present state of the law may be said only to affect the poor and the unwary.

But it is not in Scotland only, that alterations may be made with advantage to the public, on the law of personal succession. There are also various matters, which appear to require consideration and revision in the law of England, as connected with this subject.

1. It has been seen that it was well understood, that the statutes of distribution were originally penned with little correctness. (c) The decisions of the Courts have, in addition to, and in explanation of these statutes, established rules, which, in the province of Canterbury, perhaps, could not be very materially improved. But there is reason to doubt whether some of these rules, upon a revision of them, might not still be put upon a more equitable footing. I allude to the succession of the father, in total exclusion of the nearest classes of collaterals; the succession of maternal relations, as upon the same footing, in all cases, with that of the relations on the father's side; and the want of distinction,

---

(c) Supra, p. 36.

in any case, between the relations of the full and those of the half-blood.

2. But the great incongruity in England is, that the law of personal succession is placed upon a different footing in the different parts of that country.

It would be much more convenient, if the whole of England were put under the same rules of succession, instead of having, as at present, one system for the greater part of the province of Canterbury; another for the province of York; a third for the city of London; and other rules for the principality of Wales. It is true, that the universal power of disposing of personal estate by will, has tended to lessen the mischiefs arising from the present state of the law of England in this respect; but great anomalies still prevail, and, from time to time, form the subject of litigation and discussion. There can be no sound reason why these should not all be blended into one equitable common system.

In every partial alteration that may be adopted in either country, it will be highly expedient to keep in view, that it should have a tendency rather to advance than to retard that period, which sooner or later must arrive, when the rules of the law of personal succession shall be the same in every part of the empire. (d)

(d) It would have led into much too wide a field, to have attempted any inquiry in regard to the rules of the law of personal succession, established in the different dependencies and colonies of the British empire. These are of prodigious extent and variety. It is worthy of remark, that the French, when establishing their code, extended its operation, not only over the whole of France, but over every colony and dependency of the French Empire.

APPENDIX.

No. I.

THOMAS HOG, Esquire   -   -   - Appellant,

REBECCA LASHLEY and THOMAS LASHLEY, } Respondents.
Esquire, her Husband   -   -   -

Notes of what passed in the House of Lords, at the hearing of the Cause on the 20th and 30th of April, and the 4th and 7th of May, 1792.

(Taken by James Allan Park, Esq. Barrister at Law.)

MR. GRANT * for the Appellant.

This case is brought under the consideration of your Lordships, in order to settle some points of very general importance in the law of Scotland.

By that law, a person having neither wife nor child may dispose of his property in what manner he pleases. In marriage, if there be no special contract to exclude it, a communion of moveables takes place between husband and wife. But if a man die, leaving a wife and children, one third part of his personal property goes to the wife, which is called the *jus relictæ;* one third part to the children, which is styled the *legitim;* and the remainder, called the *dead's part*, the owner may dispose of to whom he pleases. This right of legitim may be renounced, with or without a consideration; and, upon such renunciation, the general doctrine seems to be, that the share of the child renouncing accrues to the other children, unless a contrary intention of the father has been manifested. From

---

* Afterwards Sir William Grant.

what has been said, it appears that the right of legitim goes to one half of whatever personal property the father dies possessed of, that is not affected by the *jus relictæ*.

In this case five points will arise : —

1st, What will be the effect of an implied renunciation, supposing it to exist in fact in this case?

2dly, Whether the right of the children to legitim may not be barred by a deed *inter vivos*, executed by the father in his lifetime?

3dly, Whether the share of a child renouncing does not accrue to the father, so as to enable him to dispose of it by will?

4thly, Whether, though the deed executed by Mr. Hog be ineffectual in Scotland, it will not operate as a will in England, so as to convey the personal property in that country, according to the deceased's intention?

5thly, If not, on the ground that the *lex domicilii* is to prevail, then, whether the property in the English funds is not to be considered as immoveable property, and descendible to the heir, which would be the case of any fund in Scotland having a *tractus futuri temporis?*

If either of the two first points be decided for the appellant, it will render the consideration of all the latter ones unnecessary, as they both go to the whole question: but the latter questions only go to the quantum of the sum to which Mrs. Lashley will be entitled. Such are the questions arising out of the facts I am going to state to the House.

[Here Mr. Grant stated the facts from the printed case.]

The marriage of the late Mr. Hog was contracted in England, by parties resident in England, and domiciled there; therefore there was no communion of goods between Mr. Hog and his wife, because a settlement was executed upon the marriage, having a respect to English property and to a marriage in England. It further appears, that all the children were born in England; at their birth, therefore, no right to legitim could attach, but, if it ever attached at all, it must have been subsequent to their birth.

At one period since her marriage, it is clear that Mrs. Lashley had no idea of a right to legitim, for in her letter of 27th February 1771, she speaks of 65*l.*, being the interest at five per cent. *for the remaining* 1300*l. of my fortune*, which words certainly imply ' all that she ever expected to receive from her father, or thought she had any right to ;" and by such expressions, every idea of a mere temporary allowance to a child is removed. Mr. Hog himself certainly entertained the same idea, for in 1775, he executed formal bonds of provision in favour of Mrs. Lashley and his other daughters, in which he mentions 2000*l.* to be in full satisfaction of the legitim. In 1785, he made a further provision, also excluding the legitim.

It must be admitted, that if this were entirely the case of a Scotch succession, and no will, there would have been a division amongst the younger children, unless they had renounced. But in this case, the Appellant, Mr. Hog, proved the deed, which was executed in his favour by his father in 1787, as a will of personal property in England. Soon after the death of her father, Mrs. Lashley brought this action. In the Court below, several defences were set up by Mr. Hog, the Appellant.

First, it was contended, that Mrs. Lashley's claim to the legitim was wholly excluded by her acceptance of the provision made by her father; and that the facts and circumstances in this case amounted to a renunciation.

The second answer made to her demand was, that Mr. Hog, the father, had not left his property to be disposed of by the law, but that he had disposed of it by a rational deed *inter vivos*, which it was competent for him to do. These two defences, if either of them had prevailed, would have been an answer to the whole of Mrs. Lashley's demand.

But it was further contended below, by way of partial defence, that, as there was property in England, upon which the deed executed by Mr. Hog could operate as a will, that property must be excluded from the claim of legitim.

It was further insisted, that a renunciation by the other children had no effect to increase Mrs. Lashley's share of legitim, but only gave Mr. Hog, the father, a power to dispose of it.

Lastly, it was contended, that the property in the English funds would go to the heir, and not to the executor; for it was either affected by the will, which gave it to Mr. Hog, the Appellant; or, if the law of the domicil prevented the will from having its due operation, the same law must be resorted to, to show how it must descend; and that law in this case would carry it to the heir.

These were the points rested upon below; but I must admit they were all decided against us, and I am now to trouble your Lordships with arguments in support of them.

The first point is as to the effect of Mrs. Lashley's acceptance. The correspondence contained in the second and third pages of the Appellants' printed case, proves, by the uniform expressions, Mr. Hog's intention to give Mrs. Lashley the same, and no larger fortune, than he bestowed upon his other daughters; and also Mrs. L.'s intention to accept it as her *fortune*. Fortune is a word of a particular import, and is always used to signify the whole sum that a parent means to bestow upon a child.

The renunciation of various rights may be collected from facts and circumstances, as well as by deed, unless there be some express law to the contrary, which is not pretended to exist in this case. The other children of Mr. Hog were executing formal deeds of provision, and in them a clause of renunciation was inserted. She, not being with her father, did not execute such an instrument, and therefore there is no formal renunciation; but words are frequently used by Mrs. Lashley and her husband tantamount to it. In her bills drawn for 65*l.* per annum, she mentions it *as interest due to her*, which proves she could not be speaking of a bounty or temporary provision. Mr. Hog having acquiesced in the statement of 2000*l.* as her fortune, if an action had been brought against him or his executors for that sum, they could not have defended themselves against such a demand. If so, the obligation must be mutual, and I contend, that Mrs. Lashley is debarred from her legitim, because she consents to accept of 2000*l.* as her fortune. But, supposing your Lordships to hold that there must be an *express* renunciation, then I contend,

Secondly, that by a rational deed executed *inter vivos, in liege poustie*, not upon death-bed, the father may exclude the legitim. Mr. Erskine (book iii. tit. 9. s. 16.) says, "that rational deeds granted by the father in relation to his moveable estate, if they be executed in the form of a disposition *inter vivos*, are sustained, though their effect should be suspended till his death." Is there any thing irrational in Mr. Hog's settlement?

Erskine's position is supported and confirmed by adjudged cases;

The case of Johnston v. Johnston, from Fountainhall, mentioned in Dict. of Dec. vol. i. tit. Legitim, p. 545.*

To the same point is the case of Lady Balmain, in the same

---

* Lord Kames's Dictionary of Decisions is here referred to.

page, which was to this effect: A disposition by a husband to his wife of the stocking that should be upon his mains at the time of his decease, being objected to by his children as in prejudice of their legitim, being of a testamentary nature, revocable, as not having been a delivered evident; it was answered, that the form of the deed is *per modum actus inter vivos*, whereby a present right is conveyed, though suspended till the grantor's death, and being done *in liege poustie*, it cannot be reached by the law of deathbed, and there lies no other bar to the father's power of alienation.

These cases are in point, and no contrary determination has been stated, where the claim of the children has prevailed against a rational disposition of the father. Formerly a man could not disappoint the heir as to the descent of real estate, but the power of disposal as to such property has increased, by merely using words of disposition instead of words of devising. If the shackles are thus taken off as to real estate, it is strange that they should still be continued upon personal property. To establish so absurd a principle, your Lordships will think it necessary to be furnished with a long chain of concurrent authorities, and even that will hardly be sufficient in a matter so contrary to reason. In the law of Scotland till lately, the *lex loci rei sitæ* was supposed to be the law that was to govern, and all the decisions are uniformly that way; but now, by a decision of your Lordships, in *Bruce* v. *Bruce* *, the rule of the *lex domicilii* has been established. Therefore, even if the decisions were against me, which I have shown they are not, your Lordships ought to decide for the appellant, upon the principle of removing as much as possible all restraints upon property, and the disposition of it.

Thirdly, as to the effect of the renunciation of the other children. When a father advances a fortune to one child, that child and the father are the only parties to the contract, and the other children have no right to interfere. If any advantage results from that agreement, the father ought to have the benefit of it, and he ought also to have the power of disposing. I admit it is laid down in general, that the share renounced goes to the other children wholly, and not to the heir; but all the cases decided on that point are where the father dies intestate, and where that is the case, he is presumed

---

* Supra, p. 118.

not to have chosen to exercise the right he acquired. From making no disposition, it is evident he meant to benefit the other younger children; and whether a child shall or shall not be barred of legitim is entirely a question of intention; for even where a father makes a provision for a child, he may exempt such child from the necessity of collating such provision. The only case material upon the subject, is that of Henderson against Henderson (Dict. of Dec. vol. i. p. 545.), and that is apparently against me. But in that case there was no renunciation, and therefore I contend that there is no case in which a child has renounced, and the father has made a will acting upon that renounced share, to be found against me.

The fourth question is, how far the deed executed in Scotland by Mr. Hog will be effectual in England as a will, so as to bind the property in England. I am bound to admit after the decision of this house in *Bruce* v. *Bruce*, that the *lex domicilii* is the rule of decision that must prevail as to the disposition of property where the party dies intestate. For it certainly would be extremely inconvenient that many different rules should prevail in the disposition of property belonging to the same individual. It would also be probably inconsistent with the intention of the proprietor, for where he dies intestate, it may be presumed that he approved of the law of his domicil. But how is this rule to be preserved where the property is in another country, and the law of the domicil can only extend to its own territories, so as not to be able to compel the foreign state, where the property actually lies, to enforce it? It is done in this way : the foreign state adopts the law of the domicil, not as a rule binding upon them, but as the presumed will of the deceased; or they resort to a fiction, by saying that moveables have no *situs*, but are attached to the person of the owner. It is necessity only that obliges a court of justice to resort to either the one or the other of these means. But the case is very different where a disposition is made, which would be effectual to transfer property in England, if the property be actually there. For, supposing a man has made a disposition effectual by the law of the country where the property happens to be, what reason or necessity is there to resort either to the presumption of implied will, or to the fiction? The law of Scotland does not deny to the owner the power of disposition, but only the form in which it is conceived : now, that is a mere local regulation, and ought not to bind the courts of any other country.

I agree with the argument, that it would be impolitic in the commercial world, that the *lex loci* should govern the disposition of property accidentally there in a course of commerce. The opinion of Lord Hardwicke, in *Thorne* v. *Watkins*, 2 Ves. 35.*, turns entirely upon the policy in a case of intestacy. But where a man makes a will, the question of policy does not arise.

Fifthly, as to the property in the English funds. It is a clear principle of the law of Scotland, that annuities are considered as heritable, and descend to the heir; and therefore, if the *lex domicilii* is to prevail, you must apply it to the whole of the property, which will exclude Mrs. Lashley from any share of that property which is in the English funds. It is true, that by the law of England, such property is considered as personal; but then that must be with reference to cases in England, the parties being English, and domiciled there. It does not seem to have been a question much agitated by writers on general law, what rule is in general to prevail, whether the *lex domicilii* or the *lex loci*, as to the point whether the property is to be considered as moveable or immoveable. Pothier (vol. iii. p. 528. s. 85.), in treating of the communion of goods between married persons, clearly states the point, and declares it to be settled, that the law of the domicil where the creditor resides, is the rule that is to prevail, and that decision seems to be agreeable to reason. If that rule prevails, then Mrs. Lashley cannot claim legitim in the English funds, because they are not the subject of legitim, but descend to the heir.

These are all the grounds of defence upon which a partial or total reversal of the judgment is prayed.

Adjourned.

April 30th, 1792.

Mr. Anstruther spoke on same side with Mr. Grant, and took precisely the same grounds, and therefore it was not thought necessary to report his arguments.

Lord Advocate† on the side of the Respondents.

I am to trouble the House in support of a judgment which, except upon the point of testate or intestate succession, was an unanimous one in the Court below.

---

* Supra, p. 109.   † Robert Dundas, afterwards Lord Chief Baron.

The points of this cause are, —

1st, Whether Mrs. Lashley is barred of her legitim by any act of hers?

2dly, Whether the deed executed by Mr. Hog is such as to entitle his son to defeat the legitim?

3dly, Whether the shares of the children renouncing accrue to the heir?

4thly, Whether the deed executed by Mr. Hog will be effectual as a will upon the property in England?

5thly, Whether the property in the English funds is to be considered as moveable or immoveable?

1st, Homologation, by the law of Scotland, is, where a party, by actual or presumed acceptance, releases or confirms a contract. But, in order to make such an act binding, it must appear that the party releasing or confirming did so with full knowledge of what he was doing. Now, in this case, the letters that have been produced do not even state that the legitim was at all a subject even of consideration. The sum of 2000*l.*, so much spoken of, was merely a matter of bounty from the late Mr. Hog. The case did not admit of homologation; for Mrs. Lashley's legal claims were never even stated or taken notice of in the whole correspondence. The sum of 700*l.* was so far from being in part satisfaction of the legitim, that it was money lent, for which Mr. Hog took a bond, that he might at any time, even to the time of his death, have put in suit and enforced. If the 65*l.* was meant as the annual interest of Mrs. Lashley's fortune, it is strange that Mr. Hog should still talk of the 700*l.* as a debt, which he does in all his letters. As late as the year 1772 he speaks of the 65*l.* per annum as an annuity and bounty during pleasure. Erskine (book iii. tit. 9. s. 23.) expressly declares, that a virtual renunciation of the legitim will not do, in the following terms, after stating that it may be renounced by a child, even without satisfaction: — " As this right of legitim is strongly founded in nature, the renunciation of it is not to be inferred by implication. It is not to be presumed either from the child's marriage, or his carrying on a trade by himself, or even his acceptance of a special provision from the father at his marriage, if he have not expressly accepted of the provision in full satisfaction of the legitim." This right, though it be not necessary, in order to decide this case, to discuss the nature of it, seems to me to partake more of the *jus crediti* than a right of succession; although that *jus crediti* may certainly be defeated in the lifetime of the father.

This brings me to the second point; namely, whether Mrs. Lashley's claim to the legitim is barred by any act of her father, Mr. Hog. I contend that the instrument produced, as far as the moveable property is concerned, is really a testament, and not a deed *inter vivos*. Now it is clear, from the authority of Mr. Erskine (book iii. tit. 9. s. 16.), that a husband, though he should be in *liege poustie*, cannot dispose of his movcables to the prejudice of the *jus relictæ*, or right of legitim, by way of testament, or, indeed, by any revocable deed." The question, then, is, whether the deed in question falls under the description of a deed *inter vivos?* It is certainly good as to heritable estate; but when he comes to dispose of his personalty, it is a mere testament, for he appoints executors, &c. The cases quoted do not affect my argument, for those were cases of rational deeds *inter vivos;* but I insist upon this, as being a mere testament of personal property.

Adjourned.

May 4th, 1792.

The *Lord Advocate* proceeded.

The third point is as to the effect of the renunciation by the other children of Mr. Hog; and I contend that the benefit of that renunciation does not tend to the profit either of the father, or of the heir, but tends to increase the legitim. It has been much argued here and below upon the policy and expediency of the measure. But after authorities so numerous, and of so much weight, and the variety of decisions in support of those authorities, it is impossible to recur to arguments of general policy. The renunciation of the legitim is not understood as a bargain between the father and the child renouncing; but the child, by anticipation, receives his legitim, and, therefore, it is but justice that those who remain should have their share. The authorities quoted in the case of the Respondent, p. 10., are all unanimous.

The first is the instructions given for the guidance of the commissaries as to the confirmation of testaments in 1606.

Lord Stair, book iii. tit. 8. s. 46.

Lord Bankton, book iii. tit. 8. s. 15.

Erskine, book iii. tit. 9. s. 23.

These authorities all concur in establishing the rule, that a child's renunciation of the legitim has the same effect in regard to the younger children, as the death of the renouncer, so that his share divides equally among the rest.

This doctrine was admitted in its full extent, by all the judges in Scotland in this case, except one (Lord Dreghorn), who has argued on the contrary side upon principles of policy, and upon grounds of expediency, which are wholly inadmissible in this case.

The fourth point is, whether or not the will of Mr. Hog is to have an operation upon the property in England, notwithstanding the law of the domicil. In the case of *Bruce* v. *Bruce*, the House of Lords certainly did state an opinion upon the general point of the law of the domicil, in a case of intestate succession; but the same rule must apply to a case of testate succession. If it be admitted that moveables are supposed to be where the owner is domiciled, then the case is clearly with my client, because then the will can have no effect; for if this will were produced in Scotland, it could not defeat the legitim. Can a court of law, by a mere transmission into another country, give validity to an instrument which it could not have in the country where the party executing it resided?

In the case of Kilpatrick, before Lord Kenyon, then Master of the Rolls (Respondent's case, p. 7.)*, the matter was viewed in this very light; and the only question was, whether the will was good by the law of Scotland? Whenever that point was ascertained, the decree proceeded according to that law.

In Dirleton's Doubts (Respondent's case, p. 8.), it is said that " *testamenti factio* ought, in all reason, to follow the person."

Lord Kames (same page) puts a case as to the *jus relictæ*, and concludes with an observation equally applicable to this point. " At any rate, the *jus relictæ* must have its effect as to his moveables in Scotland; and it would be a little strange to say that his transient effects should be withdrawn, for no better reason than that they happen accidentally to be in a foreign country, where the *jus relictæ* does not obtain." Nor does this doctrine at all militate against the truth of the position, that when a person follows property into a foreign country, in any process, he must conform to the modes pointed out in that country where the debtor resides.

Fifthly, as to the question, whether the money lodged in the Five per cent. Annuities is to be considered as moveable or immoveable: It is said, that if the law of the domicil is to be resorted to on one point, namely, as to the testate or intestate

---

* Supra, p. 116.

succession, so it must on every other; and then it is insisted, that, by the law of the domicil, this particular species of property would be considered as heritable, and, consequently, must descend to the heir. But we contend, that if these funds had been locally situated in Scotland, they would still have been deemed moveable.

There are, by the law of Scotland, certain particular rights, having a *tractus futuri temporis*, and carrying a yearly profit to the creditor, without relation to any capital sum or stock, that are heritable. But the funds in question have not a *tractus futuri temporis* within the meaning of this law; for, in order to make such a subject heritable, it must be a substantive right, without relation to any *capital sum or stock*.

This question occurred in the beginning of this century, and again in 1735; and it was then solemnly decided, that the shares of the Bank of Scotland are not heritable, but simply moveable. The Five per Cent. Annuities fall precisely within Mr. Erskine's description of that species of property which is not to be considered as having a *tractus futuri temporis*. See the whole passage from book ii. tit. 2. s. 6., quoted in Respondents' case, p. 8.

Besides, if there were any doubt upon the law of Scotland, this is a British debt, and the act of 25 Geo. III. c. 32. s. 7. declares it to be personal estate.

Mr. *Solicitor-General* [*], on the same side, after stating the five points that had been made in the cause, proceeded thus:—

The claim of legitim by the law of Scotland is exactly similar to the orphan's share in the custom of London; and it is singular, that there is hardly any question which has been agitated as to the right of legitim, that has not also arisen with respect to that custom; and every decision upon it has been conformable to the decisions in Scotland.

The first point is, whether my clients, the Respondents, are barred by any homologation or acceptance.

The legitim cannot be barred by an implied assent: and, upon this point, without entering into a discussion of the law, I rely upon the fact. In the whole of the correspondence relied upon for the Appellant, no contract appears for any precise sum to be given for the legitim; and even if a sum were mentioned, no terms are imposed, nor even hinted at, that have the smallest connection with legitim.

---

[*] Sir John Scott, afterwards Lord Eldon.

The bond referred to by Mr. Hog, in his letter of September, 1768, was reserved by him in his repositories to his last moments, and might have been put in suit at any time. When, in another place, he proposes the sum of 2000*l.* as an equal share with his other daughters; he does not even state their renunciation of their claim of legitim, or his expectation that Mrs. Lashley would do the same. In another letter, Mr. Hog speaks of his *bounty* to Mrs. L.; and, so late as 1772, he says, he will *continue his bounty* so long as her behaviour merits it. In one of the deeds of provision, also, he recites that 700*l. was due by Mr. L. upon bond;* so that he himself never considered it as an advance in satisfaction of the legitim. Indeed, the idea of giving up the legitim never was the subject of consideration with any of these parties.

The *Lord Chancellor* * asked, whether it was admitted that the husband after marriage might renounce the wife's share of legitim.

Mr. *Solicitor General.*—I do not admit it; for if a husband renounced his wife's share under the custom of London, and she survived her husband, I doubt very much whether she would be barred by that renunciation.

The second point is, whether Mrs. L. is barred by any act of her father, Mr. Hog. A great many acts might be done by a freeman of London to defeat the custom: but if he did any act, which turned out to be a will, it was held to be a fraud upon the custom, and, therefore, void. So held in the case of Tomkyns *v.* Ladbroke, 2 Vezey, 561., where Lord Hardwicke said, that a freeman may by act in his life, and even *in extremis*, give away any parts of his personal estate, provided he divests himself of all property in it; though, if he reserve to himself a power over it, that is considered as void. The act of the father was of a testamentary nature, and, therefore, must be judged to be an act in fraud of the custom. So, in this case, the deed executed by Mr. Hog was in fraud of the legitim, and, therefore, void. I cannot forbear to mention in this place some other peculiarities in the custom of London, which apply to other parts of the cause. It appears that the custom attached upon property not locally situated within the city, so that the will of a freeman would no more operate upon it than if within the walls: 4 Burn, Eccles. Law, tit. Wills, p. 378.

---

* Lord Thurlow.

In the year 1734, it became a question, whether a composition with the wife for her customary part would accrue to the benefit of the father or the children. It was held, that, in such a case, it should be taken, as if the wife were dead; so that the father would have one moiety, and the children the other: 1 P. Wms. 644. In 2 Vez. 592, Lord Hardwicke enters into the history of the cases, and holds it to be settled, that a composition with the wife has the same effect as if she were dead. If, then, the father takes no peculiar or exclusive benefit by a composition with the wife, it should seem strange if a contrary rule prevailed on a composition with the children. But, from what is said in 4 Burn, tit. Wills, p. 376., the inference is, that the same rule prevails on a composition with the children.

In this case it is argued, that, as the father might easily have defeated the right of legitim, the mode he has adopted will do as well as any other, although the law of the country has said directly the contrary. The question is, has he done that act, which the law has required him to do, in order to defeat this right? Will this deed, coupled with the bond of of provision, exclude the right of legitim? The bond alone will not do, because it remained in his bureau till the moment of his death: and as to the deed, no single judge in the Court below had a doubt upon it. The deed, as to the personal estate, is merely in the form of a Scotch testament. A deed with a power of revocation vests a present interest, subject, however, to be defeated by the act of the donor. But a deed to have no effect, till the death of the donor, is very different. The cases quoted on this subject are not analogous to it. Johnstone's case, if it were analogous, is of doubtful authority. Lady Balmain's case is not applicable; and the last case upon the subject, of Henderson v. Henderson, is decisive against both the former.

The third question goes as to the extent of the legitim; and it seems that, in a case of intestate succession, Mrs. Lashley would be clearly entitled to legitim, both as to the English and Scotch effects. Taking it for granted, that the case of Bruce v. Bruce, in the House of Lords, has decided the point, that the law of the domicil must be resorted to as the rule in a case of intestate succession, it seems to me to apply much stronger in a case of testate succession. If the *lex loci* is to govern in a case of the latter sort, is it to be the *lex loci rei sitæ* at the time when the will is made, or at the time when the owner dies? If the law of the domicil is not to prevail, how many different laws are? For if it be not, the disposition of property must depend, not upon the will of the owner, but on the situation of the various persons in whose hands his effects may happen to be placed: nay, it may depend even upon their caprice, or will, rather than upon that of the owner; for a creditor will have nothing to do, but to change his place of abode, and the will of the owner is again defeated.

But I contend that this cannot be the rule; for if a man makes a will, though he uses words which, in the country where the personal property happens to lie, would convey every thing, yet it will be restrained in its operation by the law of the domicil. In other terms, if a man in Scotland devises *all* his personal estate, and the law of the country only permits him to devise the half, neither would it convey more in England. The law of Scotland, upon this point, is clear and decisive: the passages have been read to you by the Lord Advocate, and they are all stated in the Respondents' case, p. 8. The law of England is no less plain upon the point, and is fully stated by Lord Hardwicke in Thorne *v.* Watkins, 2 Vez. 35. And in that case L. H. evidently meant to allude, either to a case of testate or intestate succession; for he speaks of *probate* or *administration.*

The case of Kilpatrick, at the Rolls, must carry great weight; for although the case was not argued at the bar with much pertinacity, yet Lord Kenyon considered the subject, and founded his decree upon the report of what the rule of the Scotch law was; and that was the case of a will.

In the case of the *jus relictæ,* as well as of the legitim, there is good reason for declaring, that the law of the domicil shall prevail; for parties contracting matrimony may be reasonably supposed to have a view to those advantages and benefits, which the laws of their country, by virtue of that relation, entitle them to expect. There ought, then, to be the highest authority to say, that a man who is, and continues to be, domiciled in Scotland shall not be enabled, by placing his property in the English funds, to disappoint the reasonable expectations of his wife, who, by the law of his and her domicil, is entitled to one half of his personal estate, where there are no children; or, if there be any, to defeat both her and them of their legal claims.

In the case of the custom of London, if a freeman of London had disposed of *all* his personal estate, it was only held to mean, *all* he had a power to dispose of under the custom; and it was held that that extended to property out of, as well as within, the jurisdiction; for Lord Hardwicke says expressly, that debts due to a freeman any where are distributable according to the custom.

The fourth point is, as to the effect which the renunciation by the other children shall have. I contend that it is in the nature of a bargain made by the father with the child renouncing for the benefit of the other children. It is a contract that the child renouncing will not claim any part of the father's fortune; but it is not a contract that the father shall claim the renounced share, instead of the renouncer. It is unnecessary to argue this point as an abstract proposition, because it has been decided over and over again; and therefore it is too late to argue upon the reason of the thing, or upon the policy or expediency of such a rule having been adopted.

Fifthly, as to the question, whether the property of the late Mr. Hog in the English funds is to be considered as moveable or immoveable property; it has been assumed, in argument, that if these funds were in Scotland, they would be deemed heritable property; but that is a position which I absolutely deny. Rights of this nature, which are deemed to be heritable by the law of Scotland, are such as carry a yearly profit, without relation to any capital sum or stock. But your Lordships know that the Five per Cent. Annuities depend upon the capital stock; *for it is in respect of his capital stock* that the holder of it is entitled to an annuity. If he propose to transfer it, he does not transfer *an annuity*, but *the stock.* The legislature has expressly declared that his fund shall be considered as personal, and shall go to the executor. Shall a different rule prevail in Scotland, from what the wisdom of Parliament has pointed out? Shall they go to the Scotch executor as trustee for the heir at law, and to the English executor for the benefit of the next of kin under the statute of distributions? Upon this point the authority of Mr. Erskine (book ii. tit. 2. s. 8.) is express, where he says, that " the shares of proprietors in *any public company or corporation, constituted either by statute* or patent, are considered as moveable."

Adjourned.

May 7th, 1792.

Mr. Grant, in reply : — One great question is, whether the legitim has not been renounced. Renunciation of a right may in many cases be inferred from circumstances. It is, indeed, said that nothing but an express renunciation will do in the special instance of legitim. In this case, Mr. Hog's intention is clearly manifested from his correspondence, that Mrs. Lashley was to expect nothing but 2000*l*. The letters on the other hand state 1300*l*. to be the remainder of her fortune. *Remainder* is a relative term, and can only have a reference to a *whole*. The term *fortune* must mean something which the father intends to advance, in satisfaction of every other expectation from her father.

With respect to the question, whether the deed executed by the late Mr. Hog would, in its operation, defeat the legitim, it is admitted to be law, that, by a rational deed *inter vivos*, it may be defeated. An attempt, however, is made to distinguish that case from this, by saying that this is a testament; but the words used are not words of a testamentary nature, but words of disposition; and although there be a nomination of executor, yet that was unnecessary, as Mr. Hog's right would be complete without it. Even though there were a clause of revocation, still it would not be a testament: such a clause was, indeed, useless; for while it remained undelivered in custody of the donor, it was necessarily revocable. The case of Henderson *v.* Henderson is the only thing against us on this point: and with respect to it I can only observe, that, although it was decided long before Erskine wrote, he did not think it of sufficient weight to induce him to alter the doctrine advanced by him in the passage I formerly alluded to.

The cases on the custom of London do not apply to this point. There are personal and local customs: those of London were of the former kind, and were attached to the person of the freeman; the latter description applies to the legitim. So by the custom of York, a person, though bound by the custom as to property locally situated within the province, might dispose of property lying without the province.

The inconvenience of different laws operating upon one man's property would not arise from my argument; for, as it seems to me, if a man has in general a power of disposition, all foreign states ought to adopt it to its utmost extent. Every man who makes a will means to dispose of *all* he can; and though it may not be a good disposition as to the whole, in his own country, yet every other country ought to receive it as binding, *jure gentium*. As to Lord Hardwicke's opinion in Thorne *v.* Watkins, that foreigners would be discouraged from lodging money in the British funds if, at their death, it was to be distributed differently from the laws of their own country, I should rather think it would operate as an encouragement, that they would have a full power of disposition free from the shackles and restraints of their own local regulations.

With regard to the operation of the will upon the English funds, I conceive, clearly, if it were a Scotch fund, it would descend to the heir; for there is no capital stock which a creditor would have a right to demand : all that he could insist upon would be the payment of an annuity from government. The particular fund is not even redeemable at the will of the debtor; for the act of parliament states a certain time, within which they shall not be redeemable ; so that there is a period, during which there only exists a right to receive an annuity. It has been said, that the statute has made this *personal* estate : but has not the same statute declared it to be devisable? If you rely upon it as declaring it personalty, I also contend that it enabled Mr. Hog to devise it. Does not that act, then, operate as a repeal of the general law of legitim, as much as the act of parliament which enabled freemen of London to make a will was a repeal of the custom?

Lord Chancellor. — Supposing no act of parliament had passed to enable a freeman of London to make a will, your argument goes the length of contending, that this statute, creating the Five per Cent. Annuities, would have been a virtual repeal of the custom as to money in those funds.

Mr. Grant. — I certainly must so contend. As to the effect of the renunciation of the other children, I can find no case which has been decided where the father has died testate. And it is a little singular that, although every judge below admitted that the reasonableness was all on the side of the Appellant, they have decided against him, without any precedent in support of their judgment. It is admitted that the children have no claim over it during their father's life; and it seems very immaterial to them whether the diminution of the legitim be occasioned by the father's spending it, or advancing a child.

The Lord Chancellor moved to affirm the judgment.*

Ordered.

---

* According to the then usual practice, in a case of affirmance, nothing was said by his Lordship upon this occasion.

No. II.

Rebecca Lashley and Thomas Lashley, Esquire, her Husband, - - - } Appellants;

William Thwaites and others, Assignees of Alexander Hog, a bankrupt, deceased; and Thomas Hog Esquire, - - - } Respondents.

Notes of the Speech of the Lord Chancellor (Lord Eldon) at moving the Judgment in this Cause (4th June 1802).*

This cause came before your Lordships by the appeal of Rebecca Lashley and her husband, Thomas Lashley, for his interest, complaining of an interlocutor pronounced by the Court of Session, in an action of multiple poinding, in which her brother, Thomas Hog, was pursuer.

The circumstances of the case are these : — Roger Hog, the father of the Appellant and of Thomas Hog, died in March, 1789. Soon after this event, an action was raised by the Appellants against the Respondent Thomas Hog, as heir to his father, as representing him on some one or other of the passive titles known in law, and as universal intromitter with his goods and gear; stating that he was indebted to the pursuer, Rebecca, in the sum of 15,000*l.*, as her share of the goods in communion at her mother's death, as one of the next in kin of her mother (this part of the summons is at present under the consideration of your Lordships in another appeal); it states, also, that he was indebted to her in the further sum of 15,000*l.*, as her share of the means and estate of her father at his death, together with interest on these two sums from the date when they ought to have been paid, till payment.

Thomas Hog's defences were, that the claims were barred by the rational and ample provisions made by the father in favour of the Appellant and his other younger children, which were accepted of by them.

Mrs. Lashley claimed as one of the six children of her mother; but she claimed the whole of the legitim at the death

---

* From my own notes taken at the time.

of her father, suggesting, or insisting, that all the other
children had discharged their claims. In his defences, Mr.
Hog put on record his belief that the other children had renounced, but at the same time insisting that the benefit of
such renunciations accrued to him; and he contended that
Mrs. Lashley also had renounced her legitim; he insisted on
the points also in which Alexander Hog was interested; viz.,
" that any claim of legitim was excluded by the trust deed of
settlement executed by the father in *liege poustie;* that the
effects in England were not liable to any claim of legitim;
that, with regard to the effects in Scotland, the renunciations
of the children must operate in his (Thomas's) favour; and that
the father was domiciled in England at the time of his wife's
death." These, as also the consequence of the father having
invested a considerable part of his personal property in the
name of his son, are the subject of argument in the other depending clause.

On the 2d of December, 1790, the Court pronounced an
interlocutor, finding that Mrs. Lashley's claim of legitim was
not barred by any thing done by her, and remitting to the
Lord Ordinary to hear the parties upon the effect of the discharges of their legitim by the other children.

It is difficult to conceive, that Alexander and his assignees
did not know of this decision.

On the 7th of May, 1792, the judgment, in an appeal by
Thomas Hog from the decision of the Court of Session, was
pronounced, affirming the interlocutors which settled that the
renunciations of the other children operated in favour of the
Appellant, Rebecca, but leaving unascertained what was the
amount of the personal estate which was the subject of
the claim. This involved questions of too great magnitude to
receive an early decision; and, indeed, with regard to some of
them, I may now observe that they are not very likely yet to
be soon decided.

Mr. Hog *bonâ fide* understood that all the other children had
renounced, and also that Mrs. Lashley herself had renounced.
In consequence of the affirmance of these interlocutors, many
of the questions, which were interesting to the other children,
as well as to Mrs. Lashley, came to an end.

The assignees of Alexander now thought proper to make a
claim, by saying that he (Alexander) was entitled to legitim as
well as Mrs. Lashley, and in consequence they raised the
the same kind of action, insisting that he had done no act in

the lifetime of his father, nor since his death, which could bar his claim. Thomas Hog instituted, thereupon, an action of multiple poinding, saying that he was ready to pay the whole free personal estate to any person who might be found entitled to it, when its amount should be ascertained, but that he was likely to be harassed by the several parties claiming it; viz., Alexander and his assignees, Mr. Lashley and his wife, and also his creditors, who arrested the funds in Thomas's hands. The Court of Session, on the report of Lord Dreghorn, pronounced an interlocutor, declaring Thomas liable only in *once* and *single payment* (the point on which all multiple poindings must rest); finding also that Alexander had not discharged his claim; and, on a reclaiming petition, the Lords adhered. The causes between the parties having been conjoined with the multiple poinding, this appeal is now brought to determine the question of Alexander's right to legitim.

At first, only the assignees of Alexander were called as respondents; but it occurred to some of your Lordships that it was doubtful whether it would be right to proceed without the presence of Thomas Hog, as a question might arise whether the Court of Session could act in contradiction to the judgment in the former appeal, which adjudged the *whole* legitim to Mrs. Lashley. This doubt arose in my mind from thinking that a multiple poinding resembled a proceeding by bill of interpleader in this country: as, here, if Rebecca had stated, in a proceeding in the Court of Chancery, that only one of the children had not discharged, and if Thomas had admitted this on the record, and on that admission a decree had been founded, giving the whole subject-matter to the plaintiff, it would be found very difficult to overturn such decree. Or put the case thus: if a creditor for 10,000*l.*, due from the estate of a person deceased, stated that he was the only creditor of the deceased, and the executor admitted this averment, and that he had assets wherewith to pay it; if a decree were pronounced in consequence for payment of the debt, whether it were paid or not paid, what would be the result of a claim by another creditor? If it were paid, no other creditor could call on that creditor for a participation of the sum recovered, but he would have his claim against the executor. If it were not paid, and the executor should pay any part of the money to any other creditor, the first creditor might, nevertheless, still insist for the whole, and no bill of review could be brought; he should have made the usual enquiry for creditors. I cannot leave this part of the case without noticing that, though some of the judges of the Court of Session expressed their surprise that there could be any doubt of the propriety of the judgment in the case of the multiple poinding, I yet think that very considerable difficulty hangs about it ; and I know that a noble and learned Lord now near me (Lord Thurlow) concurs in this opinion.

With regard to the transactions of Alexander with his father during the father's life, and of himself and his assignees since his father's death, in a suit between the brother and sister, I should hold, on the principles of the doctrine of election, that Alexander had renounced. The claim of Alexander for legitim was not made till the cause between Thomas and Rebecca was finished, though he and his assignees knew that they could make such claim. Under these circumstances, what is the effect of the transactions before and after the father's death?

During the lifetime of his father, circumstances occurred which raise a considerable question whether he was not barred during the life of his father : if not, they will be of weight in viewing the later transactions which took place.

It was stated in the Court of Session, that the assignees had acted properly in not saying a word till the cause was over : one judge, indeed, wondered that there was a different opinion in regard to this notion. When I mention the circumstances of the case, you will see that this was not a mere acquiescence, but, in some degree, a case of election. What would have been the consequence had the money been paid out of the hands of the executor? or is it morally fit or proper that one child should benefit at the expense of another, while struggling, perhaps, with poverty? Would you suffer the assignees, without having provided for the expense, to benefit by the expense of Mrs. Lashley? Will you not rather consider this, in a moral point of view, as evidence of the understanding of parties.

On 29th November, 1768, Roger Hog wrote a letter to Alexander, telling him he intended to pay off *his patrimony*, without interest; " which," he says, " is the sum I always allotted to you." On 31st December, 1768, Alexander executed a discharge of the sums as the portion bestowed on him by his father : he was only a minor at this time. The entries in Roger Hog's books cannot be evidence of any thing ; and it is obvious they were no evidence against the daughter Rebecca.

On 1st March, 1779, and 1st September, 1780, Alexander obtained two loans of 2000*l.* each, making 4000*l.*, from his father, for which he granted bonds in the English form. On 30th December, 1783, Roger executed a deed, in which, after reciting these bonds, for love, favour, and affection, and other weighty causes, he resolves, in lieu of provision, to discharge these two bonds; declaring .that this should be in full of all legitim, &c. This discharge he kept in his own hands, and it was found in his repositories at his death. On the question whether Alexander had discharged the legitim in Roger's lifetime, I am of opinion, that the fact of the father's executing this discharge amounts to a demonstration that he could not mean to have contended that the discharge of 1768 amounted to a discharge of the legitim. For these reasons, there is no ground to say, that the legitim was barred in the lifetime of Roger Hog. Indeed, Roger's proving the bonds as debts on Alexander's bankrupt estate in England, is proof of a demand of 20*s.* in the pound; and, if the bankrupt receives his certificate, the payment of the dividends on his estate is full payment of the debt; for a man, proving under a statute of bankruptcy, foregoes all other modes of payment than that under the statute, so as to destroy all other remedies for payment.

Having received the first dividend, Roger Hog died. On this event, it is to be supposed that these assignees, as representing the bankrupt, the son of a Scotsman, would have a general knowledge of the rights of the bankrupt, and, among others, of his claim on his father's estate. It was their duty to have examined whether he still retained these rights. But the matter does not rest here. They received, *in græmio* of the father's discharge of the 4000*l.*, information that the child of a Scotsman had a claim, unless he had disposed of it in the lifetime of the father: for, at the father's death, his son Thomas, very properly, and in the due execution of his duty, informed the assignees of the existence of the instrument, and sent it to them. Not only was the attention of the assignees, but also of the bankrupt, drawn to this deed; for, when the discharge was carried to him by Mr. Robertson, the agent of the family, and put into the possession of Thwaites, he gave a receipt for it, which states, that it is subjoined to an " exact copy " of the discharge. He who stated the copy to be exact could not but know the contents of the deed. Alexander wrote that he approved of this receipt at the bottom of it. They who transmitted this discharge must have considered that Alexander's claim was thereby barred. There is great danger in allowing persons, who have no interest in the subject in dispute, to be plaintiffs in a multiple poinding, raised for the purpose of bringing forward claims like this. If Mrs. Lashley had failed in obtaining the legitim, I cannot but apprehend that we should have had a probability of seeing more of the circumstances of the case than are now before us, if Alexander had then started up and said, " I did not discharge, though Mrs. Lashley has; pay *me* the legitim." Though it has, therefore, hung on my mind that a multiple poinding is a dangerous proceeding in cases like this, yet the danger is much greater to get rid of authorities.

But the matter does not rest on the understanding of Thomas alone, but also on that of the assignees; they understood that, after they had received the discharge, Thomas, as executor to Roger, had no right to any future dividends, as he no longer stood as a creditor on Alexander's estate; and they therefore paid the dividends among the other creditors, passing him over.

It is matter of astonishment to me that there can be any doubt that, in making this bargain, they agreed to take the dividends in lieu of the legitim, rather than speculate on its uncertain amount; being at the same time in doubt, whether, independent of the discharge, Alexander would have been able to sustain his claim to the legitim : and there was nothing to prevent their making such a bargain. If this had been a question in the Court of Chancery, being an election, and dealt with for three years together, they would be bound by it. But they say they were at liberty to do *this:* if the dividends amounted to the legitim, well and good; if not, they contend that they were entitled to demand more. By all our books, however, they are not so entitled, and in many cases it has been decided by my predecessors, that this amounts to an election. But it is not clear that this was an imprudent act on their part, if the Court had held that the law of the *situs* was to rule the distribution, and, of course, that all the property in the bank was not liable to claims of legitim; the claim would have been very small indeed. It was even a doubt whether Alexander had not discharged in his father's lifetime. Besides, it is not material, in a case of election, to enquire whether they made an improvident bargain or not; it is sufficient that they made it with deliberation.

I have always been clear upon this point ; but, having been

counsel in this cause, nothing but necessity should have obliged me to decide it; but, even now, I act on and deliver the deliberate and well-weighed opinion of another noble and learned Lord (Thurlow).

On the Lord Chancellor's motion this judgment was pronounced : —

It is ordered and adjudged, that the interlocutors complained of, in so far as they find, that Alexander Hog's claim of legitim was not cut off, during the life of his father, be affirmed ; and that the said interlocutors be reversed, in so far as they find, that Alexander Hog's claim of legitim was not cut off by what passed, after his father's death ; and in so far as they sustain the said claim : and it is declared and found, that the assignees of the bankruptcy of the said Alexander Hog were competent to release such claim ; and that it appears, by facts proved in this cause, that they have released it : and it is further ordered and adjudged, that as to the rest, the said interlocutors be affirmed ; and that the cause be remitted back to the Court of Session to proceed accordingly.

1898.z.ch.60.   1900.a.c.21.

No. III.

REBECCA LASHLEY and THOMAS LASHLEY, Esquire, her Husband, - - } Appellants ;

THOMAS HOG, Esquire, - - - Respondent.

Et è contra.

Notes of the Speech of the Lord Chancellor (Lord Eldon) at moving the Judgment in the Cause (9th and 10th of July, 1804).[*]

Lord Chancellor. — THIS is an appeal by Rebecca Hog, otherwise Lashley, and Thomas Lashley, Esquire, her husband, against several interlocutors of the Court of Session of the 2d of July, 1793 ; the 5th of March and 25th of November,

---

[*] From the short-hand writer's notes.

I

1794; the 16th of June and 7th of July, 1795; the 23d of
May, the 8th of June, the 26th of June, and the 11th of July,
1798; the 12th of November, 1799; and the 14th of May and
the 26th of July, 1800; and also an application to your Lordships on the part of Mr. Hog, in the nature of a cross appeal
against certain interlocutors in the course of the same proceeding. That cross appeal comprehends questions which I
shall presently state, because, before it can be taken into consideration, your Lordships will have to decide whether it was
presented consistently with the rules of your Lordships' House;
and that question, though it will not much affect the principal
matter in the cause, will certainly affect one part of it; that
which relates to a claim with reference to the expenses of
confirmation in Scotland, and probate of the testator's will in
England.

This cause comprehends a great variety of questions, including many points deserving of very great attention, which
have been very eloquently argued at your Lordships' bar. My
purpose, if that shall meet with the pleasure of your Lordships,
is to go through the statement of the case, and to exhaust the
consideration of some of the points now, meaning to conclude
the consideration of the whole in the course of to-morrow.

The case, with reference to the questions between these
parties, has been long, upon some points or other, under discussion in your Lordships' House; so long, that I have had the
honour frequently of appearing at your Lordships' bar as
counsel for one of the parties in this cause. It has been,
therefore, certainly with great reluctance that my attention,
in a judicial character, has been called so imperiously to the
consideration of the questions between these parties. But
the circumstance of the absence of one noble and learned
Lord (Thurlow), and the circumstance of the occasional
absence of another noble and learned Lord (Rosslyn), whom
I am happy to see this day present in this House, have compelled me to execute that duty as well as I can, which
I never feel any inclination, under such circumstances, to
attempt to discharge, when it is not necessary that I should
take the discharge of it upon myself. Thus I address myself
to the decision of this cause, rather from matter of necessity,
than matter of choice. In the opinion, however, which I have
formed upon this subject, I have reason to think that I have
the concurrence of those who have had occasion, in different
periods, to attend to the subject-matter of this cause, and who,

whether present or absent, have in that degree attended to the consideration of this case which enables me to collect (what is of very great value unquestionably) the judicial opinion of those who may possibly be not here to express it ; and I shall have the satisfaction in expressing my own opinion in the presence of a noble and learned Lord, who has frequently had occasion to give his attention to this subject, and who, if I fall into any mistake, will be able to set your Lordships right.

It appears that, previous to the year 1737, a gentleman of the name of Roger Hog, who married in that year a lady of the name of Rachel Missing, and who were the father and mother of the Appellant, Mrs. Rebecca Lashley, and the Respondent, Mr. Thomas Hog, lived in that part of this island which is called England. Mr. Hog carried on his trade in the city of London : he was a native of Scotland, but he had unquestionably lost his Scotch domicil : he was to all intents and purposes a domiciled Englishman when he contracted, in 1737, in England, a marriage with this lady. Upon that marriage a settlement was made, and it is necessary to state particularly to your Lordships the substance of that settlement, because it has been considered as affecting the questions in this case, both in the Courts below and in the argument here at the bar; and because it appears to me, upon the best consideration I can give the subject, that, attending to the legal effect of it, it does not in any degree affect the legal consideration of this case.

Mr. Hog received with the lady a portion of 3500*l.*, and, receiving that portion, he entered into an engagement that he would, as soon as a purchase could reasonably be had, dispose of the sum of 2500*l.*, part of the 3500*l.*, in the purchase of a real estate in England, with an obligation to convey that estate to his own use for his life, and after his death to trustees to preserve contingent remainders ; with remainder to the use of his intended wife for her life, and, after the decease of himself and his wife, then to the children of the marriage, in such manner as she, notwithstanding her coverture, by deed or will, should direct and appoint ; and, in default of such direction and appointment, to the use of the children of the marriage, to be equally divided between them share and share alike ; and, in default of such issue, to the use of the lady in fee.

In looking through this settlement, a copy of which is printed in the cause, I think I am authorised to state to your Lordships that its effect is no more than this, — that this lady, being entitled to the sum of 3500*l.*; 1000*l.*, part of the 3500*l.*, was advanced to the husband for his own use; that with respect to the remaining 2500*l.*, it was to be laid out in land, which land was to be settled to the use of the husband for life; then to the use of the wife for life; with remainder to the children of the wife, whose property, your Lordships observe, purchased the estate, in such manner as she should appoint; that, in default of any appointment by her, the children were to take equally; and, if there were no children, this real estate, so purchased with 2500*l.* of her personal property, was to go to her in fee; but the settlement does not contain any declaration whatever that this was to be in lieu of her dower; and, indeed, it would have been singular if it had, for this was the purchase of her own estate with her own money. What is more to the present purpose, it does not contain any thing by way of declaration, covenant, or otherwise, that this was to be accepted in satisfaction of any right of any kind which she could acquire by her marriage or otherwise, in the personal estate of her husband. It is a pure dry settlement of that real estate which was to be purchased with the sum of 2500*l.*; and it appears to me, if I am right in collecting and stating the fact of this settlement, that in respect to any question as to what, under any circumstances, this lady would have in the personal estate of her husband, that question remains just as much open to discussion as if this settlement had never been made; this settlement has no relation whatever to that question.

It appears that, after this, Mr. Roger Hog purchased lands at Kingston upon the terms of this covenant, and those lands were conveyed to the trustees mentioned in this deed, to the uses of the deed; and it should seem that afterwards the lady made her appointment, by which she gave, subject to her husband's estate for life, as she had a power of doing, the right of the land to the present Respondent, Mr. Thomas Hog. It appears, afterwards, that when he became of age (at least, it is so suggested, and seems to have been so taken for granted throughout the whole of the proceedings in the cause), this estate was sold, and, the estate being sold, the father received the money, the price of the estate; and, the father receiving the money, the price of the estate, of course he would be debtor to the son, whose estate it was, for the price of the estate, to be paid to the son at the time his right to the possession of the estate so sold should have commenced; and

E E

that the son would, therefore, be a creditor upon the assets of his father for that sum, calculated as a sum to be paid at that time; unless it can be shown either that, by virtue of some agreement which had been entered into between the parties, this relation of debtor and creditor so entered into was cancelled, or that, by some circumstances which had taken place between them, this debt was paid; or that, from the effect of some transaction which has taken place upon the death of Mr. Roger Hog, or otherwise, this demand has been satisfied.

Mr. Hog continued to carry on trade for a considerable time; and, carrying on that trade, it appears that he purchased an estate at Newliston, in Scotland, in 1752; and it is alleged on the part of the present Appellants (the original Appellants) that he had his residence in Scotland from about the year 1752. Mr. Hog, the son, on the other hand, contends that he was after that time domiciled in England; and that question will be material for your Lordships' consideration, at what time he ceased to be, in the contemplation of law, domiciled in England, and at what time he began to be capable of being considered, and necessarily to be considered, as domiciled in Scotland, with reference more particularly to the period of February, 1760; because in February, 1760, Mrs. Hog, formerly Miss Missing, died.

The question upon the place of domicil at that period comes to be material, because upon the fact whether he was domiciled in Scotland, or domiciled in England, at that time, arises a very material question between the parties in this cause; whether she is to be considered the wife of a Scotchman, or whether she is to be considered the wife of an Englishman; it being contended, on the part of Mrs. Lashley, that her mother was to be considered, in 1760, as the wife of a Scotchman, — of a domiciled Scotchman. The consequence of that is, that, if she was the wife of a domiciled Scotchman, she was entitled, predeceasing her husband, to what they call *jus relictæ* *; that the husband could not deprive her of it, but that she had that claim, and transmitted it to her next of kin. The appellants in this case say that she was associated with her husband, and entitled to a share under the communion of goods with him, because he was a domiciled Scotchman, because the law of

---

* In the course of the appeal this was often called the *jus relictæ*; more strictly it was, in this case, Mrs. Hog's *share of the goods in communion* at the dissolution of the marriage by her death.

Scotland creates such an interest in the case of a domiciled Scotchman, his wife predeceasing him; and therefore Mrs. Lashley, as one of the children, claims to be entitled, according to her interest, in that which, according to the law at the dissolution of that connection, goes to the children of the deceased wife.

On the other hand, it is said in the cross appeal (if it can be considered as such) that there is no fact which bears them out in the assertion that Mr. Hog was domiciled in Scotland in 1760, and, if they are not supported in the fact that he was domiciled in Scotland in 1760, that there is no occasion to enquire further about the law.

But they add, if he was domiciled, in the year 1760, in Scotland, yet they contend, — first, that, because the marriage was had in England, the Scotch law, which would obtain between Scotch persons domiciled, at the death of the wife, in Scotland, when the marriage has *de facto* taken place in Scotland, will not apply to persons, though they are proved to have been domiciled in Scotland at the dissolution of the marriage, when the *locus contractus matrimonii* was actually in England; and that by the law of Scotland you are not driven to enquire what the rights of a Scotch wife would be, if she had been clothed with the character of a Scotch wife under the effect of a marriage contracted in Scotland; but if, upon the husband's death, he is to be considered as a domiciled Scotch husband, and she is to be considered as a domiciled Scotch wife; or if, upon the wife's death, she is to be considered as a domiciled Scotch wife, and her husband as a domiciled Scotch husband, you are to apply as between the estates of such a husband and wife the law of England, if those parties were married in England.

And beyond that, they contend that, in this particular case, if that is not the just view of the law, a marriage settlement having been made in England, that is to be regarded as a conventional provision, which would shut out the right to any legal provision.

It is necessary also to state to your Lordships, that the Appellant, Mrs. Rebecca Hog, in the year 1776, intermarried with the other Appellant, a gentleman of the name of Thomas Lashley, whose father was a physician in the island of Barbadoes, and that upon that occasion no contract of marriage was entered into between them. Mrs. Lashley's father made a proposal, which did not take effect, and the Appellants received from him the sum of 700*l.*, which was advanced to Mr. Lashley uponhis bond, in 1767; another sum of 300*l.* in 1779; and an annual payment of 65*l.*, from the year 1772, during the remainder of Mr. Hog's life. I state these circumstances to your Lordships because the interlocutors have relation to these facts.

Mr. Hog's other children received from him certain provisions, which they are said severally to have accepted, in full satisfaction of all they could ask or demand, by or through his decease, or the decease of their mother, in the name of legitim or otherwise. And when I advert to this fact, in passing along, it seems to me not quite immaterial that, after Mr. Hog became unquestionably a person domiciled in Scotland, and was providing for his children as a person would do who was attending to the law of the country in which he was domiciled, his men of business, whom he consulted at the time he made these provisions, certainly felt that it was matter of doubt whether the children had not a claim under their mother, considering the circumstances under which the mother had died; for the deed which he expressly required, before he paid to them the portions which he intended for them, contained a renunciation, not only of whatever they could claim through his decease; but also of whatever they could claim through the decease of their mother, in name of legitim or otherwise.

Upon the 19th of March, 1789, Mr. Hog died at Newliston, leaving a real and personal estate of very considerable value, part of which was situated in Scotland, part in England, and a small part in France; and, before his death, he had executed certain deeds of settlement. There can be no doubt his intention was to vest, as amply as he could, his property in his eldest son; and of this he was unquestionably himself the proper judge: he was the father of all the children, and, as far as the law would allow it, he had a right to decide for himself to which of his children he would give most, and to which he would give least. It was quite clear that he meant to give all that he could give to the present Respondent, Mr. Thomas Hog.

The deeds of settlement which Mr. Hog had executed were lodged in the hands of Mr. John Robertson, writer in Edinburgh, his ordinary agent. One of these was a general disposition, containing a nomination of executors, dated the 5th of February, 1787, in favour of his eldest son, the Respondent: it conveyed to him certain lands therein mentioned, together with all Mr. Hog's personal property, burdened with the payment of debts, legacies, and provisions to younger children; and it directed, — and this is the part of the disposition to be attended to by your Lordships, — " that the residue and growing interest should be employed in purchasing land to be entailed on the series of heirs specified in the entail of Newliston." I state this to your Lordships to be material, in deciding on the circumstances of this case, (and your Lordships will recollect, that, in a former stage of it, I represented it to be material,) because, if, in fact, this species of disposition was made by the settlement in 1787, that will deserve attention when your Lordships come to consider the effect of the evidence, as it bears upon the question in regard to certain shares of stock of the Bank of Scotland, to the number of eighty-one shares, which were to be disposed of, or were intended to be disposed of; which eighty-one shares, it is contended by the Respondent, Mr. Hog, had been absolutely conveyed to, and vested in him.

Two bonds were also entrusted to Mr. Robertson in favour of Mrs. Lashley, excluding her husband's *jus mariti*; one of these, for 1300*l.* sterling, contained a declaration that the same " shall be in full satisfaction to the said Rebecca Hog, my daughter, of all portion natural, legitim, bairns' part of gear, or other claim or demand from me, or from my heirs and executors, in and through my decease, or the death of Mrs. Rachel Missing, my spouse;" and here, also, it may be material for your Lordships to attend to it, that these bonds, which were executed at a period very long subsequent to that at which her mother had died, contained a declaration, that the same should be in satisfaction of all that she could claim through his decease, or the death of Mrs. Rachel Missing, his spouse. Those, therefore, who transacted this part of the testator's business, did not think it safe to make this proposition, as a proposition to a child to accept this provision in lieu of legitim, as it could be claimed through the decease of the father, who was unquestionably then a domiciled Scotchman; but they thought it right also to propose it, as a satisfaction for what could be claimed through the mother's decease, who, as I before stated, died in the year 1760. These provisions, which had been so tendered to Mr. Lashley and his wife, they were not contented with, and they raised a suit in the Court of Session against the present Mr. Hog, as representative of his father, (for he had acted as such in Scotland, and had taken probate, also, in England,) to account for one half of his father's moveables, or personal estate, in name of legitim, and for Mrs. Lashley's proportion of one third of the goods in communion at the dissolution of the marriage, to which they alleged the children of the marriage were entitled, as the next of kin to their mother.

There were several defences to this action, and these defences were met by replies; and it will be within your Lordships' recollection, that there have been several interlocutors in favour of Mr. Lashley and his wife, which have been affirmed by your Lordships sitting in judgment here; more particularly an interlocutor of the 7th of June, 1791, that "the renunciation of legitim by the younger children of the deceased Mr. Hog operated in favour of the pursuer, Mrs. Rebecca Hog, and has the same effect as the natural death of the renouncers would have had, and as she is the only younger child who did not renounce, find her entitled to the whole legitim, being one half of the free personal estate belonging to her father at the time of his decease, whether situated in Scotland or elsewhere."

Another question which arose in that case, was with respect to some part of that personal property (of what value does not signify as to the principle which was under discussion), whether the *lex loci rei sitæ*, or the *lex domicilii*, of the testator was to determine in what manner the same should be disposed of. This question, which long agitated the Court of Session, and afterwards agitated your Lordships by a discussion at your bar, and which was finally decided here, was, taking Mr. Hog, as he was found to be, domiciled in Scotland at the time of his death, whether the personalty which he had in England and in France, particularly the personalty which he had in England, and attending to the nature of it, and the property in the funds; was personalty to be distributed according to the law of England, or to be distributed according to the law of Scotland?

There were other points, and those were points with which the present case more particularly connects itself. It was, first, denied, that Mrs. Lashley had any claim to her mother's right to a share of the personal estate of her father at the dissolution of the marriage. That question was remitted by the Court of Session to the Lord Ordinary for his reconsideration before the last appeal; and I shall have occasion to state to your Lordships his judgment, and that of the Court, upon it.

Then there was another question, which becomes extremely

material in this case, which is as to the amount of that property which is to be considered as subject to the legitim; and that question chiefly respects several shares of the stock of the Bank of Scotland; and the true question upon that will be this, — whether the property in the stock of the Bank of Scotland was, at the death of Mr. Roger Hog, to be considered (for the purposes with reference to which his children can claim) as the property of Mr. Roger Hog, whatever might be the apparent ownership of it; or whether, on the other hand, it was to be considered as property with reference to which he had, to all intents and purposes connected with the question of legitim, divested himself of all ownership, and had *bonâ fide*, out and out, given that property to his son Thomas Hog in his lifetime. It cannot be denied, in any way of stating the question, that the claim of legitim attaches only on that which is the moveable property of the father at his death, and, therefore, ceased to be the property of the father at his death; the children can claim only against that which was the property of the father at his death, subject always to the consideration of what acts can be said to put an end to the property of the father previous to his death, regard being had to the principles of the law as these respect fraud upon fair claims, attending to the nature of those claims.

The first question, therefore, is, whether, under the circumstances, Mrs. Lashley has any claim under her mother?

The next question is, what is the amount of the property to which she has a claim? That depends also upon the question, what claims Mr. Thomas Hog has, and what right Mr. Thomas Hog has to call upon Mr. and Mrs. Lashley to bring into division or into collation those sums of money and those provisions which have been advanced by the father to Mr. Lashley or to Mrs. Lashley during the lifetime of the father. When these claims are settled, it will, of course, be ascertained what is the amount of that property upon which this claim of legitim attaches.

With respect to the first of these questions, it certainly is an extremely important question, which, it appears to me, has been hitherto unprejudiced by any direct decision, but, as it seems to me, by no means unaffected by the establishment of principles which have application to it: it is this, whether, when a person marries in one country, and on that marriage a contract is entered into, but which contract, in the terms of it, has no relation whatever to the personal property of the hus-

band, such as it is at the time of the marriage, such as it shall
be subsequent to the time of the marriage, or such as it may be
at the death of the husband; whether, because, in fact, the
marriage took place in England, whatever may be the change
of domicil of the husband subsequent to the marriage, and
whatever shall be said to be in law the place of his domicil at
the time of his death; the administration of his estate in that
place where he dies domiciled is to be an administration, as far
as it respects his wife, with reference, not to the law of the place
where he died domiciled, but to the law of the place where the
marriage was had; and then stating that, whatever might have
been her claims if she had been married in the place where her
husband died, let her husband die domiciled where he may, she
neither has nor can have any other rights than those which she
would have had if the husband had died domiciled in the place
where the marriage was entered into.

This question comes to be important, because your Lordships
will observe that there is a great difference, particularly in this
case, which is the case of a predeceasing wife, between the
claims of her children, and what would be the claims of her
children, if the rights of the mother are to be determined upon
by the law of Scotland, or by the law of England. Under the
law of England, I need not state to your Lordships that, where
the wife predeceases the husband, and there has been no convention or provision upon her marriage; when she dies, instead
of any body representing her, having any claim as against the
husband, her husband has a title to be her universal representative against any children she had, and all other persons in
the world. The law of Scotland is not so, because that law
recognises what is called the communion of goods in the
married state, and by virtue of that law the wife has certain
interests, if she predeceases the husband; she and her husband
being considered as entitled, in communion and society, in the
personal estate, and the society and communion expiring by
the dissolution of the marriage: in consequence of her death,
the property comes to be severed, and her children, as her
children, have a right to a part of the property of the husband,
as representing her, against the husband himself. The proportion, in the case of the wife dying after her husband, seems
to be pretty much the same as in the law of England: if he
predeceases her in England, dying intestate, leaving children,
your Lordships know her share is one third, and the children
have the other two thirds; if there are no children, her propor-

tion is a moiety ; and the next of kin, not standing in the condition of children, take the other moiety. So, in the law of Scotland, her right is different, in respect to the proportion or extent of her claim, in respect of her husband's dying with children, or without children. I think, if he dies with children, she is entitled to a third, and to a moiety if he dies without children.

In order, therefore, to state this question to your Lordships, we must consider, first, what would be the case supposing the wife had died after the husband ; and see how far the principles we shall establish to regulate that case, will apply to the case of the wife predeceasing her husband. When it was stated, at the bar here, that the *locus contractus matrimonii* must govern, one's attention was naturally called to the consideration of all the difficulties that presented themselves, as consequential upon that way of stating the proposition. I am ready to admit, there are considerable difficulties upon any state of the proposition ; and yet, to a mind informed as that of an English lawyer is, as he is informed by his habits, I own it appears to me one of the most extraordinary propositions I had ever heard, notwithstanding the passages that are found in text writers upon the subject, that it could be maintained, as an universal proposition at least, that the *locus contractus matrimonii* was to govern. It is, no doubt, one question, what is an universal proposition to be acted upon in England, Scotland, or any where else, as a principle of sound law, to be adopted every where. And another thing to say, what is to be considered as being the law of England upon the point. When one recollects what has been the universal practice in regard to the administration, in this country, of the effects of intestates, under all the circumstances which have obtained, under all the changes and mutations of instruments which parties make in their lifetimes, I believe it never occurred to any persons who have sat in those courts, in which they administer the estates and effects of intestates, to think of the question, where was the party married ? in order to decide what was the share a wife was to take of her husband's personalty.

This is very familiar to us in this country, because your Lordships know very well that the distribution of the personal estate of intestates is in different proportions in different parts of England : where a person's estate, for instance, is to be distributed as the personal estate of an individual living in that district in which the custom of the province of York obtains, the wife is there entitled to five ninths; and if the *locus contractus matrimonii* is to determine upon her rights, where there is no domicile in the province, I believe I should state a doctrine that would extremely surprise all those inhabitants of London, who have transplanted themselves from the parts to which I am now alluding, if I were to tell them, if they happened to die domiciled in the province of Canterbury, where the wife's share is one third, that it was not the circumstance of being themselves domiciled within the province of Canterbury, which was to regulate this; but that the circumstance that the marriage had been had in that part of this kingdom on which the custom of the province of York attaches, was to decide upon it; and that it was to decide upon it with no communication, and no agreement between the parties at the time of the marriage. Upon this doctrine the result would be, that if a man domiciled within the province of Canterbury should, in taking a journey northward, marry a lady within the province of York, though they went immediately home, and resided during the rest of their lives within the province of Canterbury, the wife would be entitled to five ninths of the personal estate.

Taking it the other way, we know there are persons who come from that part of the world to which the custom of the province of York extends: they happen, perhaps, not to think much about these things; in advanced life they are likely to go home again, and they take their chance. They are husband and wife, in this respect as in all others, for better and for worse; and I should conceive it to be quite clear law (though it seems to have puzzled some very learned persons in the statement of these cases), that a man might come from a particular part of the north of England and marry in the north of England, where, if he had died before he accomplished his purpose of taking his journey, his lady would unquestionably receive five ninths of the personal estate: if he came up to London to better his fortune (as we north country people are apt to do), and died in London, his wife would take her one third according to the custom of the province of Canterbury; and if in his old age he had retired to the land of his nativity, and died intestate, the lady there, who, in the first instance, would have been entitled to five ninths, who had by the course of events lost that right, and become entitled in the second instance to only one third, when her husband returned again to the province of York, dying in the place in which he was born and married, would be restored again to the five ninths; her condition as a wife and her right as a wife being altered from time to time exactly as her person followed her husband's person from one place of domicil into another place of domicil, till it was at last decided, by his death, where he left his residence in this world. I take that to be quite clear law.

I think it was as long ago as 1704, unless I mistake the import of the case, that, as amongst French people, the law of England had decided this; for, in the case of Foubert v. Turst, in Brown's Parliamentary Cases, 38., this case occurred:— A French lady and gentleman married at Paris; and, having married there, there was a written agreement, by which certain sums of money were disposed of; and, with respect to the other property which the parties had or should acquire, that was by this agreement, according to the construction put upon it in our courts, to go according to the custom of Paris. After the marriage was had, the lady and gentleman thought London was a better place to reside in than Paris, and came here. They lived here some years: at length the wife died, and the question arose upon her death, how the property was to be distributed. It first came on in the Court of Chancery. The Lord Chancellor was of opinion, that it was not the intent of that agreement to attach, under all the circumstances, the rule which the custom of Paris afforded as to the distribution of the property; and he held that, the parties being domiciled in this country, the law of this country must decide the right to his share in his wife's property. That was afterwards reversed in this House. But upon what principle was it afterwards reversed in this House? Why, upon a principle which showed what the conception of this House was as to the law, if there had been no rule for the application of that principle; for it is distinctly admitted, in the printed reasons, by the counsel on both sides, but especially in the printed reasons by the gentleman who was of counsel for the husband, that, though the parties married at Paris, the custom of Paris would not follow them; and the ground upon which the Lord Chancellor's decree was taken to be wrong was this (and an extremely clear ground it is), that there the parties had in Paris come to a written agreement, the true construction of which written agreement was, that, wherever the parties died, the custom of Paris should regulate the distribution; therefore, said this House, it is not the regard which the law here administering property has to the custom of Paris, but the rule is founded in the contract which the parties themselves had entered into; and that contract, which they there entered into, will travel with them, though the custom will not follow them. The contract will attach upon the property after the death of the parties. The meaning of the parties was, that it should so attach upon the property after death; and there can be no reason in the world why the parties should not say, by express contract, that the *locus contractus matrimonii* should decide. They may do so if they please, in a written agreement, which shall describe what shall be the share of the wife in the property of her husband, when he is dead.

It seems to me, also, that that case was recognised to be very good law in a subsequent case, Freemoult *v.* Dedire, in. Peere Williams's Reports.* The result of the case may be stated to show this, that it was the opinion of the Court, at that day, that, where the marriage had been had in Holland, the distribution in this country, if the party died domiciled in this country, would be certainly according to the law of Holland, if you showed there were articles saying the distribution should be according to the law of Holland. But they seem to have refused, in that case, to make the distribution according to the law of Holland, because it had not been proved as a fact in the cause, what was the law of Holland, which those articles had stipulated between the parties should furnish the rule of distribution.

Your Lordships have already gone the length of deciding, in the former stages of this cause, that, with respect to the. children's shares upon the death of the father, it is the *locus domicilii*, at the death of the father, that must decide what they are to take. In this case, the marriage was had in England. Some of the children were, I believe, born in England; and Mr. Hog having altered his domicil, and dying domiciled in Scotland, your Lordships held, that, because they were the children of a father domiciled in Scotland, notwithstanding that was not the *locus contractus matrimonii*, the law of Scotland must decide upon the rights of those children. I believe it. would be next to impossible to say, that there is any distinction to be made between the legitim of the children, as taking by such succession, and the *jus relictæ* of the widow as taking by the same. It would be absolutely impossible, if the wife survived the husband, that you should say, that, though the marriage was in England, the children of that marriage should

---

* 1 P. Wms. 429.

take according to the law of Scotland, where the man was domiciled; but that the wife should take according to the law of England, where the man was married. Unless you could say, in the case of the wife surviving the husband, that her interest was to be decided by the law of England, where the marriage was had, although the right of the children, who, in a sort, derived their title under that marriage, depended on the law of Scotland, that is, that the surviving wife took according to the *locus contractus matrimonii*, and the children according to the *locus domicilii*, it would be difficult to distinguish between what the wife takes in the character of wife, if she happens to die in the lifetime of her husband, and what she takes in the same character, and under the same title, if she happens to survive the husband. It seems to me, therefore, when a distinction is taken between the *legitim* and the *jus relictæ*, in the manner in which it has been taken in this case, that the distinction is not substantial enough to be acted upon.

A vast number of ingenious difficulties have been stated upon this subject, which may deserve a great deal of consideration; but one may here lay out of consideration all those cases upon which it has been asked,—What are to be the consequences if a man marries in one place and goes immediately to dwell in another? If any persons were to go into Scotland, get married at Gretna Green, or any where else, and come back to England; or if they came from Scotland and were married in England; in the one case, if the parties returned immediately, and became domiciled in England; or, in the other case, if the parties returned, and became domiciled in Scotland; in both these cases the place of marriage is a mere incident in the form of the contract, and would not alter the law, which says, that the place where the parties *bonâ fide* reside, and that I shall call the *bonâ fide* residence of the *husband*, will decide upon the rights both of the wife and the children.

But it is said, that, if there be no express contract when the marriage is entered into, there must be an implied contract, and it is assumed that that implied contract is this, — that the distribution which the law would make of the property of the husband, if he were to die *eo instanti* that the marriage was celebrated, is the distribution which must be made of the property of the husband dying intestate at any distance of time from the period when the marriage was contracted, and under all the circumstances of mutation and change which might have taken place.

It appears to me, that those who say, that there is such an implied contract, beg the whole question, because the question is, whether the implied contract is not precisely the contrary. This being a contract attaching upon property in consequence of its being personal estate, whether the true implied contract must not be taken to be that the condition of the wife, in respect to her expectations, should change as the condition of the husband changes, with reference to the law of the country in which they are resident.

Cases of great hardship may be put with respect to Scotch and English ladies. They tell you, with reference to a marriage in England, the moment the husband contracts that marriage, all the debts due to the wife, and property in the wife, attach to him; but that in the case of a marriage in Scotland, with respect to all debts due to the wife, the husband must take the trouble of taking his hat off, to request the payment of that money from those from whom it is due to her, before he vests a right to it in himself. But, really, the difference is not very considerable, because, although it be that the husband, if he happens to die, without having done any act to stamp the character of his own peculiar ownership upon the property of his wife, is taken to have chosen to let it go to the wife, because he chooses to forbear to take that which previously to the connection was hers; yet, on the other hand, there is nothing more clear, than that the law supposes he may receive it when he pleases; for a man cannot, without evidence, be supposed to forego that which he takes in right of his wife: he may assign it for valuable considerations, or he may make it his own to all intents and purposes; and the moment he chooses so to make it his own, he may assign it to persons in trust for the wife, who may have, in this country, the special equity of claiming to have some provision made out of it for herself.

But the true question is, whether it is not of necessity that the husband and wife, or the one of them, and if the one of them, which of them, is to determine in what manner, and in what place, the husband is to struggle for the means of provision for himself and his family whilst he lives, and for all the means of provision for the family he shall leave behind him after he is dead. And when you say that, both in England and in Scotland (about which there can be no doubt), it is competent for the husband to spend every shilling of the property, to alien *bonâ fide* every shilling of the property;

what does that amount to but this, that the husband, if he pleases, has it in his power to make it of as little consequence to both his wife and children in what country they resided at his death, as if they were in no country at all? The true point seems to be this,—whether there is any thing irrational in saying that as the husband, during the whole of his life, has the absolute disposition over the property; that as to him the policy of the law has given the direction of the family as to the place of residence; that as he has therefore this species of command over his own actions, and over the actions of the family, and property which is his own, and which is to remain his own, or to become that of his family, according to his will; why should it be thought an unreasonable thing that, where there is no express contract, the implied contract shall be taken to be, that the wife is to look to the law of the country where the husband dies, for the rights she is to enjoy, in case the husband thinks proper to die intestate?

This has been the principle which, it seems to me, has been adopted, as far as we can collect what has been the principle adopted, in cases in those parts of the island with which we are best acquainted; and, not being aware that there has been any decision which will countervail this, — thinking that it squares infinitely better with those principles upon which your Lordships have already decided in this case, — it does appear to me, attending to the different sentiments to be found in the text writers upon the subject, that it is more consonant to our own laws, and more consonant to the general principle, to say that the implied contract is, that the rights of the wife shall shift with the change of residence of the wife, that change of residence being accomplished by the will of the husband, whom, by the marriage contract, in this instance, she is bound to obey.

Is there any inconvenience in this? None in the world; because it is an equally acknowledged principle, that, though the custom of the place may not follow the parties to this contract, which places them in the relation of husband and wife and children, yet it is undeniable law, that they may contract under hand and seal that the custom of the place shall follow them. Whether it will be convenient, in ninety-nine cases out of a hundred, that there should be such a convention and such a contract; or whether it will not be mightily inconvenient to the affairs of families to form such a contract or convention; is a question which persons viewing it may think

very differently about; but if there be any inconvenience in
the circumstance of such a convention not being formed upon
the marriage, it is an inconvenience neither of a higher nor
less nature than any other which attaches upon that relation
which is to be left to the providence of parties when they
enter into that relation; but which can be met by the providence of parties when they enter into that relation, and to
which inconvenience they expose themselves if they do not
think proper at the time to provide against it.

It may be said, in this case, and truly may be said, in ninety-
nine cases out of a hundred of a similar sort, if they arise, that
this is a surprise upon the parties. The true answer to that
is, that I believe the parties never thought of it; when they
entered into this marriage they entered into no contract by
which this lady was to take one penny of the husband's property; but they entered into a contract by which she was to
have somewhat more than two thirds of her own property converted into land, with a power to her to give this to any of her
children that deserved best of her: they could not but have
considered that Mr. Hog must die somewhere, that he was
likely to die in England; but there is no stipulation that she
shall have one shilling left to her: she takes her chance, under
the effect of the marriage, whether she shall or shall not receive
any thing, even upon the casualty of the husband dying intestate. If he had thought proper to lay out all his money
upon land, and had taken the caution to lay it out in the name
of a trustee, instead of in his own name, she would not have
had what the Scotch called terce, and we call dower; on the
other hand, if Mr. Hog had that which it appears he had for
a great number of years, a very strong inclination and a fixed
purpose to reside in Scotland, where he was born, and to die
there, one should think, if he thought proper to attend to this
subject with caution, he would have asked what would be the
state of his wife if he did die there. But the truth is, that parties do not think upon this subject when they enter into these
contracts; they get a bit of a settlement made, and very important interests remain unattended to.

But I think it appears that this claim could not be matter of
much surprise, when your Lordships come to see how this
matter was regarded by men of business in Scotland; because,
though this lady died in 1760, and though Mr. Hog unquestionably became afterwards a domiciled Scotchman, having
realised property in land in that country, whenever provisions

were tendered to the other children, or to the Appellant herself, your Lordships observe the persons who drew those instruments thought there might be at least some colour of claim under their mother's decease; and that circumstance, that there might be that colour of claim, whilst it contains an intimation, upon the point at law, that at least it was doubted by the lawyers in Scotland whether this might not be supported, is also a material circumstance, in another respect, — that it contains a strong intimation as to what they believed to be the fact, with respect to the domicil of the father at the decease of the mother.*

Without entering, therefore, into a great variety of very nice cases, which might be put, and which might be all reasoned down, in my apprehension, to the single question,—which is the principle that you are to imply from the contract of marriage, whether is it to be considered that the rights of the wife must vary with the rights which attach upon her residence in different places, and that her rights to succeed to her husband must depend upon the domicil which he had at the time of her death, if she is dead, or the time of his death, if she survived him: or, on the other hand, that the *locus contractus matrimonii* is to regulate the distribution of the property, and, through all the changes in future life, her right is to remain unaltered in a case in which there is no express contract at all? It does appear to me that the rule we have adopted in this country is the better rule; and therefore I shall presume upon that part of the case, in the application of that principle, to submit to your Lordships the propriety of altering the interlocutors, so far as they deny Mrs. Hog's right to transmit to her next of kin, she predeceasing her husband, the usual shares in the goods of that husband.

But this cannot be done without deciding a question of fact; because, if it be true that this gentleman was not domiciled in Scotland in 1760, then for the same reason it must follow that, if he was at that time domiciled in England, she could not claim, because she must be bound by the law of the place of his then residence; as in the case I put before of a change of residence from a place in the province of York to a place where the law of the province of Canterbury applies, it might be that her rights might change twenty different times during

---

* The discharges were according to the common form of such discharges in the law of Scotland; perhaps, on that account, little could be founded on this circumstance.

her life. I have little doubt that, without any suspicion of it, there are many persons who have different places of residence, who are changing their residences repeatedly (each of which they call their fixed place of residence); and whose property, if they happen to die without a written disposition of it by them, must be distributed according to the law in the province in which their decease takes place. So, in the case I put, I feel no difficulty in saying, that if I were to marry in London to-morrow and afterwards to go and be domiciled in Scotland, and then I were to come up to London again, and afterwards to go to Scotland again, as it appears to me, the principle must apply from time to time, according to the place of my residence, and not perhaps as I choose it should apply; but then it is entirely the consequence of my own act that it does so apply.

The question whether Mr. Hog had his domicil in Scotland in 1760 is, however, a question which your Lordships must decide before you can say, as I before stated, that there is any room for a decision in this case, founded upon the communion of goods. This point of the domicil is argued, with another point, under the cross appeal taken by Mr. Hog in this cause. I beg distinctly to state to your Lordships these two points, in order that the rule of this House, as to cross appeals, may be understood, not thinking, in my poor view of the case, that it is very important to the parties what the rule of the House is as to this point of the domicil; but because there is another question in this case which your Lordships may, perhaps, think deserves attention, with reference to whether you can alter the decision, and whether this cross appeal be rightly or wrongly presented to your Lordships' consideration.

The two points contained in that cross appeal are the question as to the domicil at the death of Mrs. Hog, which Thomas Hog contends, upon his cross appeal, ought to be held to be a domicil, not in Scotland, but in England; and the other is upon the expences of the confirmation in Scotland and the probate in England. It is insisted by Mr. Hog that those expences ought to be so thrown upon the personal estate that some share of those expences may fall upon those who are interested in the claim to the *jus relictæ* and the legitim. The Court of Session seem to have thought otherwise. I will not take upon myself to say how it may be in the law of Scotland, — that is a question your Lordships may decide; but in this country, I take it, it would be quite clear that the expences of confirming or of clothing yourself with that character which somebody must have, in order to deal and to transact with the personal estate (whoever may have a claim beneficially to enjoy the personal estate), would be a charge upon the whole fund. It would be in the nature of a debt upon the whole fund; and I should considerably doubt — and I beg my noble and learned friend's attention to this part of the case — I cannot help entertaining a doubt, whether that part of the case is rightly decided against Mr. Hog.

With respect to the question of domicil, it is of no importance whether this appeal was brought in time or not; because those who state to your Lordships that, under Mrs. Hog, they were entitled to claim in respect of the communion of goods, must make out, on their part, that Mr. Hog was domiciled in Scotland at the time the wife died. The question, therefore, whether Mr. Hog was domiciled in Scotland at the time Mrs. Hog died, is a question just as open to your Lordships, whether there is a cross appeal or not a cross appeal. That is the material question in this cause between the parties; and one should have had to lament that we could not get at a question of that kind in some cases that might have occurred, because the cross appeal did not come in time. Certainly in this case the question, though great and important, does not administer occasion for that feeling, because it seems to me impossible that those who contend for this community of goods can make out their title without satisfying your Lordships what was the residence at the time; and when they undertake to satisfy your Lordships that such was the residence at the time, they let in an opportunity for those contending with them to say that such was not the residence.

With reference to the question whether Scotland was or was not the residence of Mr. Hog at the time of Mrs. Hog's death, that depends upon a very minute attention to all the circumstances which are disclosed as matter of evidence in this cause. With respect to the mind and intention of the party upon that part of the case, I shall not give your Lordships the trouble of going through an accurate statement of the whole of the evidence, because I have not perceived in your Lordships' House, from the beginning of this cause to the end of it, any tendency to doubt, in the mind of any one of your Lordships, whether those interlocutors that have declared him to be domiciled in Scotland at the time of the death of his wife, were or were not well founded. It seems to me that the whole of the passages which are to be collected from the letters, and which have been relied upon at the bar, amount to no more than such as would entitle your Lordships to represent this matter thus: — This gentleman had originally come from Scotland to make his fortune in England; he seems to have been a very sensible and a very industrious man; he had succeeded in trade to a great extent; but throughout his whole life he seems to have been influenced by a determination to spend as much of his life, and particularly the latter days of that life, as he could in his native country. He meant to take there his *summa rerum*, — he meant that his establishment should be there, and he was acting upon that intention when he went there. It is always a very nice question, if you are called upon to decide it immediately after a change of residence, whether that change of residence has actually operated a change of the testator's domicil; but we have not such difficulty in the present case. It is admitted that Mr. Hog was domiciled in Scotland at the time of his own death. Upon the whole, I see no reason to doubt that he was domiciled in Scotland at the death of his wife.

In regard to the other point taken under the cross appeal, the expences of the confirmation in Scotland and of the probate in England, there are two questions which will occur. The first will be whether it has been decided upon a right principle, that is, whether the expence of confirmation in Scotland and probate in England has been thrown upon the right fund; and if it has not, whether, considering the time when this appeal was brought here, subject to a protest made at the bar, you can consider, with reference to the consequences of that protest, that the appeal has been brought at such time as that your Lordships can give relief upon that part of the case.

The rest of this case calls for your Lordships to apply your consideration to a very important branch of the law of Scotland, and the facts of the case which give rise to the consideration of that important question of law will require a very minute and accurate detail. It is the question, what is the amount of the legitim? In order to determine that question, your Lordships are to decide whose property the various shares in the bank stock, which at one time were undoubtedly the property of old Mr. Hog, were to be taken to be at his death; and there are minor questions, and questions with respect to the money arising from the sale of the Kingston estate, a question as to a debt of 1000*l.* out of what fund that debt is to be paid, and the question with respect to bringing into contribution what has been advanced to the children. These all fall under another distinct head; and, as I am sure I shall not be able so accurately to detail all the circumstances which relate to the state of facts upon which these questions are to be decided, as it seems expedient they should be detailed, or to bring before your Lordships' consideration the points of law which are to be applied to the decision of these questions in such a way as I should wish to do, if I were to call for your Lordships' further attention upon that part of this case to-night, I should hope your Lordships will not think it improper, if I were here to leave this statement of what I shall humbly propose to your Lordships, meaning to proceed with what remains of the case in the course of to-morrow afternoon.

Adjourned.

July 10th, 1804.

Lord Chancellor. I adjourned the consideration to the present day, of the question as to the amount of the funds out of which the legitim is to be paid. That question subdivides itself into several.

The first and most important one is most extremely important, not merely with reference to the parties in this cause, but with reference to the general law of Scotland upon the subject. It is, whether certain shares of the stock of the Bank of Scotland, which are admitted to have stood in the name of the Respondent, Mr. Thomas Hog, were or were not the father's moveable property at the time of his death.

Another question is, whether the Respondent was a creditor on his father's fund for 2500*l.*, which your Lordships recollect was the value of the estate at Kingston, which, under an appointment made by the mother, was conveyed to the respondent, Thomas Hog; and also the sum of 1000*l.* which he received with his wife and lent to his father, who granted him a bond for it.

A third question is slightly touched upon; which is, whether the respondent was entitled to the deduction of the expence incurred by him in obtaining confirmation in Scotland, and probate in England, of his father's will.

A fourth was, whether the sums paid by Roger Hog, in his lifetime, are to be considered as forming a part of Mrs. Lashley's share in calculating what is due to her.

With reference to this part of the case, I believe I shall be founded upon the authorities which are stated in the text writers on the law of Scotland, and the decisions of the Courts of Scotland, if I represent to your Lordships that legitim can be claimed only out of the moveable property belonging to the father at his death. This claim of the children to the legitim is a claim which leaves the father an unlimited power of disposition during his life; for it seems, that though the claim of legitim cannot be defeated by any deed executed on death-bed, or by any deed of a testamentary kind which is to take effect at the father's death, yet it does not interfere at all with the father's right of administration while he is living and in health. Thus he may disappoint his younger children in various ways; he may disappoint them by converting moveable property into heritable property; he may contract debts if he thinks proper, which debts would be a charge upon it; he may spend his estate in the most improvident manner in which he chooses to spend it; and he may give it away, if he thinks proper. Provided he makes the disposition in time, all these acts which he may do are to be considered certainly with reference to the question of the amount of the legitim. Your Lordships are still to determine whether the claim of legitim is capable of being considered as a right of property, as a *jus crediti*, or only as that which the children are to obtain under the hope and expectation of what the father may think proper to leave at his death.

The question therefore is substantially, what was his fair moveable property at his death; and that question will fall to be determined, regard being had to this consideration, that if an heir or disponee has a mere nominal interest in the property, that is, if he is in the nature of a trustee for the father, it will be not less the property of the father because it is ostensibly (if it be but ostensibly) the property of another.

The law of England furnishes a class of cases that seems to have some, though perhaps not a perfectly strict and correct analogy to the nature of the claim with reference to which I am now speaking; for it will be familiar to some of your Lordships that it is not an unusual thing for a parent, when he gives away his child in marriage, to enter into a covenant that he will leave that child a share of his property, equal to that which any other child at his death shall derive from him. Your Lordships perceive that when that sort of obligation is entered into by a parent he leaves to himself as complete, and indeed a more complete, power of administration than the father has under the general law of Scotland; because, in addition to those acts which the Scotch parent is capable of performing, and which I have enumerated to your Lordships, the English parent having bound himself under that obligation, is at liberty not only to spend every shilling of his fortune, but he may give away every shilling of that property, provided he does give it away the day before his death.

I apprehend, however, that there can be no manner of doubt that if an English parent, having entered into such an obligation, were to transfer to any one of his children, by an instrument, upon the face of it the most absolute and complete that could be conceived in terms, any part of that property, yet, if it appeared that subsequent to that gift the parent himself, from time to time, enjoyed the interest, dividend, or produce of that property, as it might yield, according to its nature, interest, dividend or produce, that the receipt of the income of it would be complete evidence that the gift was a trust for the father; and that if the father died under such circumstances, the child with whom he had entered into such a covenant as I have stated, that he would leave to that child as much as any other child should derive from him at his death, would have a right to say that that property was part of the father's property, and would have a right to claim upon the footing of considering it as part of the father's property.

I wish to mark, in this part of the case, very distinctly the doctrine which I have now presumed to state to your Lordships, for another purpose, which is this: that, although perhaps secretly between the father and the son, there might be an intention that the son, in such a case, should only pay during the life of the father the interest and produce of that property which had been so transferred to him, and that the son himself should take the property at the death of the father; yet if that agreement was not capable of being evidenced by testimony admissible for that purpose, if the inference of law was to be collected from the mere fact, that the father was permitted during that time to receive the interest, dividend, or produce of that property, the inference in law would not be that the father was entitled to that interest or property for the limited term of his life, but there being no special agreement capable of being proved that that limitation was intended to be put upon his enjoyment, the evidence which proved that he ate of the fruits of the tree would be testimony in our Courts of Justice that he was the absolute owner of the tree which produced that fruit. And we should not hear it said, in a question between his children, that the father meant in such a transaction, where there was nothing to show his meaning but this enjoyment of the produce of the property, that it was meant between the father and the son, to whom the ostensible transfer had been made, that the father was to have only a limited interest in it; that the property was given away from the moment of time the gift was made, and that the son was to be in the nature of a reversioner. There must be an express contract, I apprehend, before our law would admit that such was the nature of the intention of the parties to that transaction.

But I go a great deal further than that; because it has, I conceive, been settled by repeated decisions in this country, that if a father, upon the marriage of his child, enters into a covenant that he will leave that child as much as he gives to any other child descended from him, after he has entered into that engagement, the law allows him, if he thinks proper, to give away his property as improvidently as he pleases; but an interest of this sort would hardly be worth having if the law did not impose for the protection of that interest this guard upon the parent: that he shall not enjoy his property as beneficially himself, having given it away, or nearly as beneficially, as he would enjoy it if he had not given it away; and it would be competent for him at any moment to defeat the obligation he meant to enter into, to make an equal distribution among his children, if he could before his death say I will give the whole of my property to one child, and that child shall give me the whole produce of that property during my life; and he may contend, after my death, that, because I had given it on a day antecedent to my death, it was given in such a way as to prevent the operation of my covenant with respect to that property. I take it to have been decided in our Courts of Justice repeatedly, that that cannot be done. I have stated what I conceive to be the views of the law of England upon the subject, that due attention may be given, at least to the principles which have governed our decisions in this part of the island, upon a subject which seems to me to come the nearest to the subject of the right which falls under consideration, a question resulting out of the circumstances which I am now about to state.

Mr. Hog, the father of Mr. Thomas Hog, appears to have been, in the course of his life, in the habit of purchasing at different periods, I think from the year 1772 till a very late period of his life, various shares of stock in the Bank of Scotland; and it appears that, in point of fact, between the year 1772 and the time of his death, he had become the owner at least of a hundred and forty-four shares of the stock of that bank. When I say he became the owner of a hundred and forty-four shares, I mean that he had purchased a hundred and forty-four shares, some of which stood in his own name, and some in the name of his son. I do not presume to state to your Lordships, that if it can be contended they were a fair purchase in the name of his son and nothing more, that there the son is a trustee for his father; for the inference of the law would be that it is, *primâ facie*, a gift to his son; and therefore in the question relative to these shares of bank stock, it must be admitted that Mr. Hog, the respondent, has a right to the benefit of the principle, which is, that *primâ facie* what is bought in his name is given to him. So it would be in our law at the death of the father, having in the course of his life bought this number of shares, some standing in his own name, some standing in his son's name, some originally purchased in his son's name, some occasionally transferred into his son's name, some re-transferred into his son's name which had been transferred from his son's name into his own.

It has been made a material question between these parties, how many of these shares of stock belonged to the father of the parties who are now contending at your Lordships' bar; Mr. Hog, the respondent, insisted that there were only twenty-four shares which belonged to the father at the time of his death; that thirty-nine shares had been given to him some time before the period of his father's death; and that eighty-one shares had been given to him at a period very recent before Mr. Hog the father's death — at a period so recent before Mr. Hog's death, that, between the date of that transfer and the date of Mr. Hog's death, there had been no dividend payable on eighty-one shares; so that no evidence could arise, from the fact of the application of the dividends, what was the purpose of the transfer so made as to these eighty-one shares; and, therefore, if that transfer cannot be connected with any other circumstances, it should seem clear that, as this was a transfer made whilst the father was in *liege poustie*, and a transfer made of property, which he had a clear right to give away if he thought proper to give it away; if there were no other evidence attaching upon these eighty-one shares, with a view to show who the true owner was, it would be *primâ facie* evidence of a gift out and out to the son, and to be considered as his property.

It appears that in the year 1787, Mr. Hog, the father, had made a testamentary disposition, and by that he had conveyed to the respondent his whole personal estate for the purpose of being vested in landed property, which landed property he meant to be settled in the same manner and according to the same course of entail as that which he had before purchased, namely, the Newliston estate; but from these he excepted thirty-nine shares of stock of the Bank of Scotland, having by this disposition expressly given all shares or stock in the Company of the Bank of Scotland, and all stock in the public funds which should belong to him at the time of his decease, exclusive of thirty-nine shares of stock of the Bank of Scotland which were transferred, as he says, some time ago to the said Thomas Hog, and which he professes it is not his meaning or intention should fall under this conveyance, but that those thirty-nine shares should remain with his son as his own right and property, notwithstanding any obligation granted by him to his father concerning the same, of which obligation, or any other in regard of the said thirty-nine shares, the son was thereby acquitted and discharged. Thus the purpose of the father clearly was, at the time he made this testamentary disposition, to give to his son an interest which your Lordships have determined he could not give, as against the other children, on account of this claim of legitim, by giving to his son these shares of bank stock for the purpose of being laid out by his son in land, to be entailed in the same manner as the estate of Newliston; but either recollecting or conceiving that with respect to the thirty-nine shares, or misconceiving that with respect to the thirty-nine shares, his son had at some period of his life come under the obligation to him by which he had declared himself in effect to be but a trustee to his father, he excludes the terms of the trust so created by his testamentary disposition of thirty-nine shares; and he attempts by this testamentary disposition, in effect, to cancel and discharge the obligation, rightly conceiving or misconceiving, in making that disposition, that, by the obligation which his son had come under, he acknowledged himself to be trustee of those thirty-nine shares for his father.

It occurred to those who had in Scotland the duty of attending to the interests of Mr. and Mrs. Lashley, to contend, first, with respect to those thirty-nine shares, that they would be entitled to legitim upon them, because, in the first place, this testamentary disposition could not take effect upon them; and, in the next place, because the obligation itself was never cancelled nor meant to be cancelled; that there was, as they asserted, a sacred trust between the son and the father in respect to the thirty-nine shares, and a sacred trust also as to the father in a subsequent act as to the eighty-one shares. Mr. Hog was himself called upon, according to the forms of the law of Scotland, to give an account of what he conceived his interest to be in the shares of stock, and particularly in those shares of stock, with respect to which he had given any acknowledgment whatever to his father, and he represented in his answer to the interrogatory addressed to him for that purpose, " that about twenty years ago or upwards," (and as far as I recollect the time of his examination it would bring that back to the year 1774) — that about twenty years ago or upwards, but the precise year he does not remember, the deponent's father purchased some shares in the stock of the Bank of Scotland, which were transferred to the deponent; and some time afterwards he gave a letter to his father, the exact words of which he does not recollect, nor the number of shares to which it related, but that in general it imported that these shares were to be considered as his father's, and an obligation on the deponent to transfer these shares to him or his order when required so to do: that, some time after this, at an annual election of directors of the said bank, the deponent, who was at that election elected a director, stated to his father, that in consequence of his having granted him the above mentioned letter he could not take the oath as a proprietor or director, as not holding the said shares free and independent; upon which his father told him he need not give himself any concern on that account, as he intended the deponent should have a complete right to the said shares, to serve as a fund for providing for his younger children, and added, that he would cancel the letter or declaration which the deponent had granted, and therefore that he was at perfect liberty to take the oath required: that, upon this the deponent was satisfied, took the oaths of trust, and has continued to be elected annually, and to act as a director in his father's presence during his life and ever since; and the deponent is certain that at no subsequent period did he ever grant any letter or declaration to his father relative to the above shares, or to any others which were afterwards acquired for him by his father; and that he never saw the above-mentioned letter after he granted it to his father, and does not know or suspect where it is.

This declaration, your Lordships observe, refers to a period twenty years or upwards preceding the time at which the deposition was made; and it is but fair to observe, that upon a transaction which had so much of ambiguity about it, both as respected the father and the son, the son, in his deposition, might, without blame, be somewhat inaccurate; and the father might, without being exposed, I think, to the imputation of being an extraordinarily inaccurate man, be also in some degree inaccurate.

It has been stated, I think, at your Lordships' bar, that it requires ten shares of stock to be a director of the Bank of Scotland; and in order, therefore, to try the effect of this deposition, it becomes necessary to look very attentively to the number of shares which Mr. Hog had from time to time, throughout the period in which it appears that he was in the habit of making purchases of shares, either in his own name or in his son's name; and unless I mistake the effect of the evidence in this case, it will be extremely difficult to say that at any period of the twenty years or upwards, to which this deposition can be supposed to refer, it can be a very accurate account of the transaction, that it was the intent of the transaction, in which the letter was given, to qualify the son to be a director of the Bank of Scotland, and conscientiously to take the oath to enable him to act as such director: if he had less shares than ten, that could not be the object; if he had a great many more shares than ten, that could not be the sole object. Yet still that might be one object, among others; and it might be the intention of the father at once to qualify him for being a director of the Bank of Scotland, and also to give him a capacity of making that provision for his younger children, which this deposition asserts was the fair intention which his father's mind had conceived the means of effecting at one and the same time.

It may be misapprehension, but it will be worth while to examine the evidence upon that subject, whether it could be possible that the son can speak accurately. I do not mean to lay great stress upon the subject; if it be an inaccuracy in point of time, it is likely enough to be so without making any imputation upon the moral honesty of this gentleman. But, unless I misapprehend the fact, it will be found extremely doubtful whether any letters he could give, at that period, could have reference to such a number of shares, as could enable this gentleman to act as a director at that time.

If this were a question merely between the father and the son; and if the purpose of the father was to give such a number of shares to the son as would enable the son to act as a director, whether taking any oath or not; but much more, if it were to enable the son to take this oath and act as a director, where the father must, if he had that intent alone, be holding out his son to those who had interests to be well and duly attended to, and managed by a person properly qualified, in respect of property, to be placed in that situation in which he cannot be placed, according to the law, unless he has so many shares as to render himself properly qualified; and upon principles much more sacred and much more important, if he placed in his son's name a property, informing that son that he might pledge himself to God and man by his oath as the person really entitled to that property, in a question between the father and the son, to be determined immediately after that transaction took place, no Court of Justice would have suffered the father to have holden a language, which imported that he had not effectively done, what he promised upon the outside of the thing to do. This is quite familiar in this country. Your Lordships know there are a great many situations with reference to which qualifications are necessary. One is familiar with this, that a person cannot have a seat in Parliament in this country unless he has a clear freehold estate of three hundred pounds a year at least, at the time he takes his seat. That estate once given, it is supposed can be taken back, but it cannot be taken back as against the creditors of the man to whom it has been given; and whatever may be the question as between the party who gives and the party who receives, public considerations having determined that he shall receive that estate before he can act in the character of a Member of Parliament, I conceive that there would be no manner of doubt that every judgment which the receiver of that property had recorded against him in Westminster Hall would follow that property if it went back again, even by conveyance, into the hands of the man who granted it. For where the law requires that a man shall have a property, and where a third person intervenes to give him the qualification in order that the law may be satisfied, the law will not permit either the one or the other to disappoint the purposes for which that law was made. I take it, therefore, to be quite clear in this case, that it is impossible to touch these thirty-nine shares, if they should be found upon examination to be the subject of transfer made with this intent, if the question is to be considered as a question merely between the father and the son.

If, therefore, these thirty-nine shares had been given, whether twenty years ago or ten years ago, or at any other period, and nothing further had occurred in the case than that there was that gift; if, for instance, the dividends and profits of the thirty-nine shares had remained dead in the bank, and had been received by nobody; if there were no evidence to show that there was a re-transfer contracted for, or a trust *bonâ fide* afterwards had, it would be perfectly impossible to touch this property, unless you are to say, that whatever the rule may be between the man who makes the conveyance and the man who receives the benefit of the conveyance, the rule shall not operate to the prejudice of third persons; and it has been argued at your Lordships' bar, and strongly argued at your Lordships' bar, that although you would not permit the father to say, as against the son, that that gift which he had made in order to qualify him to act as a director, swearing to his qualification, should be looked at as any thing short of a gift perfectly absolute and perfectly consummate in its nature; yet, if the purpose of that gift was really to defraud the other children of the marriage, you would, in such a case as that, say that at their instance you would examine the real nature of the transaction; and, examining the real nature of the transaction, you would, as with respect to third persons, set it aside.

Now it appears to me, without saying more upon it, for it is not necessary, in my view of the case, to say more upon it, that it would be a difficult thing to maintain that proposition. In the case of a creditor in this country, unless he has carried forth his diligence to such an extent that he has got a lien upon a man's property, if he upon whose property the lien is conveys it to another to make a qualification, he fails in his purpose, inasmuch as it is not a qualification free from incumbrance; but, supposing the subject unfettered by any incumbrance, and to be conveyed in truth from A. to B., the creditors of A., who had no lien upon the property whilst it was in the hands of A., had no reason to complain ; it was their own fault that they had not acquired a lien. So, when it comes into the hands of B., the rights of B.'s creditors immediately attach upon it, and it cannot be the property both of A. and B. for the purpose of permitting the claims of the creditors of both one and the other to attach upon it; and it would be found extremely difficult to say, that if this matter of the thirty-nine shares had been to have been decided immediately after the transaction took place, it would have been competent for the younger children to have raised that contest which the father himself could not possibly, upon the ground of the policy of the law, have been permitted to raise in a question directly between himself and his son, to whom he had made the transfer.

But it is extremely possible that the thing may acquire a very different complexion by the subsequent transactions between the parties with respect to the property ; and it is alleged in this case that, notwithstanding these thirty-nine shares, or notwithstanding any other shares, more or less in number, were originally placed in the name of the son, or were by transfer placed in the name of the son, yet that, in point of fact, all the transactions of the father in his lifetime with reference to all the shares, whether they stood in the name of the father or stood in the name of the son, were transactions which would have taken place precisely in the same manner as they did take place, if every one of those shares, to the whole amount of a hundred and forty-four, had, from the beginning of the time that any of those shares were purchased to the end of it, stood in the name of the father and the father only.

It is said that the expence of these transfers was paid by the father ; if further subscriptions were called for, the sums paid in discharge of the further subscriptions were paid by the father, and the dividends *de facto* accounted for in the manner which I shall have occasion to take notice of. The dividends upon the whole were in fact carried to the account of the father, being received by the father's bankers, as they necessarily perhaps must be received. Some of your Lordships will know more correctly whether I am right or not, than I can say I know myself to be upon this point ; but I presume where shares stand in the name of any individual they cannot be received but by the authority of that individual. But whether the authority was or not given by both father and son, the produce of these shares, standing both in the name of the father and son, were received under such authorities by bankers who carried the whole to the account of the father; in short, they do allege that every act of ownership (independent of the circumstances of the apparent ownership created by the property standing in the name of the son) was exercised by the father during every period of his life, except as to what I have to observe with respect to the eighty-one shares which were transferred shortly before his death; and they say that that is very strongly confirmed by the date of the general disposition of the father, in which, as your Lordships observe, he attempts at least not only to give all the shares which were then purchased, either in his own name or the son's name, but attempts, by that instrument, to discharge even the thirty-nine shares from the obligation, which he supposed his son at that time to be under, respecting them.

In that view of the case, considering the proposition I have finally to make upon this subject, I think I should trespass too long upon your Lordships' time, if I were to go through all the detail of the circumstances in evidence in the cause; that view of the case creates the necessity of considering whether, if these shares were *bonâ fide* granted, at any period to be ascertained, to the son, the son must not be taken, in consequence of his subsequent transactions, to have become a trustee for his father; and, when the question is so put, whether the son must, in consequence of his subsequent transactions, be taken to have become a trustee for his father, I state again that which I apprehend would be clear in the law of England, that if you could show there was the appearance of an absolute gift, but that, at a time subsequent, the son had permitted the father, and particularly for a long course of years, to act with respect to the principal, or to the interest as if he was the owner of the principal, then the mere circumstance of the property standing in the son's name, would not determine that the property was not the property of the father.

Here I wish again to mark a distinction which is extremely important: that, although there may be a case in which the father of any *cestui que trust* may, upon the first formation of that trust, reserve what in Scotland they would call a life-rent, and we in England should call a life-interest; yet, the trustee who undertakes to prove that the *cestui que trust* had a limited interest fails in that proof, if the only evidence he can offer is, that the father of the *cestui que trust* was in the constant habit of receiving the dividends ; for the habit of receiving the dividends which Mr. Hog, the father, has taken, is evidence of the absolute ownership in the property which produces the dividends, unless the person who so pays the dividends shows that he pays the dividends in pursuance of a more limited obligation founded on some contract, which contract had been entered into when that practice of paying the dividends commenced.

I mention this the rather, because I observe that it has been stated in these cases, and very truly stated in these cases, that such has been supposed to be the power of the father, as to disappointing this claim of the legitim of the son, that in the case of Agnew *v.* Agnew*, tried in the Court of Session in Scotland, where a gentleman, having several children, some months, and but a few months before his death, made a disposition, not of all, but of a part, of his property to one of these children, this was found to be effectual. At the same time I do not lay much stress upon the circumstance that it was only a part of his property, for it was a considerable part of his property ; and, in principle, I cannot think that it would make a material difference whether that part had been more or less considerable ; but, a very few months before his death, he conveyed all the property, which he detailed, and enumerated in that detail, as a gift, being in *liege poustie*, to one of his sons, and he reserved as against the son his life rent in all the subjects he had so disposed of. His purpose seems to have been, — if it was not avowed, it would be impossible to deny that it could be easily perceived; his purpose was to disappoint the legitim ; that was his express intention ; and, it was to make this conveyance to one favourite child, taking care, however, that he should not himself suffer by the act which he did, because he reserved to himself the life rent ; and if a person has not the wish otherwise to dispose of the capital, having the life rent he is in pretty near as good a situation as if he had the capital at his own disposal. In the Court of Session in Scotland, that question was debated ; it underwent great consideration before the judges of that court ; and having undergone great consideration before men of great

---

* Agnew *v.* Agnew, 28th February, 1775. Wallace's Posthumou s Decisions.

eminence who then filled the court, they seem to have been much divided in opinion upon it.

I have no difficulty in the world in saying, that if the interest of the children in the legitim can be considered as at all analogous to the interest of a child in this country, under his father's covenant to leave him an equal share, a different rule would have been followed in this country. Such a covenant obliges the father to do nothing ; because, if I agree to leave this noble Lord an equal share with the noble Lord that sits next to him, if I leave this noble Lord nothing, I am under no obligation to leave the other noble Lord any thing ; and that leaves me at liberty, if I choose, to do so improvident an act as to throw my whole substance into the sea. But we have construed such a covenant as that, so as to make it an act which binds to some purpose ; and we have said that a disposition of property under the circumstances I have mentioned, by a person leaving himself just as comfortably situated, with respect to that property, after such a covenant, as if he had never entered into that covenant, shall be considered as in truth, though not in letter, a fraud upon the covenant ; and this will not be capable of being considered, according to our law, as that species of gift in the lifetime, which is to defeat the covenant to leave at the death.

I refer to this case of Agnew v. Agnew for the purpose of saying, with great deference and great respect, that I should wish rather to reserve what would be my opinion upon such a case as that, if it found its way to this House, than to say, at this moment, that I should accede to its doctrine. But if the doctrine of that case is the doctrine which ought to be abided by, it seems to me quite incapable of being applied to the present case, as to the thirty-nine shares or the eighty-one shares ; because there is a vast difference, in point of fact, between a case in which the person who receives the dividends with an express contract, capable of being produced to show that he receives them by virtue of a limited interest, and a case in which he receives the dividends exactly as the absolute owner would do, there being no contract produceable to show that it was intended between the parties, that he should have but a limited interest.

There can be no doubt, if I should lay out twenty thousand pounds in stock to-morrow, in the name of one of your Lordships, though it might be a possible thing you should pay me the dividends for my life, in consequence of an understanding between you and me, that I should have the dividends during my life, and you the capital upon my death; yet I conceive, if I were to die, and there was no evidence produceable but the single evidence that my money had been laid out, and that you from time to time had given me the produce of the purchase, that that would be quite sufficient evidence to satisfy a court of justice that, as a trustee for me during my life, you remained a trustee for those who represented me after my death; and it is incumbent upon those who have once acted as if they were not the owners of the property, to show under some contract of which they can give evidence, that the inference is to be different from the receipt of the dividends in the one case, to what it would be from the receipt of the dividends in the other case. This is a case in which it must be made out satisfactorily, either that Mr. Hog, the father, had parted with all interest in the thirty-nine shares and the eighty-one shares; or on the other hand, in which the judgment of law will be either that he had never parted with any interest in them; or if he had ever parted with any interest in them, then the judgment of law will be from the receipt of the subsequent dividends, during such a period as he shall appear to have acted with those subsequent dividends, that he had absolutely re-acquired a subsequent interest in the property.

There are some topics addressed to the consideration of your Lordships extremely well worthy of attention, as evidence upon the fact whether Mr. Hog, the father, did or did not receive those dividends; because, it does not necessarily follow that because the dividends come into my coffers, that, therefore, in looking at the whole of the transaction which takes place between you and me, I ought to be said in law to receive the dividends; and it has, therefore, been urged that Mr. Hog, when he received these dividends, in truth, in a shape paid them out again to the Respondent; because they say that he had come to an understanding or an agreement with the Respondent that he would pay him an annuity of five hundred pounds; and that, having engaged to pay him such annuity of five hundred pounds, it was natural enough that the father, when he made him a present of these thirty-nine shares, should say you must take the produce of the thirty-nine shares as *pro tanto* payment of that annuity from time to time as the produce arises; and, therefore, if that produce was brought to the account of Mansfield, Ramsay, and Company, in the name of the father, yet the payments which were made out of that fund, in discharge of the annuity, carried back the dividends again to the son.

That may all be very good argument, but it will require a great deal of consideration, before you can say it will be convincing argument. The natural quality of such a transaction as that would be this : — if the thirty-nine shares were in the name of the son, and the son received an annuity from his father, the son, who would be permitted to receive the interest and dividends of the thirty-nine shares, would carry them forward as *pro tanto* in discharge of the annuity. But it seems possible, and perhaps rational, to admit of a perfectly different consideration : if your Lordships perceive that these dividends are carried in a mass into the same drawers of the bankers' house which contain that which is undeniably the property of the father; if they are placed in a *congeries*, in which the one is incapable of being distinguished from the other, there can be no doubt in point of law they would, to many purposes, be the property of the father; and till they became severed by actual payment out again of the annuity, all which were so carried into this mass would be the property of the father, liable to all that could act upon the property of the father. Therefore, these were certainly permitted, for a period at least, by the son to be laid hold of by the bankers of the father, as the property of the father; and when looking to see what is the true intent and meaning of all this, you must look at all the other circumstances in the case; and if you find the father advancing the expences of the transfer; if you find the father advancing the subscriptions for those shares put into the name of the son; if you find the father estimating his property, and, in that estimate of property, attributing to himself the ownership of this property : these are all circumstances which must be considered when you are determining whether the dividends on these shares were taken into the coffers of the father's bankers, in consequence of any agreement or understanding between the father and the son, that they should be be paid out again in discharge of this annuity.

It is contended here, that it does not signify at all what had been entered in the father's book with respect to the estimate of his property ; but that is, perhaps, a proposition much more easily laid down than assented to, when the allegation here is not the mere question between the father, who was the truster, and the son the trustee — a question to which all the rules of evidence about trusts will naturally apply; but whether the transactions between the father and the son were transactions which, in point of fact, were intended between the father and the son to disappoint this claim of legitim: for a great many circumstances will, in such a case, be circumstances admissible as evidence, which circumstances would not be admissible· as evidence, if it were a dry question under the act 1696, whether there was or not a trust as between the person alleged to be the truster, and the person contending that he was in truth the *cestui que trust*.

Under all these circumstances, therefore, I conceive the true question, with respect to the thirty-nine shares, will be this: how many of these thirty-nine shares (attending to the date which the circumstance gives with respect to the transaction relating to the directorship) — how many of the thirty-nine shares will really fall under the effect of that transaction; and, with respect to those which would not fall under that transaction, as well as with respect to those which did fall under that transaction, whether the subsequent dealings between the father and the son do, or do not, amount to evidence that, in the subsequent life of the father and the son, these shares were considered as the property of the father, at least to the extent and the purpose of the father's receiving from time to time, (and I mean for himself beneficially receiving, and receiving as his own property,) the interest, dividends, and produce of those shares. If it should turn out, upon an accurate examination of the fact, that he did receive *eo modo et eo intuitu*, and that the son permitted him to receive *eo modo et eo intuitu*, it will be to be determined what is the effect of that subsequent dealing; with respect, first, to the shares which qualified him to act as a director, and with respect to which the oath was taken; and secondly, with respect to those shares which are not professed to have been transferred for that purpose.

In some points of view in which I have taken the liberty of representing this case as to the thirty-nine shares, this case does not appear to me to have been very fully examined into; and I am more anxious to state it in this way, because, in a subsequent case of *Millie* v. *Millie* *, it seems to me to be admitted, by the Court of Session, that though the father may ostensibly part with his property and allow it to stand as the property of the son, yet, if in truth,

---

* Millie *v*. Millie, 7th June, 1803, affirmed on appeal.

after he has so parted with that property, he really and substantially remains the owner of it, that will not defeat the
legitim; and I am the more anxious so to state it, because,
comparing the notes in the case of Millie v. Millie, containing the opinions of the judges, to which we look upon these
occasions, I observe that the case of Agnew v. Agnew, to which
I have before alluded, is a case not only extremely doubted of
by very high authority in the Court of Session. But I presume there must be some inaccuracy; for, in the case of Hog
v. Lashley, the opinion seems to represent that of Agnew v.
Agnew as establishing a doctrine which should govern the
decision in this case. The very same authority, if those notes
in Millie v. Millie are accurate, is made to state that to be a
decision with which the decision in Millie v. Millie would not
agree; but whether Agnew v. Agnew is to stand or not, for
the reasons I before mentioned, as it seems to me, it cannot
govern where, upon the examination of facts, there is nothing
to prove a limited interest (the conveyance being absolute),
but the mere circumstance of receiving dividends after that
conveyance had been made.

Having said thus much as to the thirty-nine shares, the
eighty-one shares fall certainly under a different consideration;
and the eighty-one shares cannot be affected by considerations
suggested by any of the doctrines to which I have been
alluding, without attending to the circumstances of dealing
that took place as to the thirty-nine shares, and that took place
as to the eighty-one shares, before these eighty-one shares
were transferred in the manner I am about to mention by
Mr. Hog the father to Mr. Hog the son.

It appears clearly by the instrument of the date to which I
have before referred, that these shares were intended by the
father to have been laid out in land; that Mr. Hog intended
that these eighty-one shares should have been vested by
trustees in the purchase of lands, to be subject to the same
species of entail as the estate of Newliston.

Between the date of that deed and his death, and so shortly
before his death that no dividends were received between the
date of the transfer and the death, he transferred them apparently absolutely to Mr. Hog the son; this must have been
either to give them to Mr. Hog the son absolutely, or to give
them to Mr. Hog the son under a confidence, and an understanding, that he, Hog the son, was to make the same disposition of them as the trustees were empowered and required

to make of them by the deed of disposition which the father had before made.

I believe there can be no doubt, that if the father intended absolutely to give them to the son, whilst he was in *liege poustie*, it was competent for him to do so; and if there were nothing more in this case than the mere circumstance of his having made the gift to the son, so soon after having intended to give so large a portion of his property to trustees, to be laid out in land to be settled upon that very son, however much your Lordships might suspect about that transaction, suspicion will not do as a ground of judgment, as it was competent for the father to alter his purpose, and by that act he sufficiently proved that he had altered his purpose; that that which he had a power to give away he had effectually given away; and you would have had nothing for the mind to address itself to, in order to consider whether this was really and absolutely a gift or not, excepting this circumstance, that in times past, that stock which had stood in the name of the son had in truth been dealt with by the father as his own, though it did stand in the name of the son; and you would have had to put the question to yourselves whether you could safely, in judgment, conjecture that he meant to deal with the eighty-one shares as he had dealt with the other shares; that is, that though he placed them in the name of his son, he meant to deal with them as if they were his own property. I humbly submit my opinion to your Lordships, that whatever you might have suspected, out of a court of justice, it would be much too strong to suspect, in a court of justice, that that, which was upon the face of it a gift, was not intended to be a gift, before you had seen any other transaction consequent upon it which authorised you to say so; that because the thirty-nine shares were so dealt with, if they were so dealt with, therefore the eighty-one shares ought to be so dealt with, and therefore they ought to be considered as the father's. But to explain myself upon this subject — and I wish to do this in the presence of my noble and learned friend, who sits near me—I do conceive that in this country, after the transfer of those eighty-one shares, if they had been shares in the Bank of England, if a day had come in which the son had received a dividend for the father's use — that one single receipt of the dividend for the father's use would have been evidence upon which you would have been authorised to say, that the receipt of the dividend

for the father's use proved that the property which produced
that dividend was the father's property; and in that case it
would not have been competent for the son to have said, if he
had put it on no other evidence than this, that because this
was a payment of a dividend only, in the life-time of the father,
therefore the interest of the father was, in the intendment of
law in such circumstances, to be taken to be only an interest
during the father's life. I conceive, on the contrary, that the
receipt in such circumstances would prove property in the
principal, because it proved property in the interest; and
that that limited sort of interest could not have been contended for on behalf of the son. But it happened in this case
that the father died before any interest was received; and
it will be for your Lordships to say, attending to the circumstances and transactions between these parties previously,
whether there was here any thing more than a transfer of
the principal by the father to the son.

But there is something more in this case, which has reference to this law of legitim, a consideration so important, in
the view I take of the case, that I should have had to lament
that it had not been taken into view, with reference to the fact
I am now about to mention, in every place in which it
could be fully and truly considered — what would be the
effect of such a circumstance upon the law of legitim? And
it seems to me to come distinctly to this; that if the deed
of disposition which had devoted this property to be laid out,
after the death of Mr. Hog the father, in the purchase of lands
at Newliston, could not take effect, the question then is, whether the transaction I am about to state would do so, provided
the evidence proves that such was the nature of that transaction; whether he who, by this disposition, had intended
that these funds should be laid out in land, could, by saying, I
will not permit my disposition to take effect, but I will give
this money in my life-time to my son, nevertheless, with an
understanding, and with a confidence, that he shall lay out
the property in the purchase of lands at Newliston as I have
directed money to be laid out in that neighbourhood;
whether a gift, connected with such an understanding and confidence as that, would or would not be sufficient to deprive the
younger children of their title to the legitim. If it would, it
appears to me that the case of Millie *v.* Millie, which was
afterwards decided, will deserve a great deal of consideration,
because that is neither more nor less than saying this; that in

one shape, after an ostensible transfer, you may hold over your property pretty nearly in an absolute dominion; and that in the other case, after such transfer, you cannot hold dominion over it, but subject to the claim of legitim. In the case of Millie v. Millie it was held, that the parent going ou of partnership, but still leaving the firm to go on in the name of the son, it being understood between the father and the son that the father had an interest, that this did not disappoint the legitim. It does appear to me, upon the principles of the case of Millie v. Millie, to deserve a great deal of consideration indeed, whether, if the gift of eighty-one shares to the son was a gift for the purpose of being laid out in land to be settled, after his death, by the son to whom he had given it in his life-time; and, if that was the purpose, whether he meant to retain power over it. If it was his purpose to lay it out after his death, it does not exclude the idea that he was to enjoy it, as he had heretofore enjoyed it, during his life. The question then will be, whether by a gift under such an understanding as that, the legitim may be defeated.

The proof of the facts, upon this part of the case, depends upon the evidence of Mr. Ramsay, the banker of old Mr. Hog, who seems to have been much in the knowledge of the intentions of this gentleman, and who, in that deposition, gives his account of this circumstance, with which I think it would be quite impossible in this country that any court of justice could be satisfied. I will read to your Lordships both parts of Mr. Ramsay's deposition. In the first instance, when he is examined as to the interrogatory which relates to this matter, " Do you know that, shortly before his death, Mr. Roger Hog executed a transfer in favour of Mr. Thomas Hog, and what shares did he so transfer? Do you know the terms upon which this transfer was made or the cause of making it ? "— he depones that, a short time before Mr. Hog's death, he told the deponent that he had received some anonymous letters of a very scurrilous nature, and which he supposed to have come from the Pursuer. The Pursuer is the party who is claiming, in right of his wife, this legitim, and there can be no doubt that if Mr. Hog had received a letter of a scurrilous nature, he was fully at liberty to disappoint that claim of legitim; but, whatever was his purpose, he could not execute that purpose except in the way in which the law would allow him to execute it.

Then Mr. Ramsay goes on to say, " That he had made a

transfer of his bank stock to his son, in order to prevent the possibility of its being attached, as mentioned in those letters; that the deponent believes there were no conditions annexed to the abovementioned transfer; and that Mr. Hog took it for granted that his son would fulfil what he knew to be his intentions, of vesting the money in land and entailing it in the same manner with the rest of the estate; depones that Mr. Hog told the deponent that he had executed a trust disposition, vesting his funds in Lord Henderland, Mr. Robert Mackintosh, and the deponent, to be laid out in the purchase of land, which was to be entailed in the same manner as the rest of his estate, but that afterwards he had acquired more confidence in his son, and had contented himself with taking the promise of his son that he would fulfil his intentions, and would consult with Lord Henderland, Mr. Mackintosh, and the deponent." And then, when Mr. Ramsay comes to the close of his other deposition, he states himself thus: " That, some time before Mr. Hog's death, he transferred a considerable number of shares of stock of the Bank of Scotland to his son, which the deponent believed to have become, from that hour, as much, and to all intents and purposes, the sole property of the son, as if the father had given him the value in cash out of his pocket; that he also believes this transfer, or the giving away in his own lifetime and with his own hand, was in consequence of the anonymous letters, and of some new opinions which prevailed, at that time, with regard to moveable property; and the deponent believes the only reason Mr. Hog had for keeping any shares in his own name was, merely to act as a Director of the Bank, in the event of his being again requested to accept of that office; depones that he has reason to think that if Mr. Hog had conceived that his English funds would not have been carried by the settlement he had made, he would also have transferred them to his son."

Now your Lordships will permit me to say, that I think it would have been utterly impossible for the Court of Chancery in this country, which is obliged either to content itself with certain depositions, or to take the means of making further enquiry, to have been contented with such depositions as these. I take them to be (I hope I am not mistaken in that circumstance) — I take them to be the depositions of the same gentleman; but I confess those depositions surprised me very much; for when Mr. Ramsay, in his last deposition, says that he believes these shares to have become, to all intents and purposes, the sole property of the son as if his father had given him cash out of his pocket, and that his only reason for keeping any shares in his own name was to act as a Director of the Bank, in the event of his being again requested to accept of that office; and, that he has reason to think, that if Mr. Hog had conceived that his English funds would not have been carried by the settlement he had made, he would also have transferred them to his son;" — one cannot help referring back to the former deposition of Mr. Ramsay; and with respect to the former deposition of Mr. Ramsay — (your Lordships will recollect that the English funds and the Scotch funds were given by the same settlement for the same purposes) — Mr. Ramsay has expressly stated, that whatever might have been the opinion of the deceased with respect to the Pursuer's letters, and though that allegation had led him to place these funds in the name of his son, yet he says, that Mr. Hog the father himself told him that he contented himself with taking the promise of his son, that he the son would fulfil his intention. That is not all; but the promise which he takes is a promise not only generally that he would fulfil his intention, but it represents the son as promising his father that he would consult with others as to fulfilling his intention; and with whom would he consult? Why, that he would consult with Lord Henderland, Mr. Mackintosh, and Mr. Ramsay himself.

According to Mr. Ramsay's deposition, Mr. Hog had executed a trust disposition, vesting the funds in Lord Henderland, Mr. Robert Mackintosh, and the deponent, to be laid out in the purchase of lands, to be entailed, together with those English funds; which English funds, Mr. Hog had been advised, could not be touched by the law of Scotland as to this legitim, as was contended for many years, till otherwise decided in this House. And then the question is, whether the fair inference from the whole be not this, — that this was a gift by the father to the son, not in this sense a gift by the father to the son, that it was to become the property of the son absolutely, but a gift of the father to the son for the purpose of the son laying out this property in the purchase of lands to be entailed in the same manner as his estate at Newliston: placing the property in hands in which it would be safe from the claim of legitim; as safe from the claim of legitim as those English funds were supposed to be. I state this, because it appears to me a question which deserves a great deal of consideration in this place, and would, I think, require great consideration elsewhere, whether it be possible that a father in Scotland, the moment before he dies, can hand over to his son apparently that property, for the very purpose to which he could not devote it, by a trust disposition, either made whilst he was in *liege poustie*, or made after he was in *liege poustie*.

My humble opinion upon that is, that it would be absolute destruction to the law of Scotland, as far as it relates to this claim of legitim, if that could be done. The course, therefore, I should propose to take, would be to come to some declaration of the principle which we conceive to be the principle of law that should govern in this case of legitim; and then to call upon the Court of Session to apply the facts as they are proved before them, or make such examination as may be necessary, in order to enable them to ascertain the fund to which the principle is to be applied, and to apply that principle of law so to be laid down in your Lordships' judgment. And it does seem to me, it should not fall short of this, that the receipt of the profits, during the life of the person, is evidence of the ownership of that person in the subject matter which produces the profits; to state that, without prejudice to what ought to be the determination in such a case as Agnew *v.* Agnew, if such a case should ever arise again. Your Lordships will at least go the length with me, guarding it against any such case as that to which I have referred, of stating, that if any number of shares were placed in the name of the son, under an understanding that the son was to execute the purposes contained in that trust deed, such a disposition as that would not be sufficient to defeat a claim of legitim. When it is said, in this case, that that was no more than the declaration of the father, it will be open to the Court of Session to consider what weight is due to this observation, where the question is, whether the father and the son are together acting a part in order to defeat third persons — whether the declaration of each must not be evidence. I think it must be evidence as between third persons and a father and son, who are both to be considered as one adverse party to those third persons. When I say I think it would, I am only stating the opinion which I at this moment entertain, and it will be open to those who have to reconsider this case, whether I am right or wrong in the opinion I at this moment entertain upon this point. In this way of considering the question your Lordships will, in point of fact, have settled some material points both on the law of evidence and the law of legitim, as far as the law of legitim is affected by a transaction of this kind.

The other questions which arise here are of minor consideration. The first is with respect to the Respondent, Thomas Hog, being a creditor for the value of the estate which his father had purchased in this country, which became his by the appointment of his mother, which was afterwards sold, and the father received the money. It is very difficult to suppose, that in the course of so many years of the lives of both spent after that transaction took place, that, somehow or other, it was not very well understood between them that the father was not a debtor to the son for that sum of money; but we must not take that for granted. The transaction clearly constituted the son a creditor on the father; and unless it can be shown, far beyond what appears upon conjecture or supposition, that that relation of creditor and debtor was made to cease and discontinue by some satisfaction or some agreement, we must act upon the fact as it originally was, for we are not authorised to say that the nature of it was changed, unless that change be distinctly proved. It appears to me, therefore, that this appeal is groundless, so far as it quarrels with the Court of Session, in considering Thomas Hog as a creditor for that sum of money.

I am also of opinion that regard must be had to the sums which were received as provisions for Mrs. Lashley, and the annuity paid to her. And it will be observed by your Lordships that the effect of the decree is, that they shall be brought into collation. This decree or interlocutor supposes that more than one younger child should be entitled to the legitim; but if there be a well-grounded apprehension, as from what has passed in this House there may be (I say no more than that there may be), that only one child will be entitled to legitim,— if your Lordships gathered, in the words of the interlocutor, that that collation is only to be with respect to the legitim. whoever shall finally receive the legitim will receive the benefit of that collation; if more than one receive the legitim, more than one will receive the benefit of the collation; if only one turns out finally to be entitled to the legitim, the collation cannot prejudice the estate of that child, because it would then be collation only to itself; for, as I read the books, the collation is between those who are entitled to the legitim.

There is another circumstance of a debt of seven hundred pounds, that, as a debt, will fall to be so dealt with. There will be no difficulty then in providing for the differences between the parties, in reference to these smaller considerations I have now been stating to your Lordships.

I would beg your Lordships' particular attention to that part of the case (though it is not a matter of very considerable value), which relates to the claim with reference to the expenses of confirmation in Scotland, and of the probate in England. I can have no manner of doubt, that, if a person die in England, as may happen in some parts of England to be the case, where a wife or a child have a claim against his property as wife or child, or where a part of his property may be undisposed of by his will, and where the wife, therefore, as wife, will take a share in the undisposed part, and the child take a share in the undisposed part; yet, inasmuch as no part of his property can be touched, but either wrongfully or rightfully; and as it ought not to be touched wrongfully, but ought to be administered rightfully—as no part of his property can be touched, if he has made a will, but by his executor; or, if he has made no will, but by his administrator—the expense of clothing the individual who is to act as such with the character that is to enable him to act as such, is an expense for the benefit of the whole estate, however distributed; and therefore, as it seems to me, that expense should fall proportionably upon the whole estate. Whether that which respects confirmation in Scotland falls under the same principle, I, perhaps, am not so competent to judge, but I should conceive that it would. The question then is, whether, in stating my own opinion to your Lordships, I should state that these interlocutors are right or wrong; and I do say that the inclination of my opinion as to both is that they are wrong.

Then this circumstance occurs, — and your Lordships must deal with it, regard being had to the circumstance that the cross appeal in this cause, which raises two points, the one not necessary to be raised by the cross appeal as I had occasion to observe yesterday in the question about domicil, because that was necessarily included in the discussion and argument upon the other appeal; and the other in respect of the expenses of the probate and confirmation, which is raised by the cross appeal; but unless your Lordships choose to relax your general rule, this matter is not properly before you; — how far you may choose to relax your rule is a matter of infinitely greater consequence to the House than a question of such a value as this can be to the parties now litigating at your Lordships' bar, — the difficulty will be where you are to stop. This, however, must be left to the sound judicial discretion of your Lordships; and when the question comes to be put, whether the interlocutor should be reversed, as to so much of that subject, your Lordships' opinion will be to be taken upon this point.

Your Lordships will observe that this leads me finally to say, that I have nothing to propose for a change of the interlocutor respecting the domicil of Mr. Hog. It will be for your Lordships to decide whether it is fit to adopt that proposition, that there should be a change of the interlocutor, as far as it is founded upon the notion that the marriage in England must decide the rights of the wife when she is transplanted to Scotland, and her husband's domicil is established there. But with respect to the domicil of the husband in the year 1760, it does not appear to me that there is any occasion to alter the interlocutor as to that part of it.

With respect to the price of the Kingston estate; with respect to the sum of 1000*l.* upon bond; with respect to the seven hundred pounds; and with respect to the provisions which have been made for Mrs. Lashley,—your Lordships will see that, if the interlocutors are to be altered at all, it will be an alteration rather in terms than in substance, an alteration which only clearly marks out how the collation is to operate, regard being had to whether it shall finally be more or fewer who shall be entitled to legitim; and with respect to the question upon the thirty-nine shares and the eighty-one shares, that it is fit for your Lordships to declare, as matter of law, the principles of evidence, and the rules which should obtain as to what shall, or what shall not, be taken to be *inter vivos* a sufficient disposition of the property, to render the property no longer capable of being considered as the moveable property of the testator at the time of his death; calling upon the Court of Session to act, upon that part of the case, upon that declaration, and to determine whether they can or cannot, upon the whole of the case, say that this property was not in the perfect enjoyment of Mr. Hog, and that the purpose of the transfer was not under an understanding, between the father and the son, that that property should be applied to the purchase of land, to be settled by entail in the same way as the estate at Newliston, of course giving their distinct attention, as they have been before called upon to do, to the thirty-nine and the eighty-one shares.

I hope your Lordships will allow me to state, that I have

thought it better to go through the case at great length, stating my opinion upon the different parts of it, than to draw out the judgment in form, before I knew whether your Lordships concurred with me in the opinion I have humbly stated. If it should be your Lordships' opinion so to do, it will not be difficult then to draw up the terms of such judgment as your Lordships may think proper to give upon the whole of the case; therefore, for the present, I shall content myself with saying what I have done, expressing, however, a wish that the noble and learned Lord who has given great attention to this case will be pleased to say how far he does or does not concur with me, because it will be very satisfactory to my mind, recollecting how long he has been in the knowledge of the law of that part of the island as well as this, if his Lordship should be of opinion that I have not mistaken the true view of this case; and, on the other hand, most thankfully shall I receive any information that may fall from the noble and learned Lord, that may tend to set me right, if, in any respect, I am mistaken in the principles I have laid down.

Earl of Rosslyn. I have the satisfaction entirely and absolutely to concur with the noble and learned Lord who has just sat down.

I am sorry to observe that, in the proceedings of the court below, there have occurred, in my opinion, several mistakes in point of law, particularly in that interlocutor which finds that the circumstance of the marriage being celebrated in England can decide upon the rights of succession that will arise to the wife and children of that marriage, in opposition to that law which, by the future events of the life of the party, may be the law of the land, to operate upon his property at the time of his death. I think there are many errors that have misled the judgment of the court upon this point.

In the first place, in this case there is an express contract, — and I have no conception, in point of law, that a lawyer is in such case to entertain a metaphysical idea of an implied contract arising from the situation in which the parties place themselves by a civil act. My general idea of law is, that in all cases where the parties make an express contract, that excludes all consideration of an implied contract: an idea of an implied contract, in all cases where there is an express contract, is to me a solecism.

But, supposing there had been no legal contract, and you were to determine upon the situation of the parties upon the mere fact of a marriage celebrated in a given place, they had no occasion to raise an implied contract : a man and a woman are united together; they take their chance of the future fortunes of each other, and particularly with regard to the wife, who can have no domicil separate from the domicil of her husband : she must follow the fortunes of her husband, wherever they happen to be placed, and must take her chance at the time when his fortune falls under the disposition of a particular law; therefore, in the general case, there is no foundation for that, (and I am sure my noble and learned friend will see the application of this observation in almost every case where that occurs,) that a metaphysical idea of an implied contract is a fallacious idea, substituting an imaginary idea, not applicable to the actual situation and relation of the parties.

With respect to the claim of the Appellant in right of the mother to that share of the estate which the law of Scotland gives under the name, not very properly applied, of *jus relictæ*, I am of opinion, with the noble and learned Lord, that the interlocutor ought to be reversed.

But upon that being reversed, then comes a matter of great consideration with regard to property, the claim of legitim to the children. Now, I take it that I have never learned, or that I have forgotten, the laws of Scotland, or that the father has a full power to dispose of his personal property in any manner he pleases : he may convert it all into land, and by that means the younger children will be defeated of their legitim; but then he must do the act himself; he must himself purchase the land, because the nature of the property that becomes the property, either of the right heir, or partly of the younger children, must be judged of at the time of the death of the father; therefore, according to my idea of the evidence in this case, — but I do not mean to say it is not a matter open to enquiry, for I will not presume to know so much as some others may on this subject, — I should say that Mr. Hog's intention to have either his stock in the Scotch Bank, or the funds in England, laid out in land after his death, by any stipulated alienation of them from him to his son for that purpose, is totally void in point of law, and can have no effect with regard to the disposition that he might make of it : he might do the act in person; he might give a provision to a child in his lifetime, without any consideration what might be the state of his moveable property at the time of his death; and that, when actually given, could not be recalled. He might advance one

H H

of his children into a certain situation in life; he might lay out his money expensively on his education; he could not be hindered from it; but he must actually give the money with which this would be done: he must divest himself of an interest in it, and he cannot retain that interest to the moment of his death consistently with law; therefore, the case of Agnew v. Agnew, I think, is totally wrong in law (I have no scruple to say so), and a bad decision. I should not be so moved by that decision, as to send this case back to the Court of Session for reconsideration; but when I am to pronounce upon a case where there are a great many papers, and a good deal of evidence which I have not examined with attention, I do not wish to apply the law in this case; but, as far as I know the evidence, and can judge of it, I think it clear that, as between Mr. Hog the father and Mr. Hog the son, there was a disposition and an understanding to reduce the claim of legitim, with a view to prevent the wife of the Appellant from having that claim which she would otherwise consider herself to be entitled to.

With regard to the debts contracted by the father, in consequence of the son's paying him the price of the estate he was entitled to by his mother, the son is fairly entitled, as a creditor, to stand upon the moveable estate of the father, and to receive the value of the estate at Kingston, and also the bond of 1000*l.*, before any distribution of it can take place.

I think there is a mistake in the interlocutors of the Court of Session with regard to a trifling sum — the expense of the probate in England and confirmation in Scotland: they are both sums of money laid out in order to acquire a legal title to that property which is to be distributed. Somebody must lay it out; and it is no matter whether the son or anybody else had done it: but I think, that the rules of your Lordships' House in the case of appeals ought to be strictly adhered to; and this may be still more trifling in the result, because it may happen that the shares of that fund to be divided may come to be equal, which, I think, will very probably be the result of this case; but he certainly had a legal claim on the fund for those expenses.

On the motion of the Lord Chancellor, on 16th July, 1804, this judgment was pronounced: —

> *It is declared by the Lords, &c. That the contract of marriage between the late Mr. Roger Hog and his wife is not so conceived as to bar a claim to legal provisions;*

and that Mr. Hog is to be considered as having his domicil in Scotland at the time of his wife's death ; and that the Pursuer has, therefore, a claim in right of her mother, the wife of the said Mr. Roger Hog, who, at the time of her death, had his domicil in Scotland, to a share of the moveable estate of her father at the time of her mother's death : And it is further declared, that such shares of the stock of the Bank of Scotland, standing in the name of the Respondent Thomas Hog at the death of the said Roger Hog, as shall appear to have been transferred to the said Thomas Hog, under any agreement or understanding that he would invest the same in land, after the death of the said Roger Hog, and also such shares, the dividends whereof shall appear, notwithstanding the transfer of the same, to have been after such transfer ordinarily received for the account of and applied for the use of, the said Roger Hog, ought to be considered as subject to the Pursuer's claim of legitim : And it is therefore ordered and adjudged, That all such parts of the interlocutors complained of in the said appeal as are inconsistent with these declarations, be, and the same are hereby reversed ; and, in so far as they are agreeable thereto, the same be, and are hereby affirmed : And it is further ordered, That the cause be remitted back to the Court of Session in Scotland, to ascertain whether any, and which, of the shares in the Bank of Scotland, agreeably to the declarations aforesaid, are subject to the Pursuer's claim of legitim, and also to ascertain the interests of the Pursuer in her father's estate, at her mother's death and at his death, regard being had to this declaration : And it is further ordered and adjudged, That it is unnecessary to consider so much of the matters complained of in the cross appeal as relates to the domicil of the said Roger Hog, touching which such declaration hath been made as is herein-before contained : And, the said appeal also not having been presented in due time, it is further ordered and adjudged, That the same be, and is hereby dismissed this House.

No. IV.

Edward Ommanney and others, Trustees and Executors of Sir Charles Douglas Baronet, deceased, - - - - } Appellants;

Mrs. Lydia Mariana Bingham, eldest Daughter of Sir Charles Douglas Baronet, and the Rev. Richard Bingham, her Husband, } Respondents.

*Note of the Speech of the Lord Chancellor (Lord Loughborough), at moving the Judgment in the House of Lords, 18th March, 1796.**

Lord Chancellor. — The question now to be determined by your Lordships is peculiarly interesting ; and every argument of compassion, every thing which tends to call forth the higher sentiments and feelings, press upon your Lordships for every possible favour to the Respondents ; for it is more than probable, that the resentment of the father, on account of this lady's rash conduct, would, under the real circumstances of the case, as they afterwards appeared, have been softened and appeased, and that his known good-nature would have induced him to pardon her indiscretion, and to annul the codicil to his will, if, to the great loss of his country, as well as his family, he had not been carried off suddenly and unexpectedly. But nothing can be so dangerous, as for a Court of Justice to suffer itself to be led away by compassion, instead of being guided by the general rules laid down as the law of the land ; and of applying, in the cases before it, that law, biassed by passion, or warped by personal consideration.

In the present case, there are two interlocutors brought under our review, in their natures essentially different from each other.

The first is on a question of pure Scotch law, by which the Court of Session have declared that the codicil, executed by Sir Charles Douglas, can have no effect, as being at variance with the law of Scotland. But, when this question was before them, unfortunately the Court overlooked another and previous question, which, therefore, forms the subject of their second

---

* It is understood that this note was given by his Lordship to the parties.

interlocutor; and that is, whether Sir Charles Douglas was domiciled in this country, or in Scotland. The question here alluded to has no reference to the particular law of Scotland; it must be decided on principles of general law; because it is now admitted, not merely in both parts of Great Britain, but in all, at least most of the civilised countries in Europe, that it is the place of a man's domicil which must give the rule for the distribution of his personal property.

Formerly, there seems to have existed in the Courts of Scotland, and in other parts of Europe, a kind of controversy in regard to the locality of personal property, as if its distribution was dependent upon this consideration. But the determinations of your Lordships, which have been acquiesced in and followed in Scotland, have now settled it as law, that the distribution of an intestate's personal estate, or the construction or effect of a will, must be governed by the law of the place where the intestate, or the testator, had his last domicil.

If, then, it shall be decided, in the present case, that Sir Charles Douglas died a domiciled Englishman, it is immaterial (as to these parties), whether the judgment of the Court of Session be right or wrong on the other question, which depends on the law of Scotland.

In viewing the life of the late Sir Charles Douglas, your Lordships will find it a life of bustle and adventure. The scenes of activity in which he was almost constantly engaged, and in the course of which he distinguished himself so remarkably for courage and good conduct, afforded him but little opportunity to settle long in any particular place. Independent of the services he rendered to this country, your Lordships will find him in the employment of two Courts, the allies of Britain; viz., Holland and Russia. In the Empress's service, he was entrusted with a very high command, which did not continue, however, for any great length of time; but, in the service of Holland, he continued for a much longer period, three or four years, — and it has been argued that he acquired a domicil in each of these countries; a question which I am not now called upon to discuss. At his return home, in both cases, he was employed in our own service, and your Lordships will perceive that he was much employed, and in various parts of the world; that he was exceedingly active at all times; and that, when at home on shore, he was so eagerly engaged in the course and pursuit of his profession, that he did not settle any where, so as to strike root very deeply; which, at first sight, makes it difficult to say where he was domiciled. But, upon a more minute investigation of the circumstances in his life, I cannot approve of the judgment pronounced by the Court of Session; and I shall now examine into the reasons on which that judgment is founded, for the purpose of showing on what grounds I am not satisfied, in doing which I shall take the inverse order in which those reasons are stated in the interlocutor.

By this arrangement, then, the first circumstance is, *that he died in Scotland, where some of his children were boarded.* This, however, of some of his children being boarded in Scotland, is not mentioned as the *ratio decidendi*, but is thrown in along with the circumstance of his death. On that circumstance, however, no stress can be laid, for nothing is more clear than that residence, purely temporary, has no effect whatever in the creation of a domicil. Precisely of this kind was the residence of Sir Charles Douglas, in Scotland, at the period of his death. He had been appointed to the command on a foreign station, and went down to Scotland to take leave of such of his children as happened to be there, with all the hurry which was the necessary consequence of a speedy and immediate return. When he set out for Scotland, he was actually appointed. He had, therefore, so very short a time to continue, that it is impossible to say or imagine, that he had the remotest thought of settling or remaining in Scotland at the time when, unfortunately, his life was closed. The time he had to spend in Scotland, at that period, was limited; his stay was circumscribed; an immediate return was indispensably requisite; and, lastly, the object he had in view, in this journey to Scotland, was definable, and is defined. He was there, therefore, without idea or intention to remain; and, consequently, his last visit to Scotland, and unexpected death, can have no influence on the point of his domicil.

The next circumstance is, that, *occasionally he had a domicil in Scotland.* But this is rather an inaccuracy, for when had he a domicil in Scotland; that is, at what period was he fixed and settled there for life, or, as the word has been explained, for a perpetuity, meaning a continuation of time, or with an intention to remain? Unless it can be shewn, that he had been settled in Scotland with such an *animus*, he can never be said to have had a domicil in that country. For there is no such thing as an occasional domicil. It is the general habit and tenor of a man's life which must be looked to ; and in no case is it possible for a man to be so situated as to admit the idea of any thing like two domicils for the purpose of succession, unless his time were so arranged as to be equally and statedly divided betwixt two countries, in each of which his residence had exactly the same appearance of permanency as in the other : a case which could hardly occur, for some shade of difference would in general appear, giving a clearer character of permanency, or established settlement, to one of the situations, than to the other. But if such a case, as I have now supposed, were brought before us, there might be some difficulty in coming at the true conclusion. It is sufficient, however, here to say, that such is by no means the present case.

The last, or rather the first, consideration in the interlocutor is, *that Sir Charles Douglas was born in Scotland.* This may be insisted upon as affording some little degree of argument ; but the Judges in Scotland were all agreed in opinion, that birth is the slightest circumstance in the formation of the domicil of a person who has arrived at the years of Sir Charles Douglas. If it could be made out, that in no part of his life the person made choice of any country, as the site of his domicil, his birth would undoubtedly fix it in the place of his nativity. But, where a man's conduct and general habits have settled him elsewhere, his having been born in another country becomes of no consideration, and cannot have the smallest effect in regard to his domicil.

Upon the case of Sir Charles Douglas, my opinion is, that he fixed himself in this part of the United Kingdom; and I have no hesitation in declaring it as my further opinion, that it does not detract from the idea of his being domiciled in England, that his professional habits and conveniency, joined to his hopes of preferment, induced him to fix and settle here in preference to Scotland. As I have already observed, Sir Charles Douglas could not be much at home ; but when he had any leisure, any opportunity of living on shore, where was it most likely, where most expedient, that he should be found ? At a great sea-port certainly ; at Gosport, or in its neighbourhood ; and it appears to me, that no officer, so eager about his profession, and of so much naval ingenuity as Sir Charles Douglas possessed (for it is well known that he was the author of some great improvements), would have chosen any other situation. Sir Charles Douglas was a public man, and one may, therefore, speak of him. I will, then, take it upon me to say, that his mind and inclinations were so attached to his profession, and his zeal and ingenuity for the improvement of the navy so great, that I am convinced he could not have been at rest for any great length of time in any situation, but where he had an opportunity of shewing and putting these in practice.

I have mentioned the probability that Sir Charles Douglas would take up his residence in this country; and, as matter of fact, he was domiciled at Gosport, that is, his family and establishment were there for seven years successively, from the year 1776, even when service called him personally to another quarter. At one period he had a guardship at the Medway. Still, however, his house and home continued at Gosport; and the general habits of his life and his conduct throughout, all tend to confirm the proposition, that his domicil was, by choice, in England, and consequently that he must be considered as an Englishman.

I shall not detain your Lordships with a discussion of the effect of the visit to his sister in 1786; but content myself with observing that, during the whole space of time which he remained in Scotland, he had no house of his own, was never master of a family; and that, previous to his departure for Scotland, he guards his sister against entertaining any idea that it was his intention to be more than a visiter, or to take up any settled residence in Scotland.

Your Lordships will at once see, that it is a very material circumstance, and takes away much of the favour of the case from the Respondents, that a man, considering himself an inhabitant of a particular country, and, acting upon that idea, has made a regular settlement of his affairs, agreeably to the laws of that country; and yet that he should be disappointed in his intention, and the disposition he had made be defeated, on the idea and supposition that his succession must be governed by the law of another country, where he happened to be born; and that such his settlement, not being agreeable to this latter law, shall be considered as good for nothing: that he shall be held as a person who has died intestate, leaving it to that law to make a will for him. In the case of Sir Charles Douglas, this hardship is particularly apparent; for, if we look to the will which he executed, and the subsequent codicil, it is impossible to conceive that he considered himself in the character of a Scotchman, having his property subject to the rules established by the law of Scotland. The opposite conclusion presents itself with irresistible force. His will is an English will in every sense of the word; and it is, therefore, an obvious conclusion that, in his opinion, the law of England was to dispose of his property.

But it is urged, that he also made a will, or disposition, in the Scotch form, of his property in Scotland. He did so, and he was well advised when he did so, because that property being *heritable*, it could only be disposed of by those forms prescribed by the law of Scotland. But, what was the object of this disposition? It was to direct that his whole property in Scotland should be *sold*, that it might be converted into personal property, and distributed and disposed of in the same manner as his property in England. Under these circumstances, it is impossible to conceive that Sir Charles Douglas had the most distant idea that his will would be set aside by his children, because, by the law of Scotland, they are entitled to legitim; or by his wife, who, probably, had no settlement by covenant, because she, by the same law, might claim her thirds. It appears, on the contrary, to be very evident, that Sir Charles Douglas, looking to the laws of this country, as the only medium by which his intention was to be carried into effect, never dreamed of these claims; and the hardship would rather be, that his disposition should not take effect, in consequence of his long residence in England. In my opinion, therefore, your Lordships ought to declare that the succession of Sir Charles Douglas must be regulated by the law of England.

Should your Lordships be of this opinion, it is then unnecessary to enter into the other question, because your judgment attaches on all the property, wherever situated, and Sir Charles Douglas's executors will be authorized to act as his personal representatives and executors in Scotland, under the authority of the Court of Session; the effect of which will be, that the Respondent, Mrs. Bingham, unfortunately will, by means of the codicil, lose the benefit which was intended for her by the will of her father. At the same time, it may not be improper to say a few words on the other question, even though it shall be declared that Sir Charles had his domicil in this country; in which opinion the noble and learned Lord (Lord Thurlow), who attended most of the pleadings, perfectly agrees with me; while, at the same time, he entertains, as I do, a very great degree of doubt whether, by the law of

Scotland, the first interlocutor of the Court of Session can possibly be supported.

I have looked with care into the text writers on the Scotch law, without being able to discover any positive declaration or opinion, different from what is to be met with in the law of this country.

Stair treats only of bonds of provision, which are materially different from deeds of a testamentary nature ; for the former constituted the provision a *debt* against the estate, subject, no doubt, to a certain condition, the legal validity of which depended upon its object and tendency. If it be a *general restraint*, it is said to be *contra libertatem matrimonii*, and, on that account, null. If it forces the grantee to marry a *particular person*, it is then termed *contra pietatem parentis :* the father has exceeded his authority ; and for this reason, the provision is sustained, while the condition is rejected.

Erskine speaks of bonds, with a condition impossible to be performed, in which case he lays it down, that the debt is constituted ; while, the condition being impossible, the bond is taken as a *pure* bond. Or, if the condition be such as a father ought not to impose, the debt in this case is likewise sustained without regard to the condition, because it is an improper one.

Then, as for their cases, there are several where the consent of particular persons, such as trustees, was declared to be necessary previous to marriage ; but there is not a single case in which it has been found that a father might not impose upon his child a reasonable condition. I shall just add, on the subject of these bonds of provision, that they do not require delivery, but are perfectly valid, and the provision contained in them becomes an existing debt, if found in the father's repositories at his death.

But there is no affinity betwixt these cases and the present. A father in Scotland can disinherit his child ; and certainly he can, with at least equal propriety, impose upon such child a condition in itself neither unreasonable nor improper. But, in fact, this is not properly the case of a condition, but rather that of the revocation of the bequest in a will by a subsequent codicil. The question, then, to be considered is, whether the legacy revoked by the codicil has been, and ought to be forfeited. The legacy, given by Sir Charles in his will, is recalled if his daughter had married, or should marry the Respondent or any of his brothers; that is, the legacy continues in force, but the codicil revokes it *sub modo*, if a certain event had happened, or should happen ; and there could be nothing unreasonable in this.

The event had happened; and, on the death of Sir Charles, his will was found to contain the legacy to his daughter, but the codicil was found to revoke it. There is no affinity betwixt this, and those cases in which the Court of Session has annulled the condition annexed to the *gift* or existing debt.

I feel much diffidence, however, in delivering this opinion. But the reversal of the interlocutor, on the legality of the condition, does not depend upon it. It is the declaration, that Sir Charles Douglas was a domiciled Englishman, which governs the case : that depends upon principles of general law ; and the reversal of the first interlocutor is a necessary consequence of the reversal of the second.

On the motion of the Lord Chancellor, this judgment was pronounced (18th March, 1796) : —

> *It is ordered and adjudged, That the said interlocutors of the 17th of December, 1793, and the 17th of February, 1794, complained of in the said appeal, be, and the same are hereby reversed ; and it is hereby declared, that the succession to the property of Sir Charles Douglas be regulated by the law of England: And it is further ordered and adjudged, That the interlocutor of the 17th of February, 1792, also complained of in the said appeal, be, and the same is hereby reversed.*

I.

INDEX

MATTERS RELATING TO THE LAW OF SCOTLAND.

II.

INDEX

MATTERS RELATING TO THE LAW OF ENGLAND.

III.

INDEX

RELATIVE TO

MATTERS OF INTERNATIONAL LAW.

THE END.

LONDON:
Printed by A. SPOTTISWOODE,
New-Street-Square.